I0826053

THE ROMAN TRAITOR:

OR, THE DAYS OF

CICERO, CATO AND CATALINE.

A TRUE TALE OF THE REPUBLIC.

BY HENRY WILLIAM HERBERT,

AUTHOR OF "CROMWELL," "MARMADUKE WYVIL," "BROTHERS," ETC.

Why not a Borgia or a Catiline?—POPE.

VOLUME I.

This is one of the most powerful Roman stories in the English language, and is of itself sufficient to stamp the writer as a powerful man. The dark intrigues of the days which Cæsar, Sallust and Cicero made illustrious; when Cataline defied and almost defeated the Senate; when the plots which ultimately overthrew the Roman Republic were being formed, are described in a masterly manner. The book deserves a permanent position by the side of the great *Bellum Catalinarium* of Sallust, and if we mistake not will not fail to occupy a prominent place among those produced in America.

Philadelphia:

T. B. PETERSON, NO. 102 CHESTNUT STREET.

PHILADELPHIA:
STEREOTYPED BY GEORGE CHARLES,
No. 9 Sansom Street.

PREFACE.

A FEW words are perhaps needed as an introduction to a work of far more ambitious character, than any which I have before attempted. In venturing to select a subject from the history of Rome, during its earlier ages, undeterred by the failure or, at the best, partial success of writers far more eminent than I can ever hope to become, I have been actuated by reasons, which, in order to relieve myself from the possible charge of presumption, I will state briefly.

It has long been my opinion, then, that there lay a vast field, rich with a harvest of material almost virgin, for the romancer's use, in the history of classic ages. And this at a period when the annals of every century and nation since the Christian era have been ransacked, and reproduced, in endless variety, for the entertainment of the hourly increasing reading world, is no small advantage.

Again, I have fancied that I could discover a cause for the imperfect success of great writers when dealing with classic fiction, in the fact of their endeavoring to be too learned, of their aiming too much at portraying Greeks and Romans, and too little at depicting men, forgetful that under all changes of custom, and costume, in all countries, ages, and conditions, the human heart is still the human heart, convulsed by the same passions, chilled by the same griefs, burning with the same joys, and, in the main, actuated by the same hopes and fears.

With these views, I many years ago deliberately selected this subject, for a novel, which has advanced by slow steps to such a degree of completeness as it has now attained.

Having determined on trying my success in classical fiction, the conspiracy of Cataline appeared to me, a theme particularly well adapted for the purpose, as being an actual event of vast importance, and in many respects unparalleled in history; as being partially familiar to every one, thoroughly understood perhaps by no one, so slender are the authentic documents concerning it which have come down to us, and so dark and mysterious the motives of the actors.

It possessed, therefore, among other qualifications, as the ground-work of a historical Romance, one almost indispensable—that of indistinctness, which gives scope to the exercise of imagination, without the necessity of falsifying either the truths or the probabilities of history.

Of the execution, I have, of course, nothing to say; but

that I have sedulously avoided being overlearned; that few Latin words will be found in the work—none whatsoever in the conversational parts, and none but the names of articles which have no direct English appellation; and that it is sufficiently simple and direct for the most unclassical reader.

I hope that the costume, the manners of the people, and the antiquarian details will be found sufficiently correct; if they be not, it is not for want of pains or care; for I have diligently consulted all the authorities to which I could command access.

To the history of the strange events related in this tale, I have adhered most scrupulously; and I believe that the dates, facts, and characters of the individuals introduced, will not be found in any material respect, erroneous or untrue; and here I may perhaps venture to observe, that, on reading the most recently published lectures of Niebuhr, which never fell in my way until very lately, I had the great satisfaction of finding the view I have always taken of the character and motives of Cataline and his confederates, confirmed by the opinion of that profound and sagacious critic and historian.

I will only add, that it is hardly probable that "the Roman Traitor" would ever have been finished had it not been for the strenuous advice of a friend, in whose opinion I have the utmost confidence, Mr. Benjamin, to whom some of the early chapters were casually shown, two or three years ago, and who almost insisted on my completing it.

It is most fitting, therefore, that it should be, as it is, introduced to the world under his auspices; since but for his favourable judgment, and for a feeling on my own part that to fail in such an attempt would be scarce a failure, while success would be success indeed, it would probably have never seen the light of day!

With these few remarks, I submit the Roman Traitor to the candid judgment of my friends and the public, somewhat emboldened by the uniform kindness and encouragement which I have hitherto met; and with some hope that I may be allowed at some future day, to lay another romance of the most famous, before the citizens of the youngest republic.

THE CEDARS

CONTENTS.

VOLUME I.

VOLUME II.

THE ROMAN TRAITOR;

OR, THE DAYS OF

CICERO, CATO AND CATALINE.

A TRUE TALE OF THE REPUBLIC.

CHAPTER I.

THE MEN.

But bring me to the knowledge of your chiefs.
MARINO FALIERO.

MIDNIGHT was over Rome. The skies were dark and lowering, and ominous of tempest; for it was a sirocco, and the welkin was overcast with sheets of vapory cloud, not very dense, indeed, or solid, but still sufficient to intercept the feeble twinkling of the stars, which alone held dominion in the firmament; since the young crescent of he moon had sunk long ago beneath the veiled horizon.

The air was thick and sultry, and so unspeakably oppressive, that for above three hours the streets had been entirely deserted. In a few houses of the higher class, lights might be seen dimly shining through the casements of the small chambers, hard beside the doorway, appropriated to the use of the Atriensis, or slave whose charge it was to guard the entrance of the court. But, for the most part, not a single ray cheered the dull murky streets, except that here and there, before the holy shrine, or vaster and more elaborate temple, of some one of Rome's hun dred gods, the votive lanthorns, though shorn of half their beams by the dense fog-wreaths, burnt perennial.

The period was the latter time of the republic, a few years after the fell democratic persecutions of the plebeian Marius had drowned the mighty city oceans-deep in patrician gore; after the awful retribution of the avenger Sylla had rioted in the destruction of that guilty faction.

He who was destined one day to support the laurelled diadem of universal empire on his bald brows, stood even now among the noblest, the most ambitious, and the most famous of the state; though not as yet had he unfurled the eagle wings of conquest over the fierce barbarian hordes of Gaul and Germany, or launched his galleys on the untried waters of the great Western sea. A dissipated, spendthrift, and luxurious youth, devoted solely as it would seem to the pleasures of the table, or to intrigues with the most fair and noble of Rome's ladies, he had yet, amid those unworthy occupations, displayed such gleams of overmastering talent, such wondrous energy, such deep sagacity, and above all such uncurbed though ill-directed ambition, that the perpetual Dictator had already, years before, exclaimed with prescient wisdom,—"In yon unzoned youth I perceive the germ of many a Marius."

At the same time, the magnificent and princely leader, who was to be thereafter his great rival, was reaping that rich crop of glory, the seeds of which had been sown already by the wronged Lucullus, in the broad kingdoms of the effeminate East.

Meanwhile, as Rome had gradually rendered herself, by the exertion of indomitable valor, the supreme mistress of every foreign power that bordered on the Mediterranean, wealth, avarice, and luxury, like some contagious pestilence, had crept into the inmost vitals of the commonwealth, until the very features, which had once made her famous, no less for her virtues than her valor, were utterly obliterated and for ever.

Instead of a paternal, poor, brave, patriotic aristocracy, she had now a nobility, valiant indeed and capable, but dissolute beyond the reach of man's imagination, boundless in their expenditures, reckless as to the mode of gaining wherewithal to support them, oppressive and despotical to their inferiors, smooth-tongued and hypocritical toward each other, destitute equally of justice and compassion toward men, and of respect and piety toward the Gods! Wealth had become the idol, the god of the whole people! Wealth—and no longer service, eloquence, daring, or integrity,—was held the requisite for office. Wealth now conferred upon its owner, all magistracies all guerdons—rank, power, command,—consulships, provinces, and armies.

The senate—once the most grave and stern and just assembly that the world had seen—was now, with but a few superb exceptions, a timid, faithless, and licentious oligarchy; while—name whilome so majestical and mighty!—the people, the great Roman people, was but a mob! a vile colluvion of the offscourings of all climes and regions—Greeks, Syrians, Africans, Barbarians from the chilly north, and eunuchs from the vanquished Orient, enfranchised slaves, and liberated gladiators—a factious, turbulent, fierce rabble!

Such was the state of Rome, when it would seem that the Gods, wearied with the guilt of her aggrandisement, sick of the slaughter by which she had won her way to empire almost universal, had judged her to destruction—had given her up to perish, not by the hands of any foreign foe, but by her own; not by the wisdom, conduct, bravery of others, but by her own insanity and crime.

But at this darkest season of the state one hope was left to Rome—one safeguard. The united worth of Cicero and Cato! The statesmanship, the eloquence, the splendid and unequalled parts of the former; the stern self-denying virtue, the unchanged constancy, the resolute and hard integrity of the latter; these, singular and severally, might have availed to prop a falling dynasty—united, might have preserved a world!

The night was such as has already been described: gloomy and lowering in its character, as was the aspect of the political horizon, and most congenial to the fearful plots, which were even now in progress against the lives of Rome's best citizens, against the sanctity of her most solemn temples, the safety of her domestic hearths, the majesty of her inviolable laws, the very existence of her institutions, of her empire, of herself as one among the nations of the earth.

Most suitable, indeed, was that dim murky night, most favorable the solitude of the deserted streets, to the measures of those parricides of the Republic, who lurked within her bosom, thirsty for blood, and panting to destroy. Nor had they overlooked the opportunity. But a few days remained before that on which the Consular elections, fixed for the eighteenth of October, were to take place in the Campus Martius—whereat, it was already understood that Sergius Cataline, frustrated the preceding year, by the election of the great orator of Arpinum to his discomfiture, was about once more to try the fortunes of himself and of the popular faction.

It was at this untimely hour, that a man might have been seen lurking beneath the shadows of an antique archway, decorated with half-obliterated sculptures of the old Etruscan school, in one of the narrow and winding streets which, lying parallel to the Suburra, ran up the hollow between the Viminal and Quirinal hills.

He was a tall and well-framed figure, though so lean as to seem almost emaciated. His forehead was unusually high and narrow, and channelled with deep horizontal lines of thought and passion, across which cut at right angles the sharp furrows of a continual scowl, drawing the corners of his heavy coal-black eyebrows into strange contiguity. Beneath these, situated far back in their cavernous recesses, a pair of keen restless eyes glared out with an expression fearful to behold—a jealous, and unquiet, ever-wandering glance—so sinister, and ominous, and above all so indicative of a perturbed and anguished spirit, that it could not be looked upon without suggesting those wild tales, which speak of fiends dwelling in the revivified and untombed carcasses of those who die in unrepented sin. His nose was keenly Roman; with a deep wrinkle seared, as it would seem, into the sallow flesh from either nostril downward. His mouth, grimly compressed, and his jaws, for the most part, firmly clinched together, spoke volumes of immutable and iron resolution; while all his under lip was scarred, in many places, with the trace of wounds, inflicted beyond doubt, in some dread paroxysm, by the very teeth it covered.

The dress which this remarkable looking individual at that time wore, was the *penula*, as it was called; a short, loose straight-cut overcoat, reaching a lttle way below the knees, not fitted to the shape, but looped by woollen frogs all down the front, with broad flaps to protect the arms, and a square cape or collar, which at the pleasure of the wearer could be drawn up so as to conceal all the lower part of the countenance, or suffered to fall down upon the shoulders.

This uncouth vestment, which was used only by men of the lowest order, or by others solely when engaged in long and toilsome journeys, or in cold wintry weather, was composed of a thick loose-napped frieze or serge, of a dark purplish brown, with loops and *fibulæ*, or frogs, of a dull dingy red.

The wearer's legs were bare down to the very feet, which were protected by coarse shoes of heavy leather, fastened about the ancles by a thong, with a clasp of marvellously ill-cleaned brass. Upon his head he had a *petasus*, or broad-brimmed hat of gray felt, fitting close to the skull, with a long fall behind, not very unlike in form to the south-wester of a modern seaman. This article of dress was, like the penula, although peculiar to the inferior classes, oftentimes worn by men of superior rank, when journeying abroad. From these, therefore, little or no aid was given to conjecture, as to the station of the person, who now shrunk back into the deepest gloom of the old archway, now peered out stealthily into the night, grinding his teeth and muttering smothered imprecations against some one, who had failed to meet him.

The shoes, however, of rude, ill-tanned leather, of a form and manufacture which was peculiar to the lowest artizans or even slaves, were such as no man of ordinary standing would under any circumstances have adopted. Yet if these would have implied that the wearer was of low plebeian origin, this surmise was contradicted by several rings decked with gems of great price and splendor —one a large deeply-engraved signet—which were distinctly visible by their lustre on the fingers of both his hands.

His air and carriage too were evidently in accordance with the nobility of birth implied by these magnificent adornments, rather than with the humble station betokened by the rest of his attire.

His motions were quick, irritable, and incessant! His pace, as he stalked to and fro in the narrow area of the archway, was agitated, and uneven. Now he would stride off ten or twelve steps with strange velocity, then pause, and stand quite motionless for perhaps a minute's space, and then again resume his walk with slow and faltering gestures, to burst forth once again, as at the instigation of some goading spirit, to the same short-lived energy and speed.

Meantime, his color went and came; he bit his lip, till the blood trickled down his clean shorn chin; he clinched his hands, and smote them heavily together, and uttered in a harsh hissing whisper the most appalling imprecations ---on his own head---on him who had deceived him---on Rome, and all her myriads of inhabitants---on earth, and sea, and heaven—on everything divine or human!

"The black plague 'light on the fat sleepy glutton!—nay, rather all the fiends and furies of deep Erebus pursue *me!*—me!—me, who was fool enough to fancy that aught of bold design or manly daring could rouse up the dull, adipose, luxurious loiterer from his wines—his concubines---his slumbers!—And now—the dire ones hunt him to perdition! Now, the seventh hour of night hath passed, and all await us at the house of Læca; and this foul sluggard sottishly snores at home!"

While he was cursing yet, and smiting his broad chest, and gnashing his teeth in impotent malignity, suddenly a quick step became audible at a distance. The sound fell on his ear sharpened by the stimulus of fiery passions and of conscious fear, long ere it could have been perceived by any ordinary listener.

"'Tis he," he said, "'tis he at last—but no?" he continued, after a pause of a second, during which he had stooped, and laid his ear close to the ground, "no! 'tis too quick and light for the gross Cassius. By all the gods! there are two! Can he, then, have betrayed me? No! no! By heavens! he dare not!"

At the same time he started back into the darkest corner of the arch, pulled up the cape of his cassock, and slouched the wide-brimmed hat over his anxious lineaments; then pressing his body flat against the dusky wall, to which the color of his garments was in some sort assimilated, he awaited the arrival of the new-comers, perhaps hoping that if foreign to his purpose they might pass by him in the gloom.

As the footsteps now sounded nearer, he thrust his right hand into the bosom of his cassock, and drew out a long broad two-edged dagger, or stiletto; and as he unsheathed it, "Ready!" he muttered to himself, "ready for either fortune!"

Nearer and nearer came the footsteps, and the blent sounds of the two were now distinctly audible—one a slow, listless tread, as of one loitering along, as if irresolute whether to turn back or proceed; the other a firm, rapid, and decided step.

"Ha! it is well!" resumed the listener; "Cassius it is; and with him comes Cethegus, though where they have joined company I marvel."

And, as he spoke, he put his weapon back into his girdle, where it was perfectly concealed by the folds of the penula.

"Ho!—stand!" he whispered, as the two men whose steps he had heard, entered the archway, "Stand, Friends and Brethren."

"Hail, Sergius!" replied the foremost; a tall and splendidly formed man, with a dark quick eye, and regular features, nobly chiselled and in all respects such—had it not been for the bitter and ferocious sneer, which curled his haughty lip, at every word—as might be termed eminently handsome.

He wore his raven hair in long and flowing curls, which hung quite down upon his shoulders—a fashion that was held in Rome to the last degree effeminate, indeed almost infamous—while his trim whiskers and close curly beard reeked with the richest perfumes, impregnating the atmosphere through which he passed with odors so strong as to be almost overpowering.

His garb was that of a patrician of the highest order; though tinctured, like the arrangement of his hair, with not a little of that soft luxurious taste which had, of latter years, begun so generally to pervade Rome's young nobility. His under dress or tunic, was not of that succinct and narrow cut, which had so well become the sturdy fathers of the new republic! but—beside being wrought of the finest Spanish wool of snowy whiteness, with the broad crimson facings indicative of his senatorial rank, known as the laticlave—fell in loose folds half way between his knee and ancle.

It had sleeves, too, a thing esteemed unworthy of a man—and was fringed at the cuffs, aud round the hem, with a deep passmenting of crimson to match the laticlave. His toga of the thinnest and most gauzy texture, and whiter even than his tunic, flowed in a series of classical and studied draperies quite to his heels, where like the tunic it was bordered by a broad crimson trimming. His feet were ornamented, rather than protected, by delicate buskins of black leather, decked with the silver *sigma*, in its old crescent shape, the proud initial of the high term senator. A golden bracelet, fashioned like a large serpent, exquisitely carved with horrent scales and forked tail, was twined about the wrist of his right arm, with a huge carbuncle set in the head, and two rare diamonds for eyes. A dozen rings gemmed with the clearest brilliants sparkled upon his white and tapering fingers; in which, to complete the picture, he bore a handkerchief of fine Egyptian cambric, or Byssus as the Romans styled it, embroidered at the edges in arabesques of golden thread.

His comrade was if possible more slovenly in his attire than his friend was luxurious and expensive. He wore no toga, and his tunic—which, without the upper robe, was the accustomed dress of gladiators, slaves, and such as were too poor to wear the full and characteristic attire of the Roman citizen—was of dark brownish woollen, threadbare, and soiled with spots of grease, and patched in many places. His shoes were of coarse clouted leather, and his legs were covered up to the knees by thongs of ill-tanned cowhide rolled round them and tied at the ancles with straps of the same material.

"A plague on both of you!" replied the person, who had been so long awaiting them, in answer to their salutation. "Two hours have ye detained me here; and now that ye have come, in pretty guise ye do come! Oh! by the gods! a well assorted pair. Cassius more filthy than the vilest and most base tatterdemalion of the stews, and with him rare Cethegus, a senator in all his bravery! Wise judgment! excellent disguises! I know not whether most to marvel at the insane and furious temerity of this one, or at the idiotic foolery of that! Well fitted are ye both for a great purpose. And now—may the dark furies hunt you to perdition!—what hath delayed you?"

"Why, what a coil is here", replied the gay Cethegus, delighted evidently at the unsuppressed anger of his confederate in crime, and bent on goading to yet more fiery wrath his most ungovernable temper. "Methinks, O pleasant Sergius, the moisture of this delectable night should have quenched somewhat the quick flames of your most amiable and placid humor! Keep thy hard words, I prithee, Cataline, for those who either heed or dread them. I, thou well knowest, do neither."

"Peace, peace! Cethegus; plague him no farther," interrupted Cassius, just as the fierce conspirator, exclaiming in a deep harsh whisper, the one word "Boy!" strode forth as if to strike him. "And thou, good Cataline, listen to reason—we have been dogged hitherward, and so came by circuitous byeways!"

"Dogged, said ye—dogged? and by whom?—doth the slave live, who dared it?"

"By a slave, as we reckon," answered Cassius, "for he wore no toga; and his tunic"—

"Was filthy—very filthy, by the gods!—most like thine own, good Cassius," interposed Cethegus. But, in good sooth, he *was* a slave, my Sergius. He passed us twice, before I thought much of it. Once as we crossed the sacred way after descending from the Palatine—and once again beside the shrine of Venus in the Cyprian street. The second time he gazed into my very eyes, until he caught my glance meeting his own, and then with a quick bounding pace he hurried onward."

"Tush!" answered Cataline, "tush! was that all? the knave was a chance night-walker, and frightened ye! Ha! ha! by Hercules! it makes me laugh—frightened the rash and overbold Cethegus!"

"It was not all!" replied Cethegus very calmly, "it was not all, Cataline. And, but that we are joined here in a purpose so mighty that it overwhelms all private interests, all mere considerations of the individual, you, my good sir, should learn what it is to taunt a man with fear, who fears not anything—least of all thee! But it was not all. For as we turned from a side lane into the Wicked* street that scales the summit of the Esquiline, my eye caught something lurking in the dark shadow cast over an angle of the wall by a large cypress. I seized the arm of Cassius, to check his speech"—

"Ha! did the fat idiot speak?—what said he?" interrupted Cataline.

"Nothing," replied the other, "nothing, at least, of any moment. Well, I caught Cassius by the arm, and was in the act of pointing, when from the shadows of the tree out sprang this self-same varlet, whereon I ——".

"Rushed on him! dragged him into the light! and smote him, thus, and thus, and thus! didst thou not, excellent Cethegus?" Cataline exclaimed fiercely in a hard stern whisper, making three lounges, while he spoke, as if with a stiletto.

"I did not any of these things," answered the other.

"And why not, I say, why not? why not?" cried Cataline with rude impetuosity.

"That shall I answer, when you give me time," said Cethegus, coolly. "Because when I rushed forth, he fled with an exceeding rapid flight; leaped the low wall into the graveyard of the base Plebeians, and there among the cypresses and overthrown sepulchres escaped me for a while. I beat about most warily, and at length started him up again from the jaws of an obscene and broken catacomb. I gained on him at every step; heard the quick panting of his breath; stretched out my left to grasp him, while my right held unsheathed and ready the good stiletto that ne'er failed me. And now—now—by the great Jove! his tunic's hem was fluttering in my clutch, when my feet tripped over a prostrate column, that I was hurled five paces at the least in advance of the fugitive; and when I rose again, sore stunned, and bruised, and breathless, the slave had vanished."

"And where, I prithee, during this well-concerted chase, was valiant Cassius?" enquired Cataline, with a hoarse sneering laugh.

"During the chase, I know not," answered Cethegus, "but when it was over, and I did return, I found him

* *Vicus sceleratus.* So called because Tullia therein drove her chariot over her father's corpse.

leaning on the wall, even in the angle whence the slave fled on our approach."

"Asleep! I warrant me—by the great gods! asleep!" exclaimed the other; "but come!—come, let us onward, —I trow we have been waited for—and as we go, tell me, I do beseech thee, what was't that Cassius said, when the slave lay beside ye?—"

"Nay, but I have forgotten—some trivial thing or other —oh! now I do bethink me, he said it was a long walk to Marcus Læca's."

"Fool! fool! Double and treble fool! and dost thou call this nothing? Nothing to tell the loitering informer the very head and heart of our design? By Erebus! but I am sick—sick of the fools, with whom I am thus wretchedly assorted! Well! well! upon your own heads be it!" and instantly recovering his temper he walked on with his two confederates, now in deep silence, at a quick pace through the deserted streets towards their perilous rendezvous.

Noiseless, with stealthy steps, they hurried onward, threading the narrow pass between the dusky hills, until they reached a dark and filthy lane which turning at right angles led to the broad thoroughfare of the more showy, though by no means less ill-famed Suburra. Into this they struck instantly, walking in single file, and keeping as nearly as possible in the middle of the causeway. The lane, which was composed of dwellings of the lowest order, tenanted by the most abject profligates, was dark as midnight; for the tall dingy buildings absolutely intercepted every ray of light that proceeded from the murky sky, and there was not a spark in any of the sordid casements, nor any votive lamp in that foul alley. The only glimpse of casual illumination, and that too barely serving to render the darkness and the filth perceptible, was the faint streak of lustre where the Suburra crossed the far extremity of the bye-path.

Scarce had they made three paces down the alley, ere the quick eye of Cataline, for ever roving in search of aught suspicious, caught the dim outline of a human figure, stealing across this pallid gleam.

"Hist! hist!" he whispered in stern low tones, which though inaudible at three yards' distance completely filled the ears of him to wh m they were addressed—"hist!

hist! Cethegus; seest thou not—seest thou not there? If it be he, he 'scapes us not again!—out with thy weapon, man, and strike at once, if that thou have a chance; but if not, do thou go on with Cassius to the appointed place. Leave him to me! and say, I follow ye! See! he hath slunk into the darkness. Separate ye, and occupy the whole width of the street, while I dislodge him!"

And as he spoke, unsheathing his broad poignard, but holding it concealed beneath his cassock, he strode on boldly, affecting the most perfect indifference, and even insolence of bearing.

Meanwhile the half-seen figure had entirely disappeared amid the gloom; yet had the wary eye of the conspirator, in the one momentary glance he had obtained, been able to detect with something very near to certainty the spot wherein the spy, if such he were, lay hidden. As he approached the place—whereat a heap of rubbish, the relics of a building not long ago as it would seem consumed by fire, projected far into the street—seeing no sign whatever of the man who, he was well assured, was not far distant, he paused a little so as to suffer his companions to draw near. Then as they came up with him, skilled in all deep and desperate wiles, he instantly commenced a whispered conversation, a tissue of mere nonsense, with here and there a word of seeming import clearly and audibly pronounced. Nor was his dark manœuvre unsuccessful; for as he uttered the word "Cicero," watching meanwhile the heap of ruins as jealously as ever tiger glared on its destined prey, he caught a tremulous outline; and in a second's space, a small round object, like a man's head, was protruded from the darkness, and brought into relief against the brighter back ground.

Then—then—with all the fury—all the lythe agile vigor, all the unrivalled speed, and concentrated fierceness of that tremendous beast of prey, he dashed upon his victim! But at the first slight movement of his sinewy form, the dimly seen shape vanished; impetuously he rushed on among the piles of scattered brick and rubbish, and, ere he saw the nature of the place, plunged down a deep descent into the cellar of the ruin.

Lucky was it for Cataline, and most unfortunate for Rome, that when the building fell, its fragments had choked three parts of the depth of that subterranean vault;

so that it was but from a height of three or four feet at the utmost, that the fierce desperado was precipitated !

Still, to a man less active, the accident might have been serious, but with instinctive promptitude, backed by a wonderful exertion of muscular agility, he writhed his body even in the act of falling so that he lighted on his feet; and, ere a second had elapsed after his fall, was extricating himself from the broken masses of cement and brickwork, and soon stood unharmed, though somewhat stunned and shaken, on the very spot which had been occupied scarcely a minute past by the suspected spy.

At the same point of time in which the conspirator fell, the person, whosoever he was, in pursuit of whom he had plunged so heedlessly into the ruins, darted forth from his concealment close to the body and within arm's length of the fierce Cethegus, whose attention was for the moment distracted from his watch by the catastrophe which had befallen his companion. Dodging by a quick movement —so quick that it seemed almost the result of instinct—so to elude the swift attempt of his enemy to arrest his progress, the spy was forced to rush almost into the arms of Cassius.

Yet this appeared not to cause him any apprehension ; for he dashed boldly on, till they were almost front to front; when, notwithstanding his unwieldy frame and inactivity of habit, spurred into something near to energy by the very imminence of peril, the worn-out debauchee bestirred himself as if to seize him.

If such, however, were his intention, widely had he miscalculated his own powers, and fatally underrated the agility and strength of the stranger—a tall, thin, wiry man, well nigh six feet in height, broad shouldered, and deep chested, and thin flanked, and limbed like a Greek Athlete.

On he dashed !—on—right on ! till they stood face to face; and then with one quick blow, into which, as it seemed, he put but little of his strength, he hurled the burly Cassius to the earth, and fled with swift and noiseless steps into the deepest gloom. Perceiving on the instant the necessity of apprehending this now undoubted spy, the fiery Cethegus paused not one instant to look after his discomfited companions; but rushed away on the traces of the fugitive, who had perhaps gained, at the very utmost, a dozen paces' start of him, in that wild midnight race—that race for life and death.

The slave, for such from his dark tunic he appeared to be, was evidently both a swift and practised runner; and well aware how great a stake was on his speed he now strained every muscle to escape, while scarce less fleet, and straining likewise every sinew to the utmost, Cethegus panted at his very heels.

Before, however, they had run sixty yards, one swifter than Cethegus took up the race; and bruised although he was, and stunned, and almost breathless when he started, ere he had overtaken his staunch friend, which he did in a space wonderfully brief, he seemed to have shaken off every ailment, and to be in the completest and most firm possession of all his wonted energies. As he caught up Cethegus, he relaxed somewhat of his speed, and ran on by his side for some few yards at a sort of springy trot, speaking the while in a deep whisper,

"Hist!" he said, "hist!—I am more swift of foot than thou, and deeper winded. Leave me to deal with this dog! Back thou, to him thou knowest of; sore is he hurt, I warrant me. Comfort him as thou best mayest, and hurry whither we were now going. 'Tis late even now—too late, I fear me much, and doubtless we are waited for. I have the heels of this same gallowsbird, that can I see already! Leave me to deal with him, and an he tells tales on us, then call me liar!"

Already well nigh out of breath himself, while the endurance of the fugitive seemed in nowise affected, and aware of the vast superiority of his brother conspirator's powers to his own, Cethegus readily enough yielded to his positive and reiterated orders, and turning hastily backward, gathered up the bruised and groaning Cassius, and led him with all speed toward the well-known rendezvous in the house of Læca.

Meanwhile with desperate speed that headlong race continued; the gloomy alley was passed through; the wider street into which it debouched, vanished beneath their quick beating footsteps; the dark and shadowy arch, wherein the chief conspirator had lurked, was threaded at full speed; and still, although he toiled, till the sweat dripped from every pore like gouts of summer rain, although he plied each limb, till every over-wrought sinew seemed to crack, the hapless fugitive could gain no ground on his inveterate pursuer; who, cool, collected and unwearied, without one drop of perspiration on his dark sallow brow, without one panting sob in his deep breath, followed on at an equable and steady pace, gaining not any thing, nor seeming to desire to gain any thing, while yet within the precincts of the populous and thickly-settled city.

But now they crossed the broad Virbian street. The slave, distinctly visible for such, as he glanced by a brightly decorated shrine girt by so many brilliant lamps as shewed its tenant idol to have no lack of worshippers, darted up a small street leading directly towards the Esquiline.

"Now! now!" lisped Cataline between his hard-set teeth, "now he is mine, past rescue!"

Up the dark filthy avenue they sped, the fierce pursuer now gaining on the fugitive at every bound; till, had he stretched his arm out, he might have seized him; till his breath, hot and strong, waved the disordered elf-locks that fell down upon the bare neck of his flying victim. And now the low wall of the Plebeian burying ground arose before them, shaded by mighty cypresses and overgrown with tangled ivy. At one wild bound the hunted slave leaped over it, into the trackless gloom. At one wild bound the fierce pursuer followed him. Scarcely a yard asunder they alighted on the rank grass of that charnel grove; and not three paces did they take more, ere Cataline had hurled his victim to the earth, and cast himself upon him; choking his cries for help by the compression of his sinewy fingers, which grasped with a tenacity little inferior to that of an iron vice the miserable wretch's gullet.

He snatched his poniard from his sheath, reared it on high with a well skilled and steady hand! Down it came, noiseless and unseen. For there was not a ray of light to flash along its polished blade. Down it came with almost the speed and force of the electric fluid. A deep, dull, heavy sound was heard, as it was plunged into the yielding flesh, and the hot gushing blood spirted forth in a quick jet into the very face and mouth of the fell murderer. A terrible convulsion, a fierce writhing spasm followed—so strong, so muscularly powerful, that the stern gripe of Cataline was shaken from the throat of his victim, and from his dagger's hilt!

In the last agony the murdered man cast off his slayer from his breast; started erect upon his feet! tore out, from the deep wound, the fatal weapon which had made it; hurled it far—far as his remaining strength permitted—into the rayless night; burst forth into a wild and yelling cry, half laughter and half imprecation; fell headlong to the earth—which was no more insensible than he, what time he struck it, to any sense of mortal pain or sorrow—and perished there alone, unpitied and unaided.

"HABET!—he hath it!" muttered Cataline, quoting the well-known expression of the gladiatorial strife; "he hath it!—but all the plagues of Erebus, light on it—my good stiletto lies near to him in the swart darkness, to testify against me; nor by great Hecate! is there one chance to ten of finding it. Well! be it so!" he added, turning upon his heel, "be it so, for most like it hath fallen in the deep long grass, where none will ever find it; and if they do, I care not!"

And with a reckless and unmoved demeanor, well pleased with his success, and casting not one retrospective thought toward his murdered victim, not one repentant sigh upon his awful crime, he too hurried away to join his dread associates at their appointed meeting.

CHAPTER II.

THE MEASURES.

For what then do they pause?
An hour to strike.
MARINO FALIERO.

THE hours of darkness had already well nigh passed, and but for the thick storm-clouds and the drizzling rain, some streaks of early dawn might have been seen on the horizon, when at the door of Marcus Læca, in the low grovelling street of the Scythemakers—strange quarter for the residence of a patrician, one of the princely Porcii—the arch-conspirator stood still, and glared around with keen suspicious eyes, after his hurried walk.

It was, however, yet as black as midnight; nor in that wretched and base suburb, tenanted only by poor laborious artizans, was there a single artificial light to relieve the gloom of nature.

The house of Læca! How little would the passer-by who looked in those days on its walls, decayed and moss-grown even then, and mouldering—how little would he have imagined that its fame would go down to the latest ages, imperishable through its owner's infamy.

The house of Læca! The days had been, while Rome was yet but young, when it stood far aloof in the gay green fields, the suburban villa of the proud Porcian house. Time passed, and fashions changed. Low streets and squalid tenements supplanted the rich fields and fruitful orchards, which had once rendered it so pleasant an abode. Its haughty lords abandoned it for a more stately palace nigh the forum, and for long years it had remained tenantless, voiceless, desolate. But dice, and wine, and women, mad luxury and boundless riot, had brought its owner down to indigence, and infamy and sin.

The palace passed away from its inheritor. The ruin welcomed its last lord.

And here, meet scene for orgies such as it beheld, Rome's parricides were wont to hold their murderous assemblies.

With a slow stealthy tread, that woke no echo, Cataline advanced to the door. There was no lamp in the cell of the atriensis; no sign of wakefulness in any of the casements; yet at the first slight tap upon the stout oaken pannel, although it was scarce louder than the plash of the big raindrops from the eaves, another tap responded to it from within, so faint that it appeared an echo of the other. The rebel counted, as fast as possible, fifteen; and then tapped thrice as he had done before, meeting the same reply, a repetition of his own signal. After a moment's interval, a little wicket opened in the door, and a low voice asked "Who?" In the same guarded tone the answer was returned, "Cornelius." Again the voice asked, "Which?" and instantly, as Cataline replied, "the third," the door flew open, and he entered.

The Atrium, or wide hall in which he stood, was all in utter darkness; there was no light on the altar of the Penates, which was placed by the *impluvium*—a large shallow tank of water occupying the centre of the hall in all Roman houses—nor any gleam from the *tablinum*, or closed gallery beyond, parted by heavy curtains from the audience chamber.

There were no stars to glimmer through the opening in the roof above the central tank, yet the quick eye of the conspirator perceived, upon the instant, that two strong men with naked swords, their points within a hand's breadth of his bosom, stood on each side the doorway.

The gate was closed as silently as it had given him entrance; was barred and bolted; and till then no word was interchanged. When all, however, was secure, a deep rich voice, suppressed into a whisper, exclaimed "Sergius?" "Ay!" answered Cataline. "Come on!' and without farther parley they stole into the most secret chambers of the house, fearful as it appeared of the sounds of their own footsteps, much more of their own voices.

Thus with extreme precaution, when they had traversed several chambers, among which were an indoor *triclinium*, or dining parlor, and a vast picture gallery, groping their way along in utter darkness, they reached a small square court, surrounded by a peristyle or colonnade, containing a dilapidated fountain. Passing through this, they reached a second dining room, where on the central table they found a small lamp burning, and by the aid of this, though still observing the most scrupulous silence, quickly attained their destination—a low and vaulted chamber entirely below the surface of the ground, accessible only by a stair defended by two doors of unusual thickness.

That was a fitting place for deeds of darkness, councils of desperation, such as they held, who met within its gloomy precincts. The moisture, which dripped constantly from its groined roof of stone, had formed stalactites of dingy spar, whence the large gouts plashed heavily on the damp pavement; the walls were covered with green slimy mould; the atmosphere was close and fœtid, and so heavy that the huge waxen torches, four of which stood in rusty iron candelabra, on a large slab of granite, burned dim and blue, casting a faint and ghastly light on lineaments so grim and truculent, or so unnaturally excited by the dominion of all hellish passions, that they had little need of anything extraneous to render them most hideous and appalling. There were some twenty-five men present, variously clad indeed, and of all ages, but evidently —though many had endeavoured to disguise the fact by poor and sordid garments—all of the higher ranks.

Six or eight were among them, who feared not, nor were ashamed to appear there in the full splendor of their distinctive garb as Senators, prominent among whom was the most rash and furious of them all, Cethegus.

He, at the moment when the arch-conspirator, accompanied by Læca and the rest of those who had admitted him, entered the vault, was speaking with much energy and even fierceness of manner to three or four who stood apart a little from the rest with their backs to the door, listening with knitted brows, clenched hands, and lips compressed and bloodless, to his tremendous imprecations launched at the heads of all who were for any, even the least, delay in the accomplishment of their dread scheme of slaughter.

One among them was a large stately looking personage, somewhat inclined to corpulence, but showing many a sign of giant strength, and vigor unimpaired by years or habit. His head was large but well shaped, with a broad and massive forehead, and an eye keen as the eagle's when soaring in his pride of place. His nose was prominent, but rather aquiline than Roman. His mouth, wide and thick-lipped, with square and fleshy jaws, was the worst featnre in his face, and indicative of indulged sensuality and fierceness, if not of cruelty combined with the excess of pride.

This man wore the plain toga and white tunic of a private citizen; but never did plebeian eye and lip flash with such concentrated haughtiness, curl with so fell a sneer, as those of that fallen consular, of that degraded senator, the haughtiest and most ambitious of a race never deficient in those qualities, he who, drunk with despairing pride, and deceived to his ruin by the double-tongued Sibylline prophecies, aspired to be that third Cornelius, who should be master of the world's mistress, Rome.

The others were much younger men, for Lentulus was at that period already past his prime, and these—two more especially who looked mere boys—had scarcely reached youth's threshold; though their pale withered faces, and brows seared deeply by the scorching brand of evil passions, showed that in vice at least, if not in years, they had lived long already.

Those two were senators in their full garniture, the sons of Servius Sylla, both beautiful almost as women, with soft and feminine features, and long curled hair, and lips of coral, from which in flippant and affected accents fell words, and breathed desires, that would have made the blood stop and turn stagnant at the heart of any one, not utterly polluted and devoid of every humane feeling.

This little knot seemed fierce for action, fiery and panting with that wolfish thirst, to quench which blood must flow. But all the rest seemed dumb, and tongue-tied, and crest-fallen. The sullenness of fear brooded on every other face. The torpor of despairing crime, already in its own fancy baffled and detected, had fallen on every other heart. For, at the farther end of the room, whispering to his trembling hearers dubious and dark suspicions, with terror on his tongue, stood Cassius, exaggerating the adventures of the night.

Such was the scene, when Cataline stalked into that bad conclave. The fires of hell itself could send forth no more blasting glare, than shot from his dark eyes, as he beheld, and read at half a glance their consternation. Bitter and blighting was the sneer upon his lip, as he stood motionless, gazing upon them for a little space. Then flinging his arm on high and striding to the table he dashed his hand upon it, that it rang and quivered to the blow.

"What are ye?" he said slowly, in tones that thrilled to every heart, so piercing was their emphasis. "Men?—No, by the Gods! men rush on death for glory!—Women? They risk it, for their own, their children's, or their lover's safety!—Slaves?—Nay! even these things welcome it for freedom, or meet it with revenge! Less then, than men! than women, slaves, or beasts!—Perish like cattle, if ye will, unbound but unresisting, all armed but unavenged! —And ye—great Gods! I laugh to see your terror-blanched, blank visages. I laugh, but loathe in laughing! The destined dauntless sacrificers, who would imbue your knives in senatorial, consular gore! kindle your altars on the downfallen Capitol! and build your temples on the wreck of Empire! Ha! do you start? and does some touch of shame redden the sallow cheeks that courage had left bloodless? and do ye grasp your daggers, and rear your drooping heads? are ye men, once again? Why should ye not? what do ye see, what hear, whereat to falter? What oracle, what portent? Now, by the Gods! methought they spoke of victory and glory. Once more, what do ye fear, or wish? What, in the name of Hecate and Hades! What do ye wait for?"

"A leader!" answered the rash Cethegus, excited now even beyond the bounds of ordinary rashness. "A day, a place, a signal!"

"Have them, then, all," replied the other, still half scornfully. "Lo! I am here to lead; the field of Mars will give a place; the consular elections an occasion; the blood of Cicero a signal!"

"Be it so!" instantly replied Cethegus; "be it so! thou hast spoken, as the times warrant, boldly; and upon my head be it, that our deeds shall respond to thy daring words, with equal daring!"

And a loud hum of general assent succeeded to his stirring accents; and a quick fluttering sound ran through the whole assemblage, as every man, released from the constraint of deep and silent expectation, altered his posture somewhat, and drew a long breath at the close. But the conspirator paused not. He saw immediately the effect which had been made upon the minds of all, by what had passed. He perceived the absolute necessity of following that impulse up to action, before, by a revulsion no less sudden than the late change from despondency to fierceness, their minds should again subside into the lethargy of doubt and dismay.

"But say thou, Sergius," he continued, "how shall it be, and who shall strike the blow that is to seal Rome's liberty, our vengeance?"

"First swear we!" answered Cataline. "Læca, the eagle, and the bowl!"

"Lo! they are here, my Sergius," answered the master of the house, drawing aside a piece of crimson drapery, which covered a small niche or recess in the wall, and displaying by the movement a silver eagle, its pinions wide extended, and its talons grasping a thunderbolt, placed on a pedestal, under a small but exquisitely sculptured shrine of Parian marble. Before the image there stood a votive lamp, fed by the richest oils, a mighty bowl of silver half filled with the red Massic wine, and many *pateræ*, or sacrificial vessels of a yet richer metal.

"Hear, bird of Mars, and of Quirinus"—cried Cataline, without a pause, stretching his hands toward the glittering effigy—"Hear thou, and be propitious! Thou, who didst all-triumphant guide a yet greater than Quirinus to deeds of might and glory; thou, who wert worshipped by the charging shout of Marius, and consecrated by the gore of Cimbric myriads; thou, who wert erst enshrined on the Capitoline, what time the proud patricians veiled their haughty crests before the conquering plebeian; thou, who shalt sit again sublime upon those ramparts, meet aery for thine unvanquished pinion; shalt drink again libations, boundless libations of rich Roman life-blood, hot from patrician hearts, smoking from every kennel! Hear and receive our oaths—listen and be propitious!"

He spoke, and seizing from the pedestal a sacrificial knife, which lay beside the bowl, opened a small vein in his arm, and suffered the warm stream to gush into the wine. While the red current was yet flowing, he gave the weapon to Cethegus, and he did likewise, passing it in his turn to the conspirator who stood beside him, and he in like manner to the next, till each one in his turn had shed his blood into the bowl, which now mantled to the brim with a foul and sacrilegious mixture, the richest vintage of the Massic hills, curdled with human gore.

Then filling out a golden goblet for himself, "Hear, God of war," cried Cataline, "unto whose minister and omen we offer daily worship; hear, mighty Mars, the homicide and the avenger; and thou, most ancient goddess, hear, Nemesis! and Hecate, and Hades! and all ye powers of darkness, Furies and Fates, hear ye! For unto ye we swear, never to quench the torch; never to sheath the brand; till all our foes be prostrate, till not one drop shall run in living veins of Rome's patricians; till not one hearth shall warm; one roof shall shelter; till Rome shall be like Carthage, and we, like mighty Marius, lords and spectators of her desolation! We swear! we taste the consecrated cup! and thus may his blood flow, who shall, for pity or for fear, forgive or fail or falter—his own blood, and his wife's, and that of all his race forever! May vultures tear their eyes, yet fluttering with quick vision; may wolves tug at their heart-strings, yet strong with vigorous life; may infamy be their inheritance, and Tartarus receive their spirits!"

And while he spoke, he sipped the cup of horror with unreluctant lips, and dashed the goblet with the residue over the pedestal and shrine. And there was not one there who shrank from that foul draught. With ashy cheeks indeed, but knitted brows, and their lips reeking red with the abomination, but fearless and unfaltering, they pledged in clear and solemn tones, each after each, that awful imprecation, and cast their goblets down, that the floor swam in blood; and grasped each others' hands, sworn comrades from that hour even to the gates of hell.

A long and impressive silence followed. For every heart there, even of the boldest, recoiled as it were for a moment on itself, not altogether in regret or fear, much less in anything approaching to compunction or remorse; but in a sort of secret horror, that they were now involved beyond all hope of extrication, beyond all possibility of turning back or halting! And Cataline, endowed with almost superhuman shrewdness, and himself quite immovable of purpose, perceived the feelings that actuated all the others—which he felt not, nor cared for—and called on Læca to bring wine.

"Wine, comrades," he exclaimed, "pure, generous, noble wine, to wash away the rank drops from our lips, that are more suited to our blades! to make our veins leap cheerily to the blythe inspiration of the God! and last, not least, to guard us from the damps of this sweet chamber, which alone of his bounteous hospitality our Porcius has vouchsafed to us!" And on the instant, the master—for they dared trust no slaves—bore in two earthen vases, one of strong Chian from the Greek Isle of the Egean, the other of Falernian, the fruitiest and richest of the Italian wines, not much unlike the modern sherry, but having still more body, and many cyathi, or drinking cups; but he brought in no water, wherewith the more temperate ancients were wont to mix their heady wines, even in so great a ratio as nine to one of the generous liquor.

"Fill now! fill all!" cried Cataline, and with the word he drained a brimming cup. "Rare liquor this, my Marcus," he continued; "whence had'st thou this Falernian? 'tis of thine inmost brand, I doubt not. In whose consulship did it imbibe the smoke?"

"The first of Caius Marius."

"Forty-four years, a ripe age," said Cethegus, "but twill be better forty years hence. Strange, by the Gods! that of the two best things on earth, women and wine, the nature should so differ. The wine is crude still, when the girl is mellow; but it is ripe, long after she is ——"

"Rotten, by Venus!"—interposed Cæparius, swearing the harlot's oath; "Rotten, and in the lap of Lamia!"

"But heard ye not," asked Cataline, "or hearing, did ye not accept the omen!—in whose first Consulship this same Falernian jar was sealed?"

"Marius! By Hercules! an omen! oh, may it turn out well!" exclaimed the superstitious Lentulus.

"Sayest thou, my Sura? well! drink we to the omen, and may we to the valour and the principles of Marius unite the fortunes of his rival—of all-triumphant Sylla!"

A burst of acclamations replied to the happy hit, and seeing now his aim entirely accomplished, Cataline checked the revel; their blood was up; no fear of chilling counsels!

"Now then," he said, "before we drink like boon companions, let us consult like men; there is need now of counsel; that once finished"——

"Fulvia awaits me," interrupted Cassius, "Fulvia, worth fifty revels!"

"And me Semperonia," lisped the younger and more beautiful of the twin Sylla.

"Meanwhile," exclaimed Autronius, "let us comprehend, so shall we need no farther meetings—each of which risks the awakening of suspicion, and it may well be of discovery. Let us now comprehend, that, when the time comes, we may all perform our duty. Speak to us, therefore, Sergius."

No farther exhortation was required; for coolly the conspirator arose to set before his desperate companions, the plans which he had laid so deeply, that it seemed scarcely possible that they should fail; and not a breath or whisper interrupted him as he proceeded.

"Were I not certain of the men," he said, "to whom I speak, I could say many things that should arouse you, so that you should catch with fiery eagerness at aught that promised a more tolerable position. I could recount the luxuries of wealth which you once knew; the agonies of poverty beneath which, to no purpose, you lie groaning. I could point out your actual inability to live, however basely—deprived of character and credit—devoid of any relics of your fortunes! weighed to the very earth by debts, the interest alone of which has swallowed up your patrimonies, and gapes even yet for more! fettered by bail-bonds, to fly which is infamy, and to abide them ruin! shunned, scorned, despised, and hated, if not feared by all men. I could paint, to your very eyes, ourselves in rags or fetters! our enemies in robes of office, seated on curule chairs, swaying the fate of nations, dispensing by a nod the wealth of plundered provinces! I could reverse the picture. But, as it is, your present miseries and your past deeds dissuade me. Your hopelessness and daring, your wrongs and valor, your injuries and thirst of vengeance, warn me, alike, that words are weak, and exhortation needless. Now understand with me, how matters stand. The stake for which we play, is fair before your eyes:—learn how our throw for it is certain. The consular elections, as you all well know, will be held, as proclaimed already, on the fifteenth day before the calends of November. My rivals are Sulpicius, Muræna, and Silanus. Antonius and Cicero will preside—the first, my friend! a bold and noble Roman! He waits but an occasion to declare for us. Now, mark me. Caius Manlius—you all do know the man, an old and practised soldier, a scar-seamed veteran of Sylla,—will on that very day display yon eagle to twenty thousand men, well armed, and brave, and desperate as ourselves, at Fiesolè. Septimius of Camerinum writes from the Picene district, that thirty thousand slaves will rise there at his bidding; while Caius Julius, sent to that end into Apulia, has given out arms and nominated leaders to twice five thousand there. Ere this, they have received my mandate to collect their forces, and to march on that same day toward Rome. Three several armies, to meet which there is not one legion on this side of Cisalpine Gaul! What, then, even if all were peace in Rome, what then could stand against us? But there shall be that done here, here in the very seat and heart, as I may say, of Empire, that shall dismay and paralyse all who would else oppose us. Cethegus, when the centuries are all assembled in the field of Mars, with fifteen hundred gladiators well armed and exercised even now, sets on the guard in the Janiculum, and beats their standard down. Then, while all is confusion, Statilius and Gabinius with their households,—whom, his work done, Cethegus will join straightway—will fire the city in twelve several places, break open the prison doors, and crying "Liberty to slaves!" and "Abolition of all debts!"—rush diverse throughout the streets, still gathering numbers as they go. Meanwhile, with Lentulus and Cassius, the clients of your houses being armed beneath their togas with swords and breast-plates, and casques ready to be donned, I will make sure of Cicero and the rest. Havoc, and slaughter, and flames every where will make the city ours. Then ye, who have no duty set, hear, and mark this: always to kill is to do something! the more, and nobler, so much the better deed! Remembering this, that sons have ready access to their sires, who for the most part are their bitterest foes! and that to spare none we are sworn—how, and how deeply, it needs not to remind you. More words are bootless, since to all here it must be evident that these things, planned thus far with deep and prudent council, once executed with that dauntless daring, which alone stands for armor, and for weapons, and, by the Gods! for bulwarks of defence, must win us liberty and glory, more over wealth, and luxury, and power, in which names is embraced the sum of all felicity. Therefore, now, I exhort you not; for if the woes which you would shun, the prizes which you shall attain, exhort you not, all words of man, all portents of the Gods, are dumb, and voiceless, and in vain! Mark the day only, and remember, that if not ye, at least your sires were Romans and were men!"

"Bravely, my Sergius, hast thou spoken, and well done!" cried at once several voices of the more prominent partisans.

"By the Gods! what a leader!" whispered Longinus Cassius to his neighbor.

"Fabius in council," cried Cethegus, "Marcellus in the field!"

"Moreover, fellow-soldiers," exclaimed Lentulus, "hear this: although he join not with us now, through policy, Antonius, the Consul, is in heart ours, and waits but for the first success to declare himself for the cause in arms. Crassus, the rich—Cæsar, the people's idol—have heard our counsels, and approve them. The first blow struck, their influence, their names, their riches, and their popularity, strike with us—trustier friends, by Pollux! and more potent, than fifty thousand swordsmen!"

A louder and more general burst of acclamation and applause than that which had succeeded Cataline's address, burst from the lips of all, as those great names dropped from the tongue of Lentulus; and one voice cried aloud—it was the voice of Curius, intoxicated as it were with present triumph—

"By all the Gods! Rome is our own! our own, even now, to portion out among our friends, our mistresses, our slaves!"

"Not Rome—but Rome's inheritance, the world!" exclaimed another. "If we win, all the universe is ours—and see how small the stake; when, if we fail"—

"By Hades, we'll not fail!" Cataline interrupted him, in his deep penetrating tones. "We cannot, and we will not! and now, for I wax somewhat weary, we will break up this conclave. We meet at the comitia!"

"And the Slave?" whispered Cethegus, with an inquiring accent, in his ear—"the Slave, my Sergius?"

"Will tell no tales of us," replied the other, with a hoarse laugh, "unless it be to Lamia."

Thus they spoke as they left the house; and ere the day had yet begun to glimmer with the first morning twilight—so darkly did the clouds still muster over the mighty city—went on their different ways toward their several homes, unseen, and, as they fondly fancied, unsuspected.

CHAPTER III.

THE LOVERS.

Fair lovers, ye are fortunately met.
MIDSUMMER NIGHT'S DREAM.

ON the same night, and almost at the same hour of the night, wherein that dreadful conclave was assembled at the house of Læca, a small domestic group, consisting indeed only of three individuals, was gathered in the tablinum, or saloon, of an elegant though modest villa, situate in the outskirts of the city, fronting the street that led over the Mulvian bridge to the Æmilian way, and having a large garden communicating in the rear with the plebeian cemetery on the Esquiline.

It was a gay and beautiful apartment, of small dimensions, but replete with all those graceful objects, those manifold appliances of refined taste and pleasure, for which the Romans, austere and poor no longer, had, since their late acquaintance with Athenian polish and Oriental uxury, acquired a predilection—ominous, as their sterner atriots fancied, of personal degeneracy and national deay.

Divided from the hall of reception by thick soft curtains, woven from the choice wool of Calabria, and glowing with the richest hues of the Tyrian crimson; and curtained with hangings of the same costly fabric around the windows, both of which with the doorway opened upon a peristyle; that little chamber wore an air of comfort, that charmed the eye more even than its decorations. Yet these were of no common order; for the floor was tesselated in rare patterns of mosaic work, showing its exquisite devices and bright colors, where they were not concealed by a footstool of embroidered tapestry. The walls were portioned out into compartments, each framed by a broad border of gilded scroll-work on a crimson ground, and containing an elaborately finished fresco painting; which, could they have been seen by any critical eye of modern days, would have set at rest for ever the question as to the state of this art among the ancients. The subject was a favorite one with all artists of all ages,—from the world-famous Iliad: the story of the goddess-born Achilles. Here tutored by the wise Centaur, Chiron, in horsemanship and archery, and all that makes a hero; here tearing off the virgin mitre, to don the glittering casque proffered, with sword and buckler, among effeminate wares, by the disguised Ulysses; there wandering in the despondent gloom of injured pride along the stormy sea, meet listener to his haughty sorrows, while in the distance, turning her tearful eyes back to her lord, Briseis went unwilling at the behest of the unwilling heralds. Again he was presented, mourning with frantic grief over the corpse of his beloved Patroclus—grief that called up his Nereid mother from the blue depths of her native element; and, in the last, chasing with unexampled speed the flying Hector, who, stunned and destined by the Gods to ruin, dared not await his onset, while Priam veiled his face upon the ramparts, and Hecuba already tore her hair, presaging the destruction of Troy's invincible unshaken column.*

A small wood fire blazed cheerfully upon the hearth, round which were clustered, in uncouth attitudes of old Etruscan sculpture, the grim and grotesque figures of the household Gods. Two lamps of bronze, each with four burners, placed on tall candelabra exquisitely carved in the same metal, diffused a soft calm radiance through the room, accompanied by an aromatic odor from the perfumed vegetable oil which fed their light. Upon a circular table of dark-grained citrean wood, inlaid with ivory and silver, were several rolls of parchment and papyrus, the books of the day, some of them splendidly emblazoned and illuminated; a lyre of tortoiseshell, and near to it the slender plectrum by which its cords were wakened to melody. Two or three little flasks of agate and of onyx containing some choice perfumes, a Tuscan vase full of fresh-gathered flowers, and several articles yet more decidedly feminine,

* Τροιας; αμαχον αθιραβη κιονα.—PINDAR

were scattered on the board; needles, and thread of var ous hues, and twine of gold and silver, and some embroidery, half finished, and as it would seem but that instant laid aside. Such was the aspect of the saloon wherein three persons were sitting on that night; who, though they were unconscious, nay, even unsuspicious of the existence of conspiracy and treason, were destined, ere many days should elapse, to be involved in its desperate mazes; to act conspicuous parts and undergo strange perils, in the dread drama of the times.

They were of different years and sex—one, a magnificent and stately matron, such as Rome's matrons were when Rome was at the proudest, already well advanced in years, yet still possessing not merely the remains of former charms, but much of real beauty, and that too of the noblest and most exalted order. Her hair, which had been black in her youth as the raven's wing, was still, though mixed with many a line of silver, luxuriant and profuse as ever. Simply and closely braided over her broad and intellectual temples, and gathered into a thick knot behind, it displayed admirably the contour of her head, and suited the severe and classic style of her strictly Roman features. The straight-cut eye-brows, the clear and piercing eye, the aquiline nose, and the firm thin lips, spoke worlds of character and decision; yet that which might have otherwise seemed stern and even harsh, was softened by a smile of singular sweetness, and by a lighting up of the whole countenance, which at times imparted to those high features an expression of benevolence, gentle and feminine in the extreme.

Her stature was well suited to the style of her lineaments; majestically tall and stately, and though attenuated something by the near approach of old age, preserving still the soft and flowing outlines of a form, which had in youth been noted for roundness and voluptuous symmetry.

She wore the plain white robes, bordered and zoned with crimson, of a patrician lady, but save one massive signet on the third finger of her right hand she had no gem or ornament whatever; and as she sat a little way aloof from her younger companions, drawing the slender threads with many a graceful motion from the revolving distaff into the basket by her side, she might have passed for her, whose proud prayer, that she might be known not as the daughter of the Scipios but as the mother of the Gracchi, was but too fatally fulfilled in the death-earned celebrity of those her boasted jewels.

The other lady was smaller, slighter, fairer, and altogether so different in mien, complexion, stature, and expression, that it was difficult even for those who knew them well to believe that they were a mother and her only child. For even in her flush of beauty, the elder lady, while in the full splendor of Italian womanhood, must ever have been calculated to inspire admiration, not all unmixed with awe, rather than tenderness or love. The daughter, on the other hand, was one whose every gesture, smile, word, glance, bespoke that passion latent in itself, which it awakened in the bosom of all beholders.

Slightly above the middle stature, and with a waist of scarce a span's circumference, her form was exquisitely full and rounded; the sweeping outlines of her snow-white and dimpled arms, bare to the shoulders, and set off by many strings of pearl, which were themselves scarcely whiter than the skin on which they rested; the swan-like curvature of the dazzling neck; the wavy and voluptuous development of her bust, shrouded but not concealed by the plaits of her white linen *stola*, fastened on either shoulder by a clasp of golden fillagree, and gathered just above her hips by a gilt zone of the Grecian fashion; the small and shapely foot, which peered out with its jewelled sandal under her gold-fringed draperies; combined to present to the eye a very incarnation of that ideal loveliness, which haunts enamored poets in their dreams, the girl just bursting out of girlhood, the glowing Hebe of the soft and sunny south. But if her form was lovely, how shall the pen of mortal describe the wild romantic beauty of her soul-speaking features. The rich redundancy of her dark auburn hair, black where the shadows rested on it as the sable locks of night, but glittering out wherever a wandering ray glanced on its glossy surface like the bright tresses of Aurora. The broad and marble forehead, the pencilled brows, and the large liquid eyes fraught with a mild and lustrous languor; the cheeks, pale in their wonted mood as alabaster, yet eloquent at times with warm and passionate blushes. The lips, redder than aught on earth which shares both hue and softness; and, more than all, the deep and indescribable expression which genius prints on every lineament of those, who claim that rarest and most godlike of endowments.

She was a thing to dream of, not describe; to dream of in some faint and breathless eve of early summer, beside the margin of some haunted streamlet, beneath the shade of twilight boughs in which the fitful breeze awakes that whispering melody, believed by the poetic ancients to be the chorus of the wood-nymph; to dream of and adore—even as she was adored by him who sat beside her, and watched each varying expression, that swept across her speaking features; and hung upon each accent of the low silvery voice, as if he feared it were the last to which his soul should thrill responsive.

He was a tall and powerful youth of twenty-four or five years; yet, though his limbs were sinewy and lithe, and though his deep round chest, thin flanks, and muscular shoulders gave token of much growing strength, it was still evident that, his stature having been prematurely gained, he lacked much of that degree of power of which his frame gave promise. For though his limbs were well formed they were scarcely set, or furnished, as we should say in speaking of an animal; and the strength, which he in truth possessed, was that of elasticity and youthful vigor, capable rather of violent though brief exertion, than that severe and trained robustness, which can for long continuous periods sustain the strongest and most trying labor.

His hair was dark and curling—his eye bright, clear, and penetrating; yet was its glance at times wavering and undetermined, such as would indicate perhaps a want of steadiness of purpose, not of corporeal resolution, for that was disproved by one glance at the decided curve of his bold clean-cut mouth, and the square outlines of his massive jaw, which seemed almost to betoken fierceness. There was a quick short flash at times, keen as the falcon's, in the unsteady eye, that told of energy enough within and stirring spirit to prompt daring deeds, the momentary irresolution conquered. There was a frank and cheery smile that oftentimes belied the auguries drawn from the other features; and, more than all, there was a tranquil sweet expression, which now and then pervaded the whole countenance, altering for the better its entire character, and betokening more mind and deeper feelings, than would at first have been suspected from his aspect.

His dress was the ordinary tunic of the day, of plain white woollen stuff, belted about the middle by a girdle, which contained his ivory tablets, and the metallic pencil used for writing on their waxed surface, together with his handkerchief and purse; but nothing bearing the semblance of a weapon, not so much even as a common knife. His legs and arms were bare, his feet being protected merely by sandals of fine leather having the clasps or fibulæ of gold; as was the buckle of his girdle, and one huge signet ring, which was his only ornament.

His toga, which had been laid aside on entering the saloon, as was the custom of the Romans in their own families, or among private friends, hung on the back of an armed chair; of ample size and fine material, but undistinguished by the marks of senatorial or equestrian rank. Such was the aspect, such the bearing of the youth, who might be safely deemed the girl's permitted suitor, from his whole air and manner, as he listened to the soft voice of his beautiful mistress. For as they sat there side by side, perusing from an illuminated scroll the elegies of some long-perished, long-forgotten poet, now reading audibly the smooth and honeyed lines, now commenting with playful criticism on the style, or carrying out with all the fervor and romance of young poetical temperament the half obscure allusions of the bard, no one could doubt that they were lovers; especially if he marked the calm and well-pleased smile that stole from time to time across the proud features of that patrician lady; who, sitting but a little way apart, watched—while she reeled off skein after skein of the fine Byssine flax in silence—the quiet happiness of the young pair.

Thus had the evening passed, not long nor tediously to any of the party; and midnight was at hand; when there entered from the atrium a grey-headed slave bearing a tray covered with light refreshments—fresh herbs, endive and mallows sprinkled with snow, ripe figs, eggs and anchovies, dried grapes, and cakes of candied honey; while two boys of rare beauty followed, one carrying a flagon of Chian wine diluted with snow water, the other a platter richly chased in gold covered with cyathi, or drinking cups, some of plain chrystal, some of that unknown myrrhine fabric,* which is believed by many scholars to have been highly vitrified and half-transparent porcelain.

A second slave brought in a folded stand, like a camp stool in shape, on which the tray was speedily deposited, while on a slab of Parian marble, near which the two boys took their stand, the wine and goblets were arranged in glittering order.

So silently, however, was all this done, that, their preparations made, the elder slaves had retired with a deep genuflexion, leaving the boys only to administer at that unceremonious banquet, ere the young couple, whose backs were turned towards the table, perceived the interruption.

The brilliant smile, which has been mentioned, beamed from the features of the elder lady, as she perceived how thoroughly engrossed, even to the unconsciousness of any passing sound, they were, whom, rising for the purpose, and laying by her work, she now proceeded to recall to sublunary matters.

"Paullus," she said, "and you, my Julia, ye are unconscious how the fleeting hours have slipped away. The night hath far advanced into the third watch. I would not part ye needlessly, nor over soon, especially when you must so soon perforce be severed; but we must not forget how long a homeward walk awaits our dear Arvina. Come, then, and partake some slight refreshment, before you say farewell.

"How thoughtless in me, to have detained you thus, and with a mile to walk this murky and unpleasant night They say, too, that the streets are dangerous of late, haunted by dissolute night-revellers—that villain Clodius and his infamous co-mates. I tremble like a leaf if I but meet them in broad day—and what if you should fall in with them, when flushed with wine, and ripe for any outrage?"

"Fie! dear one, fie!" answered the young man with a smile—"a sorry soldier wouldst thou make of me, who am within so short a space to meet the savages of Pontus, under our mighty Pompey! There is no danger, Julia, here in the heart of Rome; and my stout freedman Thrasea

* That it was such, can scarce be doubted, from the line of Martial: "Myrrheaque in Parthis pocula cocta focis."

awaits me with his torch. Nor is it so far either to my house, for those who cross, as I shall do, the cemetery on the Esquiline. 'Tis but a step across the sumptuous Carinæ to the Cælian."

"But surely, surely, Paul," exclaimed the lovely girl, laying her hand upon his arm, "thou wouldst not cross that fearful burying-ground, haunted by all things awful and obscene, thus at the dead of night. Oh! do not, dearest," she continued, "thou knowest not what wild terrible tales are rife, of sounds and sights unnatural and superhuman, encountered in those loathsome precincts. 'Tis a mere tempting of the Dark Ones, to brave the horrors of that place!"

"The Gods, my Julia," replied the youth unmoved by her alarm, "the Gods are never absent from their votaries, so they be innocent and pure of spirit. For me! I am unconscious of a wilful fault, and fear not anything."

"Well said, Paullus Arvina," exclaimed the elder lady, "and worthily of your descent from the Cæcilii"—for from that noble house his family indeed derived its origin. "But, although I," she added, "counsel you not to heed our Julia's girlish terrors, I love you not to walk by night so slenderly accompanied. Ho! boy, go summon me the steward, and bid him straightway arm four of the Thracian slaves."

"No! by the Gods, Hortensia!" the young man interrupted her, his whole face flushing with excitement, "you do shame to my manhood, by your caution. There is in truth no shadow of danger. Besides," he added, laughing at his own impetuosity, "I shall be far beyond the Esquiline ere excellent old Davus could rouse those sturdy knaves of yours, or find the armory key; for lo! I will but tarry to taste one cup of your choice of Chian to my Julia's health, and then straight homeward. Have a care, my fair boy, that flagon is too heavy to be lifted safely by such small hands as thine, and its contents too precious to be wasted. Soh! that's well done; thou'lt prove a second Ganymede! Health, Julia, and good dreams—may all fair things attend thee, until we meet again."

"And when shall that be, Paul," whispered his mistress, a momentary flush shooting across brow, neck, and bosom, as she spoke, and leaving her, a second afterward, even paler than her wont, between anxiety and fear, and the pain even of this temporary parting—"when shall that be? to-morrow?"

"Surely, to-morrow! fairest," he replied, clasping her little hand with a fond pressure, "unless, which may the Gods avert! anything unforeseen prevent me. Give me my toga, boy," he added, "and see if Thrasea waits, and if his torch be lighted."

"Bid him come hither, Geta," Hortensia interposed, addressing the boy as he left the room, "and tell old Davus to accompany him, bringing the keys of the peristyle and of the garden gate. So shalt thou gain the Es quiline more easily."

Her orders were obeyed as soon as they were spoken, and but few moments intervened before the aged steward, and the freedman with his staff and torch, the latter so prepared by an art common to the ancients as to set almost any violence of wind or rain at defiance, stood waiting their commands.

Familiar and kind words were interchanged between those high-born ladies and the trustworthy follower of young Arvina. For those were days, when no cold etiquette fettered the freedom of the tongue, and when no rank, how stately or how proud soever, induced austerity of bearing or haughtiness toward inferiors; and these concluded, greetings, briefer but far more warm, followed between the master and his intended bride.

"Sweet slumbers, Julia, and a happy wakening attend you! Farewell, Hortensia; both of ye farewell!" and passing into the colonnade through the door which Davus had unlocked, he drew the lappet of his toga over his head after the fashion of a hood to shield it from the drizzling rain—for, except on a journey, the hardy Romans never wore any hat or headgear—and hastened with a firm and regular step along the marble peristyle. This portico, or rather piazza, enclosed, by a double row of Tuscan columns, a few small flower beds, and a fountain springing high in the air from the conch of a Triton, and falling back into a large shell of white marble, which it was so contrived as to keep ever full without at any time overflowing.

Beyond this was a summer triclinium or dining room facing the north, and provided with the three-sided couch, from which it took its name, embracing a circular table. Through this they passed into a smaller court adorned like the other by a jet d'eau, surrounded by several small boudoirs and bed chambers luxuriously decorated, which were set apart to the use of the females of the family, and guarded night and day by the most trusty of the slaves.

Hence a strong door gave access to a walled space, throughout the length of which on either hand ran a long range of offices, and above them the dormitories of the slaves, with a small porter's lodge or guard room by the gate, opening on the orchard in the rear.

Therein were stationed the four Thracians, mentioned by Hortensia, whose duty it was to keep watch alternately over the safety of the postern, although the key was not entrusted to their charge; and he, whose watch it was, started up from a bench on which he had been stretched, and looked forth torch in hand at the sound of approaching footsteps. Seeing, however, who it was, and that the steward attended him, he lent his aid in opening the postern, and reverently bowed the knee to Arvina, as he departed from the hospitable villa.

The orchard through which lay his onward progress, occupied a considerable extent of ground, laid out in terraces adorned with marble urns and statues, long bowery walks sheltered by vine-clad trellices, and rows of fruit trees interspersed with many a shadowy clump of the rich evergreen holm-oak, the tufted stone-pine, the clustering arbutus, and smooth-leaved laurestinus. This lovely spot was separated from the plebeian cemetery only—as has been said already—by a low wall; and therefore in those days of universal superstition, the lower orders and the slaves, and many too of their employers, would have eschewed it as a place ominous of evil, if not unsafe and perilous.

The mind of Paul, however, if not entirely free from any touch of superstitious awe, which at that period of the world would have been a thing altogether unnatural and impossible, was at least of too firm a mould to shake at mere imaginary terrors; and he strode on, lighted by his torch-bearer, through the dark mazes of the orchard, with all his thoughts engrossed by the pleasant reminiscences of the past evening. Thoughtless, however, as he was, and bold, he yet recoiled a step, and the blood rushed tumultuously to his heart, as a loud yelling cry, protracted strangely, and ending in a sound midway between a groan and a burst of horrid laughter, rose awfully upon the silent night; and it required an effort to man his heart against a feeling, which crept through him, nearly akin to fear.

But with the freedman Thrasea it was a very different matter, for he shook so much with absolute terror, that he had well nigh dropped the torch; while, drawing nearer to his master's side, with teeth that chattered as if in an ague fit, and a face deserted by every particle of color, he besought him in faltering accents, "by all the Gods! to turn back instantly, lest evil might come of it!"

His entreaties were, however, of no avail with the brave youth, who in a moment had shaken off his transitory terror, and was now resolute, not only to proceed on his homeward route, but to investigate the cause and meaning of the outcry.

"Silence!" he said, somewhat sternly, in answer to the reiterated prayers of the trembling servitor, "Silence! and follow, idiot! That was no superhuman voice—no yell of nightly lemures, but the death-cry, if I err not more widely, of some frail mortal like ourselves. There may be time, however, yet to save him, and I so truly marked the quarter whence it rose, that I doubt not we may discover him. Advance the light; lo! we are at the wall. Lower thy torch now, that I may undo the wicket. Give me thy club and keep close at my heels bearing the flambeau high!"

And with the words he strode out rapidly into the wide desolate expanse of the plebeian grave yard. It was a broad bleak space, comprising the whole table land and southern slope of the Esquiline hill, broken with many deep ravines and gulleys, worn by the wintry rains, covered with deep rank grass and stunted bushes, with here and there a grove of towering cypresses, or dark funereal yews, casting a deeper shadow over the gloomy solitude. So rough and broken was the surface of the ground, so numerous the low mounds which alone covered the ashes of the humbler dead, that they were long in reaching the vicinity of the spot where that fell deed had been done so recently. When they had come, however, to the foot of the descent, where it swept gently downward to the boundary wall, the young man took the torch from his attendant, and waving it with a slow movement to and fro, surveyed the ground with close and narrow scrutiny. He had not moved in this manner above a dozen paces, before a bright quick flash seemed to shoot up from the long thick herbage as the glare of the torch passed over it. Another step revealed the nature and the cause of that brief gleam; a ray had fallen full on the polished blade of Cataline's stiletto, which lay, where it had been cast by the expiring effort of the victim, hilt downward in the tangled weeds.

He seized it eagerly, but shuddered, as he beheld the fresh dark gore curdling on the broad steel, and clotted round the golden guard of the rich weapon.

"Ha!" he exclaimed, "I am right, Thrasea. Foul murder hath been done here! Let us look farther."

Several minutes now were spent in searching every foot of ground, and prying even into the open vaults of several broken graves; for at first they had taken a wrong direction in the gloom. Quickly, however, seeing that he was in error, Arvina turned upon his traces, and was almost immediately successful; for there, scarce twenty feet from the spot where he had found the dagger, with his grim gory face turned upward as if reproachfully to the dark quiet skies, the black death-sweat still beaded on his frowning brow, and a sardonic grin distorting his pale lips, lay the dead slave. Flat on his back, with his arms stretched out right and left, his legs extended close together to their full length, he lay even as he had fallen; for not a struggle had convulsed his limbs after he struck the earth; life having actually fled while he yet stood erect, battling with all the energies of soul and body against man's latest enemy. The bosom of his gray tunic, rent asunder, displayed the deep gash which had let out the spirit, whence the last drops of the thick crimson life-blood were ebbing with a slow half-stagnant motion.

On this dread sight Paul was still gazing in that motionless and painful silence, with which the boldest cannot fail to look upon the body of a fellow creature from which the immortal soul has been reluctantly and forcefully expelled, when a loud cry from Thrasea, who, having lagged a step or two behind, was later in discovering the corpse, aroused him from his melancholy stupor.

"Alas! alas! ah me!" cried the half-sobbing freedman, "my friend, my more than friend, my countryman, my kinsman, Medon!"

"Ha! dost thou recognize the features? didst thou know him who lies so coldly and inanimately here before us?" cried the excited youth, "whose slave was he? speak, Thrasea, on thy life! this shall be looked to straightway; and, by the Gods! avenged."

"As I would recognize mine own in the polished brass, as I do know my father's sister's son! for such was he, who lies thus foully slaughtered. Alas! alas! my countryman! wo! wo! for thee, my Medon! Many a day, alas! many a happy day have we two chased the elk and urus by the dark-wooded Danube; the same roof covered us; the same board fed; the same fire warmed us; nay! the same fatal battle-field robbed both of liberty and country. Yet were the great Gods merciful to the poor captives. Thy father did buy me, Arvina, and a few years of light and pleasant servitude restored the slave to freedom. Medon was purchased by the wise consul, Cicero, and was to have received his freedom at the next Saturnalia. Alas! and wo is me, he is now free forever from any toils on earth, from any mortal master."

"Nay! weep not so, my Thrasea," exclaimed the generous youth, laying his left hand with a friendly pressure on the freedman's shoulder, "thou shalt have all means to do all honor to his name; all that can now be done by mortals for the revered and sacred dead. Aid me now to remove the body, lest those who slew him may return, and carry off the evidences of their crime."

Thus speaking, he thrust the unlighted end of the torch into the ground, and lifting up the shoulders of the carcase, while Thrasea raised the feet, bore it away a hundred yards or better, and laying it within the open arch-way of an old tomb, covered the mouth with several boughs torn from a neighboring cypress.

Then satisfied that it would thus escape a nearer search than it was likely would be made by the murderers, when

5

they should find that it had been removed, he walked away very rapidly toward his home.

Before he left the burial ground, however, he wiped the dagger carefully in the long grass, and hid it in the bosom of his tunic.

No more words were exchanged—the master buried in deep thought, the servant stupified with grief and terror—until they reached the house of Paullus, in a fair quarter of the town, near to the street of Carinæ, the noblest and most sumptuous in Rome.

A dozen slaves appeared within the hall, awaiting the return of their young lord, but he dismissed them all; and when they had departed, taking a small night lamp, and ordering Thrasea to waken him betimes to-morrow, that he might see the consul, he bade him be of good cheer, for that Medon's death should surely be avenged, since the gay dagger would prove a clue to the detection of his slayer. Then, passing into his own chamber, he soon lost all recollection of his hopes, joys, cares, in the sound sleep of innocence and youth.

CHAPTER IV

THE CONSUL.

Therefore let him be Consul; The Gods give
Him joy, and make him good friend to the people.
CORIOLANUS.

THE morning was yet young, when Paullus Arvina, leaving his mansion on the Cælian hill by a postern door, so to avoid the crowd of clients who even at that early hour awaited his forth-coming in the hall, descended the gentle hill toward the splendid street called Carinæ, from some fanciful resemblance in its shape, lying in a curved hollow between the bases of the Esquiline, Cælian, and Palatine mounts, to the keel of a galley.

This quarter of the city was at that time unquestionably the most beautiful in Rome, although it still fell far short of the magnificence it afterward attained, when the favourite Mecænas had built his splendid palace, and laid out his unrivalled gardens, on the now woody Esquiline; and it would have been difficult indeed to conceive a view more sublime, than that which lay before the eyes of the young patrician, as he paused for a moment on the highest terrace of the hill, to inhale the breath of the pure autumnal morning.

The sun already risen, though not yet high in the east, was pouring a flood of mellow golden light, through the soft medium of the half misty atmosphere, over the varied surface of the great city, broken and diversified by many hills and hollows; and bringing out the innumerable columns, arches, and aqueducts, that adorned almost every street and square, in beautiful relief.

The point at which the young man stood, looking directly northward, was one which could not be excelled, if it indeed could be equalled for the view it commanded, embracing nearly the whole of Rome, which from its commanding height, inferior only to the capitol, and the Quirinal hill, it was enabled to overlook.

Before him, in the hollow at his feet, on which the morning rays dwelt lovingly, streaming in through the deep valley to the right over the city walls, lay the long street of the Carinæ, the noblest and most sumptuous of Rome, adorned with many residences of the patrician order, and among others, those of Pompey, Cæsar, and the great Latin orator. This broad and noble thoroughfare, from its great width, and the long rows of marble columns, which decked its palaces, all glittering in the misty sunbeams, shewed like a waving line of light among the crowded buildings of the narrower ways, that ran parallel to it along the valley and up the easy slope of the Cælian mount, with the Minervium, in which Arvina stood, leading directly downward to its centre. Beyond this sparkling line, rose the twin summits Oppius and Cispius, of the Esquiline hill, still decked with the dark foliage of the ancestral groves of oak and sweet-chesnut, said to derive their origin from Servius Tullius, the sixth king of Rome, and green with the long grass and towering cypresses of the plebeian cemetery, across which the young man had come home, from the villa of his lady-love, but a few hours before.

Beyond the double hill-tops, a heavy purple shadow indicated the deep basin through which ran the ill-famed Suburra, and the "Wicked-Street", so named from the tradition, that therein Tullia compelled her trembling charioteer to lash his reluctant steeds over the yet warm body of her murdered father. And beyond this again the lofty ridge of the Quirinal mount stood out in fair relief with all its gorgeous load of palaces and columns; and the great temple of the city's founder, the god Romulus Quirinus; and the stupendous range of walls and turrets, along its northern verge, flashing out splendidly to the new-risen sun.

So lofty was the post from which Paullus gazed, as he overlooked the mighty town, that his eye reached even beyond the city-walls on the Quirinal, and passing over the broad valley at its northern base, all glimmering with uncertain lights and misty shadows, rested upon the Collis Hortulorum, or mount of gardens, now called Monte Pincio, which was at that time covered, as its name indicates, with rich and fertile shrubberies. The glowing hues of these could be distinctly made out, even at this great distance, by the naked eye. For it must be remembered that there was in those days no sea-coal to send up its murky smoke-wreaths, blurring the bright skies with its inky pall; no factories with tall chimnies, vomiting forth, like mimic Etnas, their pestilential breath, fatal to vegetable life. Not a cloud hung over the great city; and the charcoal, sparingly used for cookery, sent forth no visible fumes to shroud the daylight. So that, as the thin purplish haze was dispersed by the growing influence of the sunbeams, every line of the far architecture, even to the carved friezes of the thousand temples, and the rich foliage of the marble capitals could be observed, distinct and sharp as in a painted picture.

Nor was this all the charm of the delicious atmosphere; for so pure was it, that the odours of that flowery hill, wafted upon the wings of the light northern breeze, blent with the coolness which they caught from the hundreds of clear fountains, plashing and glittering in every public place, came to the brow of the young noble, more like the breath of some enchanted garden in the far-famed Hesperides, than the steam from the abodes of above a million of busy mortals.

Before him still, though inclining a little to the left hand, lay a broader hollow, presenting the long vista of the sacred way, leading directly to the capitol, and thence to the Campus Martius, the green expanse of which, bedecked with many a marble monument and brazen column, and already studded with quick moving groups, hurling the disc and javelin, or reining the fierce war-horse with strong Gaulish curbs, lay soft and level for half a league in length, till it was bounded far away by a gleaming reach of the blue Tiber.

Still to the left of this, uprose the Palatine, the earliest settled of the hills of Rome, with the old walls of Romulus, and the low straw-built shed, wherein that mighty son of Mars dwelt when he governed his wild robber-clan; and the bidental marking the spot where lightning from the monarch of Olympus, called on by undue rites, consumed Hostilius and his house; were still preserved with reverential worship, and on its eastern peak, the time-honoured shrine of Stator Jove.

The ragged crest of this antique elevation concealed, it is true, from sight the immortal space below, once occupied by the marsh of the Velabrum, but now filled by the grand basilicæ and halls of Justice surrounding the great Roman forum, with all their pomp of golden shields, and monuments of mighty deeds performed in the earliest ages; but it was far too low to intercept the view of the grand Capitol, and the Tarpeian Rock.

The gilded gates of bronze and the gold-plated roof of the vast national temple—gold-plated at the enormous cost of twenty-one thousand talents, the rich spoil of Carthage—the shrine of Jupiter Capitoline, and Juno, and Minerva, sent back the sun-beams in lines too dazzing to be borne by any human eye; and all the pomp of statues grouped on the marble terraces, and guarding the ascent of the celebrated hundred steps, glittered like forms of indurated snow.

Such was the wondrous spectacle, more like a fairy show than a real scene of earthly splendour, to look on which Arvina paused for one moment with exulting gladness, before descending toward the mansion of the consul. Nor was that mighty panorama wanting in moving crowds, and figures suitable to the romantic glory of its scenery.

Here, through the larger streets, vast herds of cattle were driven in by mounted herdsmen, lowing and trampling toward the forum; here a concourse of men, clad in the graceful toga, the clients of some noble house, were hastening along to salute their patron at his morning levee; there again, danced and sang, with saffron colored veils and flowery garlands, a band of virgins passing in sacred pomp toward some favourite shrine; there in sad order swept along, with mourners and musicians, with womon wildly shrieking and tearing their long hair, and players and buffoons, and liberated slaves wearing the cap of freedom, a funeral procession, bearing the body of some *young* victim, as indicated by the morning hour, to the funereal pile beyond the city walls; and far off, filing in, with the spear heads and eagles of a cohort glittering above the dust wreaths, by the Flaminian way, the train of some ambassador or envoy, sent by submissive monarchs or dependent states, to sue the favour and protection of the great Roman people.

The blended sounds swept up, in a confused sonorous murmur, like the sea; the shrill cry of the water-carriers, and the wild chant of the choral songs, and the keen clangour of the distant trumpets ringing above the din, until the ears of the youth, as well as his eyes, were filled with present proofs of his native city's grandeur; and his whole soul was lapped in the proud conscious joy, arising from the thought that he too was entitled to that boastful name, higher than any monarch's style, of Roman citizen.

"Fairest and noblest city of the universe," cried the enthusiastic boy, spreading his arms abroad over the glorious view, which, kindling all the powers of his imaginative mind, had awakened something of awe and veneration, "long may the everliving gods watch over thee; long may they guard thy liberties intact, thy hosts unconquered! long may thy name throughout the world be synonimous with all that is great, and good, and glorious! Long may the Roman fortune and the Roman virtue tread, side by side, upon the neck of tyrants; and the whole universe stand mute and daunted before the presence of the sovereign people."

"The sovereign slaves!" said a deep voice, with a strangely sneering accent, in his ear; and as he started in amazement, for he had not imagined that any one was near him, Cataline stood at his elbow.

Under the mingled influence of surprise, and bashfulness at being overheard, and something not very far removed from alarm at the unexpected presence of one so famed for evil deeds as the man beside him, Arvina recoiled a pace or two, and thrust his hand into the bosom of his toga, disarranging its folds for a moment, and suffering the eye of the conspirator to dwell on the hilt of a weapon, which he recognized instantly as the stiletto he had lost in the struggle with the miserable slave on the Esquiline.

No gleam in the eye of the wily plotter betrayed his intelligence; no show of emotion was discoverable in his dark paleness; but a grim smile played over his lips for a moment, as he noted, not altogether without a sort of secret satisfaction, the dismay caused by his unexpected presence.

"How now," he said jeeringly, before the smile had yet vanished from his ill-omened face—"what aileth the bold

Paullus, that he should start, like an unruly colt scared by a shadow, from the approach of a friend?"

"A friend," answered the young man in a half doubtful tone, but instantly recovering himself, "Ha! Cataline, I was surprised, and scarce saw who it was. Thou art abroad betimes this morning. Whither so early? but what saidst thou about slaves?"

"I thought thou didst not know me," replied the other, "and for the rest, I am abroad no earlier than thou, and am perhaps bound to the same place with thee!"

"By Hercules! I fancy not," said Paullus.

"Wherefore, I pray thee, not?" Who knoweth? Perchance I go to pay my vows to Jupiter upon the capitol! perchance," he added with a deep sneer, "to salute our most eloquent and noble consul!"

A crimson flush shot instantly across the face and temples of Arvina, perceiving that he was tampered with, and sounded only; yet he replied calmly and with dignity, "Thither indeed, go I; but I knew not that thou wert in so much a friend of Cicero, as to go visit him."

"Men sometimes visit those who be not their friends," answered the other. "I never said he was a friend to me, or I to him. By the gods, no! I had lied else."

"But what was that," asked the youth, moved, by an inexplicable curiosity and excitement, to learn something more of the singular being with whom chance had brought him into contact, "which thou didst say but now concerning slaves?"

"That all these whom we see before us, and around us, and beneath us, are but a herd of slaves; gulled and vainglorious slaves!"

"The Roman people?" exclaimed Paullus, every tone of his voice, every feature of his fine countenance, expressing his unmitigated horror and astonishment. "The great, unconquered Roman people; the lords of earth and sea, from frosty Caucasus to the twin rocks of Hercules; the tramplers on the necks of kings; the arbiters of the whole world! The Roman people, slaves?"

"Most abject and most wretched!"

"To whom then?" cried the young man, much excited, "to whom am I, art thou, a slave? For we are also of the Roman people?"

"The Roman people, and thou, as one of them, and I, Paullus Cæcilius, are slaves one and all; abject and base and spirit-fallen slaves, lacking the courage even to spurn against our fetters, to the proud tyrannous rich aristocracy."

"By the Gods! we are of it."

"But not the less, for that, slaves to it!" answered Cata line! See! from the lowest to the highest, each petty pelting officer lords it above the next below him; and if the tribunes for a while, at rare and singular moments, uplift a warning cry against the corrupt insolence of the patrician houses, gold buys them back into vile treasonable silence! Patricians be we, and not slaves, sayest thou? Come tell me then, did the patrician blood of the grand Gracchi preserve them from a shameful doom, because they dared to speak, as free-born men, aloud and freely? Did his patrician blood save Fulvius Flaccus? Were Publius Antonius, and Cornelius Sylla, the less ejected from their offices, that they were of the highest blood in Rome; the lawful consuls by the suffrage of the people? Was I, the heir of Sergius Silo's glory, the less forbidden even to canvass for the consulship, that my great grandsire's blood was poured out, like water, upon those fields that witnessed Rome's extremest peril, Trebia, and the Ticinus, and Thrasymene and Cannæ? Was Lentulus, the noblest of the noble, patrician of the eldest houses, a consular himself, expelled the less and stricken from the rolls of the degenerate senate, for the mere whining of a mawkish wench, because his name is Cornelius? Tush, Tush! these be but dreams of poets, or imaginings of children!—the commons be but slaves to the nobles; the nobles to the senate; the senate to their creditors, their purchasers, their consuls; the last at once their tools, and their tyrants! Go, young man, go. Salute, cringe, fawn upon your consul! Nathless, for thou hast mind enough to mark and note the truth of what I tell thee; thou wilt think upon this, and perchance one day, when the time shall have come, wilt speak, act, strike, for freedom!"

And as he finished speaking, he turned aside with a haughty gesture of farewell; and wrapping his toga closely about his tall person, stalked away slowly in the direction neither of the capitol nor of the consul's house; turning his head neither to the right hand nor to the left; and taking no more notice of the person to whom he had been speaking, than if he had not known him to be there, and gazing toward him half-bewildered in anxiety and wonder!

"Wonderful! by the Gods!" he said at last. "Truly he is a wonderful man, and wise withal! I fain would know if all that be true, which they say of him—his bitterness, his impiety, his blood-thirstiness! By Hercules! he speaks well! and it is *true* likewise. Yea! true it is, that we, patricians, and free, as we style ourselves, may not speak any thing, or act, against our order; no! nor indulge our private pleasures, for fear of the proud censors! Is this, then, freedom? True, we are lords abroad; our fleets, our hosts, everywhere victorious; and not one land, wherein the eagle has unfurled her pinion, but bows before the majesty of Rome—but yet—is it, is it, indeed, true, that we are but slaves, sovereign slaves, at home?"

The whole tenor of the young man's thoughts was altered by the few words, let fall for that very purpose by the arch traitor. Ever espying whom he might attach to his party by operating on his passions, his prejudices, his weakness, or his pride; a most sagacious judge of human nature, reading the character of every man as it were in a written book, Cataline had long before remarked young Arvina. He had noted several points of his mental constitution, which he considered liable to receive such impressions as he would—his proneness to defer to the thoughts of others, his want of energetic resolution, and not least his generous indignation against every thing that savored of cruelty or oppression. He had resolved to operate on these, whenever he might find occasion; and should he meet success in his first efforts, to stimulate his passions, minister to his voluptuous pleasures, corrupt his heart, and make him in the end, body and soul, his own.

Such were the intentions of the conspirator, when he first addressed Paullus. His desire to increase the strength of his party, to whom the accession of any member however humble of the great house of Cæcilii could not fail to be useful, alone prompting him in the first instance. But, when he saw by the young man's startled aspect that he was prepossessed against him, and had listened probably to the damning rumors which were rife everywhere concerning him, a second motive was added, in his pride of seduction and sophistry, by which he was wont to boast, that he could bewilder the strongest minds, and work them to his will. When by the accidental disarrangement of Arvina's gown, and the discovery of his own dagger, he perceived that the intended victim of his specious arts was probably cognizant in some degree of his last night's crime, a third and stronger cause was added, in the instinct of self-preservation. And as soon as he found out that Paullus was bound for the house of Cicero, he considered his life, in some sort, staked upon the issue of his attempt on Arvina's principles.

No part could have been played with more skill, or with greater knowledge of his character whom he addressed. He said just enough to set him thinking, and to give a bias and a colour to his thoughts, without giving him reason to suspect that he had any interest in the matter; and he had withdrawn himself in that careless and half contemptuous manner, which naturally led the young man to wish for a renewal of the subject.

And in fact Paul, while walking down the hill, toward the house of the Consul, was busied in wondering why Cataline had left so much unsaid, departing so abruptly; and in debating with himself upon the strange doctrines which he had then for the first time heard broached.

It was about the second hour of the Roman day, corresponding nearly to eight o'clock before noon—as the winter solstice was now passed—when Arvina reached the magnificent dwelling of the Consul in the Carinæ at the angle of the Cærolian place, hard by the foot of the Sacred Way.

This splendid building occupied a whole *insula*, as it was called, or space between four streets, intersecting each other at right angles; and was three stories in height, the two upper supported by columns of marble, with a long range of glass windows, at that period an unusual and expensive luxury. The doors stood wide open; and on either hand the vestibule were arranged the lictors leaning upon their fasces, while the whole space of the great Corinthian hall within, lighted from above, and adorned with vast black pillars of Lucullean marble, was crowded with the white robes of the consul's plebeian clients tendering their morning salutations; not unmixed with the crimson fringes and broad crimson facings of senatorial visitors.

Many were there with gifts of all kinds; countrymen from his Sabine farm and his Tusculan retreat, some bringing lambs; some cages full of doves; cheeses, and bowls of fragrant honey; and robes of fine white linen the produce of their daughters' looms; for whom perchance they were seeking dowers at the munificence of their noble patron; artizans of the city, with toys or pieces of furniture, lamps, writing cases, cups or vases of rich workmanship; courtiers with manuscripts rarely illuminated, the work of their most valuable slaves; travellers with gems, and bronzes, offerings known to be esteemed beyond all others by the high-minded lover of the arts, and unrivalled scholar, to whom they were presented.

These presents, after being duly exhibited to the patron himself, who was seated at the farther end of the hall, concealed from the eyes of Paullus by the intervening crowd, were consigned to the care of the various slaves, or freedmen, who stood round their master, and borne away according to their nature, to the storerooms and offices, or to the library and gallery of the consul; while kind words and a courteous greeting, and a consideration most ample and attentive even of the smallest matters brought before him, awaited all who approached the orator; whether he came empty handed, or full of gifts, to require an audience.

After a little while, Arvina penetrated far enough through the crowd to command a view of the consul's seat; and for a time he amused himself by watching his movements and manner toward each of his visitors, perhaps not altogether without reference to the conversation he had recently held with Catiline; and certainly not without a desire to observe if the tales he had heard of shameless bribery and corruption, as practiced by many of the great officers of the republic, had any confirmation in the conduct of Cicero.

But he soon saw that the courtesies of that great and virtuous man were regulated neither by the value of the gifts offered, nor by the rank of the visitors; and that his personal predilections even were not allowed to interfere with the division of his time among all worthy of his notice.

Thus he remarked that a young noble, famed for his dissoluteness and evil courses, although he brought an exquisite sculpture of Praxiteles, was received with the most marked and formal coldness, and his gift, which could not be declined, consigned almost without eliciting a glance of approbation, to the hand of a freedman; while, the next moment, as an old white-headed countryman, plainly and almost meanly clad, although with scrupulous cleanliness, approached his presence, the consul rose to meet him; and advancing a step or two took him affectionately by the hand, and asked after his family by name, and listened with profound consideration to the garrulous narrative of the good farmer, who, involved in some petty litigation, had come to seek the advice of his patron; until he sent him away happy and satisfied with the promise of his protection.

By and by his own turn arrived; and, although he was personally unknown to the orator, and the assistance of the nomenclator, who stood behind the curule chair, was required before he was addressed by name, he was received with the utmost attention; the noble house to which the young man belonged being as famous for its devotion to the common weal, as for the ability and virtue of its sons.

After a few words of ordinary compliment, Paullus proceeded to intimate to his attentive hearer that his object in waiting at his levee that morning was to communicate momentous information. The thoughtful eye of the great orator brightened, and a keen animated expression came over the features, which had before worn an air almost of lassitude; and he asked eagerly—

"Momentous to the Republic—to Rome, my good friend?"—for all his mind was bent on discovering the plots, which he suspected even now to be in process against the state.

"Momentous to yourself, Consul," answered Arvina.

"Then will it wait," returned the other, with a slight look of disappointment, "and I will pray you to remain, until I have spoken with all my friends here. It will not be very long, for I have seen nearly all the known faces. If you are, in the mean time, addicted to the humane arts, Davus here will conduct you to my library, where you shall find food for the mind; or if you have not breakfasted, my Syrian will shew you where some of my youthful friends are even now partaking a slight meal."

Accepting the first offer, partly perhaps from a sort of pardonable hypocrisy, desiring to make a favourable impression on the great man, with whom he had for the first time spoken, Arvina followed the intelligent and civil freedman to the library, which was indeed the favourite apartment of the studious magistrate. And, if he half repented, as he went by the chamber wherein several youths of patrician birth, one or two of whom nodded to him as he passed, were assembled, conversing merrily and jesting around a well spread board, he ceased immediately to regret the choice he had made, when the door was thrown open, and he was ushered into the shrine of Cicero's literary leisure.

The library was a small square apartment; for it must be remembered that books at this time being multiplied by manual labor only, and the art being comparatively rare and very costly, the vast collections of modern times were utterly beyond the reach of individuals; and a few scores of volumes were more esteemed than would be as many thousands now, in these days of multiplying presses and steam power. But although inconsiderable in size, not being above sixteen feet square, the decorations of the apartment were not to be surpassed or indeed equalled by anything of modern splendor; for the walls,* divided into compartments by mouldings, exquisitely carved and overlaid with burnished gilding, were set with panels of thick plate glass glowing in all the richest hues of purple, ruby, emerald, and azure, through several squares of which the light stole in, gorgeously tinted, from the peristyle, there being no distinction except in this between the windows and the other compartments of the wainscot, if it

* It must not be imagined that this is fanciful. Rooms were fitted up in this manner, and termed *cameræ vitreæ*, and the panels *vitreæ quadraturæ*. But a few years later than the period of the text, B. C. 58, M Æmilius Scaurus built a theatre capable of containing 80,000 persons, the scena of which, composed of three stories, had one, the central, made entirely of colored glass in this fashion.

may be so styled; and of the ceiling, which was finished in like manner with slabs of stained glass, between the intersecting beams of gilded scroll work.

The floor was of beautiful mosaic, partially covered by a foot-cloth woven from the finest wool, and dyed purple with the juice of the cuttle-fish; and all the furniture corresponded, both in taste and magnificence, to the other decorations of the room. A circular table of cedar wood, inlaid with ivory and brass, so that its value could not have fallen far short of ten thousand sesterces*, stood in the centre of the floor-cloth; with a *bisellium*, or double settle, wrought in bronze, and two beautiful chairs of the same material not much dissimilar in form to those now used. And, to conclude, a bookcase of polished maple wood, one of the doors of which stood open, displayed a rare collection of about three hundred volumes, each in its circular case of purple parchment, having the name inscribed in letters of gold, silver, or vermilion.

A noble bust in bronze of the Phidian Jupiter, with the sublime expanse of brow, the ambrosian curls and the beard loosely waving, as when he shook Olympus by his nod, and the earth trembled and the depth of Tartarus, stood on a marble pedestal facing the bookcase; and on the table, beside writing materials, leaves of parchment, an ornamental letter-case, a double inkstand and several reed pens, were scattered many gems and trinkets; signets and rings engraved in a style far surpassing any effort of the modern graver, vases of onyx and cut glass, and above all, the statue of a beautiful boy, holding a lamp of bronze suspended by a chain from his left hand, and in his right the needle used to refresh the wick.

Nurtured as he had been from his youth upward among the magnates of the land, accustomed to magnificence and luxury till he had almost fancied that the world had nothing left of beautiful or new that he had not witnessed, Paul stood awhile, after the freedman had departed, gazing with mute admiration on the richness and taste displayed in all the details of this the scholar's sanctum. The very atmosphere of the chamber, filled with the perfume of the

* About £90 sterling. See Pliny Hist. Nat. 13, 16, for a notice of this very table, which was preserved to his time.

cedar wood employed as a specific against the ravages o the moth and bookworm, seemed to the young man redolent of midnight learning; and the superb front of the presiding-god, calm in the grandeur of its ineffable benignity, who appeared to his excited fancy to smile serene protection on the pursuits of the blameless consul, inspired him with a sense of awful veneration, that did not easily or quickly pass away.

For some moments, as he gradually recovered the elasticity of his spirits, he amused himself by examining the exquisitely wrought gems on the table; but after a little while, when Cicero came not, he crossed the room quietly to the bookshelves, and selecting a volume of Homer, drew it forth from its richly embossed case, and seating himself on the bronze settle with his back toward the door, had soon forgotten where he was, and the grave business which brought him thither, in the sublime simplicity of the blind rhapsodist.

An hour or more elapsed thus; yet Paul took no note of time, nor moved at all except to unroll with his right hand the lower margin of the parchment as he read, while with the left he rolled up the top; so that nearly the same space of the manuscript remained constantly before his eyes, although the reader was continually advancing in the poem.

At length the door opened noiselessly, and with a silent foot, shod in the light slippers which the Romans always wore when in the house, Cicero entered the apartment.

The consul was at this time in the very prime of intellectual manhood, it having been decreed* about a century before, that no person should be elected to that highest office of the state, who should not have attained his forty-third year. He was a tall and elegantly formed man, with nothing especially worthy of remark in his figure, if it were not that his neck was unusually long and slender, though not so much so as to constitute any drawback to his personal appearance, which, without being what would exactly be termed handsome, was both elegant and graceful.

* By the *Lex annalis*, B. C. 180, passed at the instance of the tribune L. V. Tappulus.

His features were not, indeed, very bold or striking; but intellect was strongly and singularly marked in every line of the face; and the expression,—calm, thoughtful, and serene,—though it had not the quick and restless play of ever-varying lights and shadows which belongs to the quicker and more imaginative temperaments among men of the highest genius,—could not fail to impress any one with the conviction, that the mind which informed it must be of eminent capacity, and depth, and power.

He entered, as I have said, silently; and although there was nothing of stealthiness in his gait, which being very light and slow was yet both firm and springy, nor any of that cunning in his manner which is so often coupled to a prowling footstep, he yet advanced so noiselessly over the soft floor-cloth, that he stood at Arvina's elbow, and overlooked the page in which he was reading, before the young man was aware of his vicinity.

"Ha!" he exclaimed, after standing a moment, and observing with a soft pleasant smile the abstraction of his visitor, "so thou readest Greek, and art thyself a poet."

"A little of the first, my consul," replied Arvina, arising quickly to his feet, with the ingenuous blood rushing to his brow at the detection. "But wherefore shouldst thou believe me the second?"

"We statesmen," answered the consul, "are wont to study other men's characters, as other men are wont to study books; and I have learned by practice to draw quick conculsions from small signs. But in this instance, the light in your eye, the curl of your expanded nostril, the half frown on your brow, and the flush on your cheek, told me beyond a doubt that you are a poet. And you are so, young man. I care not whether you have penned as yet an elegy, or no—nevertheless, you are in soul, in temperament, in fantasy, a poet. Do you love Homer?"

"Beyond all other writers I have ever met, in my small course of reading. There is a majesty, a truth, an ever-burning fire, lustrous, yet natural and most beneficent, like the sun's glory on a summer day, in his immortal words, that kindles and irradiates, yet consumes not the soul; a grand simplicity, that never strains for effect; a sweet pathos, that elicits tears without evoking them; a melody that flows on, like the harmony of the eternal sea, or, if we may call fancy to our aid, the music of the spheres, telling us that like these the blind bard sang, because song was his nature—was within, and must out—not bound by laws, or measured by pedantic rules, but free, unfettered, and spontaneous as the billows, which in its wild and many-cadenced sweep it most resembles."

"Ah! said I not," replied Cicero, "that you were a poet? And you have been discoursing me most eloquent poetry; though not attuned to metre, rythmical withal, and full of fancy. Ay! and you judge aright. He is the greatest, as the first of poets; and surpassed all his followers as much in the knowledge of the human heart with its ten thousands of conflicting passions, as in the structure of the kingly verse, wherein he delineated character as never man did, saving only he. But hold, Arvina. Though I could willingly spend hours with thee in converse on this topic, the state has calls on me, which must be obeyed. Tell me, therefore, I pray you, as shortly as may be, what is the matter you would have me know. Shortly, I pray you, for my time is short, and my duties onerous and manifold."

Laying aside the roll, which he had still held open during that brief conversation, and laying aside with it his enthusiastic and passionate manner, the young man now stated, simply and briefly, the events of the past night, the discovery of the murdered slave, and the accident by which he had learned that he was the consul's property; and in conclusion, laid the magnificently ornamented dagger which he had found, on the board before Cicero; observing, that the weapon might give a clue to poor Medon's death.

Cicero was moved deeply—moved, not simply, as Arvina fancied, by sorrow for the dead, but by something approaching nearly to remorse. He started up from the chair, which he had taken when the youth began his tale, and clasping his hands together violently, strode rapidly to and fro the small apartment.

"Alas, and wo is me, poor Medon! Faithful wert thou, and true, and very pleasant to mine eyes! Alas! that thou art gone, and gone too so wretchedly! And wo is me, that I listened not to my own apprehensions, rather than to thy trusty boldness. Alas! that I suffered thee to go, for they have murdered thee! ay, thine own zeal betrayed thee; but by the Gods that govern in Olympus, they shall rue it!"

After this burst of passion he became more cool, and, resuming his seat, asked Paullus a few shrewd and pertinent questions concerning the nature of the ground whereon he had found the corpse, the traces left by the mortal struggle, the hour at which the discovery was made, and many other minute points of the same nature; the answers to which he noted carefully on his waxed tablets. When he had made all the inquiries that occurred to him, he read aloud the answers as he had set them down, and asked if he would be willing at any moment to attest the truth of those things.

"At any moment, and most willingly, my consul," the youth replied. "I would do much myself to find out the murderers and bring them to justice, were it only for my poor freedman Thrasea's sake, who is his cousin-german."

"Fear not, young man, they *shall* be brought to justice," answered Cicero. "In the meantime do thou keep silence, nor say one word touching this to any one that lives. Carry the dagger with thee; wear it as ostentatiously as may be—perchance it shall turn out that some one may claim or recognise it. Whatever happeneth, let me know privately. Thus far hast thou done well, and very wisely: go on as thou hast commenced, and, hap what hap, count Cicero thy friend. But above all, doubt not—I say, doubt not one moment,—that as there is One eye that seeth all things in all places, that slumbereth not by day nor sleepeth in the watches of night, that never waxeth weak at any time or weary—as there is One hand against which no panoply can arm the guilty, from which no distance can protect, nor space of time secure him, so surely shall they perish miserable who did this miserable murder, and their souls rue it everlastingly beyond the portals of the grave, which are but the portals of eternal life, and admit all men to wo or bliss, for ever and for ever!"

He spoke solemnly and sadly; and on his earnest face there was a deep and almost awful expression, that held Arvina mute and abashed, he knew not wherefore; and when the great man had ceased from speaking, he made a silent gesture of salutation and withdrew, thus gravely warned, scarce conscious if the statesman noted his departure; for he had fallen into a deep reverie, and was perhaps musing on the mysteries yet unrevealed of the immortal soul, so totally careless did he now appear of all sublunary matters.

CHAPTER V.

THE CAMPUS.

Eques ipso melior Bellerophonte,
Neque pugno neque segni pede victus,
Simul unctos Tiberinis humeros lavit in undis.
HORACE. OD. III. 12.

"WHAT ho! my noble Paullus," exclaimed a loud and cheerful voice, "whither afoot so early, and with so grave a face?"

Arvina started; for so deep was the impression made on his mind by the last words of Cicero, that he had passed out into the Sacred Way, and walked some distance down it, toward the Forum, in deep meditation, from which he was aroused by the clear accents of the merry speaker.

Looking up with a smile as he recognised the voice, he saw two young men of senatorial rank—for both wore the crimson laticlave on the breast of their tunics—on horseback, followed by several slaves on foot, who had overtaken him unnoticed amid the din and bustle which had drowned the clang of their horses' feet on the pavement.

"Nay, I scarce know, Aurelius!" replied the young man, laughing; "I thought I was going home, but it seems that my back is turned to my own house, and I am going toward the market-place, although the Gods know that I have no business with the brawling lawyers, with whom it is alive by this time."

"Come with us, then," replied the other; "Aristius. here, and I, have made a bet upon our coursers' speed.

He fancies his Numidian can outrun my Gallic beauty. Come with us to the Campus; and after we have settled this grave matter, we will try the *quinquertium*,* or a foot race in armor, if you like it better, or a swim in the Tiber, until it shall be time to go to dinner."

"How can I go with you, seeing that you are well mounted, and I afoot, and encumbered with my gown? You must consider me a second Achilles to keep up with your fleet coursers, clad in this heavy toga, which is a worse garb for running than any panoply that Vulcan ever wrought."

"We will alight," cried the other youth, who had not yet spoken, "and give our horses to the boys to lead behind us; or, hark you, why not send Geta back to your house, and let your slaves bring down your horse too? If they make tolerable speed, coming down by the back of the Cœlian, and thence beside the *Aqua Crabra*† to the Carmental gate, they may overtake us easily before we reach the Campus. Aurelius has some errand to perform near the Forum, which will detain us a few moments longer. What say you?"

"He will come, he will come, certainly," cried the other, springing down lightly from the back of his beautiful courser, which indeed merited the eulogium, as well as the caresses which he now lavished on it, patting his favorite's high-arched neck, and stroking the soft velvet muzzle, which was thrust into his hand, with a low whinnying neigh of recognition, as he stood on the raised foot path, holding the embroidered rein carelessly in his hand.

"I will," said Arvina, "gladly; I have nothing to hinder me this morning; and for some days past I have been detained with business, so that I have not visited the campus, or backed a horse, or cast a javelin—by Hercules! not since the Ides, I fancy. You will all beat me in the field, that is certain, and in the river likewise. But come,

* The *Quinquertium*, the same as the Greek Pentathlon, was a conflict in five successive exercises—leaping, the discus, the foot race, throwing the spear, and wrestling.

† The *Aqua Crabra* was a small stream flowing into the Tiber from the south-eastward, now called *Maranna*. It entered the walls near the Capuan gate, and passing through the *vallis Murcia* between the Aventine and Palatine hills, where it supplied the Circus Maximus with water for the *naumachia*, fell into the river above the Palatine bridge.

Fuscus Aristius, if it is to be as you have plannea it, jump down from your Numidian, and let your Geta ride him up the hill to my house. I would have asked Aurelius, but he will let no slave back his white NOTUS."

"Not I, by the twin horsemen! nor any free man either —plebeian, knight, or noble. Since first I bought him of the blue-eyed Celt, who wept in his barbarian fondness for the colt, no leg save only mine has crossed his back, nor ever shall, while the light of day smiles on Aurelius Victor."

Without a word Fuscus leaped from the back of the fine blood-bay barb he bestrode, and beckoning to a confidential slave who followed him, "Here," he said, "Geta, take Xanthus, and ride straightway up the Minervium to the house of Arvina; thou knowest it, beside the Alban Mansions, and do as he shall command you. Tell him, my Paullus."

"Carry this signet, my good Geta," said the young man, drawing off the large seal-ring which adorned his right hand, and giving it to him, "to Thrasea, my trusty freedman, and let him see that they put the housings and gallic wolf-bit on the black horse Aufidus, and bring him thou, with one of my slaves, down the slope of Scaurus, and past the Great Circus, to the Carmental Gate, where thou wilt find us. Make good speed, Geta."

"Ay, do so," interposed his master, "but see that thou dost not blow Xanthus; thou wert better be a dead slave, Geta, than let me find one drop of sweat on his flank. Nay! never grin, thou hang-dog, or I will have thee given to my Congers*; the last which came out of the fish pond were but ill fed; and a fat German, such as thou, would be a rare meal for them."

The slave laughed, knowing well that his master was but jesting, mounted the horse, and rode him at a gentle trot, up the slope of the Cælian hill, from which Arvina had but a little while before descended. In the mean time, Aristius gave the rein of his dappled grey to one of

* The *Murœna Helena*, which we commonly translate Lamprey, was a sub-genus of the Conger; it was the most prized of all the Roman fish, and grew to the weight of twenty-five or thirty pounds. The value set upon them was enormous; and it is said that guilty slaves were occasionally thrown into their stews, to fatten these voracious dainties.

his followers, desiring him to be very gentle with him, and the three young men sauntered slowly on along the Sacred Way toward the Forum, conversing merrily and interchanging many a smile and salutation with those whom they met on their road.

Skirting the base of the Palatine hill, they passed the old circular temple of Remus to the right hand, and the most venerable relic of Rome's infancy, the Ruminal Fig tree, beneath which the she-wolf was believed to have given suck to the twin progeny of Mars and the hapless Ilia. A little farther on, the mouth of the sacred grotto called Lupercal, surrounded with its shadowy grove, the favourite haunt of Pan, lay to their left; and fronting them, the splendid arch of Fabius, surnamed Allobrox for his victorious prowess against that savage tribe, gave entrance to the great Roman Forum.

Immediately at their left hand as they entered the archway, was the superb Comitium, wherein the Senate were wont to give audience to foreign embassies of suppliant nations, with the gigantic portico, three columns of which may still be seen to testify to the splendor of the old city, in the far days of the republic. Facing them were the steps of the Asylum, with the Mamertine prison and the grand façade of the temple of Concord to the right and left; and higher above these the portico of the gallery of records, and higher yet the temple of the thundering Jupiter, and glittering above all, against the dark blue sky, the golden dome, and white marble columns of the great capitol itself. Around in all directions were basilicæ, or halls of justice; porticoes filled with busy lawyers; bankers' shops glittering with their splendid wares, and bedecked with the golden shields taken from the Samnites; statues of the renowned of ages, Accius Nævius, who cut the whetstone with the razor; Horatius Cocles on his thunderstricken pedestal, halting on one knee from the wound which had not hindered him from swimming the swollen Tiber; Clælia the hostage on her brazen steed; and many another, handed down inviolate from the days of the ancient kings. Here was the rostrum, beaked with the prows of ships, a fluent orator already haranguing the assembled people from its platform—there, the seat of the city Prætor, better known as the *Puteal Libonis,* with that officer in session on his curule chair, his six lictors leaning on their fasces at his back, as he promulgated his irrevocable edicts.

It was a grand sight, surely, and one to gaze on which men of the present day would do and suffer much; and judge themselves most happy if blessed with one momentary glance of the heart, as it were, of the old world's mistress. But these young men, proud as they were, and boastful of the glories of their native Rome, had looked too often on that busy scene to be attracted by the gorgeousness of the place, crowded with buildings, the like of which the modern world knows not, and thronged with nations of every region of the earth, each in his proper dress, each seeking justice, pleasure, profit, fame, as it pleased him, free, and fearless, and secure of property and person. Casting a brief glance over it, they turned short to the left, by a branch of the Sacred Way, which led, skirting the market place, between the Comitium, or hall of the ambassadors, and the abrupt declivity of the Palatine, past the end of the Atrium of Liberty, and the cattle mart, toward the Carmental gate.

"Methought you said, my Fuscus, that our Aurelius had some errand to perform in the Forum; how is this, is it a secret?" inquired Paullus, laughing.

"No secret, by the Gods!" said Aurelius, "it is but to buy a pair of spurs in Volero's shop, hard by Vesta's shrine."

"He will need them," cried Fuscus, "he will need them, I will swear, in the race."

"Not to beat Xanthus," said Aurelius; "but oh! Jove! walk quickly, I beseech you; how hot a steam of cooked meats and sodden cabbage, reeks from the door of yon cook-shop. Now, by the Gods! it well nigh sickened me! Ha! Volero," he exclaimed, as they reached the door of a booth, or little shop, with neat leathern curtains festooned up in front, glittering with polished cutlery and wares of steel and silver, to a middle aged man, who was busy burnishing a knife within, "what ho! my Volero, some spurs—I want some spurs; show me some of your sharpest and brightest."

"I have a pair, noble Aurelius, which I got only yesterday in trade with a turbaned Moor from the deserts beyond Cyrenaica. By Mulciber, my patron god! the fairest pair my eyes ever looked upon. Right loath was the swart barbarian to let me have them, but hunger, hunger is a great tamer of your savage; and the steam of good Furbo's cook-shop yonder was suggestive of savory chops and greasy sausages—and—and—in short, Aurelius, I got them at a bargain."

While he was speaking, he produced the articles in question, from a strong brass-bound chest, and rubbing them on his leather apron held them up for the inspection of the youthful noble.

"Truly," cried Victor, catching them out of his hand, "truly, they are good spurs."

"Good spurs! good spurs!" cried the merchant, half indignantly, "I call them splendid, glorious, inimitable! Only look you here, it is all virgin silver; and observe, I beseech you, this dragon's neck and the sibilant head that holds the rowels; they are wrought to the very life with horrent scales, and erected crest; beautiful! beautiful!—and the rowels too of the best Spanish steel that was ever tempered in the cold Bilbilis. Good spurs indeed! they are well worth three *aurei*.* But I will keep them, as I meant to do at first, for Caius Cæsar; he will know what they are worth, and give it too."

"Didst ever hear so pestilent a knave?" said Victor, laughing; "one would suppose I had disparaged the accursed things! But, as I said before, they are good spurs, and I will have them; but I will not give thee three aurei, master Volero; two is enough, in all conscience; or sixty denarii at the most. Ho! Davus, Davus! bring my purse, hither, Davus," he called to his slaves without; and, as the purse-bearer entered, he continued without waiting for an answer, "Give Volero two aurei, and ten denarii, and take these spurs."

"No! no!" exclaimed Volero, "you shall not—no! by the Gods! they cost me more than that!"

"Ye Gods! what a lie! cost thee—and to a barbarian! I dare be sworn thou didst not pay him the ten denarii alone."

---

* The aureus was a gold coin, as the name implies, worth twenty-five denarii, or about seventeen shillings and nine pence sterling.

"By Hercules! I did, though," said the other, "and thou shouldst not have them for three *aurei* either, but that it is drawing near the Calends of November, and I have moneys to pay then."

"Sixty-five I will give thee—sixty-five denarii!"

"Give me my spurs; what, art thou turning miser in thy youth, Aurelius.?"

"There, give him the gold, Davus; he is a regular usurer. Give him three *aurei*, and then buckle these to my heel. Ha! that is well, my Paullus, here come your fellows with black Aufidus, and our friend Geta on the Numidian. They have made haste, yet not sweated Xanthus either. Aristius, your groom is a good one; I never saw a horse that shewed his keeping or condition better. Now then, Arvina, doff your toga, you will not surely ride in that."

"Indeed I will not," replied Paullus, "if master Volero will suffer me to leave it here till my return."

"Willingly, willingly; but what is this?" exclaimed the cutler, as Arvina unbuckling his toga and suffering it to drop on the ground, stood clad in his succinct and snow-white tunic only, girded about him with a zone of purple leather, in which was stuck the sheathless dirk of Cataline. "What is this, noble Paullus, that you carry at your belt, with no scabbard? If you go armed, you should at least go safely. See, if you were to bend your body somewhat quickly, it might well be that the keen point would rend your groin. Give it me, I can fit it with a sheath in a moment."

"I do not know but it were as well to do so," answered Paullus, extricating the dagger from his belt, "if you will not detain us a long time."

"Not even a short time!" said the cutler, "give it to me, I can fit it immediately." And he stretched out his hand and took it; but hardly had his eye dwelt on it, for a moment, when he cried, "but this is not yours—this is—where got you this, Arvina?"

"Nay, it is nought to thee; perhaps I bought it, perhaps it was given to me; do thou only fit it with a scabbard."

"Buy it thou didst not, Paullus, I'll be sworn; and I

think it was never given thee; and, see, see here, what is this?—there has been blood on the blade!"

"Folly!" exclaimed the young man, turning first very red and then pale, so that his comrades gazed on him with wonder, "folly, I say. It is not blood, but water that has dimmed its shine;—and how knowest thou that I did not buy it?"

"How do I know it?—thus," answered the artizan, drawing from a cupboard under his counter, a weapon precisely the facsimile in every respect of that in his hand: "There never were but two of these made, and I made them; the scabbard of this will fit that; see how the very chased work fits!" I sold this, but not to you, Arvina; and I do not believe that it was given to you."

"Filth that thou art, and carrion!" exclaimed the young man fiercely, striking his hand with violence upon the counter, "darest thou brave a nobleman? I tell thee, I doubt not at all that there be twenty such in every cutler's shop in Rome!—but to whom did'st thou sell this, that thou art so certain?"

"Paullus Cæcilius," replied the mechanic gravely but respectfully, "I brave no man, least of all a patrician; but mark my words—I did sell this dagger; here is my own mark on its back; if it was given to thee, thou must needs know the giver; for the rest, this *is* blood that has dimmed it, and not water; you cannot deceive me in the matter; and I would warn you, youth,—noble as you are, and plebeian I,—that there are laws in Rome, one of them called Cornelia de Sicariis, which you were best take care that you know not more nearly. Meantime, you can take this scabbard if you will," handing to him, as he spoke, the sheath of the second weapon; "the price is one sestertium; it is the finest silver, chased as you see, and overlaid with pure gold."

"Thou hast the money," returned Paullus, casting down on the counter several golden coins, stamped with a helmed head of Mars, and an eagle on the reverse, grasping a thunderbolt in its talons—"and the sheath is mine. Then thou wilt not disclose to whom it was sold?"

"Why should I, since thou knowest without telling?"

"Wilt thou, or not?"

"Not to thee, Paullus."

"Then will I find some one, to whom thou wilt fain disclose it!" he answered haughtily.

"And who may that be, I beseech you?" asked the mechanic, half sneeringly. "For my part, I fancy you will let it rest altogether; some one was hurt with it last night, as you and *he*, we both know, can tell if you will! But I knew not that you were one of his men."

There was an insolent sneer on the cutler's face that galled the young nobleman to the quick; and what was yet more annoying, there was an assumption of mutual intelligence and equality about him, that almost goaded the patrician's blood to fury. But by a mighty effort he subdued his passion to his will; and snatching up the weapon returned it to his belt, left the shop, and springing to the saddle of his beautiful black horse, rode furiously away. It was not till he reached the Carmental Gate, giving egress from the city through the vast walls of Cyclopean architecture, immediately at the base of the dread Tarpeian rock, overlooked and commanded by the outworks and turrets of the capitol, that he drew in his eager horse, and looked behind him for his friends. But they were not in sight; and a moment's reflection told him that, being about to start their coursers on a trial of speed, they would doubtless ride gently over the rugged pavement of the crowded streets.

He doubted for a minute, whether he should turn back to meet them, or wait for their arrival at the gate, by which they must pass to gain the campus; but the fear of missing them, instantly induced him to adopt the latter course, and he sat for a little space motionless on his well-bitted and obedient horse beneath the shadow of the deep gate-way.

Here his eye wandered around him for awhile, taking note indeed of the surrounding objects, the great temple of Jupiter Stator on the Palatine; the splendid portico of Catulus, adorned with the uncouth and grisly spoils of the Cimbric hordes slaughtered on the plains of Vercellæ; the house of Scaurus, toward which a slow wain tugged by twelve powerful oxen was even then dragging one of the pondrous columns which rendered his hall for many years the boast of Roman luxury; and on the other tall buildings that stood every where about him; although in truth he scarce observed what for the time his eye dwelt upon.

At length an impatient motion of his horse caused him to turn his face toward the black precipice of the huge rock at whose base he sat, and in a moment it fastened upon his mind with singular vividness—singular, for he had paused fifty times upon that spot before, without experiencing such feelings—that he was on the very pavement, which had so often been bespattered with the blood of despairing traitors. The noble Manlius, tumbled from the very rock, which his single arm had but a little while before defended, seemed to lie there, even at his feet, mortally maimed and in the agony of death, yet even so too proud to mix one groan with the curses he poured forth against Rome's democratic rabble. Then, by a not inapt transition, the scene changed, and Caius Marcius was at hand, with the sword drawn in his right, that won him the proud name of Coriolanus, and the same rabble that had hurled Caius Manlius down, yelling and hooting "to the rock with him! to the rock!" but at a safe and respectful distance; their factious tribunes goading them to outrage and new riot.

It was strange that these thoughts should have occurred so clearly at this moment to the excited mind of the young noble; and he felt that it was strange himself; and would have banished the ideas, but they would not away; and he continued musing on the inconstant turbulence of the plebeians, and the unerring doom which had overtaken every one of their idols, from the hands of their own partizans, until his companions at length rode slowly up the street to join him.

There was some coldness in the manner of Aristius Fuscus, as they met again, and even Aurelius seemed surprised and not well pleased; for they had in truth been conversing earnestly about the perturbation of their friend at the remarks of the artizan, and the singularity of his conduct in wearing arms at all; and he heard Victor say just before they joined company—

"No! that is not so odd, Fuscus, in these times. It was but two nights since, as I was coming home something later than my wont from Terentia's, that I fell in with Clodius reeling along, frantically drunk and furious, with half a dozen torch-bearers before, and half a score wolfish looking gladiators all armed with blade and buckler, and all half-drunk, behind him. I do assure you that I almost swore I would go out no more without weapons."

"They would have done you no good, man," said Aristius, "if some nineteen or twenty had set upon you. But an they would, I care not; it is against the law, and no good citizen should carry them at all."

"Carry arms, I suppose you mean, Aristius," interrupted Paullus boldly. "Ye are talking about me, I fancy—is it not so?"

"Ay, it is," replied the other gravely. "You were disturbed not a little at what stout Volero said."

"I was, I was," answered Arvina very quickly, "because I could not tell him; and it is not pleasant to be suspected. The truth is that the dagger is not mine at all, and that it *is* blood that was on it; for last night—but lo!" he added, interrupting himself, "I was about to speak out, and tell you all; and yet my lips are sealed."

"I am sorry to hear it," said Aristius, "I do not like mysteries; and this seems to me a dark one!"

"It is—as dark as Erebus," said Paullus eagerly, "and as guilty too; but it is not my mystery, so help me the god of good faith and honour!"

"That is enough said; surely that is enough for you, Aristius," exclaimed the warmer and more excitable Aurelius.

"For you it may be," replied the noble youth, with a melancholy smile. "You are a boy in heart, my Aurelius, and overflow so much with generosity and truth that you believe all others to be as frank and candid. I alas! have grown old untimely, and, having seen what I have seen, hold men's assertions little worth."

The hot blood mounted fiercely into the cheek of Paullus; and, striking his horse's flank suddenly with his heel, he made him passage half across the street, and would have seized Aristius by the throat, had not their comrade interposed to hinder him.

"You are both mad, I believe; so mad that all the hellebore in both the Anticyras could not cure you. Thou, Fuscus, for insulting him with needless doubts. Thou, Paullus, for mentioning the thing, or shewing the dagger at all, if you did not choose to explain."

"I do *choose* to explain," replied Cæcilius, "but I cannot; I have explained it all to Marcus Tullius."

"To Cicero," exclaimed Aristius. "Why did you not say so before? I was wrong, then, I confess my error; if Cicero be satisfied, it must needs be all well."

"That name of Cicero is like the voice of an oracle to Fuscus ever!" said Aurelius Victor, laughing. "I believe he thinks the new man from Arpinum a very god, descended from Olympus!"

"No! not a God," replied Aristius Fuscus, "only the greatest work of God, a wise and virtuous man, in an age which has few such to boast. But come, let us ride on and conclude our race; and thou, Arvina, forget what I said; I meant not to wrong thee."

"I have forgotten," answered Paullus; and, with the word, they gave their horses head, and cantered onward for the field of Mars.

The way for some distance was narrow, lying between the fortified rock of the Capitol, with its stern lines of immemorial ramparts on the right hand, and on the left the long arcades and stately buildings of the vegetable mart, on the river bank, now filled with sturdy peasants, from the Sabine country, eager to sell their fresh green herbs; and blooming girls, from Tibur and the banks of Anio, with garlands of flowers, and cheeks that outvied their own brightest roses.

Beyond these, still concealing the green expanse of the level plain, and the famous river, stood side by side three temples, sacred to Juno Matuta, Piety, and Hope; each with its massy colonnade of Doric or Corinthian, or Ionic pillars; the latter boasting its frieze wrought in bronze; and that of Piety, its tall equestrian statue, so richly gilt and burnished that it gleamed in the sunlight as if it were of solid gold.

Onward they went, still at a merry canter, their generous and high mettled coursers fretting against the bits which restrained their speed, and their young hearts elated and bounding quickly in their bosoms, with the excitement of the gallant exercise; and now they cleared the last winding of the suburban street, and clothed in its perennial verdure, the wide field lay outspread, like one sheet of emerald verdure, before them, with the bright Tiber flashing to the sun in many a reach and ripple, and the gay slope of the Collis Hortulorum, glowing with all its terraced gardens in the distance.

A few minutes more brought them to the Flaminian way, whereon, nearly midway the plain, stood the *diribitorium*, or pay-office of the troops; the porticoes of which were filled with the soldiers of Metellus Creticus, and Quintus Marcius Rex, who lay with their armies encamped on the low hills beyond the river, waiting their triumphs, and forbidden by the laws to come into the city so long as they remained invested with their military rank. Around this stately building were many colonnades, and open buildings adapted to the exercises of the day, when winter or bad weather should prevent their performance in the open mead, and stored with all appliances, and instruments required for the purpose; and to these Paullus and his friends proceeded, answering merely with a nod or passing jest the salutations of many a helmed centurion and gorgeous tribune of the soldiery.

A grand Ionic gateway gave them admittance to the hippodrome, a vast oval space, adorned with groups of sculpture and obelisks and columns in the midst; on some of which were affixed inscriptions commemorative of great feats of skill or strength or daring; while others displayed placards announcing games or contests to take place in future, and challenges of celebrated gymnasts for the cestus fight, the wrestling match, or the foot-race.

Around the outer circumference were rows of seats, shaded by plane trees overrun with ivy, and there were already seated many young men of noble birth, chatting together, or betting, with their waxed tablets and their *styli** in their hands, some waiting the commencement of the race between Fuscus and Victor, others watching with interest the progress of a sham fight on horseback between two young men of the equestrian order, denoted by the narrow crimson stripes on their tunics, who were careering to and fro, armed with long staves and circular bucklers, in all the swift and beautiful movements of the mimic combat.

* The stylus was a pointed metallic pencil used for tracing letters on the waxen surface of the table.

Among those most interested in this spectacle, the eye of Arvina fell instantly on the tall and gaunt form of Catiline, who stood erect on one of the marble benches, applauding with his hands, and now and then shouting a word of encouragement to the combatants, as they wheeled by him in the mazes of their half angry sport. It was not long, however, before their strife was brought to a conclusion; for, almost as the friends entered, the hindmost horseman of the two made a thrust at the other, which taking effect merely on the lower rim of his antagonist's *parma*, glanced off under his outstretched arm, and made the striker, in a great measure, lose his balance. As quick as light, the other wheeled upon him, feinted a pass at his breast with the point of the staff; and then, as he lowered his shield to guard himself, reversed the weapon with a swift turn of the wrist, dealt him a heavy blow with the truncheon on the head; and then, while the whole place rang with tumultuous plaudits, circled entirely round him to the left, and delivered his thrust with such effect in the side, that it bore his competitor clear out of the saddle.

"Euge! Euge! well done," shouted Catiline in ecstacy; "by Hercules! I never saw in all my life better skirmishing. It is all over with Titus Varus!"

And in truth it was all over with him; but not in the sense which the speaker meant: for, as he fell, the horses came into collision, and it so happened that the charger of the conqueror, excited by the fury of the contest, laid hold of the other's neck with his teeth, and almost tore away a piece of the muscular flesh at the very moment when the rider's spur, as he fell, cut a long gash in his flank.

With a wild yelling neigh, the tortured brute yerked out his heels viciously; and, as ill luck would have it, both took effect on the person of his fallen master, one striking him a terrible blow on the chest, the other shattering his collar bone and shoulder.

A dozen of the spectators sprang down from the seats and took him up before Paullus could dismount to aid him; but, as they raised him from the ground, his eyes were already glazing.

"Marcius has conquered me," he muttered in tones of

deep mortification, unconscious, as it would seem, of his agony, and wounded only by the indomitable Roman pride; and with the words his jaw dropped, and his last strife was ended.

"The fool!" exclaimed Cataline, with a bitter sneer; "what had he got to do, that he should ride against Caius Marcius, when he could not so much as keep his saddle, the fool!"

"He is gone!" cried another; "game to the last, brave Varus!"

"He came of a brave race," said a third; "but he rode badly!"

"At least not so well as Marcius," replied yet a fourth; "but who does? To be foiled by him does not argue bad riding."

"Who does? why Paullus, here," cried Aurelius Victor; "I'll match him, if he will ride, for a thousand sesterces—ten thousand, if you will."

"No! I'll not bet about it. I lost by this cursed chance," answered the former speaker; "but Varus did not ride badly, I maintain it!" he added, with the steadiness of a discomfited partisan.

"Ay! but he did, most pestilently," interposed Cataline, almost fiercely; "but come, come, why don't they carry him away? we are losing all the morning."

"I thought he was a friend of yours, Sergius," said another of the bystanders, apparently vexed at the heartlessness of his manner.

"Why, ay! so he was," replied the conspirator; "but he is nothing now: nor can my friendship aught avail him. It was his time and his fate! ours, it may be, will come to-morrow. Nor do I see at all wherefore our sports should not proceed, because a man has gone hence. Fifty men every day die somewhere, while we are dining, drinking, kissing our mistresses or wives; but do we stop for that? Ho! bear him hence, we will attend his funeral, when it shall be soever; and we will drink to his memory to-day. What comes next, comrades?"

Arvina, it is true, was for a moment both shocked and disgusted at the heartless and unfeeling tone; but few if any of the others evinced the like tenderness; for it must be remembered, in the first place, that the Romans, inured to sights of blood and torture daily in the gladiatorial fights of the arena, were callous to human suffering, and careless of human life at all times; and, in the second, that Stoicism was the predominant affectation of the day, not only among the rude and coarse, but among the best and most virtuous citizens of the republic. Few, therefore, left the ground, when the corpse, decently enveloped in the toga he had worn when living, was borne homewards; except the involuntary homicide, who could not even at that day in decency remain, and a few of his most intimate associates, who covering their faces in the lappets of their gowns, followed the bearers in stern and silent sorrow.

Scarcely then had the sad procession threaded the marble archway, before Catiline again asked loudly and imperiously,

"What is to be the next, I pray you? are we to sit here like old women by their firesides, croaking and whimpering till dinner time?"

"No! by the gods," cried Aurelius, "we have a race to come off, which I propose to win. Fuscus Aristius here, and I—we will start instantly, if no one else has the ground."

"Away with you then," answered the other; "come sit by me, Arvina, I would say a word with you."

Giving his horse to one of his grooms, the young man followed him without answer; for although it is true that Catiline was at this time a marked man and of no favorable reputation, yet squeamishness in the choice of associates was never a characteristic of the Romans; and persons, the known perpetrators of the most atrocious crimes, so long as they were unconvicted, mingled on terms of equality, unshunned by any, except the gravest and most rigid censors. Arvina, too, was very young; and very young men are often fascinated, as it were, by great reputations, even of great criminals, with a passionate desire to see them more closely, and observe the stuff they are made of. So that, in fact, Catiline being looked upon in those days much as a desperate gambler, a celebrated duellist, or a famous seducer of our own time, whom no one shuns though every one abuses, it was not perhaps very wonderful if this rash, ardent, and inexperienced youth should have conceived himself flattered by such notice, from one of whom all the world was talking; and should have followed him to a seat with a sense of gratified vanity, blended with eager curiosity.

The race, which followed, differed not much from any other race; except that the riders having no stirrups, that being a yet undiscovered luxury, much less depended upon jockeyship—the skill of the riders being limited to keeping their seats steadily and guiding the animals they bestrode—and much more upon the native powers, the speed and endurance of the coursers.

So much, however, was Arvina interested by the manner and conversation of the singular man by whose side he sat, and who was indeed laying himself out with deep art to captivate him, and take his mind, as it were, by storm, now with the boldest and most daring paradoxes; now with bursts of eloquent invective against the oppression and aristocratic insolence of the cabal, which by his shewing governed Rome; and now with sarcasm and pungent wit, that he saw but little of the course, which he had come especially to look at.

"Do you indeed ride so well, my Paullus?" asked his companion suddenly, as if the thought had been suggested by some observation he had just made on the competitors, as they passed in the second circuit. "So well, I mean, as Aurelius Victor said; and would you undertake the combat of the horse and spear with Caius Marcius?"

"Truly I would," said Arvina, blushing slightly; "I have interchanged many a blow and thrust with young Varro, whom our master-at-arms holds better with the pear than Marcius; and I feel myself his equal. I have oeen practising a good deal of late," he added modestly; "for, though perhaps you know it not, I have been elected *decurio*:* and, as first chosen, leader of a troop, and am to take the field with the next reinforcements that go out to Pontus to our great Pompey."

"The next reinforcements," replied Catiline with a meditative air: "ha! that may be some time distant."

"Not so, by Jupiter! my Sergius; we are already

* The cavalry attached to every legion, consisting of three hundred men, was divided into ten troops, *turmæ* of thirty each, which were subdivided into decuriæ of ten, commanded by a decurio, the first elected of whom was called *dux turmæ*, and led the troop.

ordered to hold ourselves in readiness to march for Brundusium, where we shall ship for Pontus. I fancy we shall set forth as soon as the consular comitia have been held."

"It may be so," said the other; "but I do not think it. There may fall out that which shall rather summon Pompey homeward, than send more men to join him. That is a very handsome dagger," he broke off, interrupting himself suddenly—"where did you get it? I should like much to get me such an one to give to my friend Cethegus, who has a taste for such things. I wonder, however, at your wearing it so openly."

Taken completely by surprise, Arvina answered hastily, "I found it last night; and I wear it, hoping to find the owner."

"By Hercules!" said the conspirator laughing; "I would not take so much pains, were I you. But, do you hear, I have partly a mind myself to claim it."

"No! you were better not," said Paullus, gravely; "besides, you can get one just like this, without risking any thing. Volero, the cutler, in the Sacred Way, near Vesta's temple, has one precisely like to this for sale. He made this too, he tells me; though he will not tell me to whom he sold it; but that shall soon be got out of him, notwithstanding."

"Ha! are you so anxious in the matter? it would oblige you, then, if I should confess myself the loser! Well, I don't want to buy another; I want this very one. I believe I must claim it."

He spoke with an emphasis so singular; impressive, and at the same time half-derisive, and with so strangely-meaning an expression, that Paullus indeed scarcely knew what to think; but, in the mean time, he had recovered his own self-possession, and merely answered—

"I think you had better not; it would perhaps be dangerous!"

"Dangerous? Ha! that is another motive. I love danger! verily, I believe I must; yes! I must claim it."

"What!" exclaimed Paullus, turning pale from excitement; "Is it yours? Do you say that it is yours?"

"Look! look!" exclaimed Catiline, springing to his feet; "here they come, here they come now; this is the last round. By the gods! but they are gallant horses, and well matched! See how the bay courser stretches himself, and how quickly he gathers! The bay! the bay has it for five hundred sesterces!"

"I wager you," said a dissolute-looking long-haired youth; "I wager you five hundred, Catiline. I say the gray horse wins."

"Be it so, then," shouted Catiline; "the bay, the bay! spur, spur, Aristius Fuscus, Aurelius gains on you; spur, spur!"

"The gray, the gray! There is not a horse in Rome can touch Aurelius Victor's gray South-wind!" replied the other.

And in truth, Victor's Gallic courser repaid his master's vaunts; for he made, though he had seemed beat, so desperate a rally, that he rushed past the bay Arab almost at the goal, and won by a clear length amidst the roars of the glad spectators.

"I have lost, plague on it!" exclaimed Catiline; "and here is Clodius expects to be paid on the instant, I'll be sworn."

And as he spoke, the debauchee with whom he had betted came up, holding his left hand extended, tapping its palm with the forefinger of the right.

"I told you so," he said, "I told you so; where be the sesterces?"

"You must needs wait a while; I have not my purse with me," Catiline began. But Paullus interrupted him—

"I have, I have, my Sergius; permit me to accommodate you." And suiting the action to the word, he gave the conspirator several large gold coins, adding, "you can repay me when it suits you."

"That will be never," said Clodius with a sneer; "you don't know Lucius Catiline, I see, young man."

"Ay, but he does!" replied the other, with a sarcastic grin; "for Catiline never forgets a friend, or forgives a foe. Can Clodius say the same?"

But Clodius merely smiled, and walked off, clinking the money he had won tauntingly in his hand.

"What now, I wonder, is the day destined to bring forth?" said the conspirator, making no more allusion to the dagger.

"A contest now between myself, Aristius, and Aurelius, in the five games of the *quinquertium*, and then a foot race in the heaviest panoply."

"Ha! can you beat them?" asked Catiline, regarding Arvina with an interest that grew every moment keener, as he saw more of his strength and daring spirit.

"I can try."

"Shall I bet on you?"

"If you please. I can beat them in some, I think; and, as I said, I will try in all."

More words followed, for Paullus hastened away to strip and anoint himself for the coming struggle; and in a little while the strife itself succeeded.

To describe this would be tedious; but suffice it, that while he won decidedly three games of the five, Paullus was beat in none; and that in the armed foot race, the most toilsome and arduous exercise of the Campus, he not only beat his competitors with ease; but ran the longest course, carrying the most ponderous armature and shield, in shorter time than had been performed within many years on the Field of Mars.

Catiline watched him eagerly all the while, inspecting him as a purchaser would a horse he was about to buy; and then, muttering to himself, "We must have him!" walked up to join him as he finished the last exploit.

"Will you dine with me, Paullus," he said, "to-day, and meet the loveliest women you can see in Rome, and no prudes either?"

"Willingly," he replied; "but I must swim first in the Tiber!"

"Be it so, there is time enough; I will swim also." And they moved down in company toward the river.

CHAPTER VI.

THE FALSE LOVE.

Fie, fie, upon her;
There's a language in her eye, her cheek, her lip;
Nay, her foot speaks, her wanton spirits look out
At every joint and motive of her body.

TROILUS AND CRESSIDA.

ABOUT three hours later than the scene in the Campus Martius, which had occurred a little after noon, Catiline was standing richly dressed in a bright saffron* robe, something longer than the ordinary tunic, flowered with sprigs of purple, in the inmost chamber of the woman's apartments, in his own heavily mortgaged mansion. His wife, Aurelia Orestilla, sat beside him on a low stool, a woman of the most superb and queenly beauty—for whom it was believed that he had plunged himself into the deepest guilt—and still, although past the prime of Italian womanhood, possessing charms that might well account for the most insane passion.

A slave was listening with watchful and half terrified attention to the injunctions of his lord—for Catiline was an unscrupulous and severe master—and, as he ceased speaking, he made a deep genuflexion and retired.

No sooner had he gone than Catiline turned quickly to the lady, whose lovely face wore some marks of displeasure, and said rather shortly,

"You have not gone to her, my Aurelia. There is no time to lose; the young man will be here soon, and if they meet, ere you have given her the cue, all will be lost."

* The guests at Roman banquets usually brought their own napkins, *mappæ*, and wore robes of bright colors, usually flowered, called *cœnatoriæ* or *cubitoriæ*.

"I do not like it, my Sergius," said the woman, rising, but making no movement to leave the chamber.

"And why not, I beseech you, madam?" he replied angrily; "or what is there in that which I desire you to tell the girl to do, that you have not done twenty times yourself, and Fulvia, and Sempronia, and half Rome's noblest ladies? Tush! I say, tush! go do it."

"She is my daughter, Sergius," answered Aurelia, in a tone of deep tenderness; "a daughter's honor must be something to every mother!"

"And a son's life to every father!" said Catiline with a fierce sneer. "I had a son once, I remember. You wished to enter an **empty* house on the day of your marriage feast. I do not think you found him in your way! Besides, for honor—if I read Lucia's eyes rightly, there is not much of that to emperil."

When he spoke of his son, she covered her face in her richly jewelled hands, and a slight shudder shook her whole frame. When she looked up again, she was pale as death, and her lips quivered as she asked—

"Must I, then? Oh! be merciful, my Sergius."

"You must, Aurelia!" he replied sternly, "and that now. Our fortunes, nay, our lives, depend on it!"

"*All*—must she give all, Lucius?"

"All that he asks! But fear not, he shall wed her, when our plans shall be crowned with triumph?"

"Will you swear it?"

"By all the Gods! he shall! by all the Furies, if you will, by Earth, and Heaven, and Hades!"

"I will go," she replied, something reassured, "and prepare her for the task!"

"The task!" he muttered with his habitual sneer. "Daintily worded, fair one; but it will not, I fancy, prove a hard one; Paullus is young and handsome; and our soft Lucia has, methinks, something of her mother's yielding tenderness.'

"Do you reproach me with it, Sergius?"

"Nay! rather I adore thee for it, loveliest one; but go and prepare our Lucia." Then, as she left the room, the dark scowl settled down on his black brow, and he clinched his hand as he said—

* Pro certo creditur, necato filio, *vacuam* domum scelestis nuptiis fecisse.

" She waxes stubborn—let her beware! She is not half so young as she was; and her beauty wanes as fast as my passion for it; let her beware how she crosses me!"

While he was speaking yet a slave entered, and announced that Paullus Cæcilius Arvina had arrived, and Curius, and the noble Fulvia; and as he received the tidings the frown passed away from the brow of the conspirator, and putting on his mask of smooth, smiling dissimulation, he went forth to meet his guests.

They were assembled in the tablinum, or saloon, Arvina clad in a violet colored tunic, sprinkled with flowers in their natural hues, and Curius—a slight keen-looking man, with a wild, proud expression, giving a sort of interest to a countenance haggard from the excitement of passion, in one of rich crimson, fringed at the wrists and neck with gold. Fulvia, his paramour, a woman famed throughout Rome alike for her licentiousness and beauty, was hanging on his arm, glittering with chains and carcanets, and bracelets of the costliest gems, in her fair bosom all too much displayed for a matron's modesty; on her round dazzling arms; about her swan-like neck; wreathed in the profuse tresses of her golden hair—for she was that unusual and much admired being, an Italian blonde—and, spanning the circumference of her slight waist. She was, indeed, a creature exquisitely bright and lovely, with such an air of mild and angelic candor pervading her whole face, that you would have sworn her the most innocent, the purest of her sex. Alas! that she was indeed almost the vilest! that she was that rare monster, a woman, who, linked with every crime and baseness that can almost unsex a woman, preserves yet in its height, one eminent and noble virtue, one half-redeeming trait amidst all her infamy, in her proud love or country! Name, honor, virtue, conscience, womanhood, truth, piety, all, all, were sacrificed to her rebellious passions. But to her love of country she could have sacrificed those very passions! That frail abandoned wretch was still a Roman—might have been in a purer age a heroine of Rome's most glorious.

" Welcome, most lovely Fulvia," exclaimed the host, gliding softly into the room. " By Mars! the most favored of immortals! You must have stolen Aphrodite's cestus! Saw you her ever look so beautiful, my Paullus? You do well to put those sapphires in your hair, for they wax pale and dim besides the richer azure of your eyes; and the dull gold in which they are enchased sets off the sparkling splendor of your tresses. What, Fulvia, know you not young Arvina—one of the great Cæcilii? By Hercules! my Curius, he won the best of the quinquertium from such competitors as Victor and Aristius Fuscus, and ran twelve stadii, with the heaviest breast-plate and shield in the armory, quicker than it has been performed since the days of Licinius Celer. I prithee, know, and cherish him, my friends, for I would have him one of us. In truth I would, my Paullus."

The flattering words of the tempter, and the more fascinating smiles and glances of the bewitching siren, were not thrown away on the young noble; and these, with the soft perfumed atmosphere, the splendidly voluptuous furniture of the saloon, and the delicious music, which was floating all the while upon his ears from the blended instruments and voices of unseen minstrels, conspired to plunge his senses into a species of effeminate and luxurious languor, which suited well the ulterior views of Catiline.

"One thing alone has occurred," resumed the host, after some moments spent in light jests and trivial conversation, "to decrease our pleasure: Cethegus was to have dined with us to-day, and Decius Brutus, with his inimitable wife Sempronia. But they have disappointed us; and, save Aurelia only, and our poor little Lucia, there will be none but ourselves to eat my Umbrian boar."

"Have you a boar, my Sergius?" exclaimed Curius, eagerly, who was addicted to the pleasures of the table, almost as much as the charms of women. "By Pan, the God of Hunters! we are in luck to-day!"

"But wherefore comes not Sempronia?" inquired Fulvia, not very much displeased by the absence of a rival beauty.

"Brutus is called away, it appears, suddenly to Tarentum upon business; and she"—

"Prefers entertaining our Cethegus, alone in her own house, I fancy," interrupted Fulvia.

"Exactly so," replied Catiline, with a smile of meaning.

"Happy Cethegus," said Arvina.

"Do you think her so handsome?" asked Fulvia, favoring him with one of her most melting glances.

"The handsomest woman," he replied, "with but one exception, I ever had the luck to look upon."

"Indeed!—and pray, who is the exception?" asked the lady, very tartly.

There happened to be lying on a marble slab, near to the place where they were standing, a small round mirror of highly polished steel, set in a frame of tortoiseshell and gold. Paullus had noticed it before she spoke; and taking it up without a moment's pause, he raised it to her face.

"Look!" he said, "look into that, and blush at your question."

"Prettily said, my Paullus; thy wit is as fleet as thy foot is speedy," said the conspirator.

"Flatterer!" whispered the lady, evidently much delighted; and then, in a lower voice she added, "Do you indeed think so?"

"Else may I never hope."

But at this moment the curtains were drawn aside, and Orestilla entered from the gallery of the peristyle, accompanied by her daughter Lucia.

The latter was a girl of about eighteen years old, and of appearance so remarkable, that she must not be passed unnoticed. In person she was extremely tall and slender, and at first sight you would have supposed her thin; until the wavy outlines of the loose robe of plain white linen which she wore, undulating at every movement of her form, displayed the exquisite fulness of her swelling bust, and the voluptuous roundness of all her lower limbs. Her arms, which were bare to the shoulders, where her gown was fastened by two studs of gold, were quite unadorned, by any gem or bracelet, and although beautifully moulded, were rather slender than full.

Her face did not at first sight strike you more than her person, as being beautiful; for it was singularly still and inexpressive when at rest—although all the features were fine and classically regular—and was almost unnaturally pale and hueless. The mouth only, had any thing of warmth, or color, or expression; and what expression there was, was not pleasing, for although soft and winning, it was sensual to the last degree.

Her manner, however, contradicted this; for she slided into the circle, with downcast eyes, the long dark silky lashes only visible in relief against the marble paleness of her cheek, as if she were ashamed to raise them from the ground; her whole air being that of a girl oppressed with verwhelming bashfulness, to an extent almost painful.

"Why, what is this, Aurelia," exclaimed Catiline, as if he were angry, although in truth the whole thing was carefully preconcerted. "Wherefore is Lucia thus strangely clad? Is it, I pray you, in scorn of our noble guests, that she wears only this plain morning stola?"

"Pardon her, I beseech you, good my Sergius," answered his wife, with a painfully simulated smile; "you know how over-timid she is and bashful; she had determined not to appear at dinner, had I not laid my commands on her. Her very hair, you see, is not braided."

"Ha! this is ill done, my girl Lucia," answered Catiline. "What will my young friend, Arvina, think of you, who comes hither to-day, for the first time? For Curius and our lovely Fulvia, I care not so much, seeing they know your whims; but I am vexed, indeed, that Paullus should behold you thus in disarray, with your hair thus knotted like a slave girl's, on your neck."

"Like a Dryad's, rather, or shy Oread's of Diana's train—beautiful hair!" replied the youth, whose attention had been called to the girl by this conversation; and who, having thought her at first unattractive rather than otherwise, had now discovered the rare beauties of her lythe and slender figure, and detected, as he thought, a world of passion in her serpent-like and sinuous motions.

She raised her eyes to meet his slowly, as he spoke; gazed into them for one moment, and then, as if ashamed of what she had done, dropped them again instantly; while a bright crimson flush shot like a stream of lava over her pallid face, and neck, and arms; yes, her arms blushed, and her hands to the finger ends! It was but one moment, that those large lustrous orbs looked full into his, swimming in liquid Oriental languor, yet flashing out beams of consuming fire.

Yet Paullus Arvina felt the glance, like an electrical influence, through every nerve and artery of his body, and trembled at its power.

it was a minute before he could collect himself enough to speak to her, for all the rest had moved away a little, and left them standing together; and when he did so, his voice faltered, and his manner was so much agitated, that she must have been blind, indeed, and stupid, not to perceive it.

And Lucia was not blind nor stupid. No! by the God of Love! an universe of wild imaginative intellect, an ocean of strange whirling thoughts, an Etna of fierce and fiery passions, lay buried beneath that calm, bashful, almost awkward manner. Many bad thoughts were there, many unmaidenly imaginings, many ungoverned and most evil passions; but there was also much that was partly good; much that might have been all good, and high and noble, had it been properly directed; but alas! as much pains had been taken to corrupt and deprave that youthful understanding, and to inflame those nascent passions, as are devoted by good parents to developing the former, and repressing the growth of the latter.

As it was, self indulged, and indulged by others, she was a creature of impulse entirely, ill regulated and ungovernable.

Intended from the first to be a tool in his own hands, whenever he might think fit to use her, she had in no case hitherto run counter to the views of Catiline; because, so long as his schemes were agreeable to her inclinations, and favorable to her pleasures, she was quite willing to be his tool; though by no means unconscious of the fact that he meant her to be such.

What might be the result should his wishes cross her own, the arch conspirator had never given himself the pains to enquire; for, like the greater part of voluptuaries, regarding women as mere animals, vastly inferior in mind and intellect to men, he had entirely overlooked her mental qualifications, and fancied her a being of as small moral capacity, as he knew her to be of strong physical organization.

He was mistaken; as wise men often are, and deeply, perhaps fatally.

There was not probably a girl in all Italy, in all the world, who would so implicitly have followed his directions, as long as to do so gratified her passions, and clashed not with her indomitable will, to the sacrifiee of all principle, and with the most total disregard of right or wrong, as Lucia Orestilla; but certainly there was not one, who would have resisted commands, threats, violence, more pertinaciously or dauntlessly, than the same Lucia, should her will and his councils ever be set at twain.

While Paullus was yet conversing in an under tone with this strange girl, and becoming every moment more and more fascinated by the whole tone of her remarks, which were free, and even bold, as contrasted with the bashful air and timid glances which accompanied them, the curtains of the Tablinum were drawn apart, and a soft symphony of flutes stealing in from the atrium, announced that the dinner was prepared.

"My Curius," exclaimed Catiline, "I must entreat you to take charge of Fulvia; I had proposed myself that pleasure, intending that you should escort Sempronia, and Decius my own Orestilla; but, as it is, we will each abide by his own lady; and Paullus here will pardon the youth and rawness of my Lucia."

"By heaven! I would wish nothing better," said Curius, taking Fulvia by the hand, and leading her forward. "Should you Arvina?"

"Not I, indeed," replied Paullus, "if Lucia be content." And he looked to catch her eye, as he took her soft hand in his own, but her face remained cold and pale as marble, and her eye downcast.

As they passed out, however, into the fauces, or passage leading to the dining-room, Catiline added,

"As we are all, I may say, one family and party, I have desired the slaves to spread couches only; the ladies will recline with us, instead of sitting at the board."

At this moment, did Paullus fancy it? or did that beautiful pale girl indeed press his fingers in her own? he could not be mistaken; and yet there was the downcast eye, the immoveable cheek, and the unsmiling aspect of the rosy mouth. But he returned the pressure, and that so significantly, that she at least could not be mistaken; nor was she, for her eye again met his, with that deep amorous languid glance; was bashfully withdrawn; and then met his again, glancing askance through the dark fringed lids, and a quick flashing smile, and a burning blush followed; and in a second's space she was again as cold, as impassive as a marble statue.

They reached the triclinium, a beautiful oblong apartment, gorgeously painted with arabesques of gold and scarlet upon a deep azure ground work. A circular table, covered with a white cloth, bordered with a deep edge of purple and deeper fringe of gold, stood in the centre, and around it three couches, nearly of the same height with the board, each the segment of a circle, the three forming a horse-shoe.

The couches were of the finest rosewood, inlaid with tortoiseshell and ivory and brass, strewed with the richest tapestries, and piled with cushions glowing with splendid needlework. And over all, upheld by richly moulded shafts of Corinthian bronze, was a canopy of Tyrian purple, tasselled and fringed with gold.

The method of reclining at the table was, that the guests should place themselves on the left side, propped partly by the left elbow and partly by a pile of cushions; each couch being made to contain in general three persons, the head of the second coming immediately below the right arm of the first, and the third in like manner; the body of each being placed transversely, so as to allow space for the limbs of the next below in front of him.

The middle place on each couch was esteemed the most honorable; and the middle couch of the three was that assigned to guests of the highest rank, the master of the feast, for the most, occupying the central position on the third or left hand sofa. The slaves stood round the outer circuit of the whole, with the cupbearers; but the carver, and steward, if he might so be termed, occupied that side of the table which was left open to their attendance.

On this occasion, there being but six guests in all, each gentleman assisted the lady under his charge to recline, with her head comfortably elevated, near the centre of the couch; and then took his station behind her, so that, if she leaned back, her head would rest on his bosom, while he was enabled himself to reach the table, and help himself or his fair partner, as need might be, to the delicacies offered in succession.

Curius and Fulvia, he as of senatorial rank, and she as a noble matron, occupied the highest places; Paullus and

Lucia reclined on the right hand couch, and Catiline with Orestilla in his bosom, as the phrase ran, on the left.

No sooner were they all placed, and the due libation made of wine, with an offering of salt, to the domestic Gods—a silver group of statues occupying the centre of the board, where we should now place the *plateau* and *epergne*, than a louder burst of music ushered in three beautiful female slaves, in succinct tunics, like that seen in the sculptures of Diana, with half the bosom bare, dancing and singing, and carrying garlands in their hands of roses and myrtle, woven with strips of the philyra, or inner bark of the linden tree, which was believed to be a specific against intoxication. Circling around the board, in time to the soft music, they crowned each of the guests, and sprinkled with rich perfumes the garments and the hair of each; and then with more animated and eccentric gestures, as the note of the flute waxed shriller and more piercing, they bounded from the banquet hall, and were succeeded by six boys with silver basins, full of tepid water perfumed with costly essences, and soft embroidered napkins, which they handed to every banqueter to wash the hands before eating.

This done, the music died away into a low faint close, and was silent; and in the hush that followed, an aged slave bore round a mighty flask of Chian wine, diluted with snow water, and replenished the goblets of stained glass, which stood beside each guest; while another dispensed bread from a lordly basket of wrought gilded scroll work.

And now the feast commenced, in earnest; as the first course, consisting of fresh eggs boiled hard, with lettuce, radishes, endive and rockets, olives of Venafrum, anchovies and sardines, and the choicest luxury of the day—hot sausages served upon gridirons of silver, with the rich gravy dripping through the bars upon a sauce of Syrian prunes and pomegranate berries—was placed upon the board.

For a time there was little conversation beyond the ordinary courtesies of the table, and such trifling jests as were suggested by occurrences of the moment. Yet still in the few words that passed from time to time, Paullus continued often to convey his sentiments to Lucia in words of double meaning; keenly marked, it is true, but seemingly unobserved by the wily plotter opposite; and more than once in handing her the goblet, or loading her plate with dainties, he took an opportunity again and again of pressing her not unwilling hand. And still at every pressure he caught that soft momentary glance, was it of love and passion, or of mere coquetry and girlish wantonness, succeeded by the fleeting blush pervading face, neck, arms, and bosom.

Never had Paullus been so wildly fascinated; his heart throbbed and bounded as if it would have burst his breast; his head swam with a sort of pleasurable dizziness; his eyes were dim and suffused; and he scarce knew that he was talking, though he was indeed the life of the whole company, voluble, witty, versatile, and at times eloquent, so far as the topics of the day gave room for eloquence.

And now, to the melody of Lydian lutes, two slaves introduced a huge silver dish, loaded by the vast brawn of the Umbrian boar, garnished with leaves of chervil, and floating in a rich sauce of anchovies, the dregs of Coan wine, white pepper, vinegar, and olives. The carver brandished his knife in graceful and fantastic gestures, proud of his honorable task; and as he plunged it into the savory meat, and the delicious savor rushed up to his nostrils, he laid down the blade, spread out his hands in an ecstacy, and cried aloud, " ye Gods, how glorious!"

"Excellent well, my Glycon," cried Curius, delighted with the expressive pantomine of the well skilled Greek; " smells it so savory?"

" I have carved many a boar from Lucania and from Umbria also; to say nothing of those from the Laurentian marshes, which are bad, seeing that they are fed on reeds only and marsh grass; most noble Curius; and never put I knife into such an one as this. There are two inches on it of pure fat, softer than marrow. He was fed upon holm acorns, I'll be sworn, and sweet chesnuts, and caught in a mild south wind!"

" Fewer words, you scoundrel," exclaimed Catiline, laughing at the fellow's volubility, " and quicker carving, if you wish not to visit the pistrinum. You have set Curius' mouth watering, so that he will be sped with longing, before you have helped Fulvia and your mistress. Fill up, you knaves, fill up; nay! not the Chian now; the Falernian from the Faustian hills, or the Cæcuban? Which shall it be, my Curius?"

"The Cæcuban, by all the Gods! I hold it the best vintage ever, and yours is curious. Besides, the Falernian is too dry to drink before the meat. Afterward, if, as Glycon says, the boar hath a flavor of the south, it will be excellent, indeed."

"Are as you as constant, Paullus, in your love for the boar, as these other epicures?" cried Fulvia, who, despite the depreciating tone in which she spoke, had sent her own plate for a second slice.

"No! by the Gods! Fulvia," he replied, "I am but a sorry epicure, and I love the boar better in his reedy fen, or his wild thicket on the Umbrian hills, with his eye glaring red in rage, and his tusks white with foam, than girt with condiments and spices upon a golden dish."

"A strange taste," said Curius, "I had for my part rather meet ten on the dining table, than one in the oak woods."

"Commend me to the boar upon the table likewise," said Catiline; "still, with my friend Arvina at my side, and a good boarspear in my hand, I would like well to bide the charge of a tusker! It is rare sport, by Hercules!"

"Wonderful beings you men are," said Fulvia, mincing her words affectedly, "ever in search of danger; ever on the alert to kill; to shed blood, even if it be your own! by Juno, I cannot comprehend it."

"I can, I can," cried Lucia, raising her voice for the first time, so that it could be heard by any others than her nearest neighbor; "right well can I comprehend it; were I a man myself, I feel that I should pant for the battle. The triumph would be more than rapture; and strife, for its own sake, maddening bliss! Heavens! to see the gladiators wheel and charge; to see their swords flash in the sun; and the red blood gush out unheeded; and the grim faces flushed and furious; and the eyes greedily devouring the wounds of the foeman, but all unconscious of their own; and the play of the muscular strong limbs; and the terrible death grapple! And then the dull hissing sound of the death stroke; and the voiceless parting of the bold spirit! Ye Gods! ye Gods! it is a joy, to live, and almost to die for!"

Paullus Arvina looked at her in speechless wonder. The eyes so wavering and downcast were now fixed, and steady, and burning with a passionate clear light; there was a fiery flush on her cheek, not brief and evanescent; her ripe red mouth was half open, shewing the snow white teeth biting the lower lip in the excitement of her feelings. Her whole form seemed to be dilated and more majestic than its wont.

"Bravo! my girl; well said, my quiet Lucia!" exclaimed Catiline. "I knew not that she had so much of mettle in her."

"You must have thought, then, that I belied my race," replied the girl, unblushingly; "for it is whispered that you are my father, and I think *you* have looked on blood, and shed it before now!"

"Boar's blood, ha! Lucia; but you are blunt and brave to-night. Is it that Paullus has inspired you?"

"Nay! I know not," she replied, half apathetically; "but I do know, that if I ever love, it shall be a hero; a man that would rather lie in wait until dawn to receive the fierce boar rushing from the brake upon his spear, than until midnight to enfold a silly girl in his embrace."

"Then will you never love me, Lucia," answered Curius.

"Never, indeed!" said she; "it must be a man whom I will love; and there is nothing manly about thee, save thy vices!"

"It is for those that most people love me," replied Curius, nothing disconcerted. "Now Cato has nothing of the man about him but the virtues; and I should like to know who ever thought of loving Cato."

"I never heard of any body loving Cato," said Fulvia, quietly.

"But I have," answered the girl, almost fiercely; "none of *you* love him; nor do I love him; because he is too high and noble, to be dishonored by the love of such as I am; but all the good, and great, and generous, do love him, and will love his memory for countless ages! I would to God, I could love him!"

"What fury has possessed her?" whispered Catiline

to Orestilla; "what ails her to talk thus? first to proclaim herself my daughter, and now to praise Cato?"

"Do not ask me!" replied Aurelia in the same tone; "she was a strange girl ever; and I cannot say, if she likes this task that you have put upon her."

"More wine, ho! bring more wine! Drink we each man to his mistress, each lady to her lover in secrecy and silence!" cried the master of the revel. "Fill up! fill up! let it be pure, and sparkling to the brim."

But Fulvia, irritated a little by what had passed, would not be silent; although she saw that Catiline was annoyed at the character the conversation had assumed, and ere the slave had filled up the beakers she addressed Lucia—

"And wherefore, dearest, would you love Cato? I could as soon love the statue of Accius Nævius, with his long beard, on the steps of the Comitium; he were scarce colder, or less comely than your Cato."

"Because to love virtue is still something, if we be vicious even; and, if I am not virtuous myself, at least I have not lost the sense that it were good to be so!"

"I never knew that you were not virtuous, my Lucia," interposed her mother; "affectionate and pious you have ever been."

"And obedient!" added Catiline, with strong emphasis. "Your mother, my Lucia, and myself, return thanks to the Gods daily for giving us so good a child."

"Do you?" replied the girl, scornfully; "the Gods must have merry times, then, for that must needs make them laugh! But good or bad, I respect the great; and, if I ever love, it will be, as I said, a great and a good man."

"I fear you will never love me, Lucia," whispered Paullus in her ear, unheard amid the clash of knives and flagons, and the pealing of a fresh strain of music, which ushered in the king of fish, the grand conger, garnished with prawns and soused in pungent sauce.

"Wherefore not?" she replied, meeting his eye with a furtive sidelong glance.

"Because I, for one, had rather watch till midnight fifty times, in the hope only of clasping Lucia, once, in my embrace; than once until dawn, to kill fifty boars of Umbria."

She made no answer; but looked up into his face as if

to see whether he was in earnest, with an affectionate and pleading glance; and then pressed her unsandalled foot against his. A moment or two afterward, he perceived the embroidered table cover had been drawn up, with the intent of protecting her dress from the sauces of the fish which she was eating, in such a manner as to conceal the greater part of her person.

Observing this, and excited beyond all restraint of ordinary prudence, by the consciousness of her manner, he profited by the chance to steal his arm about her waist; and to his surprise, almost as much as his delight, he felt his hand clasped instantly in hers, and pressed upon her throbbing heart.

The blood gushed like molten fire through his veins. The fascinations of the siren had prevailed. The voice of the charmer had been heard, charming him but too wisely. And for the moment, fool that he was, he fancied he loved Lucia, and his own pure and innocent and lovely Julia was forgotten! Forgotten, and for whom!

Catiline had not lost one word, one movement of the young couple; and he perceived, that, although there was clearly something at work in the girl's bosom which he did not comprehend, she had at least obeyed his commands in captivating Paullus; and he now doubted not but she would persevere, from vanity or passion, and bind him down a fettered captive to her will.

Determined to lose nothing by want of exertion, the traitor circulated now the fiery goblet as fast as possible, till every brain was heated more or less, and every cheek flushed, even of the women, by the inspiring influence of the wine cup.

All dainties that were known in those days ministered to his feast; oysters from Baiæ; pheasants—a rarity but lately introduced, since Pompey's conquests in the east—had been brought all the way from Phasis upon the southern shores of the Black Sea; and woodcock from the valleys of Ionia, and the watery plains of Troas, to load the tables of the luxurious masters of the world. Livers of geese, forced to an unnatural size by cramming the unhappy bird with figs; and turbot fricasseed in cream, and peacocks stuffed with truffles, were on the board of Catiline that day, as on the boards of many another noble

Roman; and the wines by which these rare dainties were diluted, differed but little, as wisest critics say, from the madeiras and the sherries of the nineteenth century. For so true is it, that under the sun there is nothing new, that in the *foix gras* of Strasburg, in the *turbot à la crême*, and in the *dindons aux truffes* of the French metropolis, the gastronomes of modern days have only reproduced the dishes, whereon Lucullus and Hortensius feasted before the Christian era.

The day passed pleasantly to all, but to Paullus Arvina it flew like a dream, like a delirious trance, from which, could he have consulted his own will, he would never have awakened.

With the dessert, and the wine cup, the myrtle branch and the lute went round, and songs were warbled by sweet voices, full of seductive thoughts and words of passion. At length the lamps were lighted, and the women arose to quit the hall, leaving the ruder sex to prolong the revel; but as Lucia rose, she again pressed the fingers of Arvina, and whispered a request that he would see her once more ere he left the house.

He promised; but as he did so, his heart sank within him; for dearly as he wished it, he believed he had promised that which would prove impossible.

But in a little while, chance, as he thought it, favored him; for seeing that he refused the wine cup, Catiline, after rallying him some time, good humoredly said with a laugh, "Come, my Arvina, we must not be too hard on you. You have but a young head, though a stout one. Curius and I are old veterans of the camp, old revellers, and love the wine cup better than the bright eyes of beauty, or the minstrel's lute. Thou, I will swear it, wouldst rather now be listening to Lucia's lyre, and may be fingering it thyself, than drinking with us roisterers! Come, never blush, boy, we were all young once! Confess, if I am right! The women you will find, if you choose to seek them, in the third chamber on the left, beyond the inner peristyle. We all love freedom here; nor are we rigid censors. Curius and I will drain a flagon or two more, and then join you."

Muttering something not very comprehensible about his exertions in the morning, and his inability to drink any more, Paullus arose, delighted to effect his escape on terms so easy, and left the triclinium immediately in quest of his mistress.

As he went out, Catiline burst into one of his sneering laughs, and exclaimed, "He is in; by Pan, the hunter's God! he is in the death-toil already! May I perish ill, if he escape it."

"Why, in the name of all the Gods, do you take so much pains with him," said Curius; "he is a stout fellow, and I dare say a brave one; and will make a good legionary, or an officer perhaps; but he is raw, and a fool to boot!"

"Raw, but no fool! I can assure you," answered Catiline; "no more a fool than I am. And we must have him, he is necessary!"

"He will be necessary soon to that girl of yours; she has gone mad, I think, for love of him. I never did believe in philtres; but this is well nigh enough to make one do so."

"Pshaw!" answered Catiline; "it is thou that art raw now, and a fool, Curius. She is no more in love with him than thou art; it was all acting—right good acting: for it did once well nigh deceive me who devised it; but still, only acting. I ordered her to win him at all hazards."

"At all hazards?"

"Aye! at *all*."

"I wish you would give her the like orders touching me, if she obey so readily."

"I would, if it were necessary; which it is not. First, because I have you as firmly mine, as need be; and secondly, because Fulvia would have her heart's blood ere two days had gone, and that would ill suit me; for the sly jade is useful."

"Take care she prove not too sly for you, Sergius. She may obey your orders in this thing; but she does so right willingly. She loves the boy, I tell you, as madly as Venus loved Adonis, or Phædra Hyppolitus; she would pursue him if he fled from her."

"She loves him no more than she loves the musty statue of my stout grandsire, Sergius Silo."

"You will see one day. Meanwhile, look that she fool you not."

While they were speaking, Paullus had reached the entrance of the chamber indicated; and, opening the door, had entered, expecting to find the three women assembled at some feminine sport or occupation. But fortune again favored him—opportune fortune!

For Lucia was alone, expecting him, prepared for his entrance at any moment; yet, when he came, how unprepared, how shocked, how terrified!

For she had unclasped her stola upon both her shoulders, and suffered it to fall down to her girdle which kept it in its place about her hips. But above those she was dressed only in a tunic of that loose fabric, a sort of silken gauze, which was called woven air, and was beginning to be worn very much by women of licentious character; this dress—if that indeed could be called a dress, which displayed all the outlines of the shape, all the hues of the glowing skin every minute blue vein that meandered over the lovely bosom—was wrought in alternate stripes of white and silver; and nothing can be imagined more beautiful than the effect of its semi-transparent veil concealing just enough to leave some scope for the imagination, displaying more than enough for the most prodigal of beauty.

She was employed in dividing her long jet-black hair with a comb of mother-of-pearl as he entered; but she dropped both the hair and comb, and started to her feet with a simulated scream, covering her beautiful bust with her two hands, as if she had been taken absolutely by surprise.

But Paullus had been drinking freely, and Paullus saw, moreover, that she was not offended; and, if surprised, surprised not unpleasantly by his coming.

He sprang forward, caught her in his arms, and clasping her to his bosom almost smothered her with kisses. But shame on her, fast and furiously as he kissed, she kissed as closely back.

"Lucia, sweet Lucia, do you then love me?"

"More than my life—more than my country—more than the Gods! my brave, my noble Paullus."

"And will you then be mine—all mine, my Lucia?"

"Yours, Paul?" she faltered, panting as if with agitation upon his bosom; "am I not yours already? but no, no, no!" she exclaimed, tearing herself from his embrace. "No no! I had forgotten. My father! no; I cannot, my father!"

"What mean you, Lucia? your father? What of your father?"

"You are his enemy. You have discovered, will betray him."

"No, by the great Gods! you are mad, Lucia. I have discovered nothing; nor if I knew him to be the slayer of my father, would I betray him! never, never!"

"Will you swear *that?*"

"Swear what?"

"Never, whatever you may learn, to betray him to any living man: never to carry arms, or give evidence against him; but faithfully and stedfastly to follow him through virtue and through vice, in life and unto death; to live for him, and die with him, unless I release you of your oath and restore you to freedom, which I will never do!"

"By all the powers of light and darkness! by Jupiter Omnipotent, and Pluto the Avenger, I swear, Lucia! May I and all my house, and all whom I love or cherish, wretchedly perish if I fail you."

"Then I am yours," she sighed; "all, and for ever!" and sank into his arms, half fainting with the violence of that prolonged excitement.

CHAPTER VII.

THE OATH.

Into what dangers
Would you lead me, Cassius?

JULIUS CÆSAR.

THE evening had worn on to a late hour, and darkness had already fallen over the earth, when Paullus issued stealthily, like a guilty thing, from Lucia's chamber. No step or sound had come near the door, no voice had called on either, though they had lingered there for hours in endearments, which, as he judged the spirit of his host, would have cost him his life, if suspected; and though he never dreamed of connivance, he did think it strange that a man so wary and suspicious as Catiline was held to be, should have so fallen from his wonted prudence, as to betray his adopted daughter's honor by granting this most fatal opportunity.

He met no member of the family in the dim-lighted peristyle; the passages were silent and deserted; no gay domestic circle was collected in the tablinum, no slaves were waiting in the atrium; and, as he stole forth cautiously with guarded footsteps, Arvina almost fancied that he had been forgotten; and that the master of the house believed him to have retired when he left the dining hall.

It was not long, however, before he was undeceived; for as he entered the vestibule, and was about to lay his hand on the lock of the outer door, a tall dark figure, which he recognized instantly to be that of his host, stepped forward from a side-passage, and stretched out his arm in silence, forbidding him, by that imperious gesture, to proceed.

"Ha! you have tarried long," he said in a deep guarded whisper, "our Lucia truly is a most soft and fascinating creature; you found her so, is it not true, my Paullus?"

There was something singular in the manner in which these words were uttered, half mocking, and half serious; something between a taunting and triumphant assertion of a fact, and a bitter question; but nothing that betokened anger or hostility, or offended pride in the speaker.

Still Paullus was so much taken by surprise, and so doubtful of his entertainer's meaning, and the extent of his knowledge, that he remained speechless in agitated and embarrassed silence.

"What, have the girl's kisses clogged your lips, so that they can give out no sound? By the gods! they were close enough to do so."

"Catiline!" he exclaimed, starting back in astonishment, and half expecting to feel a dagger in his bosom.

"Tush! tush! young man—think you the walls in the house of Catiline have no ears, nor eyes? Paullus Arvina, I know all!"

"All?" faltered the youth, now utterly aghast.

"Ay, all!" replied the conspirator, with a harsh triumphant laugh. "Lucia has given herself to you; and you have sold yourself to Catiline! By all the fiends of Hades, better it were for you, rash boy, that you had ne'er been born, than now to fail me!"

Arvina, trembling with the deep consciousness of hospitality betrayed, and feeling the first stings of remorse already, stood thunderstricken, and unable to articulate.

"Speak!" thundered Catiline; "speak! art thou not mine—mine soul and body—sworn to be mine forever?"

Alas! the fatal oath, sworn in the heat of passion, flashed on his soul, and he answered humbly, and in a faint low voice, how different from his wonted tones of high and manly confidence—

"I am sworn, Catiline!"

"See then that thou be not forsworn. Little thou

dream'st yet, unto what thou art sworn, or unto whom; but know this, that hell itself, with all its furies, would fall short of the tortures that await the traitor!"

"I am, at least, no traitor!"

"No! traitor! Ha!" cried Catiline, "is it an honest deed to creep into the bosom of a daughter of the house which entertained thee as a friend!—No! Traitor—ha! ha! ha! thou shalt ere long learn better—ha! ha! ha!"

And he laughed with the fearful sneering mirth, which was never excited in his breast, but by things perilous and terrible and hateful. In a moment, however, he repressed his merriment, and added—

"Give me that poniard thou didst wear this morning. It is mine."

"Thine!" cried the unhappy youth, starting back, as if he had received a blow; "thine, Catiline!"

"Aye!" he replied, in a hoarse voice, looking into the very eyes of Paul. "I am the slayer of the slave, and regret only that I slew him without torture. Know you whose slave he was, by any chance?"

"He was the Consul's slave," answered Arvina, almost mechanically—for he was utterly bewildered by all that had passed—"Medon, my freedman Thrasea's cousin."

"The Consul's, ha!—which Consul's? speak! fool! speak, ere I tear it from your throat; Cicero's, ha?"

"Cicero's, Catiline!"

"Here is a coil; and knows he of this matter? I mean Cicero."

"He knows it."

"That is to say, you told him. Aye! this morning, after I spoke with you. I comprehend; and you shewed him the poniard. So! so! so! Well, give it to me; I will tell you what to do, hereafter."

"I have it not with me, Sergius," he replied, thoroughly daunted and dismayed.

"See that you meet me then, bringing it with you, at Egeria's cave, as fools call it, in the valley of Muses, at the fourth hour of night to-morrow. In the meantime, beware that you tell no man aught of this, nor that the instrument was bought of Volero. Ha! dost thou hear me?"

"I hear, Catiline."

"And wilt obey?"

"And will obey."

"So shall it go well with thee, and we shall be fast friends forever. Good repose to thee, good my Paullus."

"And Lucia?" he replied, but in a voice of inquiry; for all that he had heard of the tremendous passions and vindictive fury of the conspirator, flashed on his mind, and he fancied that he knew not what of vengeance would fall on the head of the soft beauty.

"Hath played her part rarely!" answered the monster, as he dismissed him from the door, which he opened with his own hand. "Be true, and you shall see her when you will; betray us, and both you and she shall live in agonies, that shall make you call upon death fifty times, ere he relieve you."

And with a menacing gesture, he closed and barred the door behind him.

"Played her part rarely!" The words sank down into his soul with a chilling weight, that seemed to crush every energy and hope. Played her part! Then he was a dupe —the very dupe of the fiend's arch mock, to lip a wanton, and believe her chaste—the dupe of a designing harlot; the sworn tool and slave of a murderer—a monster, who had literally sold his own child's honor. For all the world well knew, that, although Lucia passed for his adopted daughter only, she was his natural offspring by Aurelia Orestilla, before their impious marriage.

Well might he gnash his teeth, and beat his breast, and tear his dark hair by handfulls from his head; well might he groan and curse.

But oh! the inconsistency of man! While he gave vent to all the anguish of his rage in curses against her, the soft partner of his guilt, and at the same time, its avenger; against the murderer and the traitor, now his tyrant; he utterly forgot that his own dereliction, from the paths of rectitude and honor, had led him into the dark toils, in which he now seemed involved beyond any hope of extrication.

He forgot, that to satisfy an insane and unjustifiable love of adventure, and a false curiosity, he had associated himself with a man whom he believed, if he did not actually know, to be infamous and capable of any crime.

He forgot, that, admitted into that man's house in friendship, he had attempted to undermine his daughter's honor; and had felt no remorse, till he learned that his success was owing to connivance—that his own treason had been met and repaid by deeper treason.

He forgot, that for a wanton's love, he had betrayed the brightest, and the purest being that drew the breath of life, from the far Alps, to the blue waters of the far Tarentum—that he had broken his soul's plighted faith—that he was himself, first, a liar, perjurer, and villain.

Alas! it is the inevitable consequence, the first fruit, as it were, of crime, that guilt is still prolific; that the commission of the first ill deed, leads almost surely to the commission of a second, of a third, until the soul is filed and the heart utterly corrupted, and the wretch given wholly up to the dominion of foul sin, and plunged into thorough degradation.

Arvina had thought lightly, if at all, of his first luxurious sin, but now to the depth of his secret soul, he felt that he was emmeshed and entangled in the deepest villainy.

All that he ever had yet heard hinted darkly or surmised of Catiline's gigantic schemes of wickedness, rushed on him, all at once! He doubted nothing any longer; it was clear to him as noonday; distinct and definite as if it had been told to him in so many words; the treason to the state concealed by individual murder; and he, a sworn accomplice—nay, a sworn slave to this murderer and traitor!

Nor was this all; his peril was no less than his guilt; equal on either side—sure ruin if he should be true to his country, and scarce less sure, if he should join its parricides. For, though he had not dared say so much to Catiline, he had already sent the poniard to the house of Cicero, and a brief letter indicating all that he had learned from Volero. This he had done in the interval between the Campus and his unlucky visit to the house of Catiline, whom he then little deemed to be the man of whom he was in quest.

Doubtless, ere this time, the cutler had been summoned to the consul's presence, and the chief magistrate of the Republic had learned that the murderer of his slave was the very person, whom he had bound himself by oaths, so strong that he shuddered at the very thought of them, to support and defend to the utmost.

What was he then to do? how to proceed, since to recede appeared impossible?

How was he to account to the conspirator for his inability to produce the poniard at their appointed meeting? how should he escape the pursuit of his determined vengeance, if he should shun the meeting?

And then, Lucia! The recollection, guilty and degraded as he knew her to be, of her soft blandishments, of her rare beauty, of her wild and inexplicable manner, adding new charms to that forbidden bliss, yet thrilled in every sense. And must he give her up? No! madness was in the very thought! so strangely had she spread her fascinations round him. And yet did he love her? no! perish the thought! Love is a high, a holy, a pure feeling—the purest our poor fallen nature is capable of experiencing; no! this fierce, desperate, guilty passion was no more like true love, than the whirlwind that upheaves the tortured billows, and hurls the fated vessel on the treacherous quicksands, is like to the beneficent and gentle breeze that speeds it to the haven of its hopes, in peace and honor.

After a little while consumed in anxious and uneasy thoughts, he determined—as cowards of the mind determine ever—to temporise, to await events, to depend upon the tide of circumstance. He would, he thought, keep the appointment with his master—for such he felt that Catiline now was indeed—however he might strive to conceal the fact; endeavor to learn what were his real objects; and then determine what should be his own course of action. Doubtful, and weak of principle, and most infirm of purpose, he shrunk alike from breaking the oath he had been entrapped into taking, and from committing any crime against his country.

His country!—To the Roman, patriotism stood for religion!—Pride, habit, education, honor, interest, all were combined in that word, country; and could he be untrue to Rome? His better spirit cried out, no! from every nerve and artery of his body. And then his evil genius whispered Lucia, and he wavered.

Meantime, had no thought crossed him of his own pure and noble Julia, deserted thus and overlooked for a mere wanton? Many times! many times, that day, had his mind reverted to her. When first he went to Cataline's house, he went with the resolution of leaving it at an early hour, so soon as the feast should be over, and seeking her, while there should yet be time to ramble among the flower-beds on the hill of gardens, or perchance, to drive out in his chariot, which he had ordered to be held in readiness, toward the falls of the Anio, or on the proud Emilian way.

Afterward, in the whirl of his mad intoxication for the fascinating Lucia, all memory of his true love was lost, as the chaste moon-light may be dimmed and drowned for a while by the red glare of the torches, brandished in some licentious orgy. Nor did he think of her again, till he found himself saddened, and self-disgusted, plunged into peril—perhaps into ruin, by his own guilty conduct; and then, when he did think, it was with remorse, and self-reproach, and consciousness of disloyalty, so bitterly and keenly painful—yet unaccompanied by that repentance, which steadily envisages past wrong, and determines to amend in future—that he shook off the recollection, whenever it returned, with wilful stubbornness; and resolved on forgetting, for the present, the being whom a few short hours before, he would have deemed it impossible that he should ever think of but with joy and rapturous anticipation.

Occupied in these fast succeeding moods and fancies, Paullus had made his way homeward from the house of Catiline, so far as to the Cerolian place, at the junction of the Sacred Way and the Carinæ. He paused here a moment; and grasping his fevered brow with his hand, recalled to mind the strange occurrences, most unexpected and unfortunate, which had befallen him, since he stood there that morning; each singly trivial; each, unconnected as it seemed with the rest, and of little moment; yet all, when united, forming a chain of circumstances by which he was now fettered hand and foot—his casual interview with Catiline on the hill; his subsequent encounter of Victor and Aristius Fuscus; the recognition of his dagger by the stout cutler Volero; the death of Varus in the hippodrome; his own victorious exercises on the plain; the invitation to the feast; the sumptuous banquet; and last, alas! and most fatal, the too voluptuous and seductive Lucia.

Just at this moment, the doors of Cicero's stately mansion were thrown open, and a long train came sweeping out in dark garments, with blazing torches, and music doleful and piercing. And women chanting the shrill funereal strain. And then, upon a bier covered with black, the rude wooden coffin, peculiar to the slave, of the murdered Medon! Behind him followed the whole household of the Consul; and last, to the extreme astonishment of Paullus, preceded by his lictors, and leaning on the arm of his most faithful freedman, came Cicero himself, doing unusual honor, for some cause known to himself alone, to the manes of his slaughtered servant.

As they passed on toward the Capuan gate of the city, the Consul's eyes fell directly on the form of Arvina, where he stood revealed in the full glare of the torch-light; and as he recognised him, he made a sign that he should join him, which, under those peculiar circumstances, he felt that he could not refuse to do.

Sadly and silently they swept through the splendid streets, and under the arched gate, and filed along the celebrated Appian way, passing the tomb of the proud Scipios on the left hand, with its superb sarcophagi—for that great house had never, from time immemorial, been wont to burn their dead—and on the right, a little farther on, the noble temple and the sacred slope of Mars, and the old statue of the god which had once sweated blood, prescient of Thrasymene. On they went, frightening the echoes of the quiet night with their wild lamentations and the clapping of their hands, sending the glare of their funereal torches far and wide through the cultured fields and sacred groves and rich gardens, until they reached at length the pile, hard by the columbarium, or slave-burying-place of Cicero's household.

Then, the rites performed duly, the dust thrice sprinkled on the body, and the farewell pronounced, the corpse was laid upon the pile, and the tall spire of blood-red flame went up, wavering and streaming through the night, rich with perfumes, and gums, and precious ointment, so noble was the liberality of the good Consul, even in the interment of his more faithful slaves.

No words were uttered to disturb the sound of the ceremony, until the flames died out, and, the smouldering embers quenched with wine, Thrasea, as the nearest relative of the deceased, gathered the ashes and inurned them, when they were duly labelled and consigned to their niche in the columbarium; and then, the final *Ilicet* pronounced, the sad solemnity was ended.

Then, though not until then, did Cicero address the young man; but then, as if to make up for his previous silence, he made him walk by his side all the way back to the city, conversing with him eagerly about all that had passed, thanking him for the note and information he had sent concerning Volero, and anticipating the immediate discovery of the perpetrators of that horrid crime.

"I have not had the leisure to summon Volero before me," he added. "I wished also that you, Arvina, should be present when I examine him. I judge that it will be best, when we shall have dismissed all these, except the lictors, to visit him this very night. He is a thrifty and laborious artisan, and works until late by lamp light; we will go thither, if you have naught to hinder you, at once."

Arvina could do no otherwise than assent; but his heart beat violently, and he could scarcely frame his words, so dreadful was his agitation. Yet, by dint of immense exertion, he contrived to maintain the outward appearance of composure, which he was very far from feeling, and even to keep up a connected conversation as they walked along. Returning home at a much quicker pace than they had gone out, it was comparatively but a short time before they arrived at the house of Cicero, and there dismissed their followers, many of the slaves and freedmen of Arvina having joined the procession in honour of their fellow-servant Thrasea.

Thence, reserving two lictors only of the twelve, the consul with his wonted activity hurried directly forward by the Sacred Way to the arch of Fabius; and then, as the young men had gone in the morning, through the Forum toward the cutler's shop, taking the shortest way, and evidently well acquainted with the spot beforehand.

"I caused the funeral to take place this night," he said to Arvina, "instead of waiting the due term of eight days, on purpose that I might create no suspicion in the minds of the slayers. They never will suspect him, we have buried even now, to be the man they slew last night, and will fancy, it may be, that the body is not discovered even."

"It will be well if it prove so," replied Paullus, feeling that he must say something, and fearful of committing himself by many words.

"It will, and I think probably it may," answered Cicero. "But see, I was right; there shines the light from Volero's shop, though all the other booths have been closed long ago, and the streets are already silent. There are but few men, even in this great city, of whom I know not something, beyond the mere names. Think upon that, young man, and learn to do likewise; cultivate memory, above all things, except virtue."

"I should have thought such things too mean to occupy a place, even, in the mind of Cicero," answered Arvina.

"Nothing, young man, that pertains to our fellow men, is too mean to occupy the mind of the noblest. Why should it, since it doth occupy the mind of the Gods, who are all great and omnipotent?"

"You lean not then to the creed of Epicurus, which teaches——"

"Who, I?" interrupted Cicero, almost indignantly. "No! by the immortal Gods! nor I trust, my young friend, do you. Believe me—but ha!" he added in a quick and altered tone, "what have we here? there is some villainy in the wind—away! away! there! lictors apprehend that fellow."

For as they came within about a bow-shot of the booth of Volero, the sound of a slight scuffle was heard from within, and the light of the lamp became very dim and wavering, as if it had been overset; and in a moment went out altogether. But its last glimmering ray shewed a tall sinewy figure making out of the door and bounding at a great pace up the street toward the Carmental gate.

Arvina caught but a momentary glance of the figure; yet was that glance enough. He recognized the spare but muscular form, all brawn and bone and sinew; he recognized the long and pardlike bounds!—It was his tyrant, and, as he thought, his Fate!

The lictors rushed away upon his track, but there seemed little chance that, encumbered with their heavy fasces, they would overtake so swift a runner, as, by the momentary sight they had of him, the fugitive appeared to be.

Arvina and the Consul speedily reached the booth.

"Volero! Volero!"

But there came forth no answer.

"Volero! what ho! Volero!"

They listened eagerly, painfully, with ears sharpened by excitement. There came a sound—a plash, as of a heavy drop of water falling on the stone floor; another, and another—the trickling of a continuous stream.

All was dark as a moonless midnight. Yet Cicero took one step forward, and laid his hand upon the counter. It splashed into a pool of some warm liquid.

"Now may the Gods avert!" he cried, "It is blood! there has been murder here! Run, my Arvina, run to Furbo's cookshop, across the way there, opposite; they sit up there all night—cry murder, ho! help! murder!"

A minute had scarcely passed before the heavy knocking of the young man had aroused the house—the neighborhood. And at the cry of murder, many men, some who had not retired for the night, and some half dressed as they had sprung up from their couches, came rushing with their weapons, snatched at random, and with torches in their hands.

It was but too true! the laborious artizan was dead; murdered, that instant, at his own counter, at his very work. He had not moved or risen from his seat, but had fallen forward with his head upon the board; and from beneath the head was oozing in a continuous stream the dark red blood, which had overflowed the counter, and trickled down, and made the paved floor one great pool!

"Ye Gods! what blood! what blood!" exclaimed the first who came in.

"Poor Volero! alas!" cried Furbo, "it is not an hour since he supped on a pound of sausages at my table, and now, all is over!"

They raised his head. His eyes were wide open; and the whole face bore an expression neither of agony or terror, so much as of wild surprise.

The throat was cut from ear to ear, dividing the windpipe, the carotid arteries, and jugular veins on both sides; and so strong had been the hand of the assassin, and so keen the weapon, that the neck was severed quite to the back bone.

Among the spectators was a gladiator; he whose especial task it was to cut the throats of the conquered victims on the arena; he looked eagerly and curiously at the wound for a moment, and then said—

"A back stroke from behind—a strong hand, and a broadbacked knife—the man has been slain by a gladia tor, or one who knows the gladiator's trick!"

"The man," said the Consul calmly, "has been killed by an acquaintance, a friend, or a familiar customer; he had not even risen from his seat to speak with him; and see, the burnisher is yet grasped in his hand, with which he was at work. Ha!" he exclaimed, as his lictors entered, panting and tired by their fruitless chase, "could you not overtake him?"

"We never saw him any more, my consul," replied both men in one breath.

"Let his head down, my friend," said Cicero, turning, much disappointed as it seemed, to Furbo, "let it lie, as it was when we found it; clear the shop, lictors; take the names of the witnesses; one of you keep watch at the door, until you are relieved; lock it and give the key to the prætor, when he shall arrive; the other, go straightway, and summon Cornelius Lentulus; he is the prætor for this ward. Go to your homes, my friends, and make no tumult in the streets, I pray you. This shall be looked to and avenged; your Consul watches over you!"

"Live! live the Consul! the good Consul, the man of the people!" shouted the crowd, as they dispersed quietly to their homes.

"Arvina, come with me. To whom told you, that you had found, and Volero sold, this dagger?" he asked very sternly.

"To no one, Cicero. Marcus Aurelius Victor, and Aristius Fuscus were with me, when he recognized it for his work?"

"No one else?"

"No one, save our slaves, and they," he added in a breath, "could not have heard what passed."

"Hath no one else seen it?"

"As I was stripping for the contests on the Campus, Catiline saw it in my girdle, and admired its fabric."

"Catiline!"

"Ay! Consul?"

"And you told *him* that Volero had made it?"

"Consul, no!" But, with the word, he turned as white as marble. Had it been daylight, his face had betrayed him; as it was, Cicero observed that his voice trembled.

"Catiline is the man!" he said solemnly, "the man who slew Medon yesternight, who has slain Volero now. Catiline is the man; but this craves wary walking. Young man, young man, beware! methinks you are on the verge of great danger. Get thee home to thy bed; and again I say, Beware!"

CHAPTER VIII.

THE TRUE LOVE.

Dear, my Lord,
Make me acquainted with your cause of grief.
JULIUS CÆSAR.

THE sun rose clear and bright on the following morning; the air was fresh and exhilarating, and full of mirthful inspiration. But Paullus Arvina rose unrefreshed and languid, with his mind ill at ease; for the reaction which succeeds ever to the reign of any vehement excitement, had fallen on him with its depressing weight; and not that only, but keen remorse for the past, and, if possible, anxiety yet keener for the future.

Disastrous dreams had beset his sleeping hours; and, at his waking, they and the true occurrences of the past day, seemed all blended and confused into one horrible and hideous vision.

Now he envisaged the whole dark reality of his past conduct, of his present situation. Lucia, the charming siren of the previous evening, appeared in her real colors, as the immodest, passionate wanton; Catiline as the monster that indeed he was!

And yet, alas! alas! as the clear perception of the truth dawned on him, it was but coupled with a despairing sense, that to these he was linked inevitably and forever.

The oath! the awful oath which he had sworn in the fierce whirl of passion, registered by the arch-traitor—the oath involving, not alone, his own temporal and eternal welfare, but that of all whom he loved or cherished; his own pure, beautiful, inimitable Julia, to whom his heart now reverted with a far deeper and more earnest tenderness, after its brief inconstancy; as he compared her strong, yet maidenly and gentle love, with the wild and ungovernable passions of the wanton, for whom he had once sacrificed her.

Paullus Arvina was not naturally, not radically evil. Far from it, his impulses were naturally virtuous and correct, his calm sober thoughts always honorable and upright; but his passions were violent and unregulated; his principles of conduct not definitively formed; and his mind wavering, unsettled, and unsteady.

His passions on the previous day had betrayed him fatally, through the dark machinations of the conspirator, and the strange fascinations of his lovely daughter, into the perpetration of a great crime. He had bound himself, by an oath too dreadful to be thought of without shuddering, to the commission of yet darker crimes in future.

And now the mists of passion had ceased to bedim his mental vision, his eyes were opened, that he saw and repented most sincerely the past guilt. How was he to avoid the future?

To no man in these days, could there be a doubt even for a moment—however great the sin of swearing such an oath! No one in these days, knowing and repenting of the crime, would hesitate a moment, or fancy himself bound, because he had committed one vile sin in pledging himself thus to guilt, to rush on deeper yet into the perpetration of wickedness.

The sin were in the swearing, not in the breaking of an oath so vile and shameful.

But those were days of dark heathenish superstition, and it was far beyond the reach of any intellect perhaps of that day to arrive at a conclusion, simple as that to which any mind would now leap, as it were instinctively.

In those days, an omitted rite, an error in the ceremonial tribute paid to the marble idol, was held a deeper sin than adultery, incest, or blood shedding. And the bare thought of the vengeance due for a broken oath would often times keep sleepless, with mere dread, the eyes of men who could have slumbered calmly on the commission of the deadliest crimes.

Such, then, was the state of Arvina's mind on that morning—grieving with deep remorse for the faults of which he confessed himself guilty; trembling at the idea of rushing into yet more desperate guilt; and at the same time feeling bound to do so, in despite of his better thoughts, by the fatal oath which bound him to the arch traitor.

While he was sitting in his lonely chamber, with his untasted meal of ripe figs, and delicate white bread, and milk and honeycomb before him, devouring his own heart in his fiery anguish, and striving with all his energies of intellect to devise some scheme by which he might escape the perils that seemed to hem him round on every side, his faithful freedman entered, bearing a little billet, on which his eye had scarcely fallen before he recognized the shapely characters of Julia's well-known writing.

He broke the seal which connected the flaxen band, and with a trembling eye, and a soul that feared it knew not what, from the very consciousness of guilt, he read as follows:

"A day has passed, my Paullus, and we have not met! The first day in which we have not met and conversed together, since that whereon you asked me to be yours! I would not willingly, my Paul, be as those miserable and most foolish girls, of whom my mother has informed me, who, given up to jealousy and doubt, torment themselves in vain, and alienate the noble spirits, which are bound to them by claims of affection only, not of compulsion or restraint. Nor am I so unreasonable as to think, that a man has no duties to perform, other than to attend a woman's leisure. The Gods forbid it! for whom I love, I would see great, and famous, and esteemed in the world's eyes as highly as in mine! The house, it is true, is our sphere —the Forum and the Campus, the great world with its toils, its strifes, and its honors, yours! All this I speak to myself often. I repeated it many, many times yesterday—it ought to have satisfied me—it did satisfy my reason, Paul, but it spoke not to my heart! That whispers ever, 'he came not yesterday to see me! he promised, yet he came not!' and it will not be answered. Are you sick, Paullus, that you came not? Surely in that case you had sent for me. Hortensia would have gone with me to visit you. No! you are not sick, else most surely I had known it! Are you then angry with me, or offended? Unconscious am I, dearest, of any fault against you in word, thought, or deed. Yet will I humble myself, if you are indeed wroth with me. Have I appeared indifferent or cold? oh! Paul, believe it not. If I have not expressed the whole of my deep tenderness which is poured out all, all on thee alone —my yearning and continued love, that counts the minutes when thou art not near me; it is not that I cease ever to think of thee, to adore thee, but that it were unmaidenly and overbold to tell thee of it. See, now, if I have not done so here; and my hand trembles, and my cheek burns, and almost I expect to see the pallid paper blush, to find itself the bearer of words so passionate as these. But you will pardon me, and come to me forthwith, and tell me, if anything, in what I have displeased thee.

"It is a lovely morning, and Hortensia has just learned from Caius Bibulus, that at high noon the ambassadors of the wild Allobroges will march in with their escort over the Mulvian Bridge. She wishes much to see the pomp, for we are told that their stature is gigantic and their presence noble, and their garb very wild, yet magnificent withal and martial. Shall we go forth and see them? Hortensia will carry me in her carpentum, and you can either ride with us on horseback, or if you be not over proud take our reins yourself as charioteer, or, what will perhaps be the best of all, come in your own car and escort us. I need not say that I wish to see you *now*, for *that* I wish always. Come, then, and quickly, if you would pleasure your own Julia."

"Sweet girl," he exclaimed, as he finished reading it, "pure as the snow upon Soracte, yet warm and tender as the dove. Inimitable Julia! And I—I—Oh, ye gods! ye gods! that beheld it!" and he smote his brow heavily with his hand, and bit his lip, till the blood almost sprang beneath the pressure of his teeth; but recovering himself in a moment, he turned to Thrasea—"Who brought this billet? doth he wait?"

"Phædon, Hortensia's Greek boy, brought it, noble Paullus. He waits for your answer in the atrium."

"Quick, then, quick, Thrasea, give me a reed and paper."

And snatching the materials he wrote hastily:

"Chance only, evil chance, most lovely Julia, and business of some weight, restrained me from you most unwilling yesterday. More I shall tell you when we meet—indeed all! for what can I wish to conceal from you, the better portion of my soul. Need I say that I come—not, alas, on the wings of my love, or I should be beside you as I write, but as quickly as the speed of horses may whirl me to your presence; until then, fare you well, and confide in the fidelity of Paullus."

"Give it to Phædon," he said, tossing the note to Thrasea, "and say to him, 'if he make not the better haste, I shall be at Hortensia's house before him.' And then, hark ye, tell some of those knaves in the hall without, to make ready with all speed my light chariot, and yoke the two black horses Aufidus and Acheron. With all speed, mark ye! And then return, good Thrasea, for I have much to say to you, before I go."

When he was left alone, he arose from his seat, walked three or four times to and fro his chamber, in anxious and uneasy thought; and then saying, "Yes! yes! I will not betray him, but I will take no step in the business any farther, and I will tell him so to-night. I will tell him, moreover, that Cicero has the dagger, for now that Volero is slain, I see not well how it can be identified. The Gods defend me from the dark ones whom I have invoked. I will not be untrue to Rome, nor to Julia, any more—perish the whole earth, rather! Ay! and let us, too, perish innocent, better than to live guilty!"

As he made up his mind, by a great effort, to the better course, the freedman returned, and announcing that the car would be ready forthwith, inquired what dress he should bring him.

Never mind that! What I have on will do well enough, with a *petasus;** for the sun shines so brightly that it will be scarce possible to drive bare headed. But I have work

*The Petasus was a broad brimmed hat of felt with a low round crown. It wat originally an article of the Greek dress, but was adopted by the Romans

for you of more importance. You know the cave of Egeria, as men call it, in the valley of the Muses?"

"Surely, my Paullus."

"I know, I know; but have you ever marked the ground especially around the cave—what opportunities there be for concealment, or the like?"

"Not carefully," he answered, "but I have noticed that there is a little gorge just beyond the grotto, broken with crags and blocks of tufo, and overgrown with much brushwood, and many junipers and ivy."

"That will do then, I warrant me," replied Arvina. "Now mark what I tell you, Thrasea; for it may be, that my life shall depend on your acting as I direct. At the fourth hour of the night, I am to meet one in the grotto, on very secret business, whom I mistrust somewhat; who it is, I may not inform you; but, as I think my plans will not well suit his councils, I should not be astonished were he to have slaves, or even gladiators, with him to attack me—but not dreaming that I suspect anything, he will not take many. Now I would have you arm all my freedmen, and some half dozen of the trustiest slaves, so as to have in all a dozen or fifteen, with corslets under their tunics, and boarspears, and swords. You must be careful that you are not seen going thither, and you were best send them out by different roads, so as to meet after nightfall. Hide yourselves closely somewhere, not far from the cavern's mouth, whence you may see, unseen yourselves, whatever passes. I will carry my light hunting horn; and if you hear its blast rush down and surround the cave, but hurt no man, nor strike a blow save in self-defence, until I bid you. Do you comprehend me?"

"I comprehend, and will obey you to the letter, Paullus," answered the grave freedman, "but will not you be armed?"

"I will, my Thrasea. Leave thou a leathern hunting helmet here on the table, and light scaled cuirass, which I will do on under my toga. I shall be there at the fourth hour precisely; but it were well that ye should be on your posts by, the second hour or soon after. For it may be, he too will lay an ambuscade, and so all may be discovered.

"It shall be done, most noble master."

"And see that ye take none but trustworthy men, and that ye all are silent—to would be ruin."

"As silent as the grave, my Paullus," answered the freedman.

"The car and horses are prepared, Paullus," exclaimed a slave, entering hastily.

"Who goes with me to hold the reins?" asked his master.

"The boy Myron."

"It is well. Fetch me a petasus, and lay the toga in the chariot. I may want it. Now, Thrasea, I rely on you! Remember—be prudent, sure, and silent."

"Else may I perish ill," replied the faithful servitor, as his master, throwing the broad brimmed hat carelessly on his curly locks, rushed out, as if glad to seek relief from his own gloomy thoughts in the excitement of rapid motion; and, scarcely pausing to observe the condition or appearance of his beautiful black coursers, sprang into the low car of bronze, shaped not much differently from an old fashioned arm chair with its back to the horses; seized the reins, and drove rapidly away, standing erect—for the car contained no seats—with the boy Myron clinging to the rail behind him.

A few minutes brought him through the Cyprian lane and the Suburra to the Virbian slope, by which he gained the Viminal hill, and the Hortensian villa; at the door of which, in a handsome street leading through the Quirinal gate to the Flaminian way, or great northern road of Italy, stood the carpentum, drawn by a pair of noble mules, awaiting its fair freight.

This was a two-wheeled covered vehicle, set apart mostly for the use of ladies; and, though without springs, was as comfortable and luxurious a carriage as the art of that day could produce; nor was there one in Rome, with the exception of those kept for public use in the sacred processions, that could excel that of the rich and elegant Hortensia.

The pannels were beautifully painted, and the arched top or tilt supported by gilded caryatides at the four corners. Its curtains and cushions were of fine purple cloth; and altogether, though far less convenient, it was a much gayer and more sumptuous looking vehicle than the perfection of modern coach building.

The ladies were both waiting in the atrium, when the young man dismounted from his car; and never had his Julia, he thought, looked more lovely than she did this morning, with the redundant masses of her rich hair confined by a net of green and gold, and a rich *pallium*, or shawl of the same colors, gracefully draped over her snowy stola, and indicating by the soft sweep of its outlines the beauties of a figure, which it might veil but could not conceal.

Joyously, in the frank openness of her pure nature, she sprung forward to meet him, with both her fair hands extended, and the ingenuous blood rising faintly to her pale cheeks.

"Dear, dearest Paul—I am so happy, so rejoiced to see you."

Nothing could be more tender, more affectionate, than all her air, her words, her manner. Love flashed from her bright eyes irrepressible, played in the dimples of her smiling mouth, breathed audible in every tone of her soft silvery voice. Yet was there nothing that the gravest and most rigid censor could have wished otherwise—nothing that he could have pronounced, even for a moment, too warm, or too free for the bearing of the chariest maiden.

The very artlessness of her emotions bore evidence to their purity, their holiness. She was rejoiced to see her permitted lover, she felt no shame in that emotion of chaste joy, and would no more have dreamed of concealing it from him whom she loved so devotedly, than of masking her devotion to the Gods under a veil of indifference or coldness.

Here was the very charm of her demeanor, as here was the difference between her manner, and that of her rival Lucia.

In Julia, every thought that sprang from her heart, was uttered by her lips in frank and fearless innocence; she had no thought she was ashamed of, no wish she feared to utter. Her clear bright eyes dwelt unabashed and fondly on the face of him she loved; and no scrutiny could have detected in their light, one glance of unquiet or immodest passion. Her manner was warm and unreserved toward Paul, because she had a right to love him, and cared not who knew that she did so. Lucia's was as cold as snow, on the contrary; yet it required no second glance to perceive that the coldness was but the cover superinduced to hide passions too warm for revelation. Her eye was downcast; yet did its stolen glances speak things, the secret consciousness of which would have debased the other in her own estimation beyond the hope of pardon. Her tongue was guarded, and her words slow and carefully selected, for her imaginations would have made the brazen face of the world blush for shame could it have heard them spoken.

Hortensia smiled to witness the manifest affection of her sweet child; but the smile was, she knew not why, half mournful, as she said—

"You are unwise, my Julia, to show this truant how much you prize his coming; how painfully his absence depresses you. Sages declare that women should not let their lords guess, even, how much they are loved."

"Why, mother," replied Julia, her bright face gleaming radiantly with the pure lustre of her artless spirit, "I *am* glad to see him; I *do* prize his coming; I *do* love Paullus. Why, then, should I dissemble, when to do so were dishonest, and were folly likewise?"

"You should not tell him so, my child," replied the mother, "I fear you should not tell him so. Men are not like us women, who love but the more devotedly, the more fondly we are cherished. There is, I fear, something of the hunter's, of the conqueror's, ardour, in their passion; the pursuit is the great allurement; the winning the great rapture; and the prize, once securely won, too often cast aside, and disregarded."

"No! no!" returned the girl eagerly, fixing her eyes on her lover's features, as if she would read therein the outward evidences of that nobility of soul, which she believed to exist within. "I will not believe it; it were against all gratitude! all honor! all heart-truth! No, I will not believe it; and if I did, Hortensia, by all the Gods, I had rather live without love, than hold it on so vile a tenure of deceit. What, treasure up the secrets of your soul from your soul's lord? No! no! I would as soon conceal my devotion from the powers of heaven, as my affections from their rightful master. I, for one, never will believe that all men are selfish and unfaithful." L

"May the Gods grant, my Julia, that sad experience shall never teach you that they they are so. I, at least, will believe, and pray, that, what his sex may be soever, our Paullus will prove worthy ever of that best gift of God, a pure woman's pure and unselfish love."

"Oh! may it be so," answered Paullus, clasping his hands fervently together. "May I die ere I wrong my Julia! and be you sure, sweet girl, that your simple trust is philosophy far truer than the sage's lore. Base must his nature be, and his heart corrupt, who remains unsubdued to artlessness and love, such as yours, my Julia."

"But tell us, now," said the elder lady, "what was it that detained you, and where were you all the day? We expected you till the seventh hour of the night, yet you came not."

"I will tell you, Hortensia," he replied, "as we drive along; for I had rather do so, where there be no ears to overhear us. You must let me be your charioteer to-day, and your venerable grey-headed coachman shall ride with my wild imp Myron, in the car, if you will permit it."

"Willingly," she replied. "Then something strange has happened. Is it not so?"

"I knew it," exclaimed Julia, clasping her snowy hands together, "I knew it; I have read it in his eye this half hour. What can it be? it is something fearful, I am certain."

"Nay! nay! be not alarmed; if there were danger, it is passed already. But come, let me assist you to the carriage; I will tell you all as we go. But if we do not make good speed, the pomp will have passed the bridge before we reach it."

The ladies made no more delay, but took their places in the carriage, Paul occupying the front seat, and guiding the sober mules with far more ease, than Hortensia's aged charioteer experienced in restraining the speed of Arvina's fiery coursers, and keeping them in their place, behind the heavier carpentum.

The narrow streets were now passed, and threading the deep arch of the Quirinal gate, they struck into a lane skirting the base of the hill of gardens, on the right hand, by which they gained the great Flaminian way, just on the farther confines of the Campus; when they drove rapidly toward the Milvian bridge, built a few years before by Æmilius Scaurus, and esteemed for many a year the masterpiece of Roman architecture.

As soon as they had cleared the confines of the busy city, within which the throng of vehicles, and the passengers, as well on foot as on horseback, compelled Arvina to give nearly the whole of his attention to the guidance of the mules—he slackened the reins, and leaving the docile and well-broken animals to choose their own way, giving only an occasional glance to their movements, commenced the detail of his adventures at the point, where he parted from them on the night before the last.

Many were the emotions of fear, and pity, and anxiety which that tale called forth; and more than once the tears of Julia were evoked by sympathy, first, with her lover's daring, then with the grief of Thrasea. But not a shade of distrust came to cloud her pure spirit, for Paullus mentioned nothing of his interview with Catiline on the Cælian, or in the Campus; much less of his dining with him, or detecting in him the murderer of the hapless Volero.

Still he did not attempt to conceal, that both Cicero and himself had suspicions of the identity of the double murderer, or that he was about to go forth that very evening, for the purpose of attempting—as he represented it—to ascertain, beyond doubt, the truth of his suspicions.

And here it was singular, that Julia evinced not so much alarm or perturbation as her mother; whether it was that she underrated the danger he was like to run, or overrated the prowess and valor of her lover. But so it was, for though she listened eagerly while he was speaking, and gazed at him wistfully after he had become silent, she said nothing. Her beautiful eyes, it is true, swam with big tear-drops for a moment, and her nether lip quivered painfully; but she mastered her feelings, and after a short space began to talk joyously about such subjects as were suggested by the pleasant scenery, through which their road lay, or the various groups of people whom they met on the way.

Ere long the shrill blast of a cavalry trumpet was heard from the direction of the bridge, and a cloud of dust surging up in the distance announced the approach of the train.

There was a small green space by the wayside, covered with short mossy turf, and overshadowed by the spreading branches of a single chesnut, beneath which Paullus drew up the mules of Hortensia's carriage, directing the old charioteer, who seemed hard set to manage his high-bred and fiery steeds, to wheel completely off the road, and hold them well in hand on the green behind him.

By this time the procession had drawn nigh, and two mounted troopers, glittering in casques of highly polished bronze, with waving crests of horsehair, corslets of burnished brass, and cassocks of bright scarlet cloth, dashed by as hard as their fiery Gallic steeds could trot, their harness clashing merrily from the rate at which they rode. Before these men were out of sight, a troop of horse rode past in serried order, five abreast, with a square crimson banner, bearing in characters of gold the well-known initials, S. P. Q. R., and surmounted by a gilded eagle.

Nothing could be more beautifully accurate than the ordered march and exact discipline of this little band, their horses stepping proudly out, as if by one common impulse, in perfect time to the occasional notes of the *lituus*, or cavalry trumpet, by which all their manœuvres were directed; and the men, hardy and fine-looking figures, in the prime of life, bestriding with an air of perfect mastery their fiery chargers, and bearing the weight of their heavy panoply beneath the burning sunshine of the Italian noon, as though a march of thirty miles were the merest child's play.

About half a mile in the rear of this escort, so as to avoid the dust which hung heavily, and was a long time subsiding in the breathless atmosphere, came the train of the ambassadors from the Gaulish Highlands, and on these men were the eyes of the Roman ladies fixed with undisguised wonder, not unmixed with admiration. For their giant stature,strong limbs, and wild barbaric dresses, were as different from those of the well-ordered legionaries, as were their long light tresses, their blue eyes, keen and flashing as a falcon's, and their fair ruddy skins, from the clear brown complexions, dark locks, and black eyes of the Italian race.

The first of these wild people was a young warrior above six feet in height, mounted on a superb grey charger, which bore his massive bulk as if it were unconscious of his burthen. His large blue eyes wandered around him on all sides with a quick flashing glance that took in everything, yet seemed surprised at nothing; though almost everything which he beheld must have been strange to him. His long red hair flowed down in wavy masses over his neck and shoulders, and his upper lip, though his cheeks and his chin were closely shaven, was clothed with an immense moustache, the ends of which curled upward nearly to his eyes.

Upon his head he wore a casque of bronze, covered with studs of silver, and crested by two vast polished horns, the spoil of the fiercest animal of Europe's forests—the gigantic and indomitable Urus. A coat of mail, composed of bright steel rings interwoven in the Gaulish fashion, covered his body from the throat downward to the hips, leaving his strong arms bare to the shoulder, though they were decorated with so many chains, bracelets, and armlets, and broad rings of gold and silver, as would have gone far to protect them from a sword cut.

His legs were clothed, unlike those of any southern people, in tightly-sitting pantaloons—*braccæ*, as they were called—of gaily variegated tartans, precisely similar to the trews of the Scottish Highlander—a much more ancient part of the costume, by the way, than the kilt, or short petticoat, now generally worn—and these trews, as well as the streaming plaid, which he wore belted gracefully about his shoulders, shone resplendent with checkers of the brightest scarlet, azure, and emerald, and white, interspersed here and there with lines and squares of darker colors, giving relief and harmony to the general effect.

A belt of leather, studded with bosses and knobs of coral and polished mountain pebbles, girded his waist, and supported a large purse of some rich fur, with a formidable dirk at the right side, and, at the left, suspended by gilt chains from the girdle, a long, straight, cutting broadsword, with a basket hilt—the genuine claymore, or great sword—to resist the sweep of which Marcellus had been fain, nearly five hundred years before, to double the strength of the Roman casque, and to add a fresh layer of wrought iron to the tough fabric of the Roman buckler.

This ponderous blade constituted, with the dagger, the whole of his offensive armature; but there was slung on his left shoulder a small round targe, of the hide of the mountain bull, bound at the rim, and studded massively with bronze, and having a steel pike projecting from the centre—in all respects the same instrument as that with which the clans received the British bayonet at Preston Pans and Falkirk.

The charger of this gallantly-attired chief was bedecked, like his rider, with all the martial trappings of the day; his bridle, mounted with bits of ponderous Spanish fabric, was covered with bosses gemmed with amber and unwrought coral; his housings, of variegated plaid, were elaborately fringed with embroideries of gold; and his rich scarlet poitrel was decked, in the true taste of the western savage, with tufts of human hair, every tuft indicating a warrior slain, and a hostile head embalmed in the coffers of the valiant rider.

"See, Julia, see," whispered Arvina, as he passed slowly by their chariot, "that must be one of their great chiefs, and a man of extraordinary prowess. Look at the horns of the mighty Urus on his helmet, a brute fiercer, and well nigh as large as a Numidian elephant. He must have slain it, single-handed in the forest, else had he not presumed to wear its trophies, which belong only to the greatest of their champions. For every stud of silver on his casque of bronze he must have fought in a pitched battle; and for each tuft of hair upon his charger's poitrel he must have slain a foe in hand-to-hand encounter. There are eighteen tufts on this side, and, I warrant me, as many on the other. Doubtless, he has already stricken down thirty-six foemen.'

"And he numbers not himself as yet so many years! Ye Gods! what monsters," exclaimed Julia, shuddering at the idea of human hair used as a decoration. "Are they not anthropophagi, the Gauls, my Paullus ?"

"No, by the Gods! Julia," answered Arvina, laughing; "but very valiant warriors, and hospitable beyond measure to those who visit their native mountains; admirers, too, of women, whom they regard as almost divine, beyond all things. I see that stout fellow looking wild admiration at you now, from his clear blue eyes, though he would fain be thought above the reach of wonder."

"Are they believers in the Gods, or Atheists, as well as barbarous ?"

"By Jupiter! neither barbarous, to speak the truth, nor Atheists; they worship Mercury and Jove, Mars and Apollo, and Diana, as we do; and though their tongues be something wild, and their usages seem strange to us, it cannot be denied that they are a brave and noble race, and at this time good friends to the Roman people. Mark that old chieftain; he is the headman of the tribe, and leader of the embassy, I doubt not."

While he was speaking, a dozen other chiefs had ridden by, accompanied by the chiefs of the Roman escort, some men in the prime of life, some grizzled and weather-beaten, and having the trace of many a hard-fought field in the scars that defaced their sunburnt visages. But the last was an old man, with long silver hair, and eyebrows and mustachios white as the snow on his native Jura; the principal personage evidently of the band, for his casque was plated with gold, and his shirt of mail richly gilded, and the very plaid which he wore, alternately checked with scarlet, black, and gold.

He also, as he passed, turned his deep grey eye toward the little group on the green, and his face lightened up, as he surveyed the athletic form and vigorous proportions of the young patrician, and he leaned toward the officer, who rode beside him, a high crested tribune of the tenth legion, and enquired his name audibly.

The soldier, who had been nodding drowsily over his charger's neck, tired by the long and dusty ride, looked up half bewildered, for he had taken no note of the spectators, but as his eyes met those of Arvina, he smiled and waved his hand, for they were old companions, and he laughed as he gave the required information to the ancient warrior.

The gaze of the old man fell next on the lovely lineaments of Julia, and dwelt there so long that the girl lowered her eyes abashed; but, when she again raised them, supposing that he had passed by, she still met the firm, penetrating, quiet gaze, rivetted on her face, for he had turned half round in the saddle as he rode along.

A milder light came into his keen, hawk-like eye, and a benignant smile illuminated his gray weather-beaten features, as he surveyed and marked the ingenuous and artless beauty of her whole form and face; and he whispered into the tribune's ear something that made him too tur back, and wave his hand to Paul, and laugh merrily.

"Now, drive us homeward, Paullus," said Hortensia, as the cohort of infantry which closed the procession, marched steadily along, dusty and dark with sweat, yet proud in their magnificent array, and solid in their iron discipline. "Drive us homeward as quickly as you may. You will dine with us, and if you must need go early to your meeting, we will not hinder you."

"Gladly will I dine with you; but I must say farewell soon after the third hour!"

They soon arrived at the hospitable villa, and shortly afterward the pleasant and social meal was served. But Paul was not himself, though the lips he loved best poured forth their fluent music in his ear, and the eyes which he deemed the brightest, laughed on him in their speaking fondness.

Still he was sad, silent, and abstracted, and Julia marked it all; and when he rose to say farewell, just as the earliest shades of night were falling, she arose too; and as she accompanied him to the door, leaning familiarly on his arm, she said—

"You have not told me all, Paullus. I thought so while you were yet speaking; but now I am sure of it. I will not vex you at this time with questions, but will devour my anxiety and grief. But to-morrow, to-morrow, Paullus, if you love me indeed, you will tell me all that disturbs you. True love has no concealment from true love. Do not, I pray you, answer me; but fare you well, and good fortunes follow you."

CHAPTER IX.

THE AMBUSH.

My friends.
That is not so. Sir, we are your enemies.
TWO GENTLEMEN OF VERONA.

IT was already near the fourth hour of the Roman night, or about a quarter past eight of our time, when Paullus issued from the Capuan gate, in order to keep his appointment with the conspirator; and bold as he was, and fearless under ordinary circumstances, it would be useless to deny that his heart beat fast and anxiously under his steel cuirass, as he strode rapidly along the Appian way to the place of meeting.

The sun had long since set, and the moon, which was in her last quarter, had not as yet risen; so that, although the skies were perfectly clear and cloudless, there was but little light by which to direct his foot-steps toward the valley of the Muses, had he not been already familiar with the way.

Stepping out rapidly, for he was fearful now of being too late at the place appointed, he soon passed the two branches of the beautiful and sparkling Almo, wherein the priests of Cybele were wont to lave the statue of their goddess, amid the din of brazen instruments and sacred song; and a little further on, arrived at the cross-road where the way to Ardea, in the Latin country, branched off to the right hand from the great Appian turnpike.

At this point there was a small temple sacred to Bacchus, and a little grove of elms and plane trees overrun with vines, on which the ripe clusters consecrated to the God were hanging yet, though the season of the vintage had elapsed, safe from the hand of passenger or truant school-boy.

Turning around the angle of this building, Arvina entered a dim lane, overshadowed by the tall trees of the grove, which wound over two or three little hillocks, and then sweeping downward to the three kindred streamlets, which form the sources of the Almo, followed their right bank up the valley of the Muses.

Had the mind of Arvina been less agitated than it was by dark and ominous forebodings, that walk had been a pleasant one, in the calm and breezeless evening. The stars were shining by thousands in the deep azure sky; the constant chirrup of the shrill-voiced cicala, not mute as yet, although his days of tuneful life were well nigh ended, rose cheerfully above the rippling murmurs of the waters, and the mysterious rustling of the herbage rejoicing to drink up the copious dew; and heard by fits and starts from the thick clumps of arbutus on the hills, or the thorn bushes on the water's brink, the liquid notes of the nightingale gushed out, charming the ear of darkness.

For the first half mile of his walk, the young patrician met several persons on the way—two or three pairs of lovers, as they seemed, of the lower orders, strolling affectionately homeward; a party of rural slaves returning from their labours on some suburban farm, to their master's house; and more than one loaded chariot; but beyond this all was lonely and silent, with the exception of the stream, the insects, and the vocal night-bird.

There was no sound or sight that would seem to indicate the vicinity of any human being, as Arvina, passing the mouth of a small gorge or hollow scooped out of the bosom of a soft green hill, paused at the arch of a low but richly ornamented grotto, hollowed out of the face of the rock, and supported by a vault of reticulated brick-work, decorated elegantly with reliefs of marble and rich stucco. The soft green mosses and dark tendrils of the waving ivy, which drooped down from the rock and curtained well nigh half the opening, rendered the grotto very dark within. And it was a moment or two before Paullus discovered that he was alone in that secluded place, or in the company only of the old marble god, who, reclining on a couch of the same material at the farther end of the cave, poured forth his bright waters from an inverted jar, into the clear cool basin which filled the centre of the place.

He was surprised not a little at finding himself the first at the place of meeting, for he was conscious that he was behind his time; and had, indeed, come somewhat late on purpose, with a view of taking his stand as if naturally during the interview, between the conspirator and the cave mouth.

It was not, however, altogether a matter of regret to him, that he had gained a little time, for the folds of his toga required some adjustment, in order to enable him to get readily at the hilt of his sword, and the mouth-piece of his hunting-horn, which he carried beneath his gown. And he applied himself to that purpose immediately, congratulating himself, as he did so, on the failure of his first project, and thinking how much better it would be for him to stand as far as possible from the entrance, so as to avoid even the few rays of dim star-light, which crept in through the tangled ivy.

This was soon done; and in accordance with his afterthought, he sat down on a projecting angle of the statue's marble couch, in the inmost corner of the vault, facing the door, and having the pool of the fountain interposed between that and himself.

For a few moments he sat thinking anxiously about the interview, which he believed, not without cause, was likely to prove embarrassing, at least, if not perilous. But, when he confessed to himself, which he was very soon compelled to do, that he could shape nothing of his own course, until he should hear what were the plans in which Catiline desired his coöperation; and when time fled and the man came not, his mind began to wander, and to think about twenty gay and pleasant subjects entirely disconnected with the purpose for which he had come thither. Then he fell gradually into a sort of waking dream, or vision, as it were, of wandering fancies, made up partly of the sounds which he actually heard with his outward ears, though his mind took but little note of them, and partly of the occurrences in which he had been mixed up, and the persons with whom he had been brought into contact within the last two or three days. The gory visage of the murdered slave, the sweet and calm expression of his own Julia, the truculent eyes and sneering lip of Catiline, and the veiled glance and voluptuous smile of his too seductive daughter, whirled still before him in a strange sort of human phantasmagoria, with the deep searching look of the consul orator, the wild glare of the slaughtered Volero, and the stern face, grand and proud in his last agony, of the dying Varus.

In this mood he had forgotten altogether where he was, and on what purpose, when a deep voice aroused him with a start, and though he had neither heard his footstep, nor seen him enter, Catiline stood beside his elbow.

"What ho!" he exclaimed, "Paullus, have I detained you long in this dark solitude."

"Nay, I know not how long," replied the other, "for I had fallen into strange thoughts, and forgotten altogether the lapse of time; but here have I been since the fourth hour."

"And it is now already past the fifth," said Cataline, "but come, we must make up for the loss of time. Some friends of mine are waiting for us, to whom I wish to introduce you, that you may become altogether one of us, and take the oaths of fidelity. Give me the dagger now, and let us be going on our way."

"I have it not with me, Catiline."

"Have it not with you! Wherefore not? wherefore not, I say, boy?" cried the conspirator, very savagely. "By all the furies in deep hell, you were better not dally with me."

"Because it is no longer in my possession; and therefore I could not bring it with me," he replied firmly, for the threats of the other only inflamed his pride, and so increased his natural courage.

"By the Gods, you brave me, then!" exclaimed Catiline; "fool! fool! beware how you tamper with your fate. Speak instantly, speak out: to whom have you dared give it?"

"There was no daring in the matter, Catiline," he answered steadily, keeping an eye on the arch-traitor's movements; "before I knew that it was yours, I sent it, as I had promised, to Cicero, with word that Volero could tell him who was the owner of it."

"Ha, didst thou so?" said the other, mastering instantly his fury, in his desire to make himself fully acquainted with all that had passed. "When was all this? has he seen Volero, and learned the secret of him, then?"

"I sent it, Catiline, within an hour of the time I left the Campus yesterday."

"Before coming to my house to dinner?"

"Before going to thy house to dinner, Sergius."

"Before seducing Lucia Orestilla?" again sneered the desperate villain.

"Before yielding," answered the young man, who was now growing angry, for his temper was not of the meekest, "to her irresistible seduction."

"Ha! yielding—well! we will speak of that hereafter. Hath the consul seen Volero?"

"He hath seen him dead; and how dead, Catiline best knoweth."

"It was, then, thou, whom I saw in the feeble lamplight with the accursed wretch that crosses my path everywhere, the dastard, drivelling dotard of Arpinum; thou that despite thine oath, didst lead him to detect the man, thou hadst sworn to obey, and follow! Thou! it is thou, then, that houndest mine enemies upon my track! By the great Gods, I know not whether most to marvel at the sublime, unrivalled folly, which could lead thee to fancy, that thou, a mere boy and tyro, couldst hoodwink eyes like mine; or at the daring which could prompt thee to rush headlong on thine own ruin in betraying me! Boy, thou hast but one course left; to join us heart and hand; to go and renew thine oath in such fashion as even thou, premeditated perjurer, wilt not presume to break, and then to seal thy faith by the blood"—

"Of whom?"

"Of this new man; this pedant consul of Arpinum."

"Aye!" exclaimed Paullus, as if half tempted to accede to his proposal; "and if I do so, what shall I gain thereby?"

"Lucia, I might say," answered Catiline, "but—seeing that possession damps something at all times the fierceness of pursuit—what if I should reply, the second place in Rome?"

"In Rome?"

"When we have beaten down the proud patricians to our feet, and raised the conquering ensign of democratic sway upon the ramparts of the capitol; when Rome and all that she contains of bright and beautiful, shall be our heritage and spoil; the second place, I say, in regenerated Rome, linked, too, to everlasting glory."

"And the first place?"

'By Mars the great avenger! dost soar so high a pitch already? ho! boy, the first is mine, by right, as by daring. How say you? are you mine?"

"If I say no!"

"Thou diest on the instant."

"I think not," replied Arvina quietly, "and I do answer No."

"Then perish, fool, in thy folly."

And leaping forward he dealt him a blow with a long two-edged dagger, which he had held in his hand naked, during the whole discussion, in readiness for the moment he anticipated; and at the same instant uttered a loud clear whistle.

To his astonishment the blade glanced off the breast of the young man, and his arm was stunned nearly to the shoulder by the unexpected resistance of the stout corslet. The whistle was answered, however, the very moment it was uttered; and just as he saw Paullus spring to the farther side of the cavern, and set his back against the wall, unsheathing a heavy broadsword of the short Roman fashion, three stout men entered the mouth of the cave, heavily armed with weapons of offence, although they wore no defensive armor.

"Give me a sword," shouted the fierce conspirator, furious at being foiled, and perceiving that his whole enterprise depended on the young man's destruction. "He is armed under his gown with a breast-plate! Give me a sword, and then set on him all at once. So that will do, now, on."

"Hold, Sergius Catiline," exclaimed Arvina, "hold, or by all the Gods you will repent it. If you have three men at your back I have full five times three within call."

"Call them, then!" answered the other, making at him, "call them! think you again to fool me? Ho, Geta and Arminius, get round the fountain and set on him! make haste I say—kill—kill."

And with the word he rushed at him, aiming a fierce blow at his head, while the others a moment afterward charged on him from the other side.

But during the brief parley Arvina had disengaged the folds of his gown from his right shoulder, and wrapped it closely about his left arm, and when Catiline rushed in he parried the blow with his sword, and raising the little horn he carried, to his lips, blew a long piercing call, which was answered by a loud shout close at hand, and by the rush of many feet without the grotto.

Catiline was himself astonished at the unexpected aid, for he had taken the words of the young patrician for a mere boast. But his men were alarmed and fell back in confusion, while Paul, profiting by their hesitation, sprang with a quick active bound across the basin of the fountain, and gained the cavern's mouth just as his stout freedman Thrasea showed himself in the entrance with a close casque and cuirass of bronze, and a boar spear in his hand, the heads and weapons of several other able-bodied men appearing close behind.

At the head of these Arvina placed himself instantly, having his late assailants hemmed in by a force, against which they now could not reasonably hope to struggle.

But Paullus showed no disposition to take undue advantage of his superiority, for he said in a calm steady voice, "I leave you now, my friend; and it will not be my fault, if aught that has passed here, is remembered any farther. None here have seen you, or know who you are; and you may rest assured that for *her* sake and mine own honor, if I join not your plans, I will not betray you, or reveal your counsels. To that I am sworn, and come what may, my oath shall not be broken."

"Tush," cried the other, maddened by disappointment, and filled with desperate apprehensions, "men trust not avowed traitors. Upon them, I say, you dogs. Let there be forty of them, but four can stand abreast in the entrance, and we can front them, four as good as they.

And he again dashed at Arvina, without waiting to see if his gladiators meant to second his attack; but they hung back, reluctant to fight against such odds; for, though brave men, and accustomed to risk their lives, without quarrel or excitement, for the gratification of the brute populace of Rome, they had come to the cave of Egeria, prepared for assassination, not for battle; and their antagonists were superior to them as much in accoutrement and arms—for their bronze head-pieces were seen distinctly glimmering in the rays of the rising moon—as in numbers.

The blades of the leaders clashed together, and several quick blows and parries had been interchanged, during which Thrasea, had he not been restrained by his young master's orders, might easily have stabbed the conspirator with his boar-spear. But he held back at first, waiting a fresh command, until seeing that none came, and that the unknown opponent was pressing his lord hard; while the gladiators, apparently encouraged by his apathy, were beginning to handle their weapons, he shifted his spear in his hands, and stepping back a pace, so as to give full scope to a sweeping blow, he flourished the butt, which was garnished with a heavy ball of metal, round his head in a figure of eight, and brought it down so heavily on the felt skull-cap of the conspirator, that his teeth jarred audibly together, a quick flash sprang across his eyes, and he fell, stunned and senseless, at the feet of his intended victim.

"Hold, Thrasea, hold," cried Paullus, "by the Gods! you have slain him."

"No, I have not. No! no! his head is too hard for that," answered the freedman; "I felt my staff rebound from the bone, which it would not have done, had the skull been fractured. No! he is not dead, though he deserved to die very richly."

"I am glad of it," replied Paullus. "I would not have him killed, for many reasons. Now, hark ye, ye scoundrels and gallows-birds! most justly are your lives forfeit, whether it seem good to me to take them here this moment, or to drag you away, and hand you over to the lictors of the city-prætor, as common robbers and assassins."

"That you cannot do, whilst we live, most noble," answered the boldest of the gladiators, sullenly; "and you cannot, I think, take our lives, without leaving some of your own on our swords' points."

"Brave me not," cried the young man, sternly, "lest you drive me to do that I would not. Your lives, I say, are forfeit; but, seeing that I love not bloodshed, I leave you, for this time, unpunished. Take up the master whom you serve, and bear him home; and, when he shall be able to re ceive it, tell him Paullus Arvina pardons his madness, pities his fears, and betrays no man's trust—least of all his. For the rest, let him choose between enmity and friendship. I care not which it be. I can defend my own life, and assail none. Beware how you follow us. If you do, by all the Gods! you die. See, he begins to stir. Come, Thrasea, call off your men; we will go, ere he come to his senses, lest worse shall befal."

And with the words he turned his back contemptuously on the crest-fallen gladiators, and strode haughtily across the threshold, leaving the fierce conspirator, as he was beginning to recover his scattered senses, to the keen agony of conscious villainy frustrated, and the stings of defeated pride and disappointed malice.

The night was well advanced, when he reached his own house, having met no interruption on the way, proud ot his well-planned stratagem, elated by success, and flattered by the hope that he had extricated himself by his own energy from all the perils which had of late appeared so dark and difficult to shun.

CHAPTER X.

THE WANTON.

Duri magno sed amore dolores
Polluto, notumque furens quid femina possit.
ÆN. V. 6. VIRGIL.

It was not till a late hour on the following day, that Catiline awoke from the heavy and half lethargic slumber, which had fallen upon him after the severe and stunning blow he received in the grotto of Egeria.

His head ached fearfully, his tongue clove to his palate parched with fever, and all his muscular frame was disjointed and unstrung, so violently had his nerves been shattered.

For some time after he awoke, he lay tossing to and fro, on his painful couch, scarce conscious of his own identity, and utterly forgetful of the occurrences of the past evening.

By slow degrees, however, the truth began to dawn upon him, misty at first and confused, until he brought to his mind fairly the attack on Arvina, and the affray which ensued; with something of an indistinct consciousness that he had been stricken down, and frustrated in his murderous attempt.

As soon as the certainty of this was impressed on him, he sprang up from his bed, with his wonted impetuosity, and inquired vehemently of a freedman, who sat in his chamber motionless as a statue in expectation of his waking—

"How came I home, Chærea? and at what hour of night?"

"Grievously wounded, Catiline; and supported in the arms of the sturdy Germans, Geta and Arminius; and, for the time, it was past the eighth hour."

"The eighth hour! impossible!" cried the conspirator; "why it was but the fifth, when that occurred. What said I, my good Chærea? What said the Germans? Be they here now? Answer me quick, I pray you."

"There was but one word on your lips, Catiline; a constant cry for water, water, so long as you were awake; and after we had given you of it, as much as you would take, and you had fallen into a disturbed and feverish sleep, you still muttered in your dreams, 'water!' The Germans answered nothing, though all the household questioned them; and, in good truth, Catiline, it was not very long that they were capable of answering, for as soon as you were in bed, they called for wine, and in less than an hour were thoroughly besotted and asleep. They are here yet, I think, sleeping away the fumes of their potent flagons."

"Call me Arminius, hither. Hold! What is the time of day."

"The sun is high already; it must be now near the fourth hour!"

"So late! you did ill, Chærea, to let me lie so long. Call me Arminius hither; and send me one of the boys; or rather go yourself, Chærea, and pray Cornelius Lentulus the Prætor, to visit me before he take his seat on the Puteal Libonis. It is his day, I think, to take cognizance of criminal matters. Begone, and do my bidding!"

Within a moment the Athenian freedman, for he was of that proud though fallen city, returned conducting the huge German gladiator, whose bewildered air and bloodshot eyes seemed to betoken that he had not as yet recovered fully from the effect of his last night's potations.

No finer contrast could be imagined by poet or painter, than was presented by those three men, each eminently striking in his own style, and characteristic of his nation. The tall spare military-looking Roman, with his hawk nose and eagle eye, and close shaved face and short black hair, his every attitude and look and gesture full of pride and dominion; the versatile and polished Greek, beautiful both in form and face, as a marble of Praxiteles, beaming with intellect, and having every feature eloquent of poetry and imagination, and something of contempt for the sterner and harder type of mind, to which he and his countryman were subjugated; and last, the wild strong-limbed yet stolid-looking German, glaring out with his bright blue eyes, full of a sort of stupid fierceness, from the long curls of his auburn hair, a type of man in his most primitive state, the hunter and the warrior of the forest, enslaved by Rome's insatiate ambition.

Catiline looked at him fiercely for a moment, and then nodded his head, as if in assent to some of his own meditations; then muttering to himself, "the boar! the mast-fed German boar!" he turned to the Greek, saying sharply—

"Art thou not gone to Lentulus? methought thou hadst been thither, and returned ere this time! Yet tarry, since thou art here still. Are any of my clients in the atrium—any, I mean, of the trustiest!"

"Rufinus, surnamed Lupus, is without, and several others. Stolo, whom you preserved from infamy, when accused of *dolus malus*, in the matter of assault with arms on Publius Natro, is waiting to solicit you, I fancy, for some favor."

"The very man—the Wolf is the very man! and your suitor for favors cannot refuse to confer what he requests. Stay my Chærea. Send Glycon to summon Lentulus, and go yourself and find out what is Stolo's suit. Assure him of my friendship and support; and, hark you, have him and Rufinus into an inner chamber, and set bread before them and strong wine, and return to me presently. Now, then, Arminius," he continued, as the Greek left the room, "what did we do last night, and what befel us?—for I can remember nothing clearly."

The giant shook his tawny locks away from his brow, and gazed into his employer's face with a look of stolid inquiry, and then answered—

"Do! we did nothing, that I know! We followed thee as in duty bound to that cave by the Almo; and when we had stayed there awhile, we brought thee back again, seeing thou couldst not go alone. What can I tell? you know yourself why you took us thither."

"Thou stupid brute!" retorted Catiline, "or worse than brute, rather—for brutes augment not their brutishness by gluttony and wine-bibbing—thou art asleep yet! see if this will awaken thee!"

And with the word he snatched up a large brazen ewer full of cold water, which stood on a slab near him, and hurled it at his head. The gladiator stood quite still, and merely bent his neck a little to avoid the heavy vessel, which almost grazed his temples, and then shook himself like a water spaniel, as the contents flashed full into his face and eyes.

"Do not do that again," he grunted, "unless you want to have your throat squeezed."

"By Pollux the pugilist! he threatens!" exclaimed Catiline, laughing at his dogged anger. "Do you not know, cut-throat, that one word of mine can have your tough hide slashed with whips in the common gaol, till your very bones are bare?"

"And do you know what difference it makes, whether my hide be slashed with dog-whips in the gaol, or with broadswords in the amphitheatre? A man can only die! and it were as well, in my mind, to die having killed a Roman in his own house, as a countryman on the arena."

"By all the Gods!" cried Catiline, "he is a philosopher! but, look you here, my German Solon, you were better regard me, and attend to what I tell you; so may you escape both gaol and amphitheatre. Tell me, briefly, distinctly, and without delay, what fell out last evening."

"You led us to assault that younker, whom you know; and when we would have set upon him, and finished his business easily, he blew a hunting horn, and fifteen or sixteen stout fellows in full armor came down the bank from behind and shut up the cave's mouth—you know as well as I do."

"So far I do, most certainly," replied the conspirator, "but what then?"

"Why, then, thou wouldest not hear reason; but, though the youth swore he would not betray thee, must needs lay on, one man against sixteen; and so, as was like, gottest thine head broken by a blow of a boar-spear from a great double-handed Thracian. For my part, I wondered he did not put the spear-head through and through you. It was a great pity that he did not; it would have saved us all, and you especially, a world of trouble."

"And you, cowardly dogs, forsook me; and held back, when by a bold rush we might easily have slain him, and cut our way through the dastard slaves."

"No! no! we could not; they were all Thracians, Dacians, and Pannonians; and were completely armed, too. We might have killed him, very likely, but we could never have escaped ourselves."

"And he, he? what became of him when I had fallen?"

"He bade us take you up," replied the German, "and carry you home, and tell you 'to fear nothing, he would betray no man, least of all you.' He is a fine young fellow, in my judgment; for he might just as well have killed us all, as not, if he had been so minded; and I can't say but that it would have served us rightly, for taking odds of four to one upon a single man. That is, I know, what you Romans call fighting; beyond the Rhine we style it cowardly and murder! Then, after that he went off with his men, leaving us scratching our heads, and looking as dastardly and crest-fallen as could be. And then we brought you home hither, after it had got late enough to carry you through the streets, without making an uproar; and then Lydon and Chærea put you to bed; and I, and Geta, and Ardaric, as for us, we got drunk, seeing there was no more work to do last night, and not knowing what might be to do, to-day. And so it is all well, very well, as I see it."

"Well, call you it, when he has got off unscathed, and lives to avenge himself, and betray me?"

"But he swore he would do neither, Catiline," answered the simple-minded son of the forest.

"Swore!" replied the conspirator, with a fell sneer.

"Ay did he, master! swore by all that was sacred he would never betray any man, and you least of all; and I believe he will keep his promise."

"So do I," answered Catiline, bitterly, "I swear he shall; not for the lack of will, but of means to do otherwise! You are a stupid brute, Arminius; but useful in your way. I have no need of you to-day, so go and tell the butler to give you wine enough to make all three of you drunk again; but mind that ye are sound, clear-headed, and alert at day-break to-morrow."

"But will he give it to me at my bidding?"

"If not, send him to me for orders; now, begone."

"I ask for nothing better," replied the gladiator, and withdrew, without any word or gesture of salutation, in truth, despising the Roman in his heart as deeply for what he deemed his over-craftiness and over-civilization, as the more polished Greek did, for what on his side he considered the utter absence of both.

Scarce had the German left the room, before the Greek returned, smiling, and seemingly well satisfied with the result of his mission.

Catiline looked at him steadily, and nodding his head, asked him quietly—

"Are they prepared, Chærea?"

"To do anything you would have them, Catiline. Stolo, it seems, is again emperilled—another charge of attempt to murder—and he wants you to screen him."

"And so I will; and will do more. I will make him rich and great, if he do my bidding. Now go, and make them understand this. They must swear that they came hither this morning to claim my aid in bringing them to speech with Lentulus, the Prætor, and then thou must be prepared to swear, Chærea, that I have had no speech or communication with them at all—which is quite true."

"That is a pity," answered the Greek, coolly; "for any one can swear steadily to the truth, but it requires genius to carry out a lie bravely."

"Oh! never fear, thou shalt have lies enough to swear to! Now mark me, when Lentulus comes hither, they must accuse to him Paullus Cæcilius Arvina, whose person, if they know him not, you must describe to them—him who dined with me, you know, the day before yesterday—of subornation to commit murder. The place where he did so, the top of the Cælian hill. The time, sunrise on that same day. The person whom he desired them to slay, Volero the cutler, who dwelt in the Sacred Way. They must make up the tale their own way, but to these facts they must swear roundly. Do you understand me?"

"Perfectly; they shall do it well, and both be in one tale. I will help them to concoct it, and dress it up with little truthful incidents that will tell. But are you sure that he cannot prove he was not there?"

"Quite sure, Chærea. For he *was* there."

"And no witnesses who can prove to whom he spoke?"

"Only one witness, and he will say nothing, unless called upon by Paullus."

"And if so called upon?"

"Will most reluctantly corroborate the tale of Stolo and Rufinus!"

"Ha! ha!" laughed the freedman, "thou shouldst have been a Greek, Catiline, thou art too shrewd to be a mere Roman."

"A *mere* Roman, hang-dog!" answered Catiline, "but thou knowest thine opportunity, and profitest by it! so let it pass! Now as for thee, seeing thou dost love lying, thou shalt have thy part. Thou shalt swear that the night before that same morning, at a short time past midnight, thou wert returning by the Wicked street, from the house of Autronius upon the Quirinal, whither I sent thee to bid him to dinner the next day—he shall confirm the tale—when thou didst hear a cry of murder from the Plebeian graveyard on the Esquiline; and hurrying to the spot, didst see Arvina, with his freedman Thrasea bearing a torch, conceal a fresh bleeding body in a broken grave; and, hidden by the stem of a great tree thyself, didst hear him say, as he left the ground, 'That dog will tell no tales!' Thou must swear, likewise, that thou didst tell me the whole affair the next morning, and that I bade thee wait for farther proof ere speaking of the matter. And again, that we visited the spot where thou saw'st the deed, and found the grass trampled and bloody, but could not find the body. Canst thou do this, thinkest thou?"

"Surely I can," said the Athenian, rubbing his hands as if well pleased, "so that no one shalt doubt the truth of it! And thou wilt confirm the truth?"

"By chiding thee for speaking out of place. See that thou blurt it out abruptly, as if unable to keep silence any longer, as soon as the others have finished their tale. Begone and be speedy. Lentulus will be here anon!"

The freedman withdrew silently, and Catiline was left alone in communion with his own bad and bitter thoughts; and painful, as it seemed, and terrible, even to himself, was that communion, for he rose up from his seat and paced the room impetuously, to and fro, gnashing and grinding his teeth, and biting his lips till the blood sprang out.

After a while, however, he mastered his passions, and began to dress himself, which he did by fits and starts in a manner perfectly characteristic of the man, uttering hide ous imprecations if the least thing ran counter to his wish es, and flinging the various articles of his attire about the chamber with almost frantic violence.

By the time he had finished dressing himself, Lentulus was announced, and entered with his dignified and haughty manner, not all unmixed with an air of indolence.

"All hail, my Sergius," he exclaimed, as he crossed the threshold. "What hast thou of so grave importance, that thou must intercept me on my way to the judgment seat? Nothing has gone wrong in our councils—ha?"

"Nothing that I know," answered Catiline, "but here are two of my trustiest clients, Stolo and Rufinus, have been these three hours waiting for my awakening, that I might gain your ear for them. They sent me word they had a very heavy charge to make to you; but for my part, I have not seen them, and know not what it is."

"Tush! tush! man; never tell me that," replied Lentulus, with a grim smile. "Do you think I will believe you have sent for me all the way hither this morning, without some object of your own to serve? No! no! my friend; with whomsoever that may pass, it will not go current with Cornelius Lentulus!"

"Just as you please," said the traitor; "you may believe me or not exactly as you choose; but it is true, nevertheless, that I have neither seen the men, nor spoken with them. Nor do I know at all what they want."

"I would, then, you had not sent for me," answered the other. "Come, let us have the knaves in. I suppose they have been robbing some one's hen-roost, and want to lay the blame on some one else!"

"What ho! Chærea."

And as he spoke the word, the curtain which covered the door-way was withdrawn, and the keen-witted freedman made his appearance.

"Admit those fellows, Stolo and Rufinus. The prætor is prepared to give them a hearing."

It would have been difficult, perhaps, to have selected from the whole population of Rome at that day, a more murderous looking pair of scoundrels.

"Well, sirrahs, what secrets of the state have you that weigh so ponderously on your wise thoughts?" asked Lentulus, with a contemptuous sneer.

"Murder, most noble Lentulus—or at least subornation thereof," answered one of the ruffians.

"Most natural indeed! I should have thought as much. Well, tell us in a word—for it is clear that nobody has murdered either of you—whom have you murdered?"

"If we have murdered no one, it was not for the lack of prompting, or of bribes either."

"Indeed! I should have thought a moderate bribe would have arranged the matter easily. But come! come! to the point! whom were ye bribed or instigated to get rid of? speak! I am in haste!"

"The cutler, Caius Volero!"

"Volero! Ha!" cried Lentulus, starting. "Indeed! indeed! that may well be. By whom, then, were you urged to the deed, and when?"

"Paulus Cæcilius Arvina tempted us to the deed, by the offer of ten thousand sesterces! We met him by appointment upon the Cælian hill, at the head of the Minervium, a little before sunrise, the day before yesterday."

"Ha!" and for a moment or two Lentulus fixed his eyes upon the ground, and pondered deeply on what he had just heard. "Have ye seen Volero since?"

"No, Prætor."

"Nor heard anything concerning him?"

"Nothing!" said Stolo. But he spoke with a confused air and in an undecided tone, which satisfied the judge that he was speaking falsely. Rufinus interposed, however, saying—

"But I have, noble Lentulus. I heard say that he *was* murdered in his own booth, that same night!"

"And having heard this, you told it not to Stolo?"

"I never thought about it any more," answered Rufinus doggedly, seeing that he had got into a scrape.

"That was unfortunate, and somewhat strange, too, seeing that you came hither together to speak about the very man. Now mark me. Volero *was* that night murdered, and it appears to me, that you are bringing this accusation against a young patrician, in order to conceal your own base handiwork in the deed. Fellows, I grievously suspect you."

"Wrongfully, then, you do so," answered Stolo, who was the bolder and more ready witted of the two. "Rufinus ever was a forgetful fool; and I trow I am not to be brought into blame for his folly."

"Well for you, if you be not brought into more than blame! Now, mark me well! can you prove where you were that night of the murder, excellent Stolo?"

"Ay! can I," answered the man boldly. "I was with stout Balatro, the fisherman, helping to mend his nets until the fourth hour, and all his boys were present, helping us. And then we went to a cookshop to get some supper in the ox forum, and thence at the sixth hour we passed across to Lydia's house in the Cyprian lane, and spent a merry hour or two carousing with her jolly girls. Will that satisfy you, Lentulus?"

"Ay, if it can be proved," returned the Prætor. "And you, Rufinus; can you also show your whereabout that evening?"

"I can," replied the fellow, "for I was sick abed; and that my wife can show, and Themison the druggist, who lives in the Sacred Way. For she went to get me an emetic at the third hour; and I was vomiting all night. A poor hand should I have made that night at murder."

"So far, then," replied Lentulus, "you have cleared yourselves from suspicion; but your charge on Arvina needs something more of confirmation, ere I dare cite a Patrician to plead to such a crime! Have you got witnesses? was any one in sight, when he spoke with you on the Minervium?"

"There was one; but I know not if he will choose to speak of it?"

"Who was it?" exclaimed Lentulus, growing a little anxious on the subject, for though he cared little enough about Arvina, he was yet unwilling to see a Patrician arraigned for so small a matter, as was in his eyes the murder of a mechanic.

"Why should he not speak? I warrant you I will find means to make him."

"It was my patron, Lentulus."

"Your patron! man!" he cried, much astonished. 'What, Catiline, here?"

"Catiline it was! my Prætor."

"And have you consulted with him, ere you spoke with me?"

"Not so! most noble, for he would not admit us!"

"Speak, Sergius. Is this so? did you behold these fellows in deep converse with Cæcilius Arvina, in the Minervium? But no! it must be folly! for what should you have been doing there at sunrise?"

"I prithee do not ask me, Lentulus," answered Catiline, with an air of well feigned reluctance. "I hate law suits and judicial inquiries, and I love young Arvina."

"Then you did see them? Nay! nay! you must speak out. I do adjure you, Catiline, by all the Gods! were you, at sunrise, on the Cœlian, and did you see Arvina and these two?"

"I was, at sunrise, on the Cælian; and I did see them."

"And heard you what they said?"

"No! but their faces were grave and earnest; and they seemed angry as they separated."

"Ha! In itself only, this were a little thing; but when it turns out that the man *was* slain that same night, the thing grows serious. You, therefore, I shall detain here as witnesses, and partially suspected. Some of your slaves must guard them, Catiline, and I will send a lictor to cite Paullus, that he appear before me after the session at the Puteal Libonis. I am in haste. Farewell!"

"Me! me! hear me! good Lentulus—hear me!" exclaimed Chærea, springing forward, all vehemence and eagerness to speak, as it would seem, ere he should be interrupted.

"Chærea?" cried Catiline, looking sternly at him, and shaking his finger, "Remember!"

"No! no!" replied Chærea—"no! no! I will not hold my peace! No! Catiline, you may kill me, if you choose, but I will speak; to keep this secret any longer would kill me, I tell you."

"If it do not, I will," answered his master, angrily.

"This must not be, my Sergius," interposed Lentulus, "let the man speak if he have any light to throw on this mysterious business. Say on, my good fellow, and I will be your mediator with your master."

The freedman needed no more exhortation, but poured out a flood of eager, anxious narrative, as had been preconcerted between himself and Catiline, speaking with so much vehemence, and displaying so much agitation in all his air and gestures, that he entirely imposed his story upon Lentulus; and that Catiline had much difficulty in restraining a smile at the skill of the Greek.

"Ha! it is very clear," said Lentulus, "he first slew the slave with his own hand, and then would have compassed—nay! I should rather say, *has* compassed—Volero's slaughter, who must some how or other have become privy to the deed. I must have these detained, and him arrested! There can be no doubt of his guilt, and the people will be, I think, disposed to make an example; there have of late been many cases of assassination!"

As soon as they were left alone, Lentulus looked steadily into the face of his fellow-conspirator for a moment, and then burst into a hoarse laugh.

"Why all this mummery, my Sergius?" he added, as soon as he had ceased from laughing, "Or wherefore would you have mystified me too?"

"I might have wished to see whether the evidence was like to seem valid to the Judices, from its effect upon the Prætor!" answered the other.

"And are you satisfied?"

"I am."

"You may be so, my Sergius, for, of a truth, until Chærea swore as he did touching Medon, I was myself deceived."

"You believe, then, that this will be sufficient to secure his condemnation?"

"Beyond doubt. He will be interdicted fire and water, if these men stick to their oaths only. It would be well, perhaps, to convict one of Arvina's slaves of the actual death of Volero. That might be done easily enough, but there must be care taken, that you select one who shall not be able to prove any alibi. But wherefore are you so bent on destroying this youth, and by the law, too, which is ever both perilous and uncertain?"

"He knows too much, to live without endangering others."

"What knows he?"

"Who slew Medon—Who slew Volero—What we propose to do, ere long, in the Campus!" answered Catiline, steadily.

"By all the Gods?" cried Lentulus, turning very pale, and remaining silent for some moments. After which he said, with a thoughtful manner, "it would be better to get rid of him quietly."

"That has been tried too."

"Well?"

"It failed! He is now on his guard. He is brave, strong, wary. It cannot be done, save thus."

"He will denounce us. He will declare the whole, ere we can spring the mine beneath him."

"No! he will not; he dares not. He is bound by oaths which ——"

"Oaths!" interrupted Lentulus, with a sneer, and in tones of contemptuous ridicule. "What are oaths? Did they ever bind you?"

"I do not recollect," answered Catiline; "perhaps they did, when I was a boy, and believed in Lemures and Lamia. But Paullus Arvina is not Lucius Catiline, nor yet Cornelius Lentulus; and I say that his oaths shall bind him, until ——"

"And I say, they shall not!" A clear high voice interrupted him, coming, apparently, through the wall of the chamber.

Lentulus started—his very lips were white, and his frame shook with agitation, if it were not with fear.

Catiline grew pale likewise; but it was rage, not terror, that blanched his swarthy brow. He dashed his hand upon the table—

"Furies of Hell!"

While the words were yet trembling on his lips, the door was thrown violently open, the curtains which concealed it torn asunder, and, with her dark eyes gleaming a strange fire, and two hard crimson spots gleaming high up on her cheek bones—the hectic of fierce passion—her bosom throbbing, and her whole frame dilated with anger and excitement, young Lucia stood before them.

"And I say," she repeated, "that they shall not bind him! By all the Gods! I swear it! By my own love! my own dishonor! I swear that they shall not! Fool! fool! did you think to outwit me? To blind a woman, whose every fear and passion is an undying eye? Go to! go to! you shall not do it."

Audacious, as he was, the traitor was surprised, almost daunted; and while Lentulus, a little reassured, when he saw who was the interlocutor, gazed on him in unmitigated wonder, he faltered out, in tones strangely dissimilar to his accustomed accents of indomitable pride and decision——

"You mistake, girl; you have not heard aright, if you have heard, at all; I would say, you are deceived, Lucia!"

"Then would you lie!" she answered, "for I am not deceived, though you would fain deceive me! Not heard? not heard?" she continued. "Think you the walls in the house of Catiline have no eyes nor ears?" using the very words which he had addressed to her lover; Lucius Catiline! I know all!

"You know all?" exclaimed Lentulus, aghast.

"And will prevent all!" replied the girl, firmly, "if you dare cross my purposes!"

"Dare! dare!" replied Catiline, who now, recovering from his momentary surprise, had regained all his natural haughtiness and vigor. "Who are you, wanton, that dare talk to us of daring?"

"Wanton!" replied the girl, turning fiery red. "Ay! But who made me the wanton that I am? Who fed my youthful passions? Who sapped my youthful principles? Who reared me in an atmosphere, whose very breath was luxury, voluptuousness, pollution, till every drop of my wholesome blood was turned to liquid flame? till every passion in my heart became a fettered earthquake? Fool! fool! you thought, in your impotence of crime, to make Lucia Orestilla your instrument, your slave! You have made her your mistress! You dreamed, in your insolence of fancied wisdom, that, like the hunter-cat of the Persian despots, so long as you fed the wanton's appetite, and basely pandered to her passions, she would leap hoodwinked on the prey you pointed her. Thou fool! that hast not half read thy villain lesson! Thou shouldst have known that the very cat, thou thoughtest me, will turn and rend the huntsman if he dare rob her of her portion! I tell you, Lucius Catiline, you thought me a mere wanton! a mere sensual thing! a soulless animal voluptuary! Fool! I say, double fool! Look into thine own heart; remem ber what blood runs in these female veins! Man! Father! Vitiator! My spirit is not female! my blood, my passions, my contempt of peril, my will indomitable and immutable, are, like my mortal body, your begetting! My crimes, and my corruption, are your teaching! Beware then, as you know the heat of your own appetites, how you presume to hinder mine! Beware, as you know your own recklessness in doing and contempt in suffering, how you stir me, your child, to do and suffer likewise! Beware, as you know the extent of your own crimes, the depth or your own pollution, how you drive me, your pupil, to outdo her master! Beware! I say! beware! This man is mine. Harm but one hair upon his head, and you shall die, like a dog, with the dogs who snarl at your bidding, and your name perish with you. I have spoken!"

There needed not one tenth part of the wisdom, which the arch-traitor really possessed, to shew him how much he had miscalculated the range of his daughter's intellect; the fierce energies of her powerful but misdirected mind.

He felt, for a moment, as the daring archimage whose spells, too potent for their master's safety, have evoked and unchained a spirit that defies their guidance. But, like that archimage, conscious that all depends on the exertion of his wonted empire, he struggled hard to regain his lost authority.

"Girl," he replied, in those firm deep tones of grave authority, which he deemed the best calculated to control her excitement, "You are mad! Mad, and ungrateful; and like a frantic dog would turn and rend the hand that feeds you, for a shadow. I never thought of making you an instrument; fool indeed had I been, to think I could hoodwink such an intellect as yours! If I have striven to clear away the mists of prejudice from before your eyes, which, in your senseless anger, you now call corrupting you, it was because I saw in you a kindred spirit to mine own, capable to soar fearless and undazzled into the very noon of reason. If I have taught you to indulge your passions, opened a universe of pleasures to your ken, it was that I saw in you a woman of mind so manly, that all the weaknesses, which fools call affections, would be but powerless to warp it from its purpose. I would have made you"——

"The world's scorn!" she interrupted him, bitterly; but he went on, without noticing the interruption—

"The equal of myself in intellect, in energy, and wisdom; else how had you dared to brave me thus, whom never man yet braved and lived to boast of it! And now for a mere girlish fancy, a weak feminine caprice for a man, who cares not for you; who has betrayed you; who, idiot and inconsistent that he is, fresh from your fiery kisses, was whimpering within an hour at the feet of his cold Julia; who has, I doubt not, boasted of your favors, while he deplored his own infatuation, to her, his promised wife!—For a fond frivolous liking of a moment, you would forego gratification, rank, greatness, power, and vengeance! Is this just toward me, wise toward yourself? Is this like Lucia Orestilla? You would preserve a traitor who deserts you, nay, scorns you in his easy triumph! You would destroy all those who love you; you would destroy yourself, to make the traitor and his minion happy! Awake! awake, my Lucia, from this soft foolish fancy! Awake, and be yourself once more! Awake to wisdom, to ambition, to revenge!"

His words were spirited and fiery; but they struck on no kindred chord in the bosom of his daughter. On the contrary, the spark had faded from her eye and the flush from her cheek, and her looks were dispirited and downcast. But as he ceased, she raised her eye and met his piercing gaze firmly, and replied in a sorrowful yet resolute tone.

"Eloquent! aye! you are eloquent! Catiline, would I had never learned it to my cost; but it is too late now! it is all too late! for the rest, I am awake; and so far, at least, am wise, that I perceive the folly of the past, and decypher clearly the sophistry of your false teaching. As for the future, hope is dead, and ambition. Revenge, I seek not; if I did so, thou art there, on whom to wreak it; for saving thou, and myself only, none have wronged me. More words are needless. See that thou lay aside thy plans, and dare not to harm him, or her. He shall not betray thee or thine; for that will I be his surety and hostage! Injure them, by deed or by word, and, one and all, you perish! I ask no promise of you—promises bind you not!—but let fear bind you, for *I* promise *you*, and be sure that my plight will be kept!"

"Can this be Lucia Orestilla?" exclaimed Catiline, "this puling love-sick girl, this timorous, repentant—I had nearly called thee—maiden! Why, thou fool, what would'st thou with the man farther? Dost think to be his wife?"

"Wife!" cried the wretched girl, clasping her hands together, and looking piteously in her destroyer's face. "Wife! wife! and me!—alas! alas! that holy, that dear, honored name!—Never! never for me the sweet sacred rites! Never for me the pure chaste kiss, the seat by the happy hearth, the loving children at the knee, the proud approving smile of—Oh! ye gods! ye just gods!—a loved and loving husband!—Wife! wife!" she continued, lashing herself, as she proceeded, into fresh anger; "there is not in the gaols of Rome the slave so base as to call Lucia Orestilla wife! And wherefore, wherefore not?—Man! man! if that thou be a man, and not a demon, but for thee, and thy cursed teachings, I might have known all this—pure bliss, and conscious rectitude, and the respect and love of men. I might have been the happy bride of an honorable suitor, the cherished matron of a respected lord, the proud glad mother of children, that should not have blushed to be sprung from the wanton Lucia! Thou! it is thou, thou only that hast done all this!—And why, I say, why should I not revenge? Beware! tempt me no farther! Do my bidding! Thou slave, that thought'st but now to be the master, obey my bidding to the letter!" And she stamped her foot on the ground, with the imperious air of a despotic queen. And in truth, crest-fallen and heavy in spirit, were the proud men whom she so superbly threatened.

She gazed at them contemptuously for a moment, and then, shaking her fore finger menacingly, "I leave ye," she said, "I leave ye, but imagine not, that I read not your councils. Me, you cannot deceive. With yourselves only it remains to succeed or to perish. For if ye dare to disobey me, the gods themselves shall not preserve you from my vengeance!"

"I fear you not, my girl," cried Catiline, "for all that you are now mad with disappointment, and with anger. So you may go, and listen if you will," he added, pointing to the secret aperture concealed in the mouldings of the wall. "We shall not speak the less freely for your hearing us."

"There is no need to listen now," she answered, "for I know everything already."

"Every thing that we *have* said, Lucia."

"Everything that you *will* do, Sergius Catiline!"

"Aye?"

"Aye! and everything that I shall do, likewise!" and with the word she left the room.

"A perilous girl, by all the Gods!" said Lentulus, in Greek, as she disappeared. "Will she do as she threatens?"

"Tush!" replied Catiline in Latin, "she speaks Greek like an Athenian. I am not sure, however, that she could understand such jargon as that is. No! she will do none of that. She is the cleverest and best girl living, only a little passionate, for which I love her all the more dearly. No! she will do none of that. Because she will not be alive, to do it, this time to-morrow," he added, putting his mouth within half an inch of the ear of Lentulus, and speaking in the lowest whisper.

Lentulus, bold as he was and unscrupulous, started in horror at his words, and his lips were white as he faltered —"Your own daughter, Lucius!"

"Ha! ha!" laughed the fierce conspirator, aloud; "ha! ha! yes, she is my own daughter, in everything but beauty She is the loveliest creature in all Rome! But we must yield, I suppose, to her wishes; the women rule us, after all is said, and I suppose I was alarmed needlessly. Doubtless Arvina will be silent. Come, I will walk with you so far on your way to the Forum. What ho! Chærea, see that Rufinus and Stolo lack nothing. I will speak with them, when I return home; and hark you in your ear. Suffer not Lucia Orestilla to leave the house a moment; use force if it be needed; but it will not. Tell her it is my orders, and watch her very closely. Come, Lentulus, it is drawing toward noon."

They left the house without more words, and walked side by side in silence for some distance, when Catiline said in a low voice, "This is unpleasant, and may be dangerous. We must, however, trust to fortune till to-morrow, when my house shall be void of this pest. Then will we proceed, as we had proposed."

Lentulus looked at him doubtfully, and asked, with a quick shudder running through his limbs, as he spoke: "And will you really?——" and there he paused, unable to complete the question.

"Remove her?" added Catiline, completing the sentence which he had left unfinished, "Ay! will I. Just as I would a serpent from my path!"

"And that done, what is to follow?" Lentulus inquired, with an assumption of coolness, which in truth he did not feel.

"We will get rid of Arvina. And then, as it wants but four days of the elections, we may keep all things quiet till the time."

"Be it so!" answered the other. "When do we meet again to settle these things finally?"

"To-morrow, at the house of Læca, at the sixth hour of night."

"Will all be there?"

"All the most faithful; until then, farewell!"

"Farewell."

And they parted; Lentulus hurrying to the Forum, to take his seat on the prætor's chair, and there preside in judgment—fit magistrate!—on men, the guiltiest of whom were pure as the spotless snow, when compared with his own conscious guilt; and Catiline to glide through dark streets, visiting discontented artizans, debauched mechanics, desperate gamblers, scattering dark and ambiguous promises, and stirring up that worthless rabble—who, with all to gain and nothing to lose by civil strife and tumult, abound in all great cities—to violence and thirst of blood.

Three or four hours at least he spent thus; and well satisfied with his progress, delighted by the increasing turbulence of the fierce and irresponsible democracy, and rejoicing in having gained many new and fitting converts to his creed, he returned homeward, ripe for fresh villainy. Chærea met him on the threshold, with his face pale and haggard from excitement.

"Catiline," he exclaimed, "she had gone forth already, before you bade me watch her!"

"She!—Who, slave? who?" and knowing perfectly who was meant, yet hoping, in his desperation, that he heard not aright, he caught the freedman by the throat, and shook him furiously.

"Lucia Orestilla," faltered the trembling menial.

"And has not returned?" thundered the traitor.

"Catiline, no!"

"Liar! and fool!" cried the other, gnashing his teeth with rage, as he gave way to his ungovernable fury, and hurling him with all his might against the marble door-post.

The freedman fell, like a dead man, with the blood gushing from his nose and mouth; and Catiline, striding across the prostrate body, retired sullenly and slowly to muse on the disappointment of this his most atrocious project, in the darkness and solitude of his own private chamber whither none dared intrude unsummoned.

CHAPTER XI.

THE RELEASE.

And, for that right is right, to follow right
Were wisdom, in the scorn of consequence.
TENNYSON. ŒNONE.

PAULLUS ARVINA sat alone in a small chamber of his own house. Books were before him, his favorites; the authors, whose words struck chords the most kindred in his soul; but though his eye rested on the fair manuscripts, it was evident that his mind was absent. The slender preparations for the first Roman meal were displayed temptingly on a board, not far from his elbow; but they were all untouched. His hair was dishevelled; his face pale, either from watching or excitement; and his eye wild and haggard. He wore a loose morning gown of colored linen, and his bare feet were thrust carelessly into unmatched slippers.

It was past noon already; nor, though his favorite freedman Thrasea had warned him several times of the lateness of the hour, had he shewn the least willingness to exert himself, so far even as to dress his hair, or put on attire befitting the business of the day.

It could not but be seen, at a glance, that he was ill at ease; and in truth he was much perturbed by what had passed on the preceding night, and very anxious with regard to the future.

Nor was it without ample cause that he was restless and disturbed; within the last three days he had by his own instability of purpose, and vacillating tastes and temper brought himself down from as enviable a position as well can be imagined, to one as insecure, unfortunate, and perilous.

That he had made to himself in Catiline an enemy, as deadly, as persevering, as relentless as any man could have upon his track; an enemy against whom force and fraud would most likely be proved equally unavailing, he entertained no doubt. But brave as he was, and fearless, both by principle and practice, he cared less for this, even while he confessed to himself, that he must be on his guard now alway against both open violence and secret murder, than he did for the bitter feeling, that he was distrusted; that he had brought himself into suspicion and ill-odor with the great man, in whose eyes he would have given so much to stand fairly, and whose good-will, and good opinion, but two little days before, he flattered himself that he had conciliated by his manly conduct.

Again, when he thought of Julia, there was no balm to his heart, no unction to his wounded conscience! What if she knew not, nor suspected anything of his disloyalty, did not he know it, feel it in every nerve? Did he not read tacit reproaches in every beam of her deep tranquil eye? Did he not fancy some allusion to it, in every tone of her low sweet voice? Did he not tremble at every air of heaven, lest it should waft the rumor of his infidelity to the chaste ears of her, whom alone he loved and honored? Did he not know that one whisper of that disgraceful truth would break off, and forever, the dear hopes, on which all his future happiness depended? And was it not most possible, most probable, that any moment might reveal to her the fatal tidings?—The rage of Catiline, frustrated in his foul designs, the revengeful jealousy of Lucia, the vigilance of the distrustful consul, might each or all at any moment bring to light that which he would have given all but life to bury in oblivion.

For a long time he had sat musing deeply on the perils of his false position, but though he had taxed every energy, and strained every faculty to devise some means by which to extricate himself from the toils, into which he had so blindly rushed, he could think of no scheme, resolve upon no course of action, which should set him at liberty, as he had been before his unlucky interview with the conspirator.

At times he dreamed of casting himself at the feet of Cicero, and confessing to that great and generous statesman all his temptations, all his trials, all his errors; of linking himself heart and soul with the determined patriots, who were prepared to live or die with the constitution, and the liberties of the republic; but the oath!—the awful imprecation, by which he had bound himself, by which he had devoted all that he loved to the Infernal Gods, recurred to his mind, and shook it with an earthquake's power. And he, the bold free thinker, the daring and unflinching soldier, bound hand and foot by a silly superstition, trembled—aye, trembled, and confessed to his secret soul that there was one thing which he ought to do, yet dared not!

Anon, maddened by the apparent hopelessness of ever being able to recur to the straight road; of ever more regaining his own self-esteem, or the respect of virtuous citizens—forced, as he seemed to be, to play a neutral part—the meanest of all parts—in the impending struggle—of ever gaining eminence or fame under the banners of the commonwealth; he dreamed of giving himself up, as fate appeared to have given him already up, to the designs of Catiline! He pictured to himself rank, station, power, wealth, to be won under the ensigns of revolt; and asked himself, as many a self-deluded slave of passion has asked himself before, if eminence, however won, be not glory; if success in the world's eyes be not fame, and rectitude and excellence.

But patriotism, the old Roman virtue, clear and undying in the hardest and most corrupt hearts, roused itself in him to do battle with the juggling fiends tempting him to his ruin; aud whenever patriotism half-defeated appeared to yield the ground, the image of his Julia—his Julia, never to be won by any indirection, never to be deceived by any sophistry, never to be deluded into smiling for one moment on a traitor—rose clear and palpable before him and the mists were dispersed instantly, and the foes of his better judgment scattered to the winds and routed.

Thus wavering, he sat, infirm of purpose, ungoverned—whence indeed all his errors—by any principle or unity of action; when suddenly the sound of a faint and hesitating knock of the bronze ring on the outer door reached his ear. The chamber, which he occupied, was far removed from the vestibule, divided from it by the whole length of the atrium, and fauces; yet so still was the interior of the house, and so inordinately sharpened was his sense of hearing by anxiety and apprehension, that he recognized the sound instantly, and started to his feet, fearing he knew not what.

The footsteps of the slave, though he hurried to undo the door, seemed to the eager listener as slow as the pace of the dull tortoise; and the short pause, which followed after the door had been opened, he fancied to be an hour in duration. Long as he thought it, however, it was too short to enable him to conquer his agitation, or to control the tumultuous beating of his heart, which increased to such a degree, as he heard the freedman ushering the new comer toward the room in which he was sitting, that he grew very faint, and turned as pale as ashes.

Had he been asked what it was that he apprehended, he could assuredly have assigned no reasonable cause to his tremors. Yet this man was as brave, as elastic in temperament, as tried steel. Oppose him to any definite and real peril, not a nerve in his frame would quiver; yet here he was, by imaginary terrors, and the disquietude of an uneasy conscience, reduced to more than woman's weakness.

The door was opened, and Thrasea appeared alone upon the threshold, with a mysterious expression on his blunt features.

"How now?" asked Paullus, "what is this?—Did I not tell you, that I would not be disturbed this morning?"

"Yes! master," answered the sturdy freedman; "but she said that it was a matter of great moment, and that she would——"

"*She!*—Who?" exclaimed Arvina, starting up from the chair, which he had resumed as his servant entered. "Whom do you mean by *She?*"

"The girl who waits in the tablinum, to know if you will receive her."

"The girl!—what girl? do you know her?"

"No, master, she is very tall, and slender, yet round withal and beautifully formed. Her steps are as light as the doe's upon the Hæmus, and as graceful. She has the finest foot and ancle mine eyes ever looked upon. I am sure too that her face is beautiful, though she is closely wrapped in a long white veil. Her voice, though exquisitely sweet and gentle, is full of a strange command, half proud and half persuasive. I could not, for my life, resist her bidding."

"Well! well! admit her, though I would fain be spared the trouble. I doubt not it is some soft votary of Flora; and I am not in the vein for such dalliance now."

"No! Paullus, no! it is a Patrician lady. I will wager my freedom on it, although she is dressed plainly, and, as I told you, closely veiled."

"Not Julia? by the Gods! it is not Julia Serena?" exclaimed the young man, in tones of inquiry, blent with wonder.

But, as he spoke, the door was opened once more; and the veiled figure entered, realizing by her appearance all the good freedman's eulogies. It seemed that she had overheard the last words of Arvina; for, without raising her veil, she said in a soft low voice, full of melancholy pathos,

"Alas! no, Paullus, it is not your Julia. But it is one, who has perhaps some claim to your attention; and who, at all events, will not detain you long, on matters most important to yourself. I have intruded thus, fearing you were about to deny me; because that which I have to say will brook no denial."

The freedman had withdrawn abruptly the very moment that the lady entered; and, closing the door firmly behind him, stood on guard out of earshot, lest any one should break upon his young lord's privacy. But Paullus knew not this; scarce knew, indeed, that they were alone; when, as she ceased, he made two steps forward, exclaiming in a piercing voice—

"Ye Gods! ye Gods! Lucia Orestilla!"

"Aye! Paul," replied the girl, raising her veil, and showing her beautiful face, no longer burning with bright amorous blushes, her large soft eyes, no longer beaming unchaste invitation, but pale, and quiet, and suffused with tender sadness, "it is indeed Lucia. But wherefore this surprise, I might say this terror? You were not, I remember, so averse, the last time we were alone together."

Her voice was steady, and her whole manner perfectly composed, as she addressed him. There was neither reproach nor irony in her tones, nor anything that betokened even the sense of injury endured. Yet was Arvina more unmanned by her serene and tranquil bearing, than he would have been by the most violent reproaches.

"Alas! alas! what shall I say to you," he faltered, "Lucia; Lucia, whom I dare not call mine."

"Say nothing, Paullus Arvina," she replied, "thou art a noble and generous soul!—Say nothing, for I know what thou would'st say. I have said it to myself many times already. Oh! wo is me! too late! too late! But I have come hither, now, upon a brief and a pleasant errand. For it *is* pleasant, let them scoff who will! I say, it *is* pleasant to do right, let what may come of it. Would God, that I had always thought so!"

"Would God, indeed!" answered the young man, "then had we not both been wretched."

"Wretched! aye! most, most wretched!" cried the girl, a large bright tear standing in either eye. "And art thou wretched, Paullus."

"Utterly wretched!" he said, with a deep groan, and buried his face for a moment in his hands. "Even before I looked upon you, thought of you, I was miserable! and now, now—words cannot paint my anguish, my self-degradation!"

"Aye! is it so?" she said, a faint sad smile flitting across her pallid lips. "Why I should feel abased and self-degraded, I can well comprehend. I, who have fallen from the high estate, the purity, the wealth, the consciousness of chaste and virtuous maidenhood! I, the despised, the castaway, the fallen! But thou, thou!—from thee I looked but for reproaches—the just reproaches I have earned by my faithless folly! I thought, indeed, to have found you wretched, writhing in the dark bonds which I, most miserable, cast around you; and cursing her who fettered you!"

"Cursing myself," he answered, "rather. Cursing my own insane and selfish passion, which alone trammelled me, which alone ruined one, better and brighter fifty fold than I!—alas! alas! Lucia."

And forgetful of all that he had heard to her disparagement from her bad father's lips, or, if he half remembered discrediting all in that moment of excitement, he flung himself at her feet, and grovelled like a crushed worm on the floor, in the degrading consciousness of guilt.

"Arise, arise for shame, young Arvina!" she said. "The ground, at a woman's feet, is no place for a man ever; least of all *such* a woman's. Arise, and mark me, when I tell you th t, which to tell you, only, I came hither. Arise, I say, an make me not scorn the man, whom I admire, whom—wo is me! I love."

Paullus regained his feet slowly, and abashed; it seemed that all the pride and haughtiness of his character had given way at once. Mute and humiliated, he sank into a chair, while she continued standing erect and self-sustained before him by conscious, though new, rectitude of pur pose.

"Mark me, I say, Arvina, when I tell you, that you are as free as air from the oath, with which I bound you. That wicked vow compels you only so long as I hold you pledged to its performance. Lo! it is nothing any more—for I, to whom alone of mortals you are bound, now and forever release you. The Gods, above and below, whom you called to witness it, are witnesses no more against you. For I annul it here; I give you back your plight. It is as though it never had been spoken!"

"Indeed? indeed? am I free?—Good, noble, generous, dear, Lucia, is it true? can it be? I am free, and at thy bidding?"

"Free as the winds of heaven, Paullus, that come whence no man knoweth, and go whither they will soever, and no mortal hindereth them! As free as the winds, Paullus," she repeated, "and I trust soon to be as happy."

"But wherefore," added the young man, "have you done this? You said you would release me *never*, and now all unsolicited you come and say 'you are free, Paullus,' almost before the breath is cold upon my lips that swore obedience. This is most singular, and inconsistent."

"What in the wide world *is* consistent, Paullus, except virtue? That indeed is immutable, eternal, one, the same on earth as in heaven, present, and past, and forever. But what else, I beseech you, is consistent, or here or anywhere, that you should dream of finding me, a weak wild wanton girl, of firmer stuff than heroes? Are you, even in your own imagination, are you, I say, consistent?"

She spoke eagerly, perhaps wildly; for the very part of self-denial, which she was playing, stirred her mind to its lowest depths; and the great change, which had been going on within for many hours, and was still in powerful progress, excited her fancy, and kindled all her strongest feelings; and, as is not unfrequently the case, all the profound vague thoughts, which had so long lain mute and dormant, found light at once, and eloquent expression.

Paullus gazed at her, in astonishment, almost in awe. Could this be the sensual, passionate voluptuary he had known two days since?—the strange, unprincipled, impulsive being, who yielded like the reed, to every gust of passion—this deep, clear, vigorous thinker! It was indeed a change to puzzle sager heads than that of Arvina! a transformation, sudden and beautiful as that from the torpid earthy grub, to the swift-winged etherial butterfly! He gazed at her, until she smiled in reply to his look of bewilderment; and then he met her smile with a sad heavy sigh, and answered—

"Most inconsistent, I! alas! that I should say it, far worse than inconsistent, most false to truth and virtue, most recreant to honor! Have not I, whose most ardent aspirations were set on glory virtuously won, whose soul, as I fancied, was athirst for knowledge and for truth, have not I bound myself by the most dire and dreadful oaths, to find my good in evil, my truth in a lie, my glory in black infamy?—Have not I, loving another better than my own life, won thee to love, poor Lucia, and won thee by base falsehood to thy ruin?"

"No! no!" she interrupted him, "this last thing you have not done, Arvina. Awake! you shall deceive yourself no longer! Of this last wrong you are as innocent as the unspotted snow; and I, I only, own the guilt, as I shall bear the punishment! Hear first, why I release you from your oath; and then, if you care to listen to a sad tale, you shall know by what infamy of others, one, who might else have been both innocent and happy, has been made infamous and foul and vile, and wretched; a thing hateful to herself, and loathsome to the world; a being with but one hope left, to expiate her many crimes by one act of virtue, and then to die! to die young, very young, unwept, unhonored, friendless, and an orphan—aye! from her very birth, more than an orphan!"

"Say on," replied the young man, "say on, Lucia; and would to heaven you could convince me that I have not wronged you. Say on, then; first, if you will, why you have released me; but above all, speak of yourself—speak freely, and oh! if I can aid, or protect, or comfort you, believe me I will do it at my life's utmost peril."

"I do believe you, Paullus. I did believe that, ere you spoke it. First, then, I set you free—and free you are henceforth, forever."

"But wherefore?"

"Because you are betrayed. Because I know all, that fell out last night. Because I know darker villainy plotted against you, yet to come; villainy from which, tramelled by this oath, no earthly power can save you. Because, I know not altogether why or how, my mind has been changed of late completely, and I will lend myself no more to projects, which I loathe, and infamy which I abhor. Because—because—because, in a word, I loveyou Paullus! Better than all I have, or hope to have on earth."

"But you must not," he replied, gravely yet tenderly, "because"——

"You love another," she interrupted him, very quickly, "You love Julia Serena, Hortensia's lovely daughter; and she loves you, and you are to be wedded soon. You see," she added, with a faint painful smile, "that I know everything about you. I knew it long since; long, long before I gave myself to you; even before I loved you, Paul—for I have loved you, also, long!"

"Loved me long!" he exclaimed, in astonishment, "how can that be, when you never saw me until the day before yesterday?"

"Oh! yes I have," she answered sadly. "I have seen you and known you many years; though you have forgotten me, if even, which I doubt, you ever noticed me at all. But I can bring it to your mind. Have you forgotten how, six summers since, as you were riding down the Collis Hortulorum, you passed a little girl weeping by the way-side ?—"

"Over a wounded kid ? No, I remember very well. A great country boor had hurt it with a stone."

"And you," exclaimed the girl, with her eyes flashing fire, "you sprang down from your horse, and chastised him, till he whined like a beaten hound, though he was twice as big as you were ; and then you bound up the kid's wound, and wiped away the tears—innocent tears they were—of the little girl, and parted her hair, and kissed her on the forehead. That little girl was I, and I have kept that kiss upon my brow, aye, and in my heart too ! until now. No lips of man or woman have ever touched that spot which your lips hallowed. From that day forth I have loved you, I have adored you, Paullus. From that day forth I have watched all your ways, unseen and unsuspected. I have seen you do fifty kind, and generous, and gallant actions ; but never saw you do one base, or tyrannous, or cowardly, or cruel—"

"Until that fatal night!" he said, with a deep groan. "May the Gods pardon me ! I never shall forgive my self."

"No ! no ! I tell you, no !" cried the girl, impetuously "I tell you, that I was not deceived, if I fell ; but I did not fall then ! I knew that you loved Julia, years ago. I knew that I never could be yours in honor ; and that put fire and madness in my brain, and despair in my heart. And my home was a hell, and those who should have been my guides and saviours were my destroyers ; and I am—*what I am;* but in that you had no share. On that night, I but obeyed the accursed bidding of the blackest and most atrocious monster that pollutes Jove's pure air by his breath !"

"Bidding," he exclaimed, starting back in horror, "Catiline's bidding ?"

"My father's," answered the miserable girl. "My own father's bidding !"

"Ye gods ! ye gods !" His own daughter's purity !"

"Purity !", she replied, with a smile of sad bitter irony

"Do you think purity could long exist in the same house with Catiline and Orestilla? Paullus Arvina, the scenes I have beheld, the orgies I have shared, the atmosphere of voluptuous sin I have breathed, almost from my cradle, had changed the cold heart of the virgin huntress into the fiery pulses of the wanton Venus! Since I was ten years old, I have been, wo is me! familiar with all luxury, all infamy, all degradation!"

"Great Nemesis!" he cried, turning up his indignant eyes toward heaven. "But, in the name of all the Gods! wherefore, wherefore? Even to the worst, the most debased of wretches, their children's honor is still dear."

"Nothing is dear to Catiline but riot, and debauchery, and murder! Sin, for its own sake, even more than for the rewards its offers to its votaries! Paullus, men called me beautiful! But what cared I for beauty, that charmed all but him, whom alone I desired to fascinate? Men called me beautifnl, I say! and in my father's sight that beauty became precious, when he foresaw that it might prove a means of winning followers to his accursed cause! Then was I educated in all arts, all graces, all accomplishments that might enhance my charms; and, as those fatal charms could avail him nothing, so long as purity remained or virtue, I was taught, ah! too easily! to esteem pleasure the sole good, passion the only guide! Taught thus, by my own parents! Curses, curses, and shame upon them! Pity me, pity me, Paullus. Oh! you are bound to pity me! for had I not loved you, fatally, desperately loved, and known that I could not win you, perchance—perchance I had not fallen. Oh! pity me, and pardon——"

"Pardon you, Lucia," he interrupted her. "What have you done to me, or who am I, that you should crave my pardon?"

"What have I done? Do you ask in mockery? Have not I made you the partaker of my sin? Have not I lured you into falsehood, momentary falsehood it is true, yet still falsehood, to your Julia? Have I not tangled you in the nets of this most foul conspiracy? Betrayed you, a bound slave, to the monster—the soul-destroyer?

Arvina groaned aloud, but made no answer, so deeply did his own thoughts afflict, so terribly did her strong words oppress him.

"But it is over—it is over now!" She exclaimed exultingly. "His reign of wickedness is over! The tool, which he moulded for his own purposes, shall be the instrument to quell him. The pitfall which he would have digged in the way of others, shall be to them a door whereby they shall escape his treason, and his ruin. You are saved, my Arvina! By all the Gods! you are saved! And, if it lost me once, it has preserved me now—my wild, unchangeable, and undying love for you, alone of men! For it has made me think! Has quenched the insane flames that burned within me! Has given me new views, new principles, new hopes! Evil no more shall be my good, nor infamy my pride! If, myself, I am most unhappy, I will live henceforth, while I do live, to make others happy! I will live henceforth for two things—revenge and retribution! By all the Gods! Julia and you, my Paullus, shall be happy! By all the Gods! he who destroyed me for his pleasure, shall be destroyed in turn, for mine!"

"Lucia! think! think! he is your father!"

"Perish the monster! I have not—never had father, or home, or——Speak not to me; speak not of him, or I shall lose what poor remains of reason his vile plots have left me. Perish!—by all the powers of hell, he shall perish, miserably!—miserably! And you, you, Paullus, must be the weapon that shall strike him!"

"Never the weapon in a daughter's hand to strike a father," answered Paullus, "no! though he were himself a parricide!"

"He is!—he is a parricide!—the parricide of Rome itself!—the murderer of our common mother!—the sacrilegious stabber of his holy country! Hear me, and tremble! It lacks now two days of the Consular election. If Catiline go not down ere that day cometh, then Rome goes down, on that day, and forever!"

"You are mad, girl, to say so."

"You are mad, youth, if you discredit me. Do not I know? am not I the sharer? the tempter to the guilt myself? and am not I the mistress of its secrets? Was it not for this, that I gave myself to you? was it not unto this that I bound you by the oath, which now I restore to you? was it not by this, that I would have held you my minion and my paramour? And is it not to reveal this, that I now have come? I tell you, I discovered, how he would yesternight have slain you by the gladiator's sword; discovered how he now would slay you, by the perverted sword of Justice, as Medon's, as Volero's murderer; convicting you of his own crimes, as he hath many men before, by his suborned and perjured clients—his comrades on the Prætor's chair! I tell you, I discovered but just now, that me too he will cut off in the flower of my youth; in the heat of the passions, he fomented; in the rankness of the soft sins, he taught me—cut me off—me, his own ruined and polluted child—by the same poisoned chalice, which made his house clear for my wretched mother's nuptials!"

"Can these things be," cried Paullus, "and the Gods yet withhold their thunder?"

"Sometimes I think," the girl answered wildly, "that there are *no* Gods, Paullus. Do you believe in Mars and Venus?"

"In Gods, whose worship were adultery and murder?" said Arvina. "Not I, indeed, poor Lucia."

"If these be Gods, there is no truth, no meaning in the name of virtue. If not these, what is God?"

"All things!" replied the young man solemnly. "Whatever moves, whatever *is*, is God. The universe is but the body, that clothes his eternal spirit; the winds are his breath; the sunshine is his smile; the gentle dews are the tears of his compassion! Time is the creature of his hand, eternity his dwelling place, virtue his law, his oracles the soul of every living man!"

"Beautiful," cried the girl. "Beautiful, if it were but true!"

"It is true—as true, as the sun in heaven; as certain as his course through the changeless seasons."

"How? how?" she asked eagerly. "What makes it certain?"

"The certainty of death!" he answered.

"Ah! death, death! that is a mystery indeed. And after that—"

"Everlasting life!"

"Ha! do you believe that too? They tell me all that is a fable, a folly, and a falsehood!"

"Perchance it would be well for them it were so."

"Yes!" she replied. "Yes! But who taught you?"

"Plato! Immortal Plato!"

"Ha! I will read him; I will read Plato."

"What! do you understand Greek too, Lucia?"

"How else should I have sung Anacreon, and learned the Lesbian arts of Sappho? But we have strayed wide of our subject, and time presses. Will you denounce, me, Catiline?"

"Not I! I will perish sooner."

"You will do so, and all Rome with you."

"Prove that to me, and—But it is impossible."

"Prove that to you, will you denounce him?"

"I will save Rome!"

"Will you denounce him?"

"If otherwise, I may preserve my country, no."

"Otherwise, you cannot. Speak! will you?"

"I must know all."

"You shall. Mark me, then judge.". And rapidly, concisely, clearly, she revealed to him the dread secret. She concealed nothing, neither the ends of the conspiracy, nor the names of the conspirators. She asseverated to him the appalling fact, that half the noblest, eldest families of Rome, were either active members of the plot, sworn to spare no man, or secret well-wishers, content at first to remain neutral, and then to share the spoils of empire. According to her shewing, the Curii, the Portii, the Syllæ, the Cethegi, the great Cornelian house, the Vargunteii, the Autronii, and the Longini, were all for the most part implicated, although some branches of the Portian and Cornelian houses had not been yet approached by the seducers. Crassus, she told him too, the richest citizen of Rome, and Caius Julius Cæsar, the most popular, awaited but the first success to join the parricides of the Republic.

He listened thoughtfully, earnestly, until she had finished her narration, and then shook his head doubtfully.

"I *think*," *he said*, "*you must be deceived*, poor Lucia. I do not see how these things can be. These men, whom you have named, are all of the first houses of the state; have all of them, either themselves or their forefathers, bled for the commonwealth. How then should they now wish to destroy it? They are men, too, of all parties and all factions; the Syllæ, the proudest and haughtiest aristocrats of Rome. Your father, also, belonged to the Dictator's faction, while the Cornelii and the Curii have belonged ever to the tribunes' party. How should this be? or how should those whose pride, whose interest, whose power alike, rest on the maintenance of their order, desire to mow down the Patrician houses, like grass beneath the scythe, and give their honors to the rabble? How, above all, should Crassus, whose estate is worth seven thousand talents,* consisting, too, of buildings in the heart of Rome, join with a party whose watch-words are fire and plunder, partition of estates, and death to the rich? You see yourself that these things cannot be; that they are not consistent. You must have been deceived by their insolent and drunken boasting!"

"Consistent!" she replied, with vehement and angry irony. "Still harping on consistency! Are virtuous men then consistent, that you expect vicious men to be so? Oh, the false wisdom, the false pride of man! You tell me these things cannot be—perhaps they cannot; but they *are!* I know it—I have heard, seen, partaken all! But if you can be convinced only by seeing that the plans of men, whose every action is insanity and frenzy, are wise and reasonable, perish yourself in your blindness, and let Rome perish with you! I can no more. Farewell! I leave you to your madness!"

"Hold! hold!" he cried, moved greatly by her vehemence, "are you indeed so sure of this? What, in the name of all the Gods, can be their motive?"

"Sure! sure!" she answered scornfully; "I thought I was speaking to a capable and clever man of action; I see that it is a mere dreamer, to whose waking senses I appeal vainly. If *you* be not sure, also, you must be weaker than I can conceive. Why, if there was no plot, would Catiline have slaughtered Medon, lest it should be revealed? Why would he, else, have striven to bind you by oaths; and to what, if not to schemes of sacrilege and treason? Why would he else have murdered Volero? why planted ambushes against your life? why would he now meditate my death, his own child's death, that I am forced

* Seven thousand talents, about 7,500,000 dollars.

to fly his house? Oh! in the wide world there is no such folly, as that of the over wise! Motive—motive enough have they! While the Patrician senate, and the Patrician Consuls hold with firm hands the government, full well they know, that in vain violence or fraud may strive to wrest it from them. Let but the people hold the reins of empire, and the first smooth-tongued, slippery demagogue, the first bloody, conquering soldier, grasps them, and is the King, Dictator, Emperor, of Rome! Never yet in the history of nations, has despotism sprung out of oligarchic sway! Never yet has democracy but yielded to the first despot's usurpation! *They* have not read in vain the annals of past ages, if you have done so, Paullus."

"Ha!" he exclaimed, "look, they so far ahead? Ambition, then, it is but a new form of ambition?"

"Will you denounce them, Paullus?"

"At least, I will warn the Consul!"

"You must denounce them, or he will credit nothing."

"I will save Rome."

"Enough! enough! I am avenged, and thou shalt be happy. Go to the Consul, straightway! make your own terms, ask office, rank, wealth, power. He will grant all! and now, farewell! Me you will see no more forever! Farewell, Paullus Arvina, fare you well forever! And sometimes, when you are happy in the chaste arms of Julia, sometimes think, Paullus, of poor, unhappy, loving, lost, lost Lucia!"

"Whither, by all the Gods, I adjure you! whither would you go, Lucia?"

"Far hence! far hence, my Paullus. Where I may live obscure in tranquil solitude, where I may die when my time comes, in peace and innocence. In Rome I were not safe an hour!"

"Tell me where! tell me Lucia, how I may aid, how guard, console, or counsel you."

"You can do none of these things, Paullus. All is arranged for the best. Within an hour I shall be journeying hence, never to pass the gates, to hear the turbulent roar, to breathe the smoky skies, to taste the maddening pleasures, of glorious, guilty Rome! There is but one thing you can do, which will minister to my well-being—but one boon you can grant me. Will you?"

"And do you ask, Lucia?"

"Will you swear?" she inquired, with a faint melancholy smile. "Nay! it concerns no one but myself. You may swear safely."

"I do, by the God of faith!"

"Never seek, then, by word or deed, to learn whither I have gone, or where I dwell. Look! I am armed," and she drew out a dagger as she spoke. "If I am tracked or followed, whether by friend or foe, this will free me from persecution; and it shall do so, by the living lights of heaven! This, after all, is the one true, the last friend of the wretched. All hail to thee, healer of all intolerable anguish!" and she kissed the bright blade, before she consigned it to the sheath; and then, stretching out both hands to Paullus, she cried, "You have sworn—Remember!"

"And you promise me," he replied, "that, if at any time you need a friend, a defender, one who would lay down life itself to aid you, you will call on me, wheresoever I may be, fearless and undoubting. For, from the festive board, or the nuptial bed, from the most sacred altar of the Gods, or from the solemn funeral pyre, I will come instant to thy bidding. 'Lucia needs Paullus,' shall be words shriller than the war-trumpet's summons to my conscious soul."

"I promise you," she said, "willingly, most willingly. And now kiss me, Paullus. Julia herself would not forbid this last, sad, pious kiss! Not my lips! not my lips! Part my hair on my brows, and kiss me on the forehead, where your lips, years ago, shed freshness, and hope that has not yet died all away. Sweet, sweet! it is pure and sweet, it allays the fierce burning of my brain. Fare you well, Paul, and remember—remember Lucia Orestilla."

She withdrew herself from his arm modestly, as she spoke, lowered her veil, turned, and was gone. Many a day and week elapsed, and weeks were merged in months, ere any one, who knew her, again saw Catiline's unhappy, guilty daughter.

CHAPTER XII.

THE FORGE.

I saw a smith stand with his hammer thus,
The whilst his iron did on anvil cool.
KING JOHN.

IT was the evening of the sixteenth day before the calends of November, or, according to modern numeration, the eighteenth of October, the eve of the consular elections, when a considerable number of rough hardy-looking men were assembled beneath the wide low-browed arch of a blacksmith's forge, situated near the intersection of the Cyprian Lane with the Sacred Way, and commanding a full view of the latter noble thoroughfare.

It was already fast growing dark, and the natural obscurity of the hour was increased by the thickness of the lowering clouds, which overspread the whole firmament of heaven, and seemed to portend a tempest. But from the jaws of the semicircular arch of Roman brick, within which the group was collected, a broad and wavering sheet of light was projected far into the street, and over the fronts of the buildings opposite, rising and falling in obedience to the blast of the huge bellows, which might be heard groaning and laboring within. The whole interior of the roomy vault was filled with a lurid crimson light, diversified at times by a brighter and more vivid glare as a column of living flame would shoot up from the embers, or long trains of radiant sparks leap from the bounding anvil. Against this clear back ground the moving figures of the strong limbed grimy giants, who plied their mighty sledges with incessant zeal on the red hot metal, were defined sharply and picturesquely; while alternately red lights and heavy shadows flickered across the forms and features of many other men, who stood around watching the progress of the work, and occasionally speaking rapidly, and with a good deal of gesticulation, at intervals when the preponderant din of hammers ceased, and permitted conversation to be carried on audibly.

At this moment, however, there was no such pause; for the embers in the furnace were at a white heat, and flashes of lambent flame were leaping out of the chimney top, and vanishing in the dark clouds overhead. A dozen bars of glowing steel had been drawn simultaneously from the charcoal, and thrice as many massive hammers were forging them into the rude shapes of weapons on the anvils, which, notwithstanding their vast weight, appeared to leap and reel, under the blows that were rained upon them faster than hail in winter.

But high above the roar of the blazing chimney, above the din of the groaning stithy, high pealed the notes of a wild Alcaic ode, to which, chaunted by the stentorian voices of the powerful mechanics, the clanging sledges made a stormy but appropriate music. "Strike, strike the iron," thus echoed the stirring strain,

Strike, strike the iron, children o' Mulciber,
Hot from the charcoal cheerily glimmering!
  Swing, swing, my boys, high swing the sledges!
    Heave at it, heave at it, all! Together!
Great Mars, the war God, watches ye laboring
Joyously. Joyous watches the gleam o' the
  Bright sparkles, upsoaring the faster,
    Faster as our merry blows revive them.
Well knoweth He that clang. It arouses him,
Heard far aloof! He laughs on us hammering
  The sword, the clear harness of iron,
    Armipotent paramour o' Venus.
Red glows the charcoal. Bend to the task, my boys,
Time flies apace, and speedily night cometh,
  When we no more may ply the anvil;
    Fate cometh eke, i' the murky midnight.

Mark ye the pines, which rooted i' rocky ground,*
Brave Euroclydon's onset at evening.
Day dawns. The tree, which stood the tallest,
Preeminent i' the leafy greenwood,
Now lies the lowest. Safely the arbutus,
Which bent before him, flourishes, and the sun
Wakens the thrush, which slept securely
Nestled in its emerald asylum.
So, when the war-shout peals i' the noon o' night,
Rousing the sleepers fearful, in ecstacy
When slaves avenge their wrongs, arising
Strong i' the name o' liberty new born,
When fury spares not beauty nor innocence,
First flame the grandest domes. I' the massacre,
First fall the noblest. Lowly virtue
Haply the shade o' poverty defends.
Forge then the broad sword. Quickly the night cometh,
When red the streets with gore o' the mightiest
Shall fiercely flow, like Tiber in flood.
Rise then, avenger, the time it hath come!
Wake bloody tyrants from merry banquetting,
From downy couches, snowy-bosomed women
And ruby wine-cups, wake—The avenger
Springs to his arms, for the time it hath come!

The wild strain ceased, and with it the clang of the hammers, the bars of steel being already beaten into the form of those short massive two-edged blades, which were the Roman's national and all victorious weapon. But, as it ceased, a deep stern hum of approbation followed, elicited probably by some real or fancied similitude between the imagery of the song, and the circumstances of the auditors, who were to a man of the lowest order of plebeians, taught from their cradles to regard the nobles, and perhaps with too much cause, as their natural enemies and oppres-

* The classical reader will perhaps object to the introduction of the Alcaic measure at this date, 62 A. C., it being generally believed that the Greek measures were first adapted to the Latin tongue by Horace, a few years later. The desire of giving a faint idea of the rhythm and style of Latin song, will, it is hoped, plead in mitigation of this very slight deviation from historical truth—the rather that, in spite of Horace's assertion,

Non ante vulgatas per artes
Verba loquor sociata chordis,

It is not certain, that no imitations of the Greek measures existed prior to his success.

sors. When the brief applause was at an end, one of the elder bystanders addressed the principal workman, at the forge, in a low voice.

"You are incautious, Caius Crispus, to sing such songs as this, and at such a time, too."

"Tush, Bassus," answered the other, "it is you who are too timid. What harm is there, I should like to know, in singing an old Greek song done into Latin words? I like the rumbling measure, for my part; it suits well with the clash and clang of our rude trade. For the song, there is no offence in it; and, for the time, it is a very good time; and, to poor men like us, a better time is coming!"

"Oh! well said. May it be so!" exclaimed several voices in reply to the stout smith's sharp words.

But the old man was not so easily satisfied, for he answered at once. "If any of the nobles heard it, they would soon find offence in it, my Caius!"

"Oh! the nobles—the nobles, and the Fathers! I am tired of hearing of the nobles. For my part, I do not see what makes them noble. Are they a whit stronger, or braver, or better man than I, or Marcus here, or any of us? I trow not."

"Wiser—they are at least wiser, Caius," said the old man once more, "in this, if in nothing else, that they keep their own councils, and stand by their own order."

"Aye! in oppressing the poor!" replied a new speaker.

"Right, Marcus," said a second; "let them wrangle as much as they may with one another, for their dice, their women, or their wine; in this at least they all agree, in trampling down the poor."

"There is a good time coming," replied the smith; "and it is very near at hand. Now, Niger," he continued, addressing one of his workmen, "carry these blades down to the lower workshop; let Rufus fit them instantly with horn handles; and then, see you to their grinding! Never heed polishing them very much, but give them right keen edges, and good stabbing points."

"I do not know," answered the other man to the first part of the smith's speech. "I am not so sure of that."

"You don't know what I mean," said Crispus, scornfully.

"Yes I do—right well. But I am not so confident, as you are, in these new leaders."

The smith looked at him keenly for a moment, and then said significantly, "*do* you know?"

"Aye! do I," said the other; and, a moment afterward, when the eyes of the bystanders were not directly fixed on him, he drew his hand edgewise across his throat, with the action of one severing the windpipe.

Caius Crispus nodded assent, but made a gesture of caution, glancing his eye toward one or two of the company, and whispering a moment afterward, "I am not sure of those fellows."

"I see, I see; but they shall learn nothing from what I say." Then raising his voice, he added, "what I mean, Caius, is simply this, that I have no so very great faith in the promises of this Sergius Catiline, even if he should be elected. He was a sworn friend to Sylla, the people's worst enemy; and never had one associate of the old Marian party. Believe me, he only wants our aid to set himself up on the horse of state authority; and when he is firm in the saddle, he will ride us down under the hoofs of patrician tyranny, as hard as any Cato, or Pompey, of them all."

Six or seven of the foremost group, immediately about the anvil when this discourse was going on, interchanged quick glances, as the man used the word elected, on which he laid a strong and singular emphasis, and nodded slightly, as indicating that they understood his more secret meaning. All, however, except Crispus, the owner of the forge, seemed to be moved by what he advanced; and the foreman of the anvil, after musing for a moment, as he leaned on his heavy sledge, said, "I believe you are right; no one but a Plebeian can truly mean well, or be truly fitted for a leader to Plebeians."

"You are no wiser than Crispus," interposed the old man, who had spoken first, in a low angry whisper. "Do you want to discourage these fellows from rising to the cry, when it shall be set up? If this be all that you can do, it were as well to close the forge at once."

"Which I shall do forthwith," said Caius Crispus; "for I have got through my work and my lads are weary; but do not you go away, my gossips; nor you either," he added, speaking to the man whom he had at first suspected, "tarry you, under one pretext or other; we will have a cup of wine, as soon as I have got rid of these fellows. Here, Aulus," turning to his foreman, "take some coin out of my purse, there it hangs by my clean tunic in the corner, and go round to the wine shop, and bring thence a skinful of the best Sabine vintage; and some of you bar up the door, all but the little wicket. And now, my friends, good night; it is very late, and I am going to shut up the shop. Good night; and remember that the only hope of us working men lies in the election of Catiline to-morrow. Be in the Campus early, with all your friends; and hark ye, you were best take your knives under your tunics, lest the proud nobles should attempt to drive us from the ballot."

"We will, we will!" exclaimed several voices. "We will not be cozened out of our votes, or bullied out of them either. But how is this? do not you vote in your class?"

"I vote *with* my class! with my fellow Plebeians and mechanics, I would say! What if I be one of the armorers of the first class, think you that I will vote with the proud senators and insolent knights? No, brethren, not one of us, nor of the carpenters either, nor of the trumpeters, or horn-blowers! Plebeians we are, and Plebeians we will vote! and let me tell you to look sharp to me, on the Campus; and whatever I do, so do ye. Be sure that good will come of it to the people!"

"We will, we will!" responded all his hearers, now unanimous. "Brave heart! stout Caius Crispus! We will have you a tribune one of these days! but good night, good night!"

And, with the words, all left the forge, except the smith and his peculiar workmen, and two or three others, all clients of the Prætor Lentulus, and all in some degree associates in the conspiracy. None of them, however, were initiated fully, except Caius himself, his foreman, Aulus, the aged Bassus, and the stranger; who, though unknown to any one present, had given satisfactory evidence that he was privy to the most atrocious portions of the plot. The wine was introduced immediately, and after a deep draught, circulated more than once, tho conversation was resumed by the initiated, who were now left alone.

"And do you believe," said the stranger, addressing Caius Crispus, "that Catiline and his companions have any real view to the redress of grievances, the regeneration of the state, or the equalization of conditions?"

"Not in the least, I," answered the swordsmith. "Do you?"

"I did once."

"I never did."

"Then, in the name of all the Gods, why did you join with them?"

"Because by the ruin of the great and noble, the poor must be gainers. Because I owe what I can never pay. Because I lust for what I can never win—luxury, beauty, wealth, and power! And if there come a civil strife, with proscription, confiscation, massacre, it shall go hard with Caius Crispus, if he achieve not greatness!"

"And you," said the man, turning short round, without replying to the smith, and addressing the aged Bassus, "why did you join the plotters, you who are so crafty, so sagacious, and yet so earnest in the cause?"

"Because I have wrongs to avenge," answered the old man fiercely; a fiery flush crimsoning his sallow face, and his eye beaming lurid rage. "Wrongs, to repay which all the blood that flows in patrician veins were but too small a price!"

"Ha?" said the other, in a tone half meditative and half questioning, but in truth thinking little of the speaker, and reflecting only on the personal nature of the motives, which seemed to instigate them all. "Ha, is it indeed so?"

"Man," cried the old conspirator, springing forward and catching him by the arm. "Have you a wife, a child, a sister? If so, listen! you can understand me! I am, as you see old, very old! I have scars, also, all in front; honorable scars, of wounds inflicted by the Moorish assagays, of Jugurtha's desert horsemen—by the huge broad swords of the Teutones and Cimbri. My son, my only son fell, as an eagle-bearer, in the front rank of the hastati of the brave tenth legion—for we had wealth in those days, and both fought and voted in the centuries of the first class. But our fields were uncultivated, while we were shedding our best blood for the state; and to complete the ruin, my rural slaves broke loose, and joined Spartacus the gladiator. Taken, they died upon the cross; and I was quite undone. Law suits and usury ate up the rest; and, for these eight years past, old Bassus has been penniless, and often cold, and always hungry. But if this had been all, it is a soldier's part to bear cold and hunger—but not to bear disgrace. Man, there have been gyves on these legs—the whip has scarred these shoulders! Ye great Gods! the whip! for what have the poor to do with their Portian or Valerian laws? Nor was this all—the eagle-bearer left a child, a sweet, fair, gentle girl, the image of my gallant boy, the only solace of my famishing old age. I told you she was fair—fatally fair—too fair for a plebeian's daughter, a plebeian's wife! Her beauty caught the lustful eyes, inflamed the brutal heart of a patrician, one of the great Cornelii. It is enough! She was torn from my house, dishonored, and sent home, to die by her own hand, that would not pardon that involuntary sin! She died; the censors heard the tale; and scoffed at the teller of it! and that Cornelius yet sits in the senate; those censors who approved his guilt yet live—I say *live!* Is not that cause enough why I should join the plotters?"

"I cannot answer, No!" replied the other; "and you, Aulus, what is your reason?"

"I would win me a noble paramour. Hortensia's Julia is very soft and beautiful."

The stranger looked at him steadily for a moment, and an expression of disgust and horror crept over his bold face. "Alas!" he said at length, speaking, it would seem, to himself rather than to the others, "poor Rome! unhappy country!"

But, as he spoke, the strong smith, whose suspicion would seem to have been excited, stepped forward and laid his hand upon the stranger's shoulder. "Look you," he said, "master. None of us know you here, I think, and we should all of us be glad to know, both who you are, and, if indeed you be of the faction, wherefore *you* joined it, that you so closely scrutinize our motives."

"Because I was a fool, Caius Crispus; because I believed that, for a great stake, Romans might yet forget *self*, base and sordid *self*, and act as becomes patriots and men! Because I dreamed, smith, till morning light came back, and I awakened, and—"

"And the dream!" asked the smith eagerly, grasping the handle of his heavy hammer firmly, and setting his teeth hard.

"Had vanished," replied the other calmly, and looking him full in the eye.

"Bar the door, Aulus," cried the smith, hastily. "This fellow must die here, or he will betray us," and he caught him by the throat, as he spoke, with an iron grip, to prevent him from calling out or giving the alarm.

But the stranger, though not to be compared in bulk or muscular proportions with the gigantic artizan, shook off his grasp with contemptuous ease, and answered with a scornful smile,

"Betray you!—tush, I am Fulvius Flaccus."

Had a thunderbolt fallen at the feet of the smith, he could not have recoiled with wilder wonder.

"What, Fulvius Flaccus, to whose great wrongs all injuries endured by us are but as flea-bites! Fulvius, the grandson of that Fulvius Flaccus, who—"

"Was murdered by Opimius, while striving for the liberties of Romans. But what is this? By Mars and Quirinus! there is something afoot without!"

And, as he uttered the words, he sprang to the wicket, which Aulus had not fastened, and gazed out earnestly into the darkness, through which the regular and steady tramp of men, advancing in ordered files, could now be heard distinctly.

The others were beside him in an instant, with terror and amazement on their faces.

They had not long to wait, before the cause of their alarm became visible. It was a band of some five hundred stout young men of the upper classes, well armed with swords and the oblong bucklers of the legion, though wearing neither casque nor cuirass, led by a curule ædile, who was accompanied by ten or twelve of the equestrian order, completely armed, and preceded by his *apparitores* or beadles, and half a dozen torch-bearers.

These men passed swiftly on, in treble file, marching as fast as they could down the Sacred Way, until they reached the intersection of the street of Apollo; by which they proceeded straight up the ascent of the Palatine, whereon they were soon lost to view, among the splendid edifices that covered its slope and summit.

"By all the Gods?" cried Caius Crispus, "This is exceedingly strange! An armed guard at this time of night!"

"Hist! here is something more."

And, as old Bassus spoke, Antonius, the consul, who was supposed to be attached to the faction of Catiline, came down a bye-street, from the lower end of the Carinæ, preceded by his torch-bearers, and followed by a lictor* with his fasces. He was in full dress too, as one of the presiding magistrates of the senate, and bore in his hand his ivory sceptre, surmounted by an eagle.

As soon as he had passed the door of the forge, Crispus stepped out into the street, motioning his guests to follow him, and desiring his foreman to lock the door.

"Let us follow the Consul, at a distance," he exclaimed, "my Bassus; for, as our Fulvius says, there is assuredly something afoot; and it may be that it shall be well for us to know it. Come, let us follow quickly."

They hurried onward, as he proposed; and keeping some twenty or thirty paces in the rear of the Consul's train, soon reached the foot of the street of Apollo. At this point, however, Antonius paused with his lictor; for, in the opposite direction coming up from the Cerolian place toward the Forum, another line of torches might be seen flaming through the darkness, and, even at that distance, the axe heads of the lictors were visible, as they flashed out by fits in the red torch-light.

"By all the Gods!" whispered Bassus, "it is the other consul, the new man from Arpinum. Believe me, my friends, this bodes no good to us! The Senate must have been convoked suddenly—and lo! here come the fathers. Look, look! this is stern Cato."

And, almost as he said the words, a powerfully made and very noble looking man passed so near as to brush the person of the mechanic with the folds of his toga. His face, which was strongly marked, was stern certainly; but it was with the sternness of gravity and deep

*The senior consul, or he whose month it was to preside, had twelve lictors; the junior but one, while within the city.

thought, coupled perhaps with something of melancholy—for it might be that he despaired at times of man's condition in this world, and of his prospects in the next—not of austerity or pride. His garb was plain in the extreme, and, although his tunic displayed the broad crimson facings, and his robe the passmenting of senatorial rank, both were of the commonest materials, and the narrowest and most simple cut.

"Hail, noble Cato!" said the mechanic, as the senator passed by; but his voice faltered as he spoke, and there was something hollow and heartless in the tones, which conveyed the greeting.

Cato raised his eyes, which had been fixed on the ground in meditation, and perused the features of the speaker with a severe and scrutinizing gaze; and then, shaking his head sternly, as if dissatisfied with the result of his observation,

"This is no time of night, sirrah smith," he said, "for thee, or such as thou, to be abroad. Thy daily work done, thou shouldst be at home with thy wife and children, not seeking profligate adventures, or breeding foul sedition in the streets. Go home! go home! for shame on thee! thou art known and marked."

And the severe and virtuous noble strode onward, unattended he by any torch-bearer, or freedman, and soon joined his worthy friend, the great Latin orator, who had come up, and having united his train to that of the other consul, was moving up the Palatine.

In the meantime senator after senator arrived, some alone, with their slaves or freedmen lighting them along the streets; others in groups of two or three, all hurrying toward the Palatine. The smith and his friends, who had been at first the sole spectators of the shew, were now every moment joined by more and more of the rabble, until a great concourse was assembled; through which the nobles had some difficulty in forcing their way toward the Temple of Apollo, in which their order was assembling, wherefore as yet they knew not.

At first the crowd was orderly enough, and quiet; but gradually beginning to ferment and grow warm, as it were by the closeness of its packing, cheers were heard, and loud acclamations, as any member of the popular faction made his way through it; and groans and yells and even curses succeeded, as any of the leaders of the aristocratic party strove to part its reluctant masses.

And now a louder burst of acclamations, than any which had yet been heard, rang through the streets, causing the very roofs to tremble.

"What foolery have we here?" said the smith very sullenly, who, though he responded nothing to it, had by no means recovered from the rebuke of Cato "Oh! yes! I see, I see," and he too added the power of his stentorian lungs to the clamor, as a young senator, splendidly dressed, and of an aspect that could not fail to attract attention, entered the little space, which had been kept open at the corner of the two streets, by the efforts of an ædile and his beadles, who had just arrived on the ground.

He was not much, if at all, above the middle size, but admirably proportioned, whether for feats of agility and strength, or for the lighter graces of society. But it was his face more especially, and the magnificent expression of his features, that first struck the beholder—the broad imaginative brow, the keen large lustrous eye, pervading, clear, undazzled as the eagle's, the bold Roman nose, the resolute curve of the clean-cut mouth, full of indomitable pride and matchless energy—all these bespoke at once the versatile and various genius of the great statesman, orator, and captain, who was to be thereafter.

At this time, however, although he was advancing toward middle age, and had already shaken off some of the trammels which luxurious vice and heedless extravagance had cast around his young puissant intellect, he had achieved nothing either of fame or power. He had, it is true, given signs of rare intellect, but as yet they were signs only. Though his friends looked forward confidently to the time, when they should see him the first citizen of the republic; and it is more than possible, that in his own heart he contemplated even now the attainment of a more glorious, if more perilous elevation.

The locks of this noble looking personage, though not arranged in that effeminate fashion, which has been mentioned as characteristic of Cethegus and some others, were closely curled about his brow—for he, as yet, exhibited no tendency to that baldness, for which in after years he was remarkable—and reeked with the choicest perfumes. He wore the crimson-bordered toga of his senatorial rank, but under it, as it waved loosely to and fro, might be observed the gaudy hues of a violet colored banqueting dress, sprinkled with flowers of gold, as if he had been disturbed from some festive board by the summons to council.

As he passed through the crowd, from which loud rose the shout, following him as he moved along—"Hail, Caius Cæsar! long live the noble Cæsar!"—his slaves scattered gold profusely among the multitude, who fought and scrambled for the glittering coin, still keeping up their clamorous greeting; while the dispenser of the wasteful largesse appearing to know every one, and to forget no face or name, even of the humblest, had a familiar smile and a cheery word for each citizen.

"Ha! Bassus, my old hero!" he exclaimed, "it is long since thou hast been to visit me. That proves, I hope, that things go better now-a-days at home. But come and see me, Bassus; I have something for thee to keep the cold from thy hearth, this freezing weather."

And he paused not to receive an answer, but moved forward a step or two, till his eye fell upon the swordsmith.

"What, Caius," he said, "sturdy Caius, absent from his forge so early—but I forgot, I forgot! you are a politician, perhaps you can tell me why they have roused me from the best cup of Massic I have tasted this ten years. What is the coil, Caius Crispus?"

"Nay! I know not," replied the mechanic, "I was about to ask the same of you, noble Cæsar!"

"I am the worst man living of whom to inquire," replied the patrician, with a careless smile. "I cannot even guess, unless perchance"—but as he spoke, he discovered, standing beside the smith, the man who had called himself Fulvius Flaccus, and interrupting himself instantly, he fixed a long and piercing gaze upon him, and then exclaimed, "Ha! is it thou?" with an expression of astonishment, not all unmixed with vexation.

The next moment he stepped close up to him, whispered a word into his ear, and hurried with an altered air up the steep street which scaled the Palatine.

A minute or two afterward, Crispus turned to address this man, but he too was gone.

In quick succession senator after senator now came up

the gentle slope of the Sacred Way, until almost all the distinguished men in Rome, whether for good or for evil, had undergone the scrutiny of the group collected around Caius Crispus.

But it was not till among the last that Catiline strode by, gnawing his nether lip uneasily, with his wild sunken eyes glaring suspiciously about him. He spoke to no one, until he came opposite the smith, on whom he frowned darkly, exclaiming, "What do you here? Go home, sirrah, go home!" and as Caius dropped his bold eyes, crest-fallen and abashed, he added in a lower tone, so that, save Bassus only, none of the crowd could hear him, "Wait for me at my house. Evil is brewing!"

Not a word more was spoken. Crispus and the old man soon extricated themselves from the throng and went their way; and in a little time afterward the multitude was dispersed, rather summarily, by a band of armed men under the Prætor Pomptinus, who cleared with very little delicacy the confines of the Palatine, whereon it was announced that the senate were now in secret session.

CHAPTER XIII.

THE DISCLOSURE.

> Maria montesque polliceri cæpit,
> Minari interdum ferro, nisi obnoxia foret.
>
> SALLUST.

> A woman, master.
>
> LOVE'S LABOUR LOST.

AMONG all those of Senatorial rank—and they were very many—who were participants of the intended treason, one alone was absent from the assemblage of the Order on that eventful night.

The keen unquiet eye of the arch-traitor missed Curius from his place, as it ran over the known faces of the conspirators, on whom he reckoned for support.

Curius was absent.

Nor did his absence, although it might well be, although indeed it *was*, accidental, diminish anything of Catiline's anxiety. For, though he fully believed him trusty and faithful to the end, though he felt that the man was linked to him indissolubly by the consciousness of common crimes, he knew him also to be no less vain than he was daring. And, while he had no fear of intentional betrayal, he apprehended the possibility of involuntary disclosures, that might be perilous, if not fatal, in the present juncture.

It has been left on record of this Curius, by one who knew him well, and was himself no mean judge of character, that he possessed not the faculty of concealing any thing he had heard, or even of dissembling his own crimes; and Catiline was not one to overlook or mistake so palpable a weakness.

But the truth was, that knowing his man thoroughly, he was aware that, with the bane, he bore about with him, in some degree, its antidote. For so vast and absurd were his vain boastings, and so needless his exaggerations of his own recklessness, blood-thirstiness, and crime, that hitherto his vaporings had excited rather ridicule than fear.

The time was however coming, when they were to awaken distrust, and lead to disclosure.

It was perfectly consistent with the audacity of Catiline—an audacity, which, though natural, stood him well in stead, as a mask to cover deep designs—that even now, when he felt himself to be more than suspected, instead of avoiding notoriety, and shunning the companionship of his fellow traitors, he seemed to covet observation, and to display himself in connection with his guilty partners, more openly than heretofore.

But neither Lentulus, nor Vargunteius, nor the Syllæ, nor any other of the plotters had seen Curius, or could inform him of his whereabout. And, ere they separated for the night, amid the crash of the contending elements above, and the roar of the turbulent populace below, doubt, and almost dismay, had sunk into the hearts of several the most daring, so far as mere mortal perils were to be encountered, but the most abject, when superstition was joined with conscious guilt to appal and confound them.

Catiline left the others, and strode away homeward, more agitated and unquiet than his face or words, or anything in his demeanor, except his irregular pace, and fitful gestures indicated.

Dark curses quivered unspoken on his tongue—the pains of hell were in his heart already.

Had he but known the whole, how would his fury have blazed out into instant action.

At the very moment when the Senate was so suddenly convoked on the Palatine, a woman of rare loveliness waited alone, in a rich and voluptuous chamber of a house not far removed from the scene of those grave deliberations.

The chamber, in which she reclined alone on a pile of

soft cushions, might well have been the shrine of that bland queen of love and pleasure, of whom its fair tenant was indeed an assiduous votaress. For there was nothing, which could charm the senses, or lap the soul in luxurious and effeminate ease, that was not there displayed.

The walls glowed with the choicest specimens of the Italian pencil, and the soft tones and harmonious colouring were well adapted to the subjects, which were the same in all—voluptuous and sensual love.

Here Venus rose from the crisp-smiling waves, in a rich atmosphere of light and beauty—there Leda toyed with the wreathed neck and ruffled plumage of the enamoured swan—in this compartment, Danaë lay warm and languid, impotent to resist the blended power of the God's passion and his gold—in that, Ariadne clung delighted to the bosom of the rosy wine-God.

The very atmosphere of the apartment was redolent of the richest perfumes, which streamed from four censers of chased gold placed on a tall candelabra of wrought bronze in the corners of the room. A bowl of stained glass on the table was filled with musk roses, the latest of the year; and several hyacinths in full bloom added their almost overpowering scent to the aromatic odours of the burning incense.

Armed chairs, with downy pillows, covered with choice embroidered cloths of Calabria, soft ottomans and easy couches, tables loaded with implements of female luxury, musical instruments, drawings, and splendidly illuminated rolls of the amatory bards and poetesses of the Egean islands, completed the picture of the boudoir of the Roman beauty.

And on a couch piled with the Tyrian cushions, which yielded to the soft impress of her lovely form, well worthy of the splendid luxury with which she was surrounded, lay the unrivalled Fulvia, awaiting her expected lover.

If she was lovely in her rich attire, as she appeared at the board of Catiline, with jewels in her bosom, and her bright ringlets of luxuriant gold braided in fair array, far lovelier was she now, as she lay there reclined, with those bright ringlets all dishevelled, and falling in a flood of wavy silken masses, over her snowy shoulders, and palpitating bosom; with all the undulating outlines of her superb form, unadorned, and but scantily concealed by a loose robe of snow-white linen.

Her face was slightly flushed with a soft carnation tinge, her blue eyes gleamed with unusual brightness. And by the fluttering of her bosom, and the nervous quivering of her slender fingers, as they leaned on a tripod of Parian marble which stood beside the couch, it was evident that she was labouring under some violent excitement.

"He comes not," she said. "And it is waxing late. He has again failed me! and if he have—ruin—ruin!—Debts pressing me in every quarter, and no hope but from him. Alfenus the usurer will lend no more—my farms all mortgaged to the utmost, a hundred thousand sesterces of interest, due these last Calends, and unpaid as yet. What can I do?—what hope for? In him there is no help—none! Nay! It is vain to think of it; for he is amorous as ever, and, could he raise the money, would lavish millions on me for one kiss. No! *he* is bankrupt too; and all his promises are but wild empty boastings. What, then, is left to me?" she cried aloud, in the intensity of her perturbation. "Most miserable me! My creditors will seize on all—all—all! and poverty—hard, chilling, bitter poverty, is staring in my face even now. Ye Gods! ye Gods! And I can not—can not live poor. No more rich dainties, and rare wines! no downy couches and soft perfumes! No music to induce voluptuous slumbers! no fairy-fingered slaves to fan the languid brow into luxurious coolness! No revelry, no mirth, no pleasure! Pleasure that is so sweet, so enthralling! Pleasure for which I have lived only, without which I must die! *Die!* By the great Gods! I *will* die! What avails life, when all its joys are gone? or what is death, but one momentary pang, and then—quiet? Yes! I will die. And the world shall learn that the soft Epicurean can vie with the cold Stoic in carelessness of living, and contempt of death—that the warm votaress of Aphrodite can spend her glowing life-blood as prodigally as the stern follower of Virtue! Lucretia died, and was counted great and noble, because she cared not to survive her honour! Fulvia will perish, wiser, as soon as she shall have outlived her capacity for pleasure!"

She spoke enthusiastically, her bright eyes flashing a

strange fire, and her white bosom panting with the strong and passionate excitement; but in a moment her mood was changed. A smile, as if at her own vehemence, curl ed her lip; her glance lost its quick, sharp wildness. She clapped her hands together, and called aloud,

"Ho! Ægle! Ægle!"

And at the call a beautiful Greek girl entered the chamber, voluptuous as her mistress in carriage and demeanor, and all too slightly robed for modesty, in garments that displayed far more than they concealed of her rare symmetry.

"Bring wine, my girl," cried Fulvia; "the richest Massic; and, hark thee, fetch thy lyre. My soul is dark to-night, and craves a joyous note to kindle it to life and rapture."

The girl bowed and retired; but in a minute or two returned, accompanied by a dark-eyed Ionian, bearing a Tuscan flask of the choice wine, and a goblet of crystal, embossed with emeralds and sapphires, imbedded, by a process known to the ancients but now lost, in the transparent glass.

A lyre of tortoiseshell was in the hands of Ægle, and a golden plectrum with which to strike its chords; she had cast loose her abundant tresses of dark hair, and decked her brows with a coronal of myrtle mixed with roses, and as she came bounding with sinuous and graceful gestures through the door, waving her white arms with the dazzling instruments aloft, she might have represented well a young priestess of the Cyprian queen, or the light Muse of amorous song.

The other girl filled out a goblet of the amber-coloured wine, the fragrance of which overpowered, for a moment, as it mantled on the goblet's brim, the aromatic perfumes which loaded the atmosphere of the apartment.

And Fulvia raised it to her lips, and sipped it slowly, and delightedly, suffering it to glide drop by drop between her rosy lips, to linger on her pleased palate, luxuriating in its soft richness, and dwelling long and rapturously on its flavour.

After a little while, the goblet was exhausted, a warmer hue came into her velvet cheeks, a brighter spark danced in her azure eves, and as she motioned the Ionian slave-girl to replenish the cup and place it on the tripod at her elbow, she murmured in a low languid tone,

"Sing to me, now—sing to me, Ægle."

And in obedience to her word the lovely girl bent her fair form over the lute, and, after a wild prelude full of strange thrilling melodies, poured out a voice as liquid and as clear, aye! and as soft, withal, as the nightingale's, in a soft Sapphic love-strain full of the glorious poetry of her own lovely language.

Where in umbrageous shadow of the greenwood
Buds the gay primrose i' the balmy spring time;
Where never silent, Philomel, the wildest
Minstrel of ether,

Pours her high notes, and caroling, delighted
In the cool sun-proof canopy of the ilex
Hung with ivy green or a bloomy dog-rose
Idly redundant,

Charms the fierce noon with melody; in the moonbeam
Where the coy Dryads trip it unmolested
All the night long, to merry dithyrambics
Blissfully timing

Their rapid steps, which flit across the knot grass
Lightly, nor shake one flower of the blue-bell;
Where liquid founts and rivulets o' silver
Sweetly awaken

Clear forest echoes with unearthly laughter;
There will I, dearest, on a bank be lying
Where the wild thyme blows ever, and the pine tree
Fitfully murmurs

Slumber inspiring. Come to me, my dearest,
On the fresh greensward, as a downy bride-bed,
Languid, unzoned, and amorous, reclining;
Like Ariadne,

When the blythe wine-God, from Olympus hoary,
Wooed the soft mortal tremulously yielding
All her enchantments to the mighty victor—
Happy Ariadne!

There will I, dearest, every frown abandon;
Nor do thou fear, nor hesitate to press me,
Since, if I chide, 'tis but a girl's reproval,
Faintly reluctant.

Doubt not I love thee, whether I return thy
Kisses in delight, or avert demurely
Lips that in truth burn to be kissed the closer,
Eyes that avoid thee,

Loth to confess how amorously glowing
Pants the fond heart. Oh! tarry not, but urge me
Coy to consent; and if a blush alarm thee,
Shyly revealing

Sentiments deep as the profound of Ocean,
If a sigh, faltered in an hour of anguish,
Seem to implore thee—pity not. The maiden
Often adores thee

Most if offending. Never, oh! believe me,
Did the faint-hearted win a girl's devotion,
Nor the true girl frown when a youth disarmed her
Dainty denial.

While she was yet singing, the curtains which covered the door were put quietly aside, and with a noiseless step Curius entered the apartment, unseen by the fair vocalist, whose back was turned to him, and made a sign to Fulvia that she should not appear to notice his arrival.

The haggard and uneasy aspect, which was peculiar to this man—the care-worn expression, half-anxious and half-jaded, which has been previously described, was less conspicuous on this occasion than ever it had been before, since the light lady loved him. There was a feverish flush on his face, a joyous gleam in his dark eye, and a self-satisfied smile lighting up all his features, which led her to believe at first that he had been drinking deeply; and secondly, that by some means or other he had succeeded in collecting the vast sum she had required of him, as the unworthy price of future favours.

In a minute or two, the voluptuous strain ended; and, ere she knew that any stranger listened to her amatory warblings, the arm of Curius was wound about her slender waist, and his half-laughing voice was ringing in her ear,

"Well sung, my lovely Greek, and daintily advised!—By my faith! sweet one, I will take thee at thy word!"

"No! no!" cried the girl, extricating herself from his arms, by an elastic spring, before his lips could touch her cheek. "No! no! you shall not kiss me. Kiss Fulvia, she is handsomer than I am, and loves you too. Come, Myrrha, let us leave them."

And, with an arch smile and coquettish toss of her pretty head, she darted through the door, and was followed instantly by the other slave-girl, well trained to divine the wishes of her mistress.

"Ægle is right, by Venus!" exclaimed Curius, drawing nearer to his mistress; "you are more beautiful to-night than ever."

"Flatterer!" murmured the lady, suffering him to enfold her in his arms, and taste her lips for a moment. But the next minute she withdrew herself from his embrace, and said, half-smiling, half-abashed, "But flattery will not pay my debts. Have you brought me the moneys for Alfenus, my sweet Curius? the hundred thousand sesterces, you promised me?"

"Perish the dross!" cried Curius, fiercely. "Out on it! when I come to you, burning with love and passion, you cast cold water on the flames, by your incessant cry for gold. By all the Gods! I do believe, that you love me only for that you can wring from my purse."

"If it be so," replied the lady, scornfully, "I surely do not love you much; seeing it is three months, since you have brought me so much as a ring, or a jewel for a keepsake! But you should rather speak the truth out plainly, Curius," she continued, in an altered tone, "and confess honestly that you care for me no longer. If you loved me as once you did, you would not leave me to be goaded by these harpies. Know you not—why do I ask? you *do* know that my house, my slaves, nay! that my very jewels and my garments, are mine but upon sufferance. It wants but a few days of the calends of November, and if they find the interest unpaid, I shall be cast forth, shamed, and helpless, into the streets of Rome!"

"Be it so!" answered Curius, with an expression which she could not comprehend. "Be it so! Fulvia; and if it be, you shall have any house in Rome you will, for your abode. What say you to Cicero's, in the Carinæ? or the grand portico of Quintus Catulus, rich with the Cimbric spoils? or, better yet, that of Crassus, with its Hymettian columns, on the Palatine? Aye! aye! the speech of Marcus Brutus was prophetic; who termed it, the other day, the house of *Venus* on the Palatine! And you, my love, shall be the goddess of that shrine! It shall be yours *to-morrow*, if you will—so you will drive away the clouds from that sweet brow, and let those eyes beam forth—by all the Gods!"—he interrupted himself—"I *will* kiss thee!"

"By all the Gods! thou shalt not—now, nor for evermore!" she replied, in her turn growing very angry.—"Thou foolish and mendacious boaster! what? dost thou deem me mad or senseless, to assail me with such drivelling folly? Begone, fool! or I will call my slaves—I *have* slaves yet, and, if it be the last deed of service they do for me, they shall spurn thee, like a dog, from my doors.—Art thou insane, or only drunken, Curius?" she added, breaking off from her impetuous railing, into a cool sarcastic tone, that stung him to the quick.

"You shall see whether of the two, Harlot!" he replied furiously, thrusting his hand into the bosom of his tunic, as if to seek a weapon.

"Harlot!" she exclaimed, springing to her feet, the hot blood rushing to her brow in torrents—"dare you say this to me?"

"Dare! do you call this daring?" answered the savage. "This? what would you call it, then, to devastate the streets of Rome with flame and falchion—to hurl the fabric of the state headlong down from the blazing Capitol—to riot in the gore of senators, patricians, consulars!—What, to aspire to be the lords and emperors of the universe?"

"What mean you?" she exclaimed, moved greatly by his vehemence, and beginning to suspect that this was something more than his mere ordinary boasting and exaggeration. "What can you mean? oh! tell me; if you do love me, as you once did, tell me, Curius!" and with rare artifice she altered her whole manner in an instant, all the expression of eye, lip, tone and accent, from the excess of scorn and hatred, to blandishment and fawning softness.

"No!" he replied sullenly. "I will not tell you—no! You doubt me, distrust me, scorn me—no! I will tell you nothing! I will have all I wish or ask for, on my own terms—you shall grant all, or die!"

And he unsheathed his dagger, as he spoke, and grasping her wrist violently with his left hand, offered the weapon at her throat with his right—"You shall grant all, or die!"

"Never!"—she answered—"never!" looking him steadily yet softly in the face, with her beautiful blue eyes. "To fear I will never yield, whatever I may do, to love or passion. Strike, if you will—strike a weak woman, and so prove your daring—it will be easier, if not so noble, as slaying senators and consuls!"

"Perdition!" cried the fierce conspirator, "I *will* kill her!" And with the word he raised his arm, as if to strike; and, for a moment, the guilty and abandoned sensualist believed that her hour was come.

Yet she shrunk not, nor quailed before his angry eye, nor uttered any cry or supplication. She would have died that moment, as carelessly as she had lived. She would have died, acting out her character to the last sand of life, with the smile on her lip, and the soft languor in her melting eye, in all things an Epicurean.

But the fierce mood of Curius changed. Irresolute, and impotent of evil, in a scarce less degree than he was sanguinary, rash, unprincipled, and fearless, it is not one of the least strange events, connected with a conspiracy the whole of which is strange, and much almost inexplicable, that a man so wise, so sagacious, so deep-sighted, as the arch traitor, should have placed confidence in one so fickle and infirm of purpose.

His knitted brow relaxed, the hardness of his eye relented, he cast the dagger from him.

The next moment, suffering the scarf to fall from her white and dazzling shoulders, the beautiful but bad enchantress flung herself upon his bosom, in the abandonment of her dishevelled beauty, winding her snowy arms about his neck, smothering his voice with kisses.

A moment more, and she was seated on his knee, with his left arm about her waist, drinking with eager and attentive ears, that suffered not a single detail to escape them, the fullest revelation of that atrocious plot, the days, the very hours of action, the numbers, names, and rank of the conspirators!

A woman's infamy rewarded the base villain's double treason! A woman's infamy saved Rome!

Two hours later, the crash and roar of the hurricane and earthquake cut short their guilty pleasures. Curius rushed into the streets headlong, almost deeming that the insurrection might have exploded prematurely, and found it—more than half frustrated.

Fulvia, while yet the thunder rolled, and the blue lightning flashed above her head, and the earth reeled beneath her footsteps, went forth, strong in the resolution of that Roman patriotism, which, nursed by the institutions of the age, and the pride of the haughty heart, stood with her, as it did with so many others, in lieu of any other principle, of any other virtue.

Closely veiled, unattended even by a single slave, that delicate luxurious sinner braved the wild fury of the elements; braved the tumultuous frenzy, and more tumultuous terror, of the disorganised and angry populace; braved the dark superstition, which crept upon her as she marked the awful portents of that night, and half persuaded her to the belief that there were Powers on high, who heeded the ways, punished the crimes of mortals.

And that strange sense grew on her more and more, though she resisted it, incredulous, when after a little while she sat side by side with the wise and virtuous Consul, and marked the calmness, almost divine, of his thoughtful benignant features, as he heard the full details of the awful crisis, heretofore but suspected, in which he stood, as if upon the verge of a scarce slumbering volcano.

What passed between that frail woman, and the wise orator, none ever fully knew. But they parted—on his side with words of encouragement and kindness—on her's with a sense of veneration approaching almost to religious awe.

And the next day, the usurer Alfenus received in full the debt, both principal and interest, which he had long despaired of touching.

But when the Great Man stood alone in his silent study, that strange and unexpected interview concluded, he turned his eyes upward, not looking, even once, toward the sublime bust of Jupiter which stood before him, serene in more than mortal grandeur; extended both his arms, and prayed in solemn accents—

"All thanks to thee, Omnipotent, Ubiquitous, Eternal, One! whom we, vain fools of fancy, adore in many forms, and under many names; invest with the low attributes of our own earthy nature; enshrine in mortal shapes, and human habitations! But thou, who wert, before the round world was, or the blue heaven o'erhung it; who wilt be, when those shall be no longer,—thou pardonest our madness, guidest our blindness, guardest our weakness. Thou, by the basest and most loathed instruments, dost work out thy great ends. All thanks, then, be to thee, by whatsoever name thou wouldest be addressed; to thee, whose dwelling is illimitable space, whose essence is in every thing that we behold, that moves, that is—to thee whom I hail, God! For thou hast given it to me to save my country. And whether I die now, by this assassin's knife, or live a little longer to behold the safety I establish, I have lived long enough, and am content to die!—Whether this death be, as philosophers have told us, a dreamless, senseless, and interminable trance; or, as I sometimes dream, a brief and passing slumber, from which we shall awaken into a purer, brighter, happier being—I have lived long enough! and when thou callest me, will answer to thy summons, glad and grateful! For Rome, at least, survives me, and shall perchance survive, 'till time itself is ended, the Queen of Universal Empire!"

CHAPTER XIV.

THE WARNINGS.

These late eclipses in the sun and moon
Portend no good to us.

KING LEAR.

The morning of the eighteenth of October, the day so eagerly looked forward to by the conspirators, and so much dreaded by the good citizens of the republic, had arrived. And now was seen, as it will oftentimes happen, that when great events, however carefully concealed, are on the point of coming to light, a sort of vague rumour, or indefinite anticipation, is found running through the whole mass of society—a rumour, traceable to no one source, possessing no authority, and deserving no credibility from its origin, or even its distinctness; yet in the main true and correct—an anticipation of I know not what terrible, unusual, and exaggerated issue, yet, after all, not very different from what is really about to happen.

Thus it was at this period; and—though it is quite certain, that on the preceding evening, at the convocation of the senate, no person except Cicero and Paullus, unconnected with the conspiracy, knew anything at all of the intended massacre and conflagration; though no one of the plotters had yet broken faith with his fellows; and though none of the leaders dared avow their schemes openly, even to the discontented populace, with whom they felt no sympathy, and from whom they expected no cordial or general coöperation—it is equally certain that for many days, and even months past, there had been a feverish and excited state of the public mind; an agitation and restlessness of the operative classes; an indistinct and vague alarm of the noble and wealthy orders; which had increased gradually until it was now at its height.

Among all these parties, this restlessness had taken the shape of anticipation, either dreadful or desirable, of some great change, of some strange novelty—though no one, either of the wishers or fearers, could explain what it was he wished or feared—to be developed at the consular comitia.

And amid this confusion, most congenial to his bold and scornful spirit, Catiline stalked, like the arch magician, to and fro, amid the wild and fantastic shapes of terror which he has himself evoked, marking the hopes of this one, as indications of an unknown, yet sure friend; and revelling in the terrors of that, as certain evidences of an enemy too weak and powerless to be formidable to his projects.

It is true, that a year before, previous to Cicero's elevation to the chief magistracy, and previous to the murder of Piso by his own adherents on his way to Spain, the designs of Catiline had been suspected dangerous; and, as such, had contributed to the election of his rival; his own faction succeeding only in carrying in Antonius, the second and least dreaded of their candidates.

Him Cicero, by rare management and much self-sacrifice, had contrived to bring over to the cause of the commonwealth; although he had so far kept his faith with Catiline, as to disclose none, if indeed he knew any of his infamous designs.

In consequence of this defeat, and this subsequent secession of one on whom they had, perhaps, prematurely reckoned, the conspirators, all but their indomitable and unwearied leader, had been for some time paralyzed. And this fact, joined to the extreme caution of their latter proceedings, had tended to throw a shade of doubt over the previous accusation, and to create a sense of carelessness and almost of disbelief in the minds of the majority, as to the real existence of any schemes at all against the commonwealth.

Under all these circumstances, it cannot be doubted, for

a moment, that had Catiline and his friends entertained any real desire of ameliorating the condition of the masses, of extending the privileges, or improving the condition, of the discontented and suffering plebeians, they could have overturned the ancient fabric of Rome's world-conquering oligarchy.

But the truth is, they dreamed of nothing less, than of meddling at all with the condition of the people; on whom they looked merely as tools and instruments for the present, and sources of plunder and profit in the future.

They could not trust the plebeians, because they knew that the plebeians, in their turn, could not trust them.

The dreadful struggles of Marius, Cinna, and Sylla, had convinced those of all classes, who possessed any stake in the well being of the country; any estate or property, however humble, down even to the tools of daily labour, and the occupation of permanent stalls for daily traffic, that it was neither change, nor revolution, nor even larger liberty—much less proscription, civil strife, and fire-raising—but rest, but tranquillity, but peace, that they required.

It was not to the people, therefore, properly so called, but to the dissolute and ruined outcasts of the aristocracy, and to the lowest rabble, the homeless, idle, vicious, drunken *poor*, who having nothing to love, have necessarily all to gain, by havoc and rapine, that the conspirators looked for support.

The first class of these was won, bound by oaths, only less binding than their necessities and desperation, sure guaranties for their good faith.

The second—Catiline well knew that—needed no winning. The first clang of arms in the streets, the first blaze of incendiary flames, no fear but they would rise to rob, to ravish, and slay—ensuring that grand anarchy which he proposed to substitute for the existing state of things, and on which he hoped to build up his own tyrannous and blood-cemented empire.

So stood affairs on the evening of the seventeenth; and, although at times a suspicion—not a fear, for of that he was incapable—flitted across the mind of the traitor, that things were not going on as he could wish them; that the alienation of Paullus Arvina, and the absence of his injured daughter, must probably work together to the discomfiture of the conspiracy; still, as hour after hour passed away, and no discovery was made, he revelled in his anticipated triumph.

Of the interview between Paullus and Lucia, he was as yet unaware; and, with that singular inconsistency which is to be found in almost every mind, although he disbelieved, as a principle, in the existence of honor at all, he yet never doubted that young Arvina would hold himself bound strictly by the pledge of secrecy which he had reiterated, after the frustration of the murderous attempt against his life, in the cave of Egeria.

Nor did he err in his premises; for had not Arvina been convinced that new and more perilous schemes were on the point of being executed against himself, he would have remained silent as to the names of the traitors; however he might have deemed it his duty to reveal the meditated treason.

With his plans therefore all matured, his chief subordinates drilled thoroughly to the performance of their parts, his minions armed and ready, he doubted not in the least, as he gazed on the setting sun, that the next rising of the great luminary would look down on the conflagration of the suburbs, on the slaughter of his enemies, and the triumphant elevation of himself to the supreme command of the vast empire, for which he played so foully.

The morning came, the long desired sun arose, and all his plots were countermined, all his hopes of immediate action paralyzed, if not utterly destroyed.

The Senate, assembled on the previous evening at a moment's notice, had been taken by surprise so completely by the strange revelations made to them by their Consul, that not one of the advocates or friends of Catiline arose to say one syllable in his defence; and he himself, quick-witted, ready, daring as he was, and fearing neither man nor God, was for once thunderstricken and astonished.

The address of the Consul was short, practical, and to the point; and the danger he foretold to the order was so terrible, while the inconvenience of deferring the elections was so small, and its occurrence so frequent—a sudden tempest, the striking of the standard on the Janiculum, the interruption of a tribune, or the slightest informality in the augural rites sufficing to interrupt them—that little objection was made in any quarter, to the motion of Cicero, that the comitia should be delayed, until the matter could be thoroughly investigated. For he professed only as yet to possess a clue, which he promised hereafter to unravel to the end.

Catiline had, however, so far recovered from his consternation, that he had risen to address the house, when the first words he uttered were drowned by a strange and unearthly sound, like the rumbling of ten thousand chaiots over a stony way, beginning, as it seemed, underneath their feet, and rising gradually until it died away over head in the murky air. Before there was time for any comment on this extraordinary sound, a tremulous motion crept through the marble pavements, increasing every moment, until the doors flew violently open, and the vast columns and thick walls of the stately temple reeled visibly in the dread earthquake.

Nor was this all, for as the portals opened, in the black skies, right opposite the entrance, there stood, glaring with red and lurid light, a bearded star or comet; which, to the terror-stricken eyes of the Fathers, seemed a portentous sword, brandished above the city.

The groans and shrieks of the multitude, rushed in with an appalling sound to increase their superstitious awe; and to complete the whole, a pale and ghastly messenger was ushered into the house, announcing that a bright lambent flame was sitting on the lance-heads of the Prætor's guard, which had been summoned to protect the Senate in its deliberations.

A fell sneer curled the lip of Catiline. He was not even superstitious. Self-vanity and confidence in his own powers, and long impunity in crime, had hardened him, had maddened him, almost to Atheism. Yet he dared not attack the sacred prejudices of the men, whom, but for that occurrence, he had yet hoped to win to their own undoing.

But, as he saw their blanched visages, and heard their mutterings of terror, he saw likewise that an impression was made on their minds, which no words of his could for the present counteract. And, with a sneering smile at fears which he knew not, and a smothered curse at the accident, as he termed it, which had foiled him, he sat down silent.

"The Gods have spoken!" exclaimed Cicero, flinging his arms abroad majestically. "The guilty are struck dumb! The Gods have spoken aloud their sympathy for Rome's peril; and will ye, ye its chosen sons, whose all of happiness and life lie in its sanctity and safety, will ye, I say, love your own country, your own mother, less than the Gods love her?"

The moment was decisive, the appeal irresistible. By acclamation the vote was carried; no need to debate or to divide the House—'that the elections be deferred until the eleventh day before the Calends, and that the Senate meet again to-morrow, shortly after sunrise, to deliberate what shall be done to protect the Republic?'

Morning came, dark indeed, and lurid, and more like the close, than the opening of day. Morning came, but it brought no change with it; for not a head in Rome had lain that night upon a pillow, save those of the unburied dead, or the bedridden. Young men and aged, sick and sound, masters and slaves, had wooed no sleep during the hours of darkness, so terribly, so constantly was it illuminated by the broad flashes of blue lightning, and the strange meteors, which rushed almost incessantly athwart the sky. The winds too had been all unchained in their fury, and went howling like tormented spirits, over the terrified and trembling city.

It was said too, that the shades of the dead had arisen, and were seen mingling in the streets with the living, scarcely more livid than the half-dead spectators of portents so ominous. No rumour so absurd or fanatical, but it found on that night, implicit credence. Some shouted in the streets and open places, that the patricians and the knights were arming their adherents for a promiscuous massacre of the people. Some, that the gladiators had broken loose, and slain thousands of citizens already! Some, that there was a Gallic tumult, and that the enemy would be at the gates in the morning! Some that the Gods had judged Rome to destruction!

And so they raved, and roared, and sometimes fought; and would have rioted tremendously; for many of the commoner conspirators were abroad, ready to take advantage of any casual incident to breed an affray; but that a strong force of civil magistrates patrolled the streets with armed attendants; and that, during the night several cohorts were brought in, from the armies of Quintus Marcius Rex, and Quintus Metellus Creticus, with all their armor and war weapons, in heavy marching order; and occupied the Capitol, the Palatine, and the Janiculum, and all the other prominent and commanding points of the city, with an array that set opposition at defiance.

So great, however, were the apprehensions of many of the nobles, that Rome was on the eve of a servile insurrection, that many of them armed their freedmen, and imprisoned all their slaves; while others, the more generous and milder, who thought they could rely on the attachment of their people, weaponed their slaves themselves, and fortified their isolated dwellings against the anticipated onslaught.

Thus passed that terrible and tempestuous night; the roar of the elements, unchained as they were, and at their work of havoc, not sufficing to drown the dissonant and angry cries of men, the clash of weapons, and the shrill clamor of women; which made Rome more resemble the Pandemonium than the metropolis of the world's most civilized and mightiest nation.

But now morning had come at length; and gradually, as the storm ceased, and the heavens resumed their natural appearance, the terrors and the fury of the multitude subsided; and, partly satisfied by the constant and well-timed proclamations of the magistrates, partly convinced that for the moment there was no hope of successful outrage, and yet more wearied out with their own turbulent vehemence, whether of fear or anger, the crowd began to retire to their houses, and the streets were left empty and silent.

As the day dawned, there was no banner hoisted on the Janiculum, although its turrets might be seen bristling with the short massive javelins of the legions, and gleaming with the tawny light that flashed from their brazen casques and corslets.

There was no augural tent pitched on the hills without the city walls, wherefrom to take the auspices.

And above all, there were no loud and stirring calls of

the brazen trumpets of the centuries, to summon forth the civic army of the Roman people to the Campus, there to elect their rulers for the ensuing year.

It was apparent therefore to all men, that the elections would not be held that day, though none knew clearly wherefore they had been deferred.

While the whole city was loud with turbulent confusion —for, as morning broke, and it was known that the comitia were postponed, the agitation of terror succeeded to that of insubordination—Hortensia and her daughter sat together, pale, anxious, and heartsick, yet firm and free from all unworthy evidences of dismay.

During the past night, which had been to both a sleepless one, they had sate listening, lone and weak women, to the roar of tumultuous streets, and expecting at every moment they knew not what of violence and outrage.

Paullus Arvina had come in once to reassure them: and informed them that the vigilance of the Consul had been crowned with success, and that the danger of a conflict in the streets was subsiding every moment.

Still, the care which he bestowed on examining the fastenings of the doors, and such windows as looked into the streets, the earnestness with which he inculcated watchful heed to the armed slaves of the household, and the positive manner in which he insisted on leaving Thrasea and a dozen of his own trustiest men to assist Hortensia's people, did more to obliterate the hopes his own words would otherwise have excited, than the words themselves to excite them.

Nor was it, indeed, to be wondered that Hortensia should be liable, above other women, not to base terror,— for of that from her high character she was incapable— but to a settled apprehension and distrust of the Roman Populace.

It was now four-and-twenty years since the city had been disturbed by plebeian violence or aristocratic vengeance. Twenty-four years ago, the avenging sword of Sylla had purged the state of its bloodthirsty demagogues, and their brute followers; twenty-four years ago his powerful hand had reestablished Rome's ancient constitution, full of checks and balances, which secured equal rights to every Roman citizen; which secured all equality, in short to all men, save that which no human laws can give, equality of social rank, and equality of wealth.

The years, however, which had gone before that restoration, the dreadful massacres and yet more dreadful proscriptions of Cinna and Marius, had left indelible and sanguinary traces on the ancestral tree of many a noble house; and on none deeper than on that of Hortensia's family.

Her brother, Caius Julius, an orator second to none in those days, had been murdered by the followers of Marius, almost before his sister's eyes, with circumstances of appalling cruelty. Her house had been forced open by the infuriate rabble, her husband hewn down with unnumbered wounds, on his own hearth-stone, and her first born child tossed upon the revolutionary pike heads.

Her husband indeed recovered, almost miraculously, from his wounds, and lived to see retribution fall upon the guilty partizans of Marius; but he was never well again, and after languishing for years, died at last of the wounds he received on that bloody day.

Good cause, then, had Hortensia to tremble at the tender mercies of the people.

Nor, though they struck the minds of these high-born ladies with less perplexity and awe than the vulgar souls without, were the portents and horrors of the heaven, without due effect. No mind in those days, however clear and enlightened, but held some lingering belief that such things were ominous of coming wrath, and sent by the Gods to inform their faithful worshippers.

It was moreover fresh in her memory, how two years before, during the consulship of Cotta and Torquatus, in a like terrible night-storm, the fire from heaven had stricken down the highest turrets of the capitol, melted the brazen tables of the law, and scathed the gilded effigy of Romulus and Remus, sucking their shaggy foster-mother, which stood on the Capitoline.

The augurs in those days, collected from Etruria and all parts of Italy, after long consultation, had proclaimed that unless the Gods should be appeased duly, the end of Rome and her empire was at hand.

And now—what though for ten whole days consecutive the sacred games went on; what though nothing had been omitted whereby to avert the immortal indignation

—did not this heaven-born tempest prove that the wrath was not soothed, that the decree yet stood firm?

In such deep thoughts, and in the strong excitement of such expectation, Hortensia and her daughter had passed that awful night; not without high instructions from the elder lady, grave and yet stirring narratives of the great men of old—how they strove fiercely, energetically, while strife could avail anything; and how, when the last hope was over, they folded their hands in stern and awful resignation, and met their fate unblenching, and with but one care—that the decorum of their deaths should not prove unworthy the dignity of their past lives.

Not without generous and noble resolutions on the part of both, that they too would not be found wanting.

But there was nothing humble, nothing soft, in their stern and proud submission to the inevitable necessity. Nothing of love toward the hand which dealt the blow —nothing of confidence in supernal justice, much less in supernal mercy! Nothing of that sweet hope, that undying trust, that consciousness of self-unworthiness, that full conviction of a glorious future, which renders so beautiful and happy the submission of a dying christian.

No! there were none of these things; for to the wisest and best of the ancients, the foreshadowings of the soul's immortality were dim, faint, and uncertain. The legends of their mythology held up such pictures of the sensuality and vice of those whom they called Gods, that it was utterly impossible for any sound understanding to accept them. And deep thinkers were consequently driven into pure Deism, coupled too often with the Epicurean creed, that the Great Spirit was too grand and too sublime to trouble himself with the brief doings of mortality.

The whole scope of the Roman's hope and ambition, then, was limited to this world; or, if there was a longing for anything beyond the term of mortality, it was for a name, a memory, an immortality of good report.

And pride, which the christian, better instructed, knows to be the germ and root of all sin, was to the Roman, the sole spring of honourable action, the sole source of virtue.

Now, with the morning, quiet was restored both to the angry skies, and to the restless city.

Worn out with anxiety, and watching, sleep fell upon the eyes of Julia, as she sat half recumbent in a large softly-cushioned chair of Etruscan bronze. Her fair head fell back on the crimson pillow, with all its wealth of auburn ringlets flowing dishevelled; and that soft still shadow, which is yet, in its beautiful serenity, half terrible, so nearly is it allied to the shadow of that sleep from which there comes no waking, fell over her pale features.

The mother gazed on her for a moment, with more gentleness in her eye, and a milder smile on her face, than her indomitable pride often permitted her to manifest.

"She sleeps"—she said, looking at her wistfully—"she sleeps! Aye! the young sleep easily, even in their affliction. They sleep, and forget their sorrows, and awaken, either to fresh woes, as soon to be obliterated, or to vain joys, yet briefer, and more fleeting. Thoughtlessness to the young—anguish to the old—such is mortality! And what beyond?—aye, what?—what that we should so toil, so suffer, to be virtuous? Is it a dream, all a dream—this futurity? I fear so"—and, with the words, she lapsed into a fit of solemn meditation, and stood for many minutes silet, and absorbed. Then a keen light came into her dark eyes, a flash of animation coloured her pale cheeks, she stretched her arms aloft, and in a clear sonorous voice—"No! no!" she said, "Honour—honour—immortal honour; thou, at least, art no dream—thou art worth dying, suffering, aye! worth *living* to obtain! For what is life but the deeper sorrow, to the more virtuous and the nobler?"

A few minutes longer she stood gazing on her daughter's beautiful face, until the sound of voices louder than usual, and a slight bustle, in the peristyle, attracted her attention. Then, after throwing a pallium, or shawl, of richly embroidered woollen stuff over the fair form of the sleeper, she opened the door leading to the garden colonnade, and left the room silently.

Scarcely had Hortensia disappeared, before the opposite door, by which the saloon communicated with the atrium, was opened, and a slave entered, bearing a small folded note, secured by a waxen seal, on a silver plate.

He approached Julia's chair, apparently in some hesitation, as if he felt that it was his duty, and was yet half afraid to awaken her. At length, however, he made up his mind, and addressed a word or two to her, which were sufficiently distinct to arouse her—for she started up and gazed wildly about her—but left no clear impression of their meaning on her mind.

This, however, the man did not appear to notice; at all events, he did not wait to observe the effect of his communication, but quitted the room hastily, and in considerable trepidation, leaving the note on the table.

Julia was sleeping very heavily, at the moment when she was so startled from her slumber; and, as is not unfrequently the case, a sort of bewilderment and nervous agitation fell upon her, as she recovered her senses. Perhaps she had been dreaming, and the imaginary events of her dream had blended themselves with the real occurrence which awakened her. But for a minute or two, though she saw the note, and the person who laid it on the table, she could neither bring it to her mind who that person was, nor divest herself of the impression that there was something both dangerous and supernatural in what had passed.

In a little while this feeling passed away, and, though still nervous and trembling, the young girl smiled at her own alarm, as she took up the billet, which was directed to herself in a delicate feminine hand, with the usual form of superscription—

"To Julia Serena, health"—

although the writer's name was omitted.

She gazed at it for a moment, wondering from whom it could come; since she had no habitual correspondent, and the hand-writing, though beautiful, was strange to her. She opened it, and read, her wonder and agitation increasing with every line—

"You love Paullus Arvina," thus it ran, "and are loved by him. He is worthy all your affection. Are you worthy of him? I know not. I love him also, but alas! less happy, am not loved again, nor hope to be, nor indeed deserve it! They tell me you are beautiful; I have seen you, and yet I know not—they told me once that I too was beautiful, and yet I know not! I know this only, that I am desperate, and base, and miserable! Yet fear me not, nor mistake me. I love Paullus, yet would not have him mine, now; no! not to be happy—as to be his would render me. Yet had it not been for you, I might have been virtuous, honourable, happy, *his*—for winning him from me, you won from me hope; and with hope virtue; and with virtue honour! Ought I not then to hate you, Julia? Perchance I ought—to do so were at least Roman—and hating to avenge! Perchance, if I *hoped*, I should. But hoping nothing, I hate nothing, dread nothing, and wish nothing.—Yea! by the Gods! I wish to know Paullus happy—yea! more, I wish, even at cost of my own misery, to make him happy. Shall I do so, by making him yours, Julia? I think so, for be sure—be sure, he loves you. Else had he yielded to my blandishments, to my passion, to my beauty! for I am—by the Gods! I am, though he sees it not, as beautiful as thou. And I am proud likewise—or was proud once—for misery has conquered pride in me; or what is weaker yet, and baser—love!

"I think you will make him happy. You can if you will. Do so, by all the Gods! I adjure you do so; and if you do not, tremble!—tremble, I say—for think, if I sacrifice myself to win bliss for him—think, girl, how gladly, how triumphantly, I would destroy a rival, who should fail to do that, for which alone I spare her.

"Spare her! nay, but much more; for I can save her—can and will.

"Strange things will come to pass ere long, and terrible; and to no one so terrible as to you.

"There is a man in Rome, so powerful, that the Gods, only, if there be Gods, can compare with him—so haughty in ambition, that stood he second in Olympus, he would risk all things to be first—so cruel, that the dug-drawn Hyrcanian tigress were pitiful compared to him—so reckless of all things divine or human, that, did his own mother stand between him and his vengeance, he would strike through her heart to gain it.

"This man hath Paullus made his foe—he hath crossed his path; he hath *foiled* him!

"HE never spared man in his wrath, or woman in his passion.

"He hateth Paullus!

"He hath looked on Julia!

"Think, then, when lust and hate spur such a man together, what will restrain him.

"Now mark me, and you shall yet be safe. All means will be essayed to win you, for he would torture Paul by making him his slave, ere he make you his victim.

"And Paul may waver. He hath wavered once. Chance only, and I, rescued him! I can do no more, for Rome must know me no longer! See, then, that thou hold him constant in the right—firm for his country! So may he defy secret spite, as he hath defied open violence.

"Now for thyself—beware of women! Go not forth alone ever, or without armed followers! Sleep not, but with a woman in thy chamber, and a watcher at thy door! Eat not, nor drink, any thing abroad; nor at home, save that which is prepared by known hands, and tasted by the slave who serves it!

"Be true to Paullus, and yourself, and you have a friend ever watchful. So fear not, nor despond!

"Fail me—and, failing truth and honour, failing to make Paullus happy, you *do* fail me! Fail me, and nothing, in the world's history or fable, shall match the greatness of my vengeance—of your anguish!

"Fail me! and yours shall be, for ages, the name that men shall quote, when they would tell of untold misery, of utter shame, and desolation, and despair.

"Farewell."

The letter dropped from her hand; she sat aghast and speechless, terrified beyond measure, and yet unable to determine, or divine, even, to what its dark warnings and darker denunciations pointed.

Just at this instant, as between terror and amazement she was on the verge of fainting, a clanging step was heard without; the crimson draperies that covered the door, were put aside; and, clad in glittering armour, Paullus Arvina stood before her.

She started up, with a strange haggard smile flashing across her pallid face, staggered a step or two to meet him, and sank in an agony of tears upon his bosom.

CHAPTER XV.

THE CONFESSION.

To err is human; to forgive—divine!

The astonishment of Paullus, at this strange burst of feeling on the part of one usually so calm, so self-controlled, and seemingly so unimpassioned as that sweet lady, may be more easily imagined than described.

That she, whose maidenly reserve had never heretofore permitted the slightest, the most innocent freedom of her accepted lover, should cast herself thus into his arms, should rest her head on his bosom, was in itself enough to surprise him; but when to this were added the violent convulsive sobs, which shook her whole frame, the flood of tears, which streamed from her eyes, the wild and disjointed words, which fell from her pale lips, he was struck dumb with something not far removed from terror.

That it was fear, which shook her thus, he could not credit; for during all the fearful sounds and rumours of the past night, she had been as firm as a hero.

Yet he knew not, dared not think, to what other cause he might attribute it.

He spoke to her soothingly, tenderly, but his voice faltered as he spoke.

"Nay! nay! be not alarmed, dear girl!" he said. The tumults are all, long since, quelled; the danger has all vanished with the darkness, and the storm. Cheer up, my own, sweet, Julia."

And, as he spoke, he passed his arm about her graceful form, and drew her closer to his bosom.

But whether it was this movement, or something in his words that aroused her, she started from his arms in a moment; and stood erect and rigid, pale still and agitated, but no longer trembling. She raised her hands to her brow, and put away the profusion of rich auburn ringlets, which had fallen down dishevelled over her eyes, and gazed at him stedfastly, strangely, as she had never gazed at him before.

"Your own Julia!" she said, in slow accents, scarce louder than a whisper, but full of strong and painful meaning. "Oh! I adjure you, by the Gods! by all you love! or hope! Are you false to me, Paullus!"

"False! Julia!" he exclaimed, starting, and the blood rushing consciously to his bold face.

"I am answered!" she said, collecting herself, with a desperate effort. "It is well—the Gods guard you!—Leave me!"

"Leave you!" he cried. "By earth, and sea, and heaven, and all that they contain! I know not what you mean."

"Know you this writing, then?" she asked him, reaching the letter from the table, and holding it before his eyes.

"No more than I know, what so strangely moves you," he answered; and she saw, by the unaffected astonishment which pervaded all his features, that he spoke truly.

"Read it," she said, somewhat more composed; "and tell me, who is the writer of it. You must know."

Before he had read six lines, it was clear to him that it must come from Lucia, and no words can describe the agony, the eager intense torture of anticipation, with which he perused it, devouring every word, and at every word expecting to find the damning record of his falsehood inscribed in characters, that should admit of no denial.

Before, however, he had reached the middle of the letter, he felt that he could bear the scrutiny of that pale girl no longer; and, lowering the strip of vellum on which it was written, met her eye firmly.

For he was resolute for once to do the true and honest thing, let what might come of it. The weaker points of his character were vanishing rapidly, and the last few eventful days had done the work of years upon his mind; and all that work was salutary.

She, too, read something in the expression of his eye, which led her to hope—what, she knew not; and she smiled faintly, as she said—

"You know the writer, Paullus?"

"Julia, I know her," he replied steadily.

"Her!" she said, laying an emphasis on the word, but how affected by it Arvina could not judge. "It *is* then a woman?"

"A very young, a very beautiful, a very wretched, girl!" he answered.

"And you love her?" she said, with an effort at firmness, which itself proved the violence of her emotion.

"By your life! Julia, I do not!" he replied, with an energy, that spoke well for the truth of his asseveration.

"Nor ever loved her?"

"Nor ever—*loved* her, Julia." But he hesitated a little as he said it; and laid a peculiar stress on the word loved, which did not escape the anxious ears of the lovely being, whose whole soul hung suspended on his speech.

"Why not?" she asked, after a moment's pause, "if she be so very young, and so very beautiful?"

"I might answer, because I never saw her, 'till I loved one more beautiful. But—"

"But you will not!" she interrupted him vehemently. "Oh! if you love me, if you *do* love me, Paullus, do not answer me so."

"And wherefore not?" he asked her, half smiling, though little mirthful in his heart, at her impetuosity.

"Because if you descend to flatter," answered the fair girl quietly, "I shall be sure that you intended to deceive me."

"It would be strictly true, notwithstanding. For though, as she says, we met years ago, she was but a child then; and, since that time, I never saw her until four or five days ago—"

"And since then, how often?" Julia again interrupted him; for, in the intensity of her anxiety, she could not wait the full answer to one question, before another suggested itself to her mind, and found voice at the instant.

"Once, Julia."

"Only once?"

"Once only, by the Gods!"

"You have not told me wherefore it was, that you never loved her!"

"Have I not told you, that I never saw her till a few days, a few hours, I might have said, ago? and does not that tell you wherefore, Julia?"

"But there is something more. There is another reason. Oh! tell me, I adjure you, by all that you hold dearest, tell me!"

"There is another reason. I told you that she was very young, and very beautiful; but, Julia, she was also very guilty!"

"Guilty!" exclaimed the fair girl, blushing fiery red, "guilty of loving you! Oh! Paullus! Paullus!" and between shame, and anger, and the repulsive shock that every pure and feminine mind experiences in hearing of a sister's frailty, she buried her face in her hands, and wept aloud.

"Guilty, before I ever heard her name, or knew that she existed," answered the young man, fervently; but his heart smote him somewhat, as he spoke; though what he said was but the simple truth, and it was well for him perhaps at the present moment, that Julia did not see his face. For there was much perturbation in it, and it is like that she would have judged even more hardly of that perturbation than it entirely deserved. He paused for a moment, and then added,

"But if the guilt of woman can be excusable at all, she can plead more in extenuation of her errors, than any of her sex that ever fell from virtue. She is most penitent; and might have been, but for fate and the atrocious wickedness of others, a most noble being—as she is now a most glorious ruin."

There was another pause, during which neither spoke or moved, Julia overpowered by the excess of her feelings—he by the painful consciousness of wrong; the difficulty of explaining, of extenuating his own conduct; and above all, the dread of losing the enchanting creature, whom he had never loved so deeply or so truly as he did now, when he had well nigh forfeited all claim to her affection.

At léngth, she raised her eyes timidly to his, and said, "This is all very strange—there must be much, that I have a right to hear."

"There is much, Julia!—much that will be very painful for me to tell; and yet more so for you to listen to."

"And will you tell it to me?"

"Julia, I will!"

"And all? and truly?"

"And all, and truly, if I tell you at all; but you—"

"First," she said, interrupting him, "read that strange letter to the end. Then we will speak more of these things. Nay?" she continued, seeing that he was about to speak, "I will have it so. It must be so, or all is at an end between us two, now, and for ever. I do not wish to watch you; there is no meanness in my mind, Paullus, no jealousy! I am too proud to be jealous. Either you are worthy of my affection, or unworthy; if the latter, I cast you from me without one pang, one sorrow;—if the first, farther words are needless. Read that wild letter to the end. I will turn my back to you." And seating herself at the table, she took up a piece of embroidery, and made as if she would have fixed her mind upon it. But Paullus saw, as his glance followed her, that, notwithstanding the firmness of her words and manner, her hand trembled so much that she could by no means thread her needle.

He gazed on her for a moment with passionate, despairing love, and as he gazed, his spirit faltered, and he doubted. The evil genius whispered to his soul, that truth must alienate her love, must sever her from him for ever. There was a sharp and bitter struggle in his heart for that moment—but it passed; and the better spirit was again strong and clear within him.

"No!" he said to himself, "No! I have done with fraud, and falsehood! I will not win her by a lie! If by the truth I must lose her, be it so! I will be true, and at least I can—die!"

Thereon, without another word, he read the letter to the end, neither faltering, nor pausing; and then walked calmly to the table, and laid it down, perfectly resolute and tranquil, for his mind was made up for the worst.

"Have you read it?" she asked, and her voice trembled, as much as her hand had done before.

"I have, Julia, to the end. It is very sad—and much of it is true."

"And who is the girl, who wrote it?"

"Her name is Lucia Orestilla."

"Orestilla! Ye Gods! ye Gods! the shameless wife of the arch villain Catiline!"

"Not so—but the wretched, ruined daughter of that abandoned woman!"

"Call her not woman! By the Gods that protect purity! call her not woman! Did she not prompt the wretch to poison his own son! Oh! call her anything but woman! But what—what—in the name of all that is good or holy, can have brought you to know that awful being's daughter?"

"First, Julia, you must promise me never, to mortal ears, to reveal what I now disclose to you."

"Have you forgotten, Paullus, that I am yet but a young maiden, and that I have a mother?"

"Hortensia!" exclaimed the youth, starting back, aghast; for he felt that from her clear eye and powerful judgment nothing could be concealed, and that her iron will would yield in nothing to a woman's tenderness, a woman's mercy.

"Hortensia," replied the girl gently, "the best, the wisest, and the tenderest of mothers."

"True? she is all that you say—more than all! But she is resolute, withal, as iron; and stern, and cold, and unforgiving in her anger!"

"And do you need so much forgiveness, Paullus?"

"More, I fear, than my Julia's love will grant me."

"I think, my Paullus, you do not know the measure of a girl's honest love. But may I tell Hortensia? If not, you have said enough. What is not fitting for a girl to speak to her own mother, it is not fitting that she should hear at all—least of all from a man, and that man—her lover!"

"It is not that, my Julia. But what I have to say contains many lives—mine among others! contains Rome's safety, nay! existence! One whisper breathed abroad, or lisped in a slave's hearing, were the World's ruin. But be it as you will—as you think best yourself and wisest. If you will, tell Hortensia."

"I shall tell her, Paullus. I tell her everything. Since I could babble my first words, I never had a secret from her!"

"Be it so, sweet one. Now I implore you, hear me to the end, before you judge me, and then judge mercifully, as the Gods are merciful, and mortals prone to error."

"And will you tell me the whole truth?"

"The whole."

"Say on, then. I will hear you to the end; and your guilt must be great, Paullus, if you require a more partial arbitress."

It was a trying and painful task, that was forced upon him, yet he went through it nobly. At every word the difficulties grew upon him. At every word the temptation, to swerve from the truth, increased. At every word the dread of losing her, the agony of apprehension, the dull cold sense of despair, waxed heavier, and more stunning. The longer he spoke, the more certain he felt that by his own words he was destroying his own hope; yet he manned his heart stoutly, resisted the foul tempter, and, firm in the integrity of his present purpose, laid bare the secrets of his soul.

Beginning from his discovery of Medon's corpse upon the Esquiline, he now narrated to her fully all that had passed, including much that in his previous tale he had omitted. He told of his first meeting with Cataline upon the Cælian; of his visit to Cicero; of his strange conversation with the cutler Volero; of his second encounter with the traitor in the field of Mars, not omitting the careless accident by which he revealed to him Volero's recognition of the weapon. He told her of the banquet, of the art with which Catiline plied him with wine, of the fascinations of that fair fatal girl. And here, he paused awhile, reluctant to proceed. He would have given worlds, had he possessed them, to catch one glance of her averted eye, to read her features but one moment. But she sat, with her back toward him, her head downcast, tranquil and motionless, save that a tremulous shivering at times ran through her frame perceptible.

He was compelled perforce to continue his narration; and now he was bound to confess that, for the moment, he had been so bewitched by the charms of the siren, that he

20

had bound himself by the fatal oath, scarce knowing what he swore, which linked him to the fortunes of the villain father. Slightly he touched on that atrocity of Catiline, by telling which aloud he dared not sully her pure ears. He then related clearly and succinctly the murder of the cutler Volero, his recognition of the murderer, the forced deception which he had used reluctantly toward Cicero, and the suspicions and distrust of that great man. And here again he paused, hoping that she would speak, and interrupt him, if it were even to condemn, for so at least he should be relieved from the sickening apprehension, which almost choked his voice.

Still, she was silent, and, in so far as he could judge, more tranquil than before. For the quick tremors had now ceased to shake her, and her tears, he believed, had ceased to flow.

But was not this the cold tranquillity of a fixed resolution, the firmness of a desperate, self-controlling effort?

He could endure the doubt no longer. And, in a softer and more humble voice,

"Now, then," he said, "you know the measure of my sin—the extent of my falsehood. All the ill of my tale is told, faithfully, frankly. What remains, is unmixed with evil. Say, then; have I sinned, Julia, beyond the hope of forgiveness? If to confess that, my eyes dazzled with beauty, my blood inflamed with wine, my better self drowned in a tide of luxury unlike aught I had ever known before, my senses wrought upon by every art, and every fascination—if to confess, that my head was bewildered, my reason lost its way for a moment—though my heart never, never failed in its faith—and by the hopes, frail hopes, which I yet cling to of obtaining you—the dread of losing you for ever! Julia, by these I swear, my heart never did fail or falter! If, I say, to confess this be sufficient, and I stand thus condemned and lost for ever, spare me the rest—I may as well be silent!"

She paused a moment, ere she answered; and it was only with an effort, choking down a convulsive sob, that she found words at all.

"Proceed," she said, "with your tale. I cannot answer you."

But, catching at her words, with all the elasticity of

youthful hope, he fancied that she *had* answered him, and cried joyously and eagerly—

"Sweet Julia, then you can, you will forgive me."

"I have not said so, Paullus," she began. But he interrupted her, ere she could frame her sentence—

"No! dearest; but your speech implied it, and—"

But here, in her turn, she interrupted him, saying—

"Then, Paullus, did my speech imply what I did not intend. For I have *not* forgiven—do not know if I can forgive, all that has passed. All depends on that which is to come. You made me promise not to interrupt your tale. I have not done so; and, in justice, I have the right to ask that you should tell it out, before you claim my final answer. So I say, once again, Proceed."

Unable, from the steadiness of her demeanour, so much even as to conjecture what were her present feelings, yet much dispirited at finding his mistake, the young man proceeded with his narrative. Gaining courage, however, as he continued speaking, the principal difficulties of his story being past, he warmed and spoke more feelingly, more eloquently, with every word he uttered.

He told her of the deep depression, which had fallen on him the following morning, when her letter had called him to the house of Hortensia. He again related the attack made on him by Catiline, on the same evening, in Egeria's grotto; and spoke of the absolute despair, in which he was plunged, seeing the better course, yet unable to pursue it; aiming at virtue, yet forced by his fatal oath to follow vice; marking clearly before him the beacon light of happiness and honour, yet driven irresistibly into the gulf of misery, crime, and destruction. He told her of Lucia's visit to his house; how she released him from his fatal oath! disclaimed all right to his affection, nay! to his respect, even, and esteem! encouraged him to hold honour in his eye, and in the scorn of consequence to follow virtue for its own sake! He told her, too, of the conspiracy, in all its terrible details of atrocity and guilt—that dark and hideous scheme of treason, cruelty, lust, horror, from which he had himself escaped so narrowly.

Then, with a glow of conscious rectitude, he proved to her that he had indeed repented; that he was now, howsoever he might have been deceived into error and to the brink of crime, firm, and resolved; a champion of the right; a defender of his country; trusted and chosen by the Great Consul; and, in proof of that trust, commissioned by him now to lead his troop of horsemen to Præneste, a strong fortress, near at hand, which there was reason to expect might be assailed by the conspirators.

"And now, my tale is ended," he said. "I did hope there would have been no need to reveal these things to you; but from the first, I have been resolved, if need were, to open to you my whole heart—to show you its dark spots, as its bright ones. I have sinned, Julia, deeply, against you! Your purity, your love, should have guarded me! Yet, in a moment of treacherous self-confidence, my head grew dizzy, and I fell. But oh! believe me, Julia, my heart never once betrayed you! Now say—can you pardon me—trust me—love me—be mine, as you promised? If not—speed me on my way, and my first battle-field shall prove my truth to Rome and Julia."

"Oh! this is very sad, my Paullus," she replied; "very humiliating—very, very bitter. I had a trust so perfect in your love. I could as soon have believed the sunflower would forget to turn to the day-god, as that Paul would forget Julia. I had a confidence so high, so noble, in your proud, untouched virtue. And yet I find, that at the first alluring glance of a frail beauty, you fall off from your truth to me—at the first whispering temptation of a demon, you half fall off from patriotism—honour—virtue! Forgive you, Paullus! I can forgive you readily. For well, alas! I know that the best of us all are very frail, and prone to evil. Love you? alas! for me, I do as much as ever—but say, yourself, how can I trust you? how can I be yours? when the next moment you may fall again into temptation, again yield to it. And then, what would then remain to the wretched Julia, but a most miserable life, and an untimely grave?"

The proud man bowed his head in bitter anguish; he buried his face in his hands; he gasped, and almost groaned aloud, in his great agony. His heart confessed the truth of all her words, and it was long ere he could answer her. Perhaps he would not have collected courage to do so at all, but would have risen in his agony of pride and despair, and gone his way to die, heart-broken, hopeless, a lost man.

But she—for her heart yearned to her lover—arose and crossed the room with noiseless step to the spot where he sat, and laid her fair hand gently on his shoulder, and whispered in her voice of silvery music,

"Tell me, Paullus, how can I trust you?"

"Because I have told you all this, truly! Think you I had humbled myself thus, had I not been firm to resist? think you I have had no temptation to deceive you, to keep back a part, to palliate? and lo! I have told you all—the shameful, naked truth! How can I ever be so bribed again to falsehood, as I have been in this last hour, by hope of winning, and by dread of losing you, my soul's idol? Because I have been true, now to the last, I think that you may trust me."

"Are you sure, Paullus?" she said, with a soft sad smile, yet suffering him to retain the little hand he had imprisoned while he was speaking—"very, very sure?"

"Will you believe me, Julia?"

"Will you be true hereafter, Paullus?"

"By all—"

"Nay! swear not by the Gods," she interrupted him; "they say the Gods laugh at the perjury of lovers! But oh! remember, Paullus, that if you were indeed untrue to Julia, she could but die!"

He caught her to his heart, and she for once resisted not; and, for the first time permitted, his lips were pressed to hers in a long, chaste, holy kiss.

"And now," he said, "my own, own Julia, I must say fare you well. My horse awaits me at your door—my troopers are half the way hence to Præneste."

"Nay!" she replied, blushing deeply, "but you will surely see Hortensia, ere you go."

"It must be, then, but for a moment," he answered. "For duty calls me; and *you* must not tempt me to break my new-born resolution. But say, Julia, will you tell all these things to Hortensia?"

She smiled, and laid her hand upon his mouth; but he kissed it, and drew it down by gentle force, and repeated his question,

"Will you?"

"Not a word of it, Paul. Do you think me so foolish?"

"Then I will—one day, but not now. Meanwhile, let us go seek for her."

And, passing his arm around her slender waist, he led her gently from the scene of so many doubts and fears, of so much happiness.

CHAPTER XVI.

THE SENATE.

Most potent, grave, and reverend Seniors.

OTHELLO.

THE second morning had arrived, after that regularly appointed for the Consular elections.

No tumult had occurred, nor any overt act to justify the apprehensions of the people; yet had those apprehensions in no wise abated. The very indistinctness of the rumored terror perhaps increased its weight; and so widespread was the vague alarm, so prevalent the dread and excitement, that in the hagard eyes and pale faces of the frustrated conspirators, there was little, if anything, to call attention; for whose features wore their natural expression, during those fearful days, each moment of which might bring forth massacre and conflagration? Whose, but the great Consul's?

The second morning had arrived; and the broad orb of the newly risen sun, lurid and larger than his wont, as it struggled through the misty haze of the Italian autumn, had scarcely gained sufficient altitude to throw its beams over the woody crest of the Esquiline into the hollow of the Sacred Way.

The slant light fell, however, full on the splendid terraces and shrines of the many-templed Palatine, playing upon their stately porticoes, and tipping their rich capitals with golden lustre.

And at that early hour, the ancient hill was thronged with busy multitudes.

The crisis was at hand—the Senate was in solemn session. The knights were gathered in their force, all armed. The younger members of the patrician houses were mustered with their clients. The fasces of the lictors displayed the broad heads of the axes glittering above the rods, which bound them—the axes, never borne in time of peace, or within the city walls, save upon strange emergency.

In the old temple of Jupiter Stator, chosen on this occasion for the strength of its position, standing on the very brink of the steep declivity of the hill where it overlooked the great Roman forum, that grand assembly sate in grave deliberation.

The scene was worthy of the actors, as were the actors of the strange tragedy in process.

It was the cella, or great circular space of the inner temple. The brazen doors of this huge hall, facing the west, as was usual in all Roman temples, were thrown open; and without these, on the portico, yet so placed that they could hear every word that passed within the building, sat on their benches, five on each side of the door, the ten tribunes* of the people.

Within the great space, surrounded by a double peristyle of tall Tuscan columns, and roofed by a vast dome, richly carved and gilded, but with a circular opening at the summit, through which a flood of light streamed down on the assembled magnates, the Senate was in session.

Immediately facing the doors stood the old Statue of the God, as old, it was believed by some, as the days of Romulus, with the high altar at its base, hung round with votive wreaths, and glittering with ornaments of gold.

Around this altar were grouped the augurs, each clad, as was usual on occasions of high solemnity, in his *trabea*, or robe of horizontal stripes, in white and purple; each holding in his hand his *lituus*, a crooked staff whereby to designate the temples of the heaven, in which to observe the omens.

---

* The Tribunes of the people were, at this period of the Republic, Senators; the Atinian law, the data of which is not exactly fixed, having undoubtedly come into operation soon after A. C. 130. I do not, however, find it mentioned, that their seats were thereupon transferred into the body of the Senate; and I presume that such was not the case; as they were not real senators, but had only the right of speaking without voting, as was the case with all who sat by the virtue of their offices, without regular election.

On every side of the circumference, except that occupied by the altar and the idol, were ranged in circular state the benches of the order.

Immediately to the right of the altar, were placed the curule chairs, rich with carved ivory and crimson cushions, of the two consuls; and behind them, erect, with their shouldered axes, stood the stout lictors.

Cicero, as the first chosen of the consuls, sat next the statue of the God; calm in his outward mien, as the severe and placid features of the marble deity, although within him the soul labored mightily, big with the fate of Rome. Next him Antonius, a stout, bold, sensual-looking soldier, filled his place—worthily, indeed, so far as stature, mien, and bearing were concerned; but with a singular expression in his eye, which seemed to indicate embarrassment, perhaps apprehension.

After these, the presiding officers of the Republic, were present, each according to his rank, the conscript fathers—first, the Prince of the Senate, and then the Consulars, Censorians, and Prætorians, down to those who had filled the lowest office of the state, that of Quæstor, which gave its occupant, after his term of occupancy expired, admission to the grand representative assembly of the commonwealth.

For much as there has been written on all sides of this subject, there now remains no doubt that, from the earliest to the latest age of Rome, the Senate was strictly, although an aristocratical, still an elective representative assembly.

The Censors, themselves, elected by the Patricians out of their own order, in the assembly of the Curiæ, had the appointment of the Senators; but from those only who had filled one of the magistracies, all of which were conferred by the popular vote of the assembly of the centuries; and all of which, at this period of the Republic, might be, and sometimes were, conferred on Plebeians—as in the case of Marius, six times elected Consul in spite of Patrician opposition.

Such was the constitution of the Senate, purely elective, though like all other portions of the Roman constitution, under such checks and balances as were deemed sufficient to ensure it from becoming a democratical assembly.

And such, in fact, it never did become. For having

been at first an elective body chosen from an hereditary aristocracy, it was at that time, save in the varying principles of individuals, wholly aristocratic in its nature. Nor, after the tenure of the various magistracies, which conferred eligibility to the Senate, was thrown open to the plebeians, did any great change follow; since the preponderance of patrician influence in the assembly of the centuries, and the force perhaps of old habit, combined to continue most of the high offices of state in the hands of members of the Old Houses. Again, when plebeians were raised to office, and became, as they were styled, New Men, they speedily were merged in the nobility; and were no less aristocratic in their measures, than the oldest members of the aristocracy.

For when have plebeians, anywhere, when elevated to superior rank, been true to their origin; been other than the fellest persecutors of plebeians?

The senate was therefore still, as it had been, a calm and conservative assembly.

It was not indeed, what it had been, before Marius first, and then Sylla, the avenger, had decimated it of their foes with the sword; and filled the vacancies with unworthy friends and partizans.

Yet it was still a grand, a wise, a noble body—when viewed as a body—and, for the most part, its decisions were worthy of its dignity and power—were sage, conservative, and patriotic.

On this occasion, all motives had conspired to produce a full house; doubt, anger, fear, excitement, curiosity, the love of country, the strong sense of right, the fiery impulses of interest, hate, vengeance, had urged all men of all parties, to be participants in the eventful business of the day.

About five hundred senators were present; men of all ages from thirty-two years* upward—that being the earliest at which a man could fill this eminent seat. But the majority were of those, who having passed the prime of active life, might be considered to have reached the highest of mental power and capacity, removed alike from the

* The age of senatorial eligibility is nowhere distinctly named. But the quæstorship, the lowest office which gave admission to the Curia, required the age of thirty-one in its occupant.

greenness of inconsiderate youth, and the imbecility of extreme old age.

The rare beauty of the Italian race—the strength and symmetry of the unrivalled warrior nation, of which these were, for the most part, the noblest and most striking specimens; the grand flow of the snow-white draperies, faced with the broad crimson laticlave—the classic grace of their positions—the absence of all rigid angular lines, of anything mean or meagre, fantastic or tawdry in the garb of the solemn concourse, rendered the meeting of Rome's Fathers a widely different spectacle from the convention of any other representative assembly, the world has ever witnessed.

There was no flippancy, no affectation, no light converse—The members, young or old, had come thither to perform a great duty, in strength of purpose, singleness of spirit—and all felt deeply the weight of the present moment, the vastness of the interests concerned. The good and the true were there convened to defend the majesty, perhaps the safety, of their country—the wicked to strive for interest, for revenge, for life itself!

For Catiline well knew, and had instilled his knowledge carefully into the minds of his confederates, that now to conquer was indeed to triumph; that now to be defeated was to fail, probably, forever—to die, it was most like, by the dread doom of the Tarpeian.

Not one of the conspirators but was in his appointed place, firm, seemingly unconscious, and unruffled; and as the eye of the great consul glanced from one to another of that guilty throng, he could not, even amid his detestation of their crimes, but admire the cool hardihood with which they sat unmoved on the brink of destruction; could not but think, within himself, how vast the good that might be wrought by such resolution, under a virtuous leader, and in an upright cause. Catiline noticed the glance; and as he marked it run along the crowded benches, dwelling a moment on the face of each one of his own confederates, he saw in an instant, that all was discovered; and, as he saw, resolved that since craft had failed to conceal, henceforth he would trust audacity alone to carry out his detected villainy.

But now the augurs had performed their rites; the day

was pronounced fortunate; the assembly formal; and nothing more remained, but to proceed to the business of the moment.

A little pause ensued, after the sanction of the augurs had been given; a short space, during which each man drew a deep breath, as though he were aware that ere long he should hear words spoken, that would thrill his every nerve with excitement, and hold him breathless with awe and apprehension.

There was not a voice, not a motion, not the rustling of a garment, through the large building; for every living form was mute, as the marble effigies around them, with intense expectation.

Every eye of conspirator, or patriot, was riveted upon the consul, the new man of Arpinum.

He rose, not unobservant of the general expectation, nor ungratified; for that great man, with all his grand genius, solid intellect, sound virtue, had one small miserable weakness; he was not proud, but vain; vain beyond the feeblest and most craving vanity of womanhood.

Yet now he showed it not—perhaps felt it, in a less degree than usual; it might be, it was crushed within him for the time, by the magnitude of vast interests, the consciousness of right motives, the necessity of extraordinary efforts.

He rose; advanced a step or two, in front of his curule chair, and in a clear slow voice gave utterance to the solemn words, which formed the exordium to all senatorial business.

"May this be good, and of good omen, happy, and fortunate to the Roman people, the Quirites; which now I lay before you, Fathers, and Conscript Senators."

He paused, emphatically, with the formula; and then raising his voice a little, and turning his eyes slowly round the house, as if in mute appeal to all the senators.

"For that," he said, "on which you must this day determine, concerns not the majesty or magnitude of Rome—the question is not now of insolent foes to be chastised, or of faithful friends to be rewarded—is not, how the city shall be made more beautiful, the state more proud and noble, the empire more enduring. No, conscript fathers; for the round world has never seen a city, so flourishing in all rare beauty, so decorated with the virtue of her living citizens, so noble in the memories of her dead heroes—the sun has never shone upon a state, so solidly established; upon an empire so majestical and mighty; extending from the Herculean columns, the far limits of the west, beyond the blue Symplegades; from Hyperborean snows, to the parched sands of Ethiopia!—no! Conscript Fathers, for we have no foes unsubdued, from the wild azure-tinctured hordes of Gaul to the swart Eunuchs of the Pontic king—for we have no friends unrewarded, unsheltered by the wings of our renown.

"No! it is not to beautify, to stablish, to augment—but to preserve the empire, that I now call upon you; that I now urge you, by all that is sweet, is sacred, is sublime in the name of our country; that I implore you, by whatever earth contains of most awful, and heaven of most holy!

"I said to preserve it! And do you ask from whom? Is there a Gallic tumult? Have Cimbric myriads again scaled the Alps, and poured their famished deluge over our devastated frontiers? Hath Mithridates trodden on the neck of Pompey? By the great gods! hath Carthage revived from her ashes? is Hannibal, or a greater one than Hannibal, again thundering at our gates, with Punic engines visible from the Janiculum?

"If it were so, I should not despair of Rome—my heart would not throb, as it now does, nor my voice tremble with anxiety.

"Cisalpine Gaul is tranquil as the vale of Arno! No bow is bended in the Teutonic forests, unless against the elk or urus! The legions have not turned their backs before the scymetars of Pontus! The salt sown in the market-place of Carthage hath borne no crop, but desolation. The one-eyed conqueror is nerveless in the silent grave!

"But were all these, now peaceful, subjugated, lifeless, were all these, I say, in arms, victorious, present, upon this soil of Italy, around these walls of Rome, I should doubt nothing, fear nothing, expect nothing, but present strife, and future victory!

"There is—there is, that spark of valor, that clear light of Roman virtue, alive in every heart; yea! even of our maids and matrons, that they would brook no hostile step even upon the threshold of our empire!

"What then do I foresee? what fear? Massacre—

parricide—conflagration—treason! Treason in Rome itself—in the Forum—in the Campus—*here!* Here in this holiest and safest spot! Here in the shrine of that great God, who, ages since, when this vast Rome was but a mud-built hamlet, that golden capitol, a straw-thatched shed, rolled back the tide of war, and stablished here, here, where my foot is fixed, the immortal seat of empire!

"Even now as I turn my eyes around me they fall abhorrent on the faces, they read indignant the designs, of their country's parricides!

"Aye! Conscript Fathers, prætorians, patricians of the great old houses, I see them in their places here; ready to vote immediately on their own monstrous schemes! I see them here, adulterers, forgers of wills, assassins, spendthrifts, poisoners, defilers of vestal virgins, contemners of the Gods, parricides of the Republic! I see them, with daggers sharpened against all true Romans, lurking beneath their fringed and perfumed tunics! Misled by strange ambition, maddened with lust, drunk with despairing guilt, athirst for the blood of citizens!

"I see them! you all see them! Will you await in coward apathy, until they shake you from your lethargy—until the outcries of your murdered children, of your ravished wives arouse you, until you awake from your sleep and find Rome in ashes?

"You hear me—you gaze on me in wonder, you ask me with your eyes what it is that I mean? who are the traitors? Lend me your ears then, and fix well your minds, lest they shrink in disgust and wonder. Lend me your ears only, and I fear not that you will determine, worthily of yourselves, and of the Republic!

"You all well know that on the 16th day before the calends of November, which should have been the eve of the consular Elections, I promised that I would soon lay before you ample proofs of the plot, which then I foretold to you but darkly.

"Mark, now, the faces of the men I shall address, and judge whether I then promised vainly; whether what I shall now disclose craves your severe attention—your immediate action."

He paused for a moment, as if to note the effect of his words; then turning round abruptly upon the spot, where

Catiline sat, writhing with rage and impatience, and gnawing his nether lip, until the blood trickled down his chin, he flung forth his arm with an indignant gesture, and instantly addressed him by his name, in tones that rang beneath the vaulted roof, over the heads of the self-convicted traitors, like heaven's own thunder, and found a fearful echo in their dismayed and guilty souls.

"Where wert thou, Catiline?" he thundered forth the charge, amid the mute astonishment of all—"Where wert thou on the evening of the Ides? what wert thou doing? Speak! Unless guilt and despair hold thee silent, I say to thee, speak, Catiline!"

Again he stopped in mid-speech, as if for an answer, fixed his eye steadily on the face of the arch conspirator. But he, though he spoke not to reply, quailed not, nor shunned that steady gaze, but met it with a terrible and portentous glare, pregnant with more than mortal hatred.

"Thou wilt not—can'st not—darest not! Now hear and tremble! Hear, and know that no step of thine, or deed, or motion escapes my eye—no, traitor, not one movement!

"On the eve of the Ides, thou wert in the street of the Scythemakers! Ha! does thy cheek burn now? In the house of a senator—of Marcus Porcus Læca. But thou wert not there, till thou hadst added one more deed of murder to those which needed no addition. Thou wert, I say, in the house of Læca; and many whom I now see around me, with trim and well-curled beards, with long-sleeved tunics and air-woven togas, many whom I could name, and will, if needs be, were there with thee!

"What beverage didst thou send around? what oath didst thou administer, thou to thy foul associates? and on the altar of what God?

"Fathers, my mind shrinks, as I speak, with horror—that bowl mantled to the brim with the gore of a human victim; those lips reeked with that dread abomination! His lips, and those of others, fitter to sip voluptuous nectar from the soft mouths of their noble paramours than to quaff such pollution!

"That oath was to destroy Rome, utterly, with fire and the sword, till not one stone should stand upon another, to mark the site of empire!

"The silver eagle was the god to whom he swore! The silver eagle, whose wings were dyed so deep in massacre by Marius—to whom he had a shrine in his own house, consecrated by what crimes, adored by what sacrilege, I say not!

"The consular election was the day fixed; and, had the people met on that day in the Campus, on that day had Rome ceased to be!

"To murder me in my robes of peace, at the Comitia, to murder the consuls elect, to murder the patricians to a man, was his own task, most congenial to his own savage nature!

"To fire the city in twelve several places was destined to his worthy comrades, whose terror my eye now beholds, whose names for the present my tongue shall not disclose. For I would give them time to repent, to change their frantic purpose, to cast away their sin—oh! that they would do so! oh! that they would have compassion on their prostrate and imploring country—compassion on themselves—on me, who beseech them to turn back, ere it be too late, to the ways of virtue, happiness, and honor!

"But names there are, which I will speak out, for to conceal them would avail nothing, since they have drawn the sword already, and raised the banner of rebellion against the majesty of Rome.

"Septimius of Camerinum has stirred the slaves even now to a fresh servile war! has given out arms! has appointed leaders! by the Gods! has a force on foot in the Picene district! Julius is soliciting the evil spirits of Apulia; and, ere four days have flown, you shall have tidings from the north, that Caius Manlius is in arms at Fæsulæ. Already he commands more than two legions; not of raw levies, not of emancipated slaves, or enfranchised gladiators—though these ere long will swell his host. No! Sylla's veterans muster under his banner—the same swords gleam around him which conquered the famed Macedonian phalanx at bloody Chæronea, which stormed the long walls of Piræus, which won Bithynia, Cappadocia, Paphlagonia, which drove great Mithridates back to his own Pontus!

"Nor is this all—for, if frustrated by the postponement of the consular comitia, believe not that the rage of the parricide is averted, or his thirst for the blood of Romans quenched forever.

"No, Fathers, he hath but deferred the day; and even now he hath determined on another. The fifth before the calends! Await that day in quiet, and ye will never rue your apathy. For none of you shall live to rue it, save those who now smile grimly, conscious of their own desperate resolve, expectant of your apathy.

"Nor is his villainy all told, even now; for so securely and so wisely has he laid his plans, that, had not the great Gods interfered and granted it to me to discover all, he must needs have succeeded! On the night of the calends themselves he would have been the master of Præneste, that rich and inaccessible strong-hold, by a nocturnal escalade! That I myself have already made impossible—the magistrates are warned, the free burghers armed, and the castle garrisoned by true men, and impregnable.

"Do ye the like, Fathers and Conscript Senators, and Rome also shall be safe, inaccessible, immortal. Give me the powers to save you, and I devote my mind, my life. I am here ready to die at this instant—far worse than death to a noble mind, ready to go hence, and be forgotten, if I may rescue Rome from this unequalled peril!"

Again, he ceased speaking for a moment, and many thought that he had concluded his oration; but in a second's space he resumed, in a tone more spirited and fiery yet, his eyes almost flashing lightning, and his whole frame appearing to expand, as he confronted the undaunted traitor.

"Dost thou not now see, Catiline, that in all things thou art my inferior? Dost thou not feel thyself caught, detected like a thief? baffled? defeated? beaten? and wilt thou not now lay down thine arms, thy rage, thy hate, against this innocent republic? wilt thou not liberate me now from great fear, great peril, and great odium?

"No! thou wilt not—the time hath flown! thou canst not repent—canst not forgive, or be forgiven—the Gods have maddened thee to thy destruction—thy crimes are full-blown, and ripening fast for harvest—earth is aweary of thy guilt—Hades yawns to receive thee!

"Tremble, then, tremble! Yea! in the depths of thy secret soul—for all thine eye glares more with hate than terror, and thy lip quivers, not with remorse but rage—

yea! thou dost tremble—for thou dost see, feel, know, thy schemes, thy confederates, thyself, detected, frustrated, devoted to destruction!

"Enough! It is for you, my Fathers, to determine; for me to act your pleasure. And if your own souls, your own lives, your own interests, yea! your own fears, cry not aloud to rouse you, with a voice stronger than the eternal thunder, why should I seek to warn you? Whom his own, his wife's, children's, country's safety, the glory of his great forefathers, the veneration of the everlasting Gods awaiting his decision from the tottering pinnacle of Rome's capitol—whom all these things excite not to action—no voice of man, no portent of the Gods themselves can stir to energy or valor; and I but waste my words in exhorting you to manhood!

"But they *will* burst the bonds of your long stupor; they *will* re-kindle, in your hearts, that blaze of Roman virtue, which may sleep for a while, but never can be all extinguished!—and ye *will* stir yourselves like men; ye *will* save your country! For this thing I do not believe; that the immortal Gods would have built up this commonwealth of Rome to such a height of beauty, of glory, of puissance, had they foredoomed it to destruction, by hands so base as those now armed against it. Nor, had it been their pleasure to abolish its great name, and make it such as Troy and Carthage, would they have placed me here, the consul, endowed by themselves with power to discern, but with no power to avert destruction!"

His words had done their work. The dismayed blank faces of all the conspirators, with the exception of the arch traitor only, whom it would seem that nothing could disconcert or dismay, confirmed the impression made upon all minds by that strong appeal. For, though he had mentioned no man's name save Catiline's and Læca's only, suspicion was called instantly to those who were their known associates in riot and debauchery; and many eyes were scrutinizing the pale features, which struggled vainly to appear calm and unconcerned.

The effect of the speech was immediate, universal. There were not three men of the order present who were not now convinced as fully in their own minds of the truth of Cicero's accusation, as they would, had it come forth in thunder from the cold lips of the marble God, who overlooked their proud assembly.

There was a long drawn breath, as he ceased speaking —one, and simultaneous through the whole concourse; and, though there were a few men there, Crassus, especially, and Caius Julius Cæsar, who, though convinced of the existence of conspiracy, would fain have defended the conspirators, in the existing state of feeling, they dared not attempt to do so.

Then Cicero called by name on the Prince of the Senate, enquiring if he would speak on the subject before the house, and on receiving from him a grave negative gesture, he put the same question to the eldest of the consulars, and thence in order, none offering any opinion or showing any wish to debate, until he came to Marcus Cato. He rose at once to speak, stern and composed, without the least sign of animation on his impassive face, without the least attempt at eloquence in his words, or grace in his gestures; yet it was evident that he was heard with a degree of attention, which proved that the character of the man more than compensated the unvarnished style and rough phraseology of the speaker.

"As it appears to me," he said, "Fathers and Conscript Senators, after the very luminous and able oration which our wise consul has this day held forth, it would be great folly, and great loss of time, to add many words to it. This I am not about to do, I assure you, but I arise in my place to say two things. Cicero has told you that a conspiracy exists, and that Catiline is the planner, and will be the executor of it. This, though I know not by what sagacity or foresight, unless from the Gods, he discovered it —this, I say, I believe confidently, clearly—all things declare it—not least the faces of men! I believe therefore, every word our consul has spoken; so do you all, my friends. Nevertheless, it is just and right, that the man, villain as he may be, shall be heard in his own behalf. Let him then speak at once, or confess by his silence! This is the first thing I would say—the next follows it! If he admit, or fail clearly to disprove his guilt, let us not be wanting to ourselves, to our country, or to the great and prudent consul, who, if man can, will save us in this crisis. Let us, I say, decree forthwith, 'THAT THE CONSULS SEE

THE REPUBLIC TAKES NO HARM!' and let us hold the consular election to-morrow, on the field of Mars—There, with our magistrates empowered to act, our clients in arms to defend us, let us see who will dare to disturb the Roman people! Let who would do so, remember that not all the power or favor of Great Marius could rescue Saturninus from the death he owed the people—remember that we have a consul no less resolute and vigorous, than he is wise and good—that there are axes in the fasces of the Lictors—that there stands the Tarpeian!"

And as he spoke, he flung wide both his arms; pointing with this hand to the row of glittering blades which shone above the head of the chief magistrate, with that, through the open door-way of the temple, to the bold front of the precipitous and fatal rock, all lighted up by the gay sunbeams, as it stood fronting them, beyond the hollow Velabrum, crowned with the ramparts of the capitol.

A general hum, as if of assent, followed, and without putting the motion to the vote, Cicero turned his eye rapidly to every face, and receiving from every senator a slight nod of assent, he looked steadily in the fierce and ghastly face of the traitor, and said to him;

"Arise, Catiline, and speak, if you will!—But take my counsel, confess your guilt, go hence, and be forgiven!"

"Forgiven!" cried the traitor, furious and desperate—"Forgiven!—this to a Roman citizen!—this to a Roman noble! Hear me, Fathers and Conscript Senators—hear me!—who am a soldier and a man, and neither driveller nor dotard. I tell you, there is no conspiracy, hath been none, shall be none—save in the addled brains of yon prater from Arpinum, who would fain set his foot upon the neck of Romans. All is, all shall be peace in Rome, unless the terror of a few dastards drive you to tyranny and persecution, and from persecution come resistance? For myself, let them who would ruin me, beware. My hand has never yet failed to protect my head, nor have many foes laughed in the end at Sergius Catiline!—unless," he added with a ferocious sneer—"they laughed in their death-pang. For my wrongs past, I have had some vengeance; for these, though I behold the axes, though I see, whence I stand, the steep Tarpeian, I think I shall have more, and live to feast my eyes with the downfall of my foes. Fathers, there are two bodies in the State, one weak, with a base but crafty head—the other powerful and vast, but headless. Urge me a little farther, and you shall find that a wise and daring head will not be wanting long, to that bold and puissant body. Urge me, and I will be that head; oppress me, and ——"

But insolence such as this, was not tolerable. There was an universal burst, almost a shout, of indignation from that assembly, the wonted mood of which was so stern, so cold, so gravely dignified, and silent. Many among the younger senators sprang to their feet, enraged almost beyond the control of reason; nor did the bold defiance of the daring traitor, who stood with his arms folded on his breast, and a malignant sneer of contempt on his lip, mocking their impotent displeasure, tend to disarm their wrath.

Four times he raised his voice, four times a cry of indignation drowned his words, and at length, seeing that he could obtain no farther hearing, he resumed his seat with an expression fiendishly malignant, and a fierce imprecation on Rome, and all that it contained.

After a little time, the confusion created by the audacity of that strange being moderated; order and silence were restored, and, upon Cato's motion, the Senate was divided.

Whatever might have been the result had Catiline been silent, the majority was overwhelming. The very partisans and favorers of the conspiracy, not daring to commit themselves more openly, against so strong a manifestation, passed over one by one, and voted with the consul.

Catiline stood alone, against the vote of the whole order. Yet stood and voted resolute, as though he had been conscious of the right.

The vote was registered, the Senate declared martial law, investing the consuls with dictatorial power, by the decree which commanded them to SEE THAT THE REPUBLIC TAKES NO HARM.

The very tribunes, factious and reckless as they were, potent for ill and powerless for good, presumed not to interpose. Not even Lucius Bestia, deep as he was in the design—Bestia, whose accusation of the consul from the rostrum was the concerted signal for the massacre, the conflagration—not Bestia himself, relied so far on the inviolability of his person, as to intrude his VETO.

The good cause had prevailed—the good Consul triumphed! The Senate was dismissed, and as the stream of patrician togas flowed through the temple door conspicuous, the rash and reckless traitor shouldered the mass to and fro, dividing it as a brave galley under sail divides the murmuring but unresisting billows.

Once in the throng he touched Julius Cæsar's robe as he brushed onward, and as he did so, a word fell on his ear in the low harmonious tones which marked the orator, second to none in Rome, save Cicero alone!—

"Fear not," it said—"another day will come!—"

"Fear!—" exclaimed the Conspirator in a hoarse cry, half fury, half contempt. "What is fear?—I know not the thing, nor the word!—Go, prate of fear to Cicero, and he will understand you!"

These words perhaps alienated one who might have served him well.

But so it ever is! Even in the shrewdest and most worldly wise of men, passion will often outweigh interest; and plans, which have been framed for years with craft and patience, are often wrecked by the impetuous rashness of a moment.

END OF VOL. I.

www.ingramcontent.com/pod-product-compliance
Lightning Source LLC
LaVergne TN
LVHW050512100826
845148LV00002B/312